WOLF'S SOUL

WOLF'S SOUL

Jane Lindskold

Obsidian Tiger Books

*Hi Dan,
One sometimes discovers one's soul when least expected.
Jane Lindskold*

WOLF'S SOUL

Copyright © 2020 Obsidian Tiger Inc

Cover Art by Julie Bell

Obsidian Tiger Books, Albuquerque, New Mexico All rights reserved. This book or any portion thereof may not be reproduced or used in any manner whatsoever without the express written permission of the publisher except for the use of brief quotations in a book review.

Cover Design and Interior Design and Formatting by

www.emtippettsbookdesigns.com

PRAISE FOR THE FIREKEEPER SAGA

"This engrossing tale of feral myth and royal intrigue from Lindskold offers plenty of action as well as fascinating anthropological detail on the social behavior of wolves. A beautiful and complex book."

—*Publisher's Weekly* on *Through Wolf's Eyes*

"The ultimate fairy tale. Captivating and well-told."

—*VOYA* on *Through Wolf's Eyes*

"Draws its greatest strength from its feral heroine, whose animal sensibilities lend a unique perspective to the foibles of human society. Rich details and intriguing sensibilities make this fantasy series a good choice."

—*Library Journal* on *Wolf's Head, Wolf's Heart*

"Highly enjoyable. A marvelous opportunity to see the peculiarities of human society through the eyes of intelligent beasts. Lindskold's wild and wonderful magic thrives in this volume."

—*Booklist* on *Wolf's Head, Wolf's Heart*

"In Lindskold's exciting third installment of her wolf-girl fantasy saga, Firekeeper finds herself deeply entangled in the politics and intrigues of her high-born human relations and even more so in the fight for survival of her alternate family, the Royal Beasts of the forest."

—*Publisher's Weekly* on *The Dragon of Despair*

"Firekeeper's dual citizenship in beast and human worlds makes her a perfect liaison…in this seamless continuation"

—*Booklist* on *The Dragon of Despair*

"Firekeeper hits her stride in the exhilarating fourth book…An increase in pace and greater character depth… give this exciting book an edge"
—*Publisher's Weekly* (starred review)

"Watching Firekeeper learn about humanity and still maintain her identity as a wolf makes for compelling reading. Intricately plotted and written, Lindskold's latest creates an utterly fascinating world that readers can lose themselves in."
—*Romantic Times* on *Wolf Captured*

"Thrilling. The intriguing plot makes for a quick and enjoyable read."
—*Publisher's Weekly* on *Wolf Hunting*

"Lindskold hones her world-building skills in this latest entry in her Firekeeper Saga, populating it with credible characters moving through an action-packed plot."
— *VOYA* on *Wolf Hunting*

"Intricately plotted, A thought-provoking tale of magic and politics, enlivened by Firekeeper's wry and wolfish point-of-view."
—*Publisher's Weekly* on *Wolf's Blood*

"Lindskold explores the philosophical question, 'What is love?'… Firekeeper has matured in mind and body throughout this fantasy epic, gaining understanding of her complex world's operation. Lindskold does a solid job of world-building, offering thought-provoking questions to underpin this well-paced chronicle"
—*VOYA* on *Wolf's Blood*

OTHER BOOKS BY
Jane Lindskold

The Artemis Awakening Series
Artemis Awakening

Artemis Invaded

The Firekeeper Series
Through Wolf's Eyes

Wolf's Head, Wolf's Heart

The Dragon of Despair

Wolf Captured

Wolf Hunting

Wolf's Blood

Wolf's Search

The Breaking the Wall Series
Thirteen Orphans

Nine Gates

Five Odd Honors

The Athanor Series
Changer

Changer's Daughter (aka Legends Walking)

Captain Ah-Lee Short Stories
Endpoint Insurance

Winner Takes Trouble

Here to There

Star Messenger **(the box set of all three short stories)**

Stand Alone Novels

The Buried Pyramid

Child of a Rainless Year

Brother to Dragons, Companion to Owls

Marks of Our Brothers

The Pipes of Orpheus

Chronomaster

Smoke and Mirrors

When the Gods are Silent

Asphodel

With Roger Zelazny

Donnerjack

Lord Demon

With David Weber

Fire Season

Treecat Wars

Nonfiction

Wanderings on Writing

For Jim for so many reasons, all of them wonderful.

And for Keladry, my most faithful assistant

ACKNOWLEDGEMENTS

First of all, there's a very special group I want to thank. Without them, *Wolf's Soul* would have taken a lot longer to be finished. These are the members of my current gaming group: Rowan Derrick, Melissa Jackson, Cale Mims, Dominique Price, and my husband, Jim Moore.

There was a point when, overwhelmed by too many projects unexpectedly coming to a head at one time, I realized I was burning out. Something had to go. Reluctantly, I realized that I was going to need to give up running our weekly game. I was crushed, because gaming may be the single activity that helps me recharge my creativity.

What can I say? I'm a storyteller. Gaming reminds me that stories are fun, not just my job.

My gamers are all seriously busy people, with high-end, stressful jobs. I figured they'd be glad for an excuse to reclaim their Sunday evenings. Instead, they insisted we keep meeting. Rowan, despite having just started a new job, took over as gamemaster. I stepped to the sidelines as one of the players. As I started working through the backlog that was weighing me down, burnout ebbed and writing *Wolf's Soul* became fun again, rather than a chore.

I also want to thank my husband, Jim Moore, for undying patience, for being my first reader, and for helping as much as possible with all the projects, not just this one.

Just about every day, Keladry cat ran for my desk as soon as she heard me turning on the computer. Despite her fondness for walking in front of the monitor, she really was my best assistant. She died completely unexpectedly as this book was going into copy edit. I will miss her forever.

My beta readers, Julie Bartel and Paul Dellinger, brought their own unique perspectives to the completed manuscript. Thanks to both of them for their thoughtful comments, especially those that led me to rewrite for greater clarity.

Sally Gwylan served as copy editor, showing dedication beyond grammatical belief.

Artist Julie Bell let me use her lovely "Three Hungry Wolves" for the cover art. Someday I'll find out how she knew what I planned to write about before I did.

Emily Mah Tippetts and her team at E.M. Tippetts Book Design made the book beautiful *and* put up with my fussing over minor details.

Thanks, again, to all of you who have been running with Firekeeper and Blind Seer these many years. If you're a member of their pack, you know it!

PROLOGUE

When had the Voice first started speaking to him? It was difficult for Kabot to remember. There had been very few ways to judge the passage of time within that channel of stony mana which had saved them from dissolution while holding them captive. Kabot recalled as if it were yesterday or eons past, how he and his small band of fellow enthusiasts had crafted their spell. What the five of them had sought to create had not been so much a gate as a tunnel, a funnel, between the ruined lands of Rhinadei and the prestigious university at which their ancestors had studied what was, in Rhinadei, forbidden lore.

They had worked their calculations with great care. Nonetheless, as soon as the spell was activated, something had gone wrong. First Phiona, the second most powerful of their number, had seemed to explode within the matrix. Caidon, who was next, had not exploded. He had slowed, then stopped, his essential essence petrifying into a living blockade that prevented Uaid and Daylily from moving forward.

Kabot had tried to retrieve his comrades, but instead he had been pulled in after them. The four of them remained stuck, vaguely aware of each other, unable to communicate or to coordinate any plan. The only aid Kabot could offer his loyal followers was to pour energy from the mana surge through the fragmenting spell to sustain them.

They'd lost Caidon next. Kabot wasn't sure when, since his only timepiece was the physical appearance of those who came to check on them. At first there had been many visitors, people he recognized as hardline supporters of Rhinadei's policy against any resurgence of the anathema art. Later, only Kabot's childhood companion, Wythcombe, had come. People don't visibly age much once they reached their middle years, a brief taste of seeming immortality before Time starts inscribing lines on face and body, mocking the wistful presumption that time's passage can be stopped. But when Caidon had exploded, Wythcombe's appearance had changed little, so Caidon must have been lost relatively early.

Kabot still felt a wash of guilt when he remembered how he'd allowed himself to hope that, with Caidon gone, whatever blocked their funnel would also vanish, letting them move along. Nothing had changed. Uaid and Daylily remained frozen, as did Kabot himself.

Kabot was drowning in despair when the visions started. The hallucinations were weird and often fragmentary, yet possessed of an internal logic, the visual equivalent of sound distorted by echoes. Kabot struggled to decipher the images. They might be crazed, but they were better than losing himself in the loop of his own thoughts.

Wythcombe's hair had been thinning when the Voice had started talking to Kabot. Initially, Kabot had dismissed the Voice as just another hallucination, one more vivid than most, his loneliness creating an imaginary friend for him. Later, Kabot had wondered if Uaid or Daylily, his remaining companions, had finally figured out a way to communicate. However, the Voice said none of the things Uaid and Daylily would certainly have mentioned.

At last, Kabot accepted that the Voice was a genuine individual, someone who could speak to him even though—perhaps especially because—he was trapped. When Kabot realized this and began to answer the Voice's many, many questions, his new life and shining purpose had been born.

Eventually, the Voice confided that, having learned of Uaid and Daylily from Kabot's worry for them, it had journeyed along the threads of mana that Kabot never had ceased to channel toward his two remaining followers. The Voice did not boast or brag. Nonetheless, Kabot had the impression that it had endured many perils in order to find a way to these stranded souls.

Later still, the Voice had linked Kabot, Uaid, and Daylily together. Their communications had not been words at first, but a prickling awareness. Kabot imagined them as three mayflies caught in a spider's web, aware of each other through the thrumming of their struggles to escape.

Wythcombe's crown was shiny bald when the Voice had managed to transform the web into a tightly woven cocoon. This cradled them, huddled tight, protected against the vicissitudes without. If Kabot had ever doubted that people had souls, this arcane unity would have convinced him of the soul's reality. He grew to appreciate his companions as their more essential selves: Daylily, a glittering rainbow shaped from tiny stars; Uaid, strong and solid as stone. Eventually, they learned to converse in a language that made as much use of images as of sounds.

Once they had perfected this manner of communication, the Voice had taken upon itself the tremendous and unrewarding chore of informing them that the university that had been their destination no longer existed. It told them of querinalo, the curse that burned through magical talent, feasting by choice upon the most powerful. It told them how their own torment was rooted in the lingering traces of this curse which—although it had abated somewhat—continued to turn a gourmet's eye upon those who were especially gifted.

Asking no credit or thanks—indeed, begging them not to reveal its existence—the Voice had shown them how they might break free of their ruined transportation spell. When at last they were able to retreat to Rhinadei, they had all been aware of the Voice's secret sorrow as it felt them leave.

Kabot had been heart-wrenchingly certain that the Voice would be terribly lonely without them, but had been far too noble to hold them back. When he had hinted that they might draw the Voice into Rhinadei with them, the only response had been wistful gratitude, coupled with the certainty that, even for sorcerers as talented as they were, this would be impossible.

Once Kabot, Daylily, and Uaid had been replenished by the power of the mana surge, Daylily had tentatively suggested that perhaps they should build a refuge for themselves in one of the wilder reaches of Rhinadei. Although their staves and charms had been lost, they still possessed basic equipment. After all, as the Voice had informed them, the community of like-minded sorcerers they had hoped to find in the Old World was no more.

"We can use the power of the mana surge to sustain us while we establish a fortress, pursue our own studies, replace the equipment we lost. We could quietly recruit others who have become unsatisfied. Surely, after all this time, there will be others. If our behavior is peaceful and scholarly, in time Rhinadei's ruling council may stop seeing us as a threat."

Kabot had shaken his head. "Do as you wish, dear Daylily, and with my blessing. I will even help you find a location for your hideaway before I depart. However, we were viewed as rebels then. Do you really think attitudes will have changed? If they had, I firmly believe Wythcombe would have rescued us, rather than staring forlornly after us every so often. When I next encounter those who rejected us, I will make sure they must treat me as an equal."

His confidence had stiffened Daylily's spine. Soon thereafter, Uaid and Daylily had joined with Kabot in designing a new spell to carry them to the ruins of the Old World university. Although the Voice had warned them that the university was no longer active, it had also hinted that there were prizes to be found amid the crumbled buildings: books and artifacts secreted by scholars of the magical arts who had believed that what they were experiencing was a passing illness, that they would return and reestablish themselves.

The spell had taken moonspans to design, a tense period during which

Kabot had both dreaded and secretly hoped that Wythcombe would come to check on them. Had he hoped to be dissuaded? Even now, Kabot wasn't sure. However, nothing had happened to interrupt their plans. This time their spell had successfully taken them to the ruined university.

The dismay Kabot had felt when he had realized that their long journey had ended not among picturesque ruins, but among raw destruction, had never entirely faded. Rhinadei had been swept by war, by spells run wild. What had been done to university at Azure Towers was an attempt to obliterate any trace of the magical arts. What had not been burned had been broken; what had refused to burn or break had been buried. That there could be anything of value left would have seemed impossible but for the Voice's hints of concealed treasure.

As the trio began their search, Kabot realized how much he missed Phiona. There had been something special between them—not just the on-again, off-again romance that had resulted in tears as often as in kisses, but a sort of creative synergy that was as difficult to define as it had been stimulating. They'd disagreed frequently and heatedly. However, in working through those disagreements, the concepts they had arrived upon had been not merely the adding together of their thoughts but a multiplication.

Uaid and Daylily were strong-minded and gifted, else they would not have been elected into Kabot's elite circle. But what Kabot shared with them was not what he had once had with Phiona. Perhaps it was his longing for Phiona that called out to the Voice which had fallen silent once they had left the cocoon it had woven to nurture and protect them. Perhaps the Voice's loneliness—enhanced rather than assuaged by the camaraderie it had shared with the three rebels from Rhinadei—had been so great that finally it had been able to answer.

At first the contact had been as tenuous as a rainbow created by a lens made from a raindrop caught within a loop of grass. First the Voice spoke to Kabot in dreams, advising, cautioning, encouraging. Later, they connected via the mindful abstraction of meditation. Then came the glorious day when

Kabot thought to himself, "I must try to ask the Voice about that," and the Voice replied, "Why wait? I am here, with you."

The Voice sounded so very much like Phiona that tears rose to Kabot's eyes, shattering the light and driving prismatic spears into his heart.

I

"You still here?" Firekeeper threw her arms around Derian as soon as she and Blind Seer cleared the gate from Rhinadei. "We think you'd be gone, taking Isende to see your family in Hawk Haven."

She checked her friend's reaction carefully. Derian had delayed making the trip to Hawk Haven the previous summer, saying, with some justification, that he was needed while the Nexus Islands established themselves as an independent nation. But she knew that Derian also dreaded showing his family what querinalo had done to him. His fight to maintain his talent against the curse had left him with features that blended those of a horse with those a human. That the horse in question was a fine chestnut did not seem to comfort Derian, although he had eventually become resigned to the change. Firekeeper—who would not have minded looking more like a wolf than a human—sometimes had to fight to remember just how much anguish Derian had initially felt about his transformation.

Not long ago, Firekeeper had also thought that Derian was being cowardly in not wanting to visit his family. After all, what was there to fear? Derian had gained honors far beyond what a mere horse carter could have expected for his son. If Derian had lost an arm in battle, Colby and Vernita Carter would not have loved him less. How was a transformed physical appearance any different?

But now Firekeeper knew how very thoughtless she had been. The people of Hawk Haven had been taught from infancy to dread magic, just as the wolves who had raised her and Blind Seer had been. As long as Blind Seer's magical gifts had been unknown, Firekeeper could ignore what their birth pack's reaction would be, but now… Now Blind Seer's power was far more than latent. He had transformed himself to have wings, and flown. He was openly studying magic under the tutelage of a human spellcaster. Now that there could be no overlooking what he was, what would their parents think? Would their welcome be any more certain than what Derian dreaded from the family he so faithfully continued to write?

Firekeeper hugged Derian tightly in mute apology.

"Soon." Derian hugged Firekeeper back, then released her to give Blind Seer a light punch in the shoulder by way of greeting. "What sort of trouble have you gotten yourself into that you were hoping I'd be gone?"

If Derian had expected laughter or denial at what had been clearly intended as a joke, he knew Firekeeper too well to miss the suppressed tension in how she tossed her tousled curls from her dark eyes.

"The others come through soon," Firekeeper said, stepping well away from the monolith that held the gate. "Then we tell all at once. I am sure you will be glad for Arasan being better with words than me before this is told." The wolf-woman glanced mournfully over at the tidy sailing vessel that would carry them from the outer island which held the Rhinadei gate to the main island of the Nexus Island chain. "Especially since I do not have any fresh seasickness medicine."

Derian dipped a hand into his vest pocket. "Frostweed sent some, just in case. Why don't you down it, so it has time to take effect? One thing. Should I expect any strangers—like that Varelle you brought last time?"

Firekeeper shook her head. "Not yet. Strangers are staying behind to finish explaining how things are to their people while we came ahead."

Narrowing his eyes—the brown orbs much more like that of a horse than a human—Derian gave a low whistle. "That doesn't sound good."

"Is not good," Firekeeper admitted, adding water to the powder in the little flask, shaking it, tossing the foul brew back in one gulp. She grimaced. "But maybe it could be worse, far worse."

Derian waited patiently while first Laria, with the falcon Farborn on her shoulder, followed by Arasan, came through the gate. None of them would seem much changed from when he had seen them last, roughly a moonspan and a half before.

Arasan had shed the extra weight he had gained during his convalescence, and his hair was a trace longer. Otherwise he appeared much as he had before: thick, dark-brown hair, showing attractive (to Firekeeper's wolfish way of thinking) accents of grey, lines accenting thoughtful brown eyes. His lightly greying close-cropped beard and mustache couldn't hide how both pain and laughter had taken their part in shaping his features. Arasan was the oldest member of their company in more ways than one. His body had experienced fifty-some years, but of his two souls, one was that of the centuries-old Meddler—a personage who, depending to whom you spoke, just might be a god, but who everyone agreed was trouble.

The merlin Farborn now flew without his remarkable crystalline talons setting him off-balance, but what couldn't be seen in the tidy little dark-brown and golden-tan falcon was how much of his self-confidence he had regained. If anything, these days Farborn tended toward a certain officious certainty that the safely of his companions depended upon him, first and foremost.

Perhaps the greatest alteration would be seen in Laria who, at fourteen, was the youngest human member of their company. That she wore a sword—carrying it as if she was accustomed to its weight—was the smallest change. Her light-brown eyes had lost their perpetually worried expression. She actually smiled at Derian when he greeted her, rather than looking down at her feet and worrying the ribbon braided into her golden-brown hair. Her skin was the lightest of their group, a golden-brown like ripe wheat.

Firekeeper knew that neither she nor Blind Seer would have changed at all. Her short, curly brown hair was a little neater, mostly because Arasan insisted on trimming it, rather than letting her go after it with her hunting knife whenever it started getting in her eyes. But her eyes were still a brown so dark as to be almost black, and if her tanned skin carried a few more scrapes and scars, no one would notice.

Wolves did not alter much after reaching full adulthood, so Blind Seer was, as always, the handsomest grey wolf ever, his markings classic, the brilliant blue of his eyes perpetually thrilling by contrast. As was true of most yarimaimalom predators, Blind Seer was larger than Cousin-kind, standing tall enough that Firekeeper could rest her arm on his back without leaning down.

After greeting everyone, Derian said, "Chaker Torn and his daughter, Symeen, sailed me over when we detected the gate activating. Shall we board the *Silver Lady*? You can tell me about your adventures while we sail back. Did Blind Seer find his teacher?"

"His teacher, yes," Firekeeper said, reluctantly climbing aboard, "and so much more."

On the *Silver Lady*, Firekeeper and Blind Seer settled where they could face into the salt-scented air. With her face and body angled forward, Firekeeper knew she looked like a peculiar figurehead, but she listened carefully as Arasan—assisted by Laria—briefed Derian on the events since they had left to find Blind Seer a teacher, and had found so much more.

"So the short version is that you have reason to believe that this Kabot and his associates are somewhere in the Old World, probably Azure Towers?" Derian rocked his head back to ease a cramp in his neck muscles. "Can you narrow down when they would have arrived there?"

Arasan shrugged. "Somewhat. The message Kabot left Wythcombe said they'd been released three moonspans before."

"But before when?"

"I'm getting to that. They were still caught within their gate spell a few years ago when Wythcombe made his last pilgrimage. Our current theory is that they were freed sometime after Virim made the most recent modifications to querinalo."

"Why then?"

"Because their spell malfunctioned after the Old World mages report that their people were beginning to survive querinalo, but that it was still strong enough to kill. Wythcombe checked on Kabot's cabal more or less regularly at first. Remember, he knew nothing about querinalo, so all he was checking was whether they were still suspended."

"Hold up. So Rhinadei didn't experience querinalo?"

"It did, but what they experienced was much milder. It abated about the time—best as I can estimate—that Virim and his associates altered querinalo to permit the reemergence of talents in the New World. Since the Rhinadeians don't practice blood magic at all—their term for it is 'the anathema art'—they wouldn't have experienced the extreme penalties suffered by those who employed blood magic. So, basically, the residents of Rhinadei have been without much in the way of restrictions on their magic for over a century."

Laria cut in. "The Rhinadeians seem to have a lot more people with magical gifts than we do—which makes sense, since their society was founded by magic users. Because of this, there are whole parts of their educational system built around learning what sort of magic children have, then teaching them. So even though Kabot was somewhere around forty when he rebelled, he was already an expert."

Derian frowned. "So we're facing rogue blood mages who trained in magic as I did horseback riding—and I could ride before I could walk. Marvelous. Going back to when this cabal might have arrived in the Old World, why do you think the timing is related to querinalo?"

When Firekeeper spoke, she was very aware of her gut jouncing as *Silver Lady* smacked over the waves. "For a long time, Wythcombe thought that Kabot had done his gate wrong. When he learn from us how when we—you and me and Blind Seer—come from the New World to the Old, and how querinalo makes us all so ill, then Wythcombe wonders: What if Kabot did not do the spell wrong? What if querinalo made them sick so they could not finish the spell?"

"Oh, I get it," Derian interjected. "Then, last year, Virim set out to make amends. So far he hasn't figured out how to cancel the curse that's at the heart of querinalo, but he's been working hard to make the victims' reactions less severe. You think that Kabot and all were somehow able to finish their spell then?"

Laria replied, "Wythcombe does. I think he's right. I couldn't get a clear reading on that place where Kabot's cabal had made their base, but they were able to get out of the snare they'd been caught in, come back, set up a nasty welcome for just about anyone who might come after them, and then leave. Wythcombe and Ranz are going to try to narrow down when Kabot reopened his gate."

Arasan nodded. "Even without that, we can estimate anywhere between the three months mentioned in the message and about six months, because that's when Virim worked his first major abatement of the curse. Derian, you look… thoughtful? I'd expected anger or even disbelief, but what's bothering you?"

Derian shook his head so hard that his forelock tumbled into his eyes. "I have a feeling that there's a reason that Azure Towers is going to be difficult to deal with on this matter, but I can't remember why. We're going to need to brief the Nexus Islands council in any case, so rather than my speculating, let's wait and consult them."

He looked to where Symeen was adjusting a sail in preparation for bringing *Silver Lady* into the dock, then back to where Chaker stood at the wheel. "If you don't mind, I'd prefer you two keep what you've heard to yourselves for now. I trust the Nexans, but today is a transit day for some of our clients. I'd just as soon that this news not get out before we've had a chance to decide what to do about it."

Symeen nodded, trying hard not to look impressed at being taken into Derian's confidence. Chaker grinned.

"No problem, Counselor. We're used to keeping mum."

Firekeeper wasn't surprised by their support. Since last summer when the Nexus Islands had established their right to rule themselves, the Nexans had not lost their unity of purpose. They knew all too well how close they'd come to losing control of the gates, to returning to life as slaves of the powerful Once Dead. Maybe in time they'd forget that lesson but, for now, as the graves of those who had died in the defense were only now being covered with the faint green of new grass, the memory was fresh and raw.

Once ashore, Firekeeper's erstwhile pack began to go their separate ways. Since it was likely that their small group would be departing before long, Laria wanted to spend time with her mother and two siblings. Blind Seer would be off to consult the jaguar, Truth, a frustrating proposition at the best of times, and one certain to be more so if—as they suspected—the currents of future events were in flux. This would leave Firekeeper and Arasan to brief the administrative council of the Nexus Islands. Farborn was remaining on the island in case anyone came through from Rhinadei. True, the gate was kept under observation by yarimaimalom gulls, but Farborn would know their friends—or at least allies—from outright intruders.

"Hard as it is for us to face," Blind Seer said as he shook the sea spray from his fur, "the gates have changed what it means to have a territory."

Firekeeper knelt so she could press her face into his fur and feel his breath warm on her skin. "Remember how Grateful Peace spoke of the gates? That in all his years as a spymaster, he had never realized that New Kelvin possessed a border in the basement of Thendulla Lypella. So it is for us all now. We have borders that cannot be easily seen—and dread the borders we have not yet discovered."

"That is so," the blue-eyed wolf agreed, stretching his torso in preparation for a run. "Truth needs to know what we have learned, if for no other reason than so she will understand why there is good reason if her visions have become more turbulent of late."

"Run to Truth, then, my sweet hunter. I will listen while Derian and the counselors repeat themselves. Perhaps in listening I will learn what has Fox Hair so troubled."

The council proved to be small. Zebel, the doctor, had expressed due thanks for being included in the ruling body, but excused himself from attending meetings unless the matter under discussion somehow pertained to the island's medical needs. Wort, the island's quartermaster, was logging in a new shipment of supplies. This left Skea, Ynamynet, Urgana, and Derian.

As Firekeeper had expected, much of what was said first was a repetition of what they had reported to Derian. One of Blind Seer's favorite proverbs ran, "Hunt when hungry, sleep when not, for hunger always returns." Until her stomach had settled from seasickness, Firekeeper had no appetite, so she drowsed while the discussion went on around her.

The wolf-woman was drawn from her doze by the voice of Ynamynet, the leading spellcaster of the Nexus Islands. Unlike many of the remaining Nexus Islands spellcasters, Ynamynet continued to wear the elaborate embroidered robes and close-fitting cloth caps that had distinguished those who practiced the magical arts. The reasons were, Firekeeper suspected, dual. Ynamynet was the Nexus Islands' highest-ranking spellcaster. In her role as one of the two heads of the very informal government, she often needed to confer with other users of magic. These would have been shocked to see her otherwise attired. Ynamynet's other reason was that, because of querinalo, she was always cold. Where others might find the heavy garment stifling, she welcomed the warmth.

"I wish I knew if Kabot's cabal actually suffered querinalo or if it simply blocked their ability to use magic," Ynamynet was saying, her pale blue-grey eyes narrowing in suspicion. "If they did suffer it, what did it do to them?"

Arasan replied, "I wish I knew. None who experience querinalo comes through undamaged—as you know all too well."

"And for far too many," Ynamynet added, "the damage is more than physical: a sense of entitlement is the least of it. Often there is paranoia, megalomania, or worse."

"Very true," Firekeeper put in, resisting the urge to yawn. "Maybe when Wythcombe comes, you could warn him his friend may be changed. You are a spellcaster who has lived through querinalo. Words from you should bear much weight."

"I'll do that," Ynamynet replied. "Most definitely."

Derian turned to Urgana. The elderly woman had come to the Nexus Islands decades before, in company with her magically gifted sister, who had been exiled from their homeland for the crime of surviving querinalo with her talent intact. After her sister's death, Urgana had served as a clerk to the Spell Wielders. Now she served the Nexus Islands as their chief archivist and librarian—a task which made use of her scholarly inclinations and took advantage of the experience of her long life as well.

"Urgana, ever since Arasan told us that it's likely that this Kabot's spell took him to Azure Towers, I've been feeling uneasy—but I can't remember why. On the surface, there doesn't seem to be a reason for it. We haven't had a great deal of contact with Azure Towers, but I can't recall anything unduly bad. In fact, if I remember correctly, Queen Anitra has an excellent reputation."

"She does and deservedly," Urgana said. "Let me give you a brief summary of Azure Tower's politics. I suspect that will explain why you're feeling uneasy." She shifted to a lecturing tone. "Azure Towers is very careful about foreign visitors, even those who can be assumed to be friendly. It shares borders with two nations—three, if one counts Tishiolo but, as Tishiolo is on the other side of a nearly impassible mountain range, that does not concern us—or them. One of Azure Towers' borders is with the Mires. However, since the conclusion of the recent war, King Bryessidan has bent himself over backwards to prove that he truly desires nothing more than peaceful trade."

Firekeeper tried to imagine the brash young monarch bending over backwards and found she could. When she had first seen him, Bryessidan had been clad in terrifying armor of silver and brass. Since then, she had seen him in other contexts, including with his wife and small children. The warrior king had been unbending to his undoing. The father king was a much more pleasant and flexible person.

Urgana continued, "On the other border is Hearthome. Queen Iline of Hearthome has always sparred with Azure Towers. Some say that she has a personal rivalry with Queen Anitra. Others say she uses the conflict as a means of keeping her extended family too busy to give her trouble. Queen Iline has repeatedly stated that she believes that Queen Anitra's tiny nation should not be custodian of the ruins of the ancient university city, that the ruins should be the property of Hearthome instead."

Derian tapped one hoof-like fingernail on the tabletop. "That's what's been bothering me—something about the university. Ruins you say?"

"Ruins," Urgana agreed. "As Arasan mentioned, Azure Towers was the site of what was considered the largest and most prestigious university specializing in the magical arts. U-Chival also had a large magical academy, but since their magical teachings were inextricably intertwined with their religious beliefs, it was never as important."

"But after the coming of querinalo, the university was destroyed, wasn't it?" Derian protested. "Ruins, you said."

"Destroyed, yes," Urgana said, "but indiscriminately, by those with no knowledge of what they damaged. There has long been speculation that the ignorant may have left behind items of great value—especially of value to those who practice the magical arts."

Ynamynet, the one spellcaster in their company, nodded. "I certainly heard such stories when I was growing up in Pelland. By the time I was born, people with magical talents were beginning to survive querinalo with their ability to use magic intact: Once Dead, as people still say."

Firekeeper saw how Ynamynet unconsciously straightened with pride at the term, for she herself was Once Dead, and a spellcaster as well. Not long before, that would have set her at the top of the hierarchy of the Nexus Islands.

Of course, she still is on top, but for very different reasons. Ynamynet's love for her husband, Skea, and their little girl caused her to side with us.

Derian flicked his horse ears flat against his skull, perhaps remembering how ruthless Once Dead Ynamynet had been, but he perked them again. When he spoke his voice held no aggression. "That's something I've wondered about for a while, Ynamynet. If I have the dates straight, people in the Old World started surviving querinalo some three or four generations ago. Didn't anyone start a new university?"

"Not a university," Ynamynet replied with a brisk shake of her head, "nothing much larger than small-scale, very secretive instruction within families or communities. If you think that that New World has bad memories of when the sorcerer monarchs of old ruled, they're nothing to what the Old World history holds. The colonies were well-established when Virim and his associates decided to protect the New World's indigenous peoples from the invaders from the Old by creating querinalo. Here in the Old World—as well as in more distant lands, such as Tey-yo, where Skea's family comes from—the sorcerers had ruled for centuries, and most felt little compassion for the peoples they dominated. When querinalo sickened those who possessed magical gifts, the attacks from the non-magical were swift and vicious—and justified as retribution.

"When those with magical talents began to survive, the fact that many were made—forgive me—apparently monstrous, by what the fevers did to them, did not reassure those without talents. Even those who, like myself, were apparently not marked were viewed as monsters. That we were born a few generations distant from the worst of the abuses kept us from being automatically slaughtered when we were discovered, but certainly not enough time had passed for the establishment of public teaching facilities."

Urgana rapped her pen on the table. "King Essidan took advantage of the negative view of those who use magic to create a refuge for the Once Dead in the Mires. You know the consequences of that well enough."

"I do indeed," Derian agreed. "So, Queen Anitra is custodian of what many believe is not just a ruin, but also a sort of repository of magical what? Books? Surely those would have burned. Artifacts like the glowstones?"

"Or that peculiar sword that Laria brought back from Rhinadei," Urgana agreed, "and possibly more powerful artifacts. Queen Anitra has declared the ruins of the old university absolutely off limits. For this reason, Queen Iline's claim that Azure Towers is an unfit custodian has always been viewed by other nations, both on the continent of Pelland and those within trading distance, such as Tavetch and u-Chival, as unfounded paranoia and envy, nothing more."

"But Queen Anitra is not likely to give us permission to send in a group to investigate if Kabot did go there." Derian snorted a very equine sigh. "No wonder I was apprehensive. Either we take the risk of a crazed mage having free run of the ruins of a magical university or we send in what could be taken as an invading force, not just by Azure Towers, but by all the other Old World nations."

"Laria, is that really, truly a magical sword?" asked Laria's youngest sibling—her five-year-old brother Kitatos—for what seemed like the hundredth time over the past several days.

"Yes, it is."

"What's its name?" Kitatos asked.

"It doesn't have one, yet," Laria answered.

"I'd call it Biter of Badness," Kitatos said, not for the first time.

Laria wished she'd just said her sword was an old one she'd found while in Rhinadei, but it was too late for that. She hadn't liked to leave the sword sitting around, but carrying it with her had, inevitably, led to questions, questions she had answered honestly.

"Can I use it?" her younger sister Nenean asked. "You said that this sword helps people who don't know how to use swords do it safely. Right? So you shouldn't be greedy."

Laria decided the time for white lies had come. "The sword can only have one owner. I'm the owner now, so it wouldn't work for you."

"You could tell it you're giving it to me," Nenean said with the covetous craft of her eleven years. "Then I'd give it back. Don't be selfish."

Ikitata, obviously regretting teaching her children to share, interjected maternal authority. "Enough, Nenean. Laria also told us that she's been practicing how to use a sword, not depending on this one's magic alone. She clearly understands that a weapon is a responsibility, not a toy. I thought you did, too, but maybe you don't. Perhaps I should withdraw you from archery classes."

That shut Nenean up right away. The Nexus Islands required all adults in its small population to train in the military arts. Even the elders had to learn the basics. Those who were too infirm to fight were trained in medical arts—learning enough to be able to tend patients or watch at the bedside of someone who had been critically wounded. Being given more than basic self-defense training was one of the first hallmarks of adulthood, and Nenean was very proud of her short bow and quiver of blunted practice arrows.

Ikitata went on. "Laria, do you remember the stories I told you when you were little? Maybe you can find a name for your sword in one of those."

"Volsyl!" A character hardly remembered, never forgotten, sprang immediately into Laria's mind.

"Not a bad choice," Ikitata said. "You always did love the stories about her."

Laria nodded. There had been stories about strong heroes, magical heroes, cunning heroes. Among these Volsyl stood out because she was none of these. All she had going for her was determination.

"Volsyl," Laria repeated, touching the sword's hilt. "I'll call it Volsyl."

"I still like Biter of Badness, better," Kitatos muttered.

Laria tousled Nenean's hair. "Want to go shoot targets? Bet I can beat you. I've been helping hunt."

The sisters were out at the archery butts when Farborn streaked down from the sky and landed on Laria's shoulder. The merlin bobbed his head down to indicate the message tube tied to his right leg.

"Thanks," Laria said as she carefully unfastened it. Experimentation had shown that, no matter how delicate the glimmering crystal appeared to be, Farborn's legs were actually armored. Nonetheless, they looked as if a breath might break the shell.

"What's it say?" Nenean asked, jumping up and down impatiently.

Laria read aloud. "*Silver Lady* has set sail to retrieve Ranz and Wythcombe from the Rhinadei gate island. Firekeeper and Blind Seer have gone missing again. Arasan and I are stuck in a meeting. Will you meet them? Derian."

Nenean went wide-eyed, all her previous sass vanishing. Although the Nexus Islanders were accustomed to transients, the idea of new arrivals from a civilization that had been forgotten long before the coming of querinalo remained exotic.

The sisters unstrung their bows, slid them into their cases, then hurried off toward the high ground where they could glimpse *Silver Lady*, her sails belled out, heading toward the small island.

"We have time to drop our archery gear at the apartment," Laria said, omitting that she wanted to comb her hair and put on less sweaty clothes. Ranz had certainly seen her looking a complete mess, but that didn't mean she didn't want to take advantage of an opportunity to look her best. She even considered changing into a dress, rather than her more usual trousers and tunic, but Nenean would be certain to notice and, after she got a look at Ranz, to tease. As far as Laria could tell, Ranz hadn't noticed that she "liked" him, but having him find out because of her little sister's sly comments would be the worst.

"Laria! *Silver Lady* is nearly to the docks! I can see the pennants clearly."

Gulping, Laria took a final quick look in the mirror—another of those little luxuries the non-ruling Islanders hadn't possessed a few months before—then hurried down the stairs, Nenean pounding after. They arrived while *Silver Lady* was loosing her sails preparatory to sliding into its berth. Junco Torn, Chaker's son and one of the few Nexans about Laria's own age, gave the sisters a casual wave as he used his one remaining arm to grab the line Symeen tossed out to him. Nenean rushed forward to assist but, despite her getting underfoot, *Silver Lady* glided smoothly to the dock. What seemed like moments—or ages—later, Ranz stepped onto the dock, then turned to lend Wythcombe a hand.

They were an ill-matched pair. Laria knew that her tendency to compare Wythcombe to a potato had a great deal to do with the fact that, when she'd first met him, he had been digging tubers in his garden. He was somewhat shorter than average, balding, with weathered brown skin, deceptively mild brown eyes, and a generally nobbly build. Wythcombe had never said just how old he was, but Laria thought he couldn't be less than seventy and maybe as much as ninety. His attire was more suited to a farmer than a spellcaster, all but for the polished, rune-inscribed staff, topped with some rough mineral, that he held in his right hand. Laria knew that Wythcombe's many-pocketed vest was designed to hold the powders and dried herbs he used to hasten the activation of various spells but, combined with brown homespun trousers and well-used boots, it added to his overall lumpy appearance.

By contrast, Ranz—his full name was Ransom, but he hated to be called that—was as handsome as a dream. Like most Rhinadeians, his skin was a warm brown. His eyes were a pale ice grey with a darker rim around the iris. He wore his silky black hair to his shoulders, held from his face by a band tied across his forehead, the ends streaming down behind. Today's band was a dark blue, similar to one Laria had filched and that now resided like a guilty secret at the bottom of her trouser pocket. In imitation of his master, Ranz wore simple clothing, but on him the multi-pocketed vest didn't look in the least lumpy. He didn't carry a staff, but Laria didn't doubt he longed for that mark of a master spellcaster.

Wythcombe accepted Ranz's assistance, although something in his slight smile suggested that he was humoring Ranz much as Junco had humored Nenean. Stepping neatly behind them came Rusty the goat, wearing Wythcombe's packs.

Laria cleared her throat. "Welcome to the Nexus Islands." Aware that she sounded ridiculously formal, she tried again. "Right? I mean, I'm sure that Chaker Torn already greeted you and all that, but… I'm glad to see you both. This…"

She indicated Nenean, who was now standing next to Junco. "…is my sister, Nenean. And this is Junco Torn. Nenean, Junco, these are Wythcombe, Ranz, and Rusty."

"Is the goat yarimaimalom?" Junco asked, interested.

"Not wise," Wythcombe replied, "merely a beast of burden, a prop for my aging years. It really would have been too much to ask Varelle to watch Rusty, so I brought him along. I figured he could be left here if we didn't choose to take him with us. Goats eat almost anything. Rusty can make do with seaweed if he must."

As if to prove the point, Rusty trotted along the dock, down to the sandy, gravelly shore, and started chewing enthusiastically on a bristly weed. Nenean hooted with enthusiasm and galloped down the dock after the goat. Laria couldn't help but grin.

"If you don't mind having Nenean take change of Rusty, the first place I'm supposed to take you to is Virim's rooms."

"That's the sorcerer who created querinalo?" Wythcombe asked.

"That's him," Laria agreed. "I know you told us that you thought you could shield yourself and Ranz from querinalo, but Virim says he can do a better job. That way you won't need to deplete your mana maintaining a shield."

Wythcombe nodded. "That might be useful. However, I'll want to discuss the nature of Virim's shield with him before he does it."

Laria laughed. "Virim will be very happy to explain what he's doing to you. He *loves* to talk. The hard part will be getting him to stop explaining, and actually work the spell. Also, I've been told that when you're rested from your travels, the council wants to speak with you—with all of us, actually. I don't know the details, but there's some disagreement as to the best way for us to go after Kabot."

WOLF'S SOUL

"Interesting," Wythcombe said, his affable expression fading. "Very well. First Virim, then the council."

"You don't need to feel too rushed," Laria said quickly. "'I'm supposed to show you to your quarters as soon as Virim has proofed you. There's a nice cottage next to Plik that we've been using as a guest house that you can have. Private bedrooms and everything."

She decided not to mention that no one had wanted to move into that particular cottage because the Spell Wielders had used it as a prison. Also, even with the gate removed from its hinges and repurposed elsewhere, not many people wanted to live surrounded by blood briar. Plik claimed not to mind. He even worked with Frostweed in tending the ferocious stuff, which—to be fair—was a valuable medicinal herb when it wasn't killing anything stupid—or ignorant—enough get too close to it.

"'Plik?' That name sounds familiar," Wythcombe mused, following Laria down the dock.

"The maimalodalu," Ranz reminded. "The one who was captured by the Spell Wielders and is now a sort of elder statesman of the Nexus Islands."

"That's right!" Wythcombe said. "If I have estimated correctly, Plik's around my age. It will be good to have another oldster around. You young people are exhausting. Where's my other apprentice, by the by?"

"Hunting," Laria replied, "with Firekeeper. On the mainland—in the New World. I'm sure someone will have sent a message that you're here and they'll be back. If they went far afield, the local yarimaimalom wolf pack will howl to them."

"Marvelous," Wythcombe said. "Absolutely marvelous."

He said that a lot over the next few hours: repeatedly as he and Virim discussed querinalo and how to proof against it; when he met Plik; when he examined the blood briar (it turned out that Rhinadei had a several different varieties of the horrible plant); when Derian came to greet him astride the yarimaimalom horse, Eshinarvash, Isende behind him, her arms around his waist. The gate complex merited a "stupendous," and the council a "deeply honored."

Ranz was a lot more quiet, but his grey eyes missed nothing. Laria guessed he was imagining what it would have been like if he'd grown up here, surrounded by people who routinely used blood magic. No doubt the Spell Wielders would have recognized his considerable ability and taken care to train him. Of course, Ranz would have suffered querinalo, and probably wouldn't have come through nearly as handsome. Then again… Laria found herself imagining Ranz transformed into a sort of Ice King: the sleet grey of his eyes paled into glinting, topaz blue; his usually unruly black hair combed back and frosted at the temples; the planes of his face sharper, as if carved from a glacier. His touch would be as cold as Ynamynet's, but hadn't she and Skea managed to…? They did have a kid.

Laria felt herself grow hot and, not for the first time lately, was glad her skin was brown enough to hide a blush.

Wythcombe had opted to take a quick tour, then visit more with Virim. However, he all but ordered Ranz to tour the Nexus Islands. Laria thought that Wythcombe was very aware that Ranz had only lived in one isolated village, which he had left in pursuit of his teacher. Certainly, there were times that—despite the fact that Ranz was more than five years older than she was—Laria felt as if he was the younger. He certainly showed that "youngness" in his first informal encounter with Ynamynet.

When evening came, Laria brought Ranz with her to the dining hall. The Nexus Islands had come a long way since the previous summer, but communal meals had become a habit. In any case, one team cooking for everyone freed up other Nexans for other, more essential jobs.

Ynamynet came to greet them, her daughter Sunshine tugging at her hand, her husband, Skea, towering behind. As always, Ynamynet was bundled in clothing more suitable for outdoors in winter, even though the dining hall was warm from hot food and many people—not all of whom were human. The yarimaimalom had taken to dining with the humans when appropriate, a way of asserting that they were people, too, not just very interesting animals.

Ranz studied Ynamynet with the most animation that he'd permitted himself to this point. "Excuse me if I'm being rude. I don't really understand the protocol, but when Arasan was explaining about querinalo and how no one survived it without paying some sort of price, he used your situation as an example of how that price was not always readily apparent. Perhaps Arasan told you that my specialization is magic related to cold? I was wondering if I might…"

Ynamynet drew in her breath sharply. Behind her, Skea stiffened, which—given his height and bulk—would be enough to make most people stop talking. Even little Sunshine stopped smiling. But Ranz had built a city from snow and ice; that single-minded focus was upon him now.

"I was thinking that I might be able to reverse the damage. What happened to you might be something like the adaptation I raise for myself when I'm working with snow and ice, so my body heat doesn't melt the snow, but somehow stuck."

To say that Ynamynet's gaze became frosty was clichéd, but Laria couldn't help but think that if a gaze could freeze someone in their tracks, Ranz would be an ice statue now.

"My situation isn't quite that simple," Ynamynet said. "Querinalo isn't. Be glad you have been spared."

Ranz stammered. "I'm sorry… I did say I didn't understand the protocol. I only…"

Sunshine tugged at her mother's hand, and whispered, "Mama, you're scaring him."

Ynaymynet drew in a deep breath. "Yes. I'm sure I am. Ranz, come and dine with us. No hard feelings, but querinalo takes hold where one is weakest, and I am still very, very weak in some ways."

Laria glanced between them. Skea gave her a broad wink and tossed his head to where Ikitata waved from where she sat with Nenean and Kitatos.

"Go on, your mama's waiting. We'll see you at the meeting tonight."

So dismissed, Laria went. She glanced back, hoping Ranz would ask her to stay, but he was staring earnestly at Ynamynet and didn't seem to notice that she'd left.

"We have chairs for you and Blind Seer," Wort said when the wolves arrived prior to the meeting. Ruddy-skinned, fair-haired, Wort still possessed his warrior's build and kept fit, but these days his frontline was likely to be one of the warehouses.

As much as Blind Seer appreciated Wort's thoughtfulness, he wasn't about to spend the next few hours sitting upright, unable to get his tail into a comfortable position. He didn't need to voice his complaint to Firekeeper. She liked sitting on chairs as little as he did.

"Cannot sit that way," Firekeeper said. "Not for meeting. Blind Seer needs his tail to talk."

That last was both true and clever. Blind Seer huffed agreement and gently butted Firekeeper with his head in thanks.

Wort looked concerned. "But if you sit on the floor, people won't be able to see you."

"*People* will," Firekeeper retorted. "Some humans may have difficulty. What say this? When we have visited the Liglimom's u-Liall, they set their tables and chairs like this." She sketched a broad curve in the air. "Those of us—like Truth when she was the jaguar of her year—who are not human but are people, we sit closer to the ground. Truth have a special pillow even, though I think she would be happy with a rug or even a blanket."

Wort rubbed his palms against his ears hard enough that Blind Seer could hear the coarse hair within rasping. Then he shrugged. Like most of the Nexus Islanders, he would not have survived the war without the intervention of various yarimaimalom.

"That would work," he said.

To show her gratitude, Firekeeper hurried over to shift tables and chairs. The days when she thought such labor beneath a wolf were long gone. Now that the Nexus Islands were the closest thing she and Blind Seer had to a pack, she gave her all, as was right and proper for a wolf.

Blind Seer still lacked hands. He swallowed a sigh at this, but the grip of his jaws could be very delicate if he wished, so he pulled various chairs into position.

"Is Truth coming to the meeting?" Wort asked, obviously considering whether he should send one of his staff to find a rug.

"Blind Seer says he thinks she will," Firekeeper replied. She stood back, hands on hips, went to move one of the perches that had been supplied for those of the wingéd folk who would be attending, then nodded, satisfied. "Me and Blind Seer, we don't need a rug. The floor is fine."

"Blind Seer and I," Derian corrected, as he entered the room, his arms full of map cases. "You wouldn't say 'Me don't need a rug,' would you?"

"Maybe," Firekeeper hung her head, then peeked up through her tousled hair. "If I forget. Did you like the venison we brought back from the mainland?"

"Did you?" Derian said, moving to where an easel had been set and pinning up maps. "I don't think that was included in tonight's meal, but I'm sure it will be delicious."

"A bit tough," Firekeeper said honestly. "Spring game is, though on the mainland where it never really gets too winter, the game is fattening up nicely."

She shared news about the wolves they had run with during their visit. Derian was as interested in the news that Onion and Half-Ear's pack had a healthy litter of pups as he would have been to learn that one of his human friends had a new baby.

The best thing about Derian, Blind Seer thought as he eased himself onto the polished boards of the floor, *is that he didn't need querinalo to make him look like a horse to begin to think of Beasts as people.*

Not long after, the rest of the council filed in, minus, as usual, the doctor, Zebel. Derian and Ynamynet took seats at the center table, near the easel with the maps. Skea sat to Ynamynet's left, with Wythcombe and Ranz to his left. Urgana and Wort sat to Derian's right, where Arasan joined them a few moments later.

There was a chair for Laria next to Ranz but, to Blind Seer's surprise—his nose told him of the girl's interest in Ranz—Laria flung herself on the floor next to himself and Firekeeper. Farborn took one of the perches. Last, when her attendance would be certain to cause a reaction, the jaguar Truth padded in and lounged regally on the folded horse blanket Wort had found for her.

Blind Seer opened his mouth in a grin wide enough to show his molars. Truth would have made an impression even if she'd been a more normal jaguar, but her bout of querinalo—during which she claimed she had fought the Liglimom's deity of fire, Ahmyn—had turned her formerly golden fur charcoal black, transformed her black spots to reddish orange tongues of flame, and altered her dark-amber eyes to white with slit pupils of blue.

"Tell that human child that she can sit on the blanket with me," Truth said. "She need not sit on bare boards."

Firekeeper passed on the invitation. Laria—acutely aware of the honor—scooted over next to Truth, scratching the jaguar behind her rounded ears when invited to do so. Blind Seer wondered which of Truth's visions had told her that it was important to build Laria up in front of those who would still be inclined to view her as a child, but he did not doubt that Truth's actions were calculated to do precisely that.

After Truth had settled and water had been poured for those who wished it, Derian started talking. "Over dinner, those of you who hadn't done so already had opportunity to meet our guests from Rhinadei: Wythcombe and Ranz. Let's get down to business then."

"Business" proved to be a short summary of the events that had brought Wythcombe and Ranz to the Nexus Islands, "so you can correct us if we have any details wrong."

After Wythcombe stated that the council understood matters better than if he himself had reported them, Ynamynet took over, reporting—with occasional references to the map on the easel—about Azure Towers and how access to the ruins of the university was forbidden. Next the discussion became general as various options were discussed. No one liked the idea of leaving Kabot and his cabal to have free run of the university ruins, so "wait and see" was immediately discarded. Another option that was discarded was informing Queen Anitra of the situation, then leaving her to decide whether or not to investigate.

"If she says 'I don't believe you' or 'I don't want to take the risk until there's reason,' what would we do?" Skea asked. "I think it's best that we narrow to how and what to ask the queen. We should make it clear that this is a matter in which Wythcombe, as a representative of Rhinadei's government, in pursuit of a fugitive, feels a strong need to assure himself Kabot isn't in the ruins."

Wythcombe scratched the bald spot on the crown of his head and said, "I think Rhinadei's government would support me as their representative in this matter, although I will admit, I didn't come here with anything like an official appointment."

"As long as you think they'll back you if asked," Skea said, "that's enough."

Ranz had been studying the map. Now he half-raised one hand. "Is there a way we could get into the ruins without being detected? With Firekeeper and Blind Seer as guides, we could travel by night or under cover. That way we wouldn't need to involve the queen at all."

All eyes moved to look at the map. Azure Towers was bordered by the Mires to the west, Hearthome to the north, mountains to the east, and a short stretch of rocky shoreline to the south. There was a thoughtful silence.

"The magical gate we know of in Azure Towers is in the City of Towers," Urgana began after consulting her notes. "It's likely there were others, possibly many others, in the university city, but we know nothing of them and none of our investigations into the sealed gates has taken us there. If we don't wish Queen Anitra to know of your intent, using Azure Towers' gate would be out of the question."

"What about those other lands?" Ranz persisted. "From the stories Arasan told us, I had the impression that the Nexus Islands were on pretty good terms with the Mires. Would the king—Bryessidan, I think his name was—would he let us in through his gate? We could make our way across the Mires into Azure Towers, maybe cling to the shore, then find our way into the ruins."

Blind Seer snorted. The journey did look simple when one was looking at a map. That was the problem with humans—they tended to forget the picture wasn't the reality. He and Firekeeper had spent a very interesting half-moonspan in the Mires and come away from it with muddy paws and a firm respect for that treacherous terrain. But even if King Bryessidan provided a guide, there was another reason this was a bad option.

"*Tell them*," Blind Seer said to Firekeeper, "*that we cannot have King Bryessidan accused of partaking in what would—after all—be an invasion. That would be poor repayment for his overtures of friendship.*"

Firekeeper translated faithfully. Ranz, who had been looking quite eager, deflated. Doubtless he had been prepared to remind them that his gift for turning water into ice would make passing through the sodden swamplands, if not easy, at least possible.

"A related argument," Skea added, giving Blind Seer a nod, general to general, "applies to our sending a team in via the southern shore or the eastern mountains. The difference would be that the Nexus Islands could be accused of invading. We're establishing good relations with the various gate-holding lands, but none of them have forgotten even for a moment that one of the yet unawakened gates might open into their backyards. Trust is our best defense, and we don't dare weaken it."

"So," Arasan said, tapping a martial rhythm on the table, "that means we either must speak with Queen Anitra, or go in via her gate, then hope to sneak into the university ruins. I think we have ample reasons to discard the latter option. So we must speak with the queen, and hope she will give us permission to do what she and her ancestors have steadfastly forbidden since querinalo caused the fall of the sorcerer monarchs of old."

Somewhere in the course of planning the embassy to Queen Anitra of Azure Towers, Firekeeper realized that Derian was intending to be one of the members. For a brief moment, the thought made her very happy. No matter how much she had come to treasure other humans, Derian was her first human friend. He had stood up for her when she hadn't even known she needed defending—indeed, when she would have heatedly argued that the last thing she needed was any weak human's defense. Firekeeper hadn't understood the risks Derian had taken for her, because she hadn't understood how humans in his society judged not only on merit, but on birth. In return for these old debts, no matter how appealing the idea of having Derian with her and Blind Seer as they set off on this new journey, Firekeeper realized that it was her role to forbid him to join the embassy.

Shortly after the decision was made to approach Queen Anitra, the meeting was adjourned until after breakfast the next day. Of course, Derian had to stop and talk with any number of people before he could leave, but Firekeeper and Blind Seer waited patiently in the shadows, then trailed Derian to the cottage he shared with Isende. The door was hardly closed behind him before Firekeeper—remembering that this was Isende's home, too, and she might not approve if Firekeeper and Blind Seer came in unannounced—knocked lightly but firmly.

Derian swung the door open a narrow crack. "Can't it wait…" He stopped midsentence when he saw the two wolves and swung the door wide to admit them. "Firekeeper, Blind Seer… What is it? It must be important if you couldn't tell me at the meeting."

Firekeeper made certain the door was closed behind them, gave Isende a deep bow to wordlessly acknowledge that they had invaded her territory, then turned to Derian.

"Is important. Very. We came to tell you that you cannot go with us to Azure Towers, not even to the court for diplomacy."

Derian looked shocked and hurt, Isende only puzzled. She recovered first, and motioned to the hearth where banked coals broke the springtime chill.

"Have a seat on the rug by the fire. I have some oatmeal raisin cookies and tea. I knew Derian would be hungry after the meeting."

Firekeeper and Blind Seer accepted the offered place by the fire, although the room was warm enough that they would have been more comfortable away from it. However, they knew when welcome was being offered, and the situation was delicate enough that they had no desire to unbalance it. Firekeeper even accepted a cookie, although she didn't have much of a taste for sweets. These little social rituals gave Derain an opportunity to recover his poise. Anyone who didn't know him so well—or have Blind Seer's keen nose for reading human moods—would have been fooled by his casual, teasing reply.

"So, I can't come with you? Certainly you don't think you're up to negotiating with queens, do you? Or do you now trust Arasan so much? Have you forgotten that the Meddler is there as well? Or do you think you have him on a choke chain?"

Firekeeper frowned as she pieced through this barrage of questions. "No. No. Yes. Not at all. No. Not anymore."

Isende sputtered with laughter, then poured tea for Derian and herself, water for Firekeeper and Blind Seer. "Derian, why don't you ask Firekeeper why she doesn't want you to go with them? Then you'll have a better foundation for arguing with her."

Blind Seer thumped his tail against the floor and Isende amended. "With them. Blind Seer clearly agrees with Firekeeper."

Derian's ears flickered as if he might pin them back in mulish refusal, then he sighed. "Very well. Firekeeper, why do you and Blind Seer think I shouldn't come with you to Azure Towers?"

Firekeeper hid her relief. She really hadn't wanted to get into a fight with Derian. "There is—are—two reasons. One is because of who you are. Even if you do not say this too loudly, you are the One of the Nexus Islands. Not a king, no, but definitely One, because everyone looks to you when a decision must be made—especially if that decision is not about magic. If you go with us, then what is just people becomes something more. A meeting of packs, of governments. I do not think you wish this thing. If we decide to do something sneaky, then it is like what Blind Seer said about King Bryessidan helping—an invasion or attack."

Derian looked uncomfortable. "Do you plan to do something 'sneaky'?"

"Plan? No. But if we must, we must. This is too big to leave alone or to leave others to deal with. I think—Blind Seer, too—from how Kabot left a message for Wythcombe and only for Wythcombe that part of what Kabot does is because of Wythcombe. Good? Bad? I don't know. But this is why we cannot leave this to Queen Anitra and her people to decide."

Blind Seer lifted his head from his paws and stared at Derian. *"Tell him, dear heart, that while I could not get much sense out of Truth, she did say that those of us who went into Rhinadei, as well as the two from Rhinadei, must be involved or worse would happen. That she risked the streams of insanity to learn this much makes me feel that she, too, feels this is not a matter we can leave to Queen Anitra."*

Firekeeper translated and Derian sighed again. "So, one reason I shouldn't go is that this matter then becomes Nexus Island business. I might argue…"

Isende cut in. "But you'd be wrong. So don't, Derian, just don't. I suspect that Firekeeper and Blind Seer are anticipating an argument that would have come up in the morning meeting. I'm interested in knowing what their other reason for not letting you go is."

"She smells of apprehension," Blind Seer said. *"The tang is strong, but I cannot tell why she feels this way."*

In reply, Firekeeper gently squeezed his shoulder with the hand that lay buried in the fur on his back, then went on, "Isende, this next is not signs and omens. It is what we two, Derian's friends, think. We think Derian needs to go home to his family. It has been too long. So much has changed and those changes are far bigger than the horse ears and handsome mane. He has found you. In the religion which is like a pack to him, Fox Hair needs to show you to his family, to his ancestors. Then you and him and any little ones will be part of the bigger pack. If going to them was impossible, then it would not matter, I think. But it is possible and, no matter how Derian makes excuses, as long as he puts off this visit, the putting off will eat at his gut."

Isende smiled and rested her hand on Derian's arm. "I think that, too, but I also understand his being nervous."

Blind Seer said and Firekeeper translated, "If we worry about the elk kicking, we will never begin the hunt."

"I understand what you mean," Derian said, "but what if I'm in doubt about the wisdom of this hunt?"

"You don't doubt," Firekeeper stated firmly. "You are only nervous. Blind Seer says to tell you there is another reason for this going. As we have said over and over, you are the One of these islands. To those in the New World, you will be the most important One, for they will not trust Ynamynet because she is a sorcerer. They must learn to know you and accept you. Grateful Peace will smooth the way in New Kelvin. I think that—much as you may doubt this— Rahniseeta will in Liglim. But for Hawk Haven and Bright Bay, you must speak for yourself, and quickly."

"Blind Seer says all of that?" Derian said, forcing a chuckle. "He has a lot more to say these days than he used to."

"Blind Seer has changed," Firekeeper admitted. "Before he viewed himself as one of our pack of two. Now we has a bigger pack."

"Ouch!" Derian said, but he was laughing as he said it. "Very well. I will make clear that not only shouldn't I be part of this embassy, neither should Ynamynet or anyone who could be taken as representing the Nexus Islands. Moreover, I will also make clear that Isende and I haven't changed our plans to go first to Liglim, then from there, by ship, to Bright Bay and Hawk Haven."

Isende visibly relaxed. Firekeeper didn't need Blind Seer's nose to know that she was pleased. And why shouldn't Isende be? She had no family other than

Derian. To remain forever on the fringe would become increasingly painful and might, in time, weaken the budding trust between them.

"This is all good," Firekeeper said. "We think everyone will feel relieved. If you can go away from the Nexus Islands, then there is nothing to fear, for they know you would never leave if you did not believe everyone will be safe."

Derian tossed back his forelock. "Now, if only I can make myself believe that."

II

"Why don't we start with sort of the truth?" Laria suggested, when the after-breakfast meeting had gone round and round regarding the best way to approach Queen Anitra without making the audience seem too important. "We've opened a gate. We've found a new land. The people from the new land want to see where their ancestors came from. Since the people of Rhinadei consider Azure Towers about as close to a homeland as they have, we want to bring them there."

There was silence as everyone considered. Then Urgana, who could be trusted to be tart if she thought the reaction was merited, gave a dry chuckle. "Perfect! I suggest we approach Loris Ambler, head of the diplomatic corps, rather than sending a request directly to the queen. We can hint that since Wythcombe and Ranz are the first members of Rhinadei to depart for centuries, they are ambassadors. As such, the queen might want to meet them, but we will leave it up to them to decide."

"But," Firekeeper said anxiously, "what if Queen Anitra doesn't want to see them?"

Arasan chuckled. When he spoke, his voice held all of his own natural music and all the Meddler's guile. "Then we hint that there are reasons Wythcombe and Ranz should meet with the queen. We could even make our request to tour the ruins to Loris Ambler. She's certain to bring *that* to the queen, especially if we hint that Wythcombe and Ranz are custodians of a dangerous secret. But I'm willing to bet my favorite thumb piano that Queen Anitra will give them an audience. She has her fair share of human curiosity."

While the council worked on the letter that would be sent to Loris Ambler, everyone else focused on finding appropriate attire for court. Wythcombe and Ranz had brought nothing fancy with them, and there was a great deal of debate on how they should be dressed. The Rhinadeian's equivalent of court dress was not too different from the elaborate robes favored by the thaumaturges of New Kelvin. This was no great surprise, since both cultures had evolved traditions rooted from the same source: the days when the sorcerers of old had been dominant.

"We could present ourselves as non-magical," Wythcombe said, "but that would only cause difficulties in the future—and I do not need to be gifted with prophesy to know that once opened, gates are not easily closed. Best not to begin our relationship with deception."

One of the two gates that communicated with the New World went into New Kelvin. Contact was made and Citrine Shield, a young woman a few years older than Laria, came through, consulted, then took back with her detailed drawings of what Wythcombe and Ranz required. She returned with the promise that her foster father, Grateful Peace, would be able to arrange for appropriate attire and took measurements. Wythcombe requested that his robes be brown touched with harvest gold and green. The obvious theme for Ranz was white, because of his affiliation with cold and snow, but he balked at something so much showier than what his master would be wearing. In the end, cool shades of blue and the dark green of deeply frozen ice were chosen.

The only payment Grateful Peace requested for this very expensive commission was an audience with Wythcombe and Ranz at their convenience—and Wythcombe found it convenient to make himself available almost immediately. Both Rhinadeians were eager to meet people from other cultures, doubtless so they could get a better sense for the world their ancestors had left behind centuries before.

This meant that Laria didn't see much of either Wythcombe or Ranz for the next few days, but she tried hard not to feel to bereft. It was actually easy enough. Getting fitted for her own court attire was surprisingly fun. It hadn't been that long ago that she'd been grateful for clothing that wasn't third or fourth hand. To have something that wasn't only new, but was made specifically for her, was exciting. The Nexus Islands hadn't settled on anything like standard formalwear, so Laria was aware that what she wore would set precedent. Right off, Ynamynet insisted that those who had a magical gift display some badge or emblem indicating this was the case.

"We have nothing to be ashamed of," Ynamynet stated firmly. "Also, in this way we cannot be accused of concealing our strengths."

Even Firekeeper surrendered to being fitted with court attire with relative grace, although she did insist that she not be swaddled up in a gown or robe—especially when they couldn't be certain of their reception. No one argued, since Firekeeper's reputation as a warrior—which the wolf-woman said was undeserved, since she wanted nothing to do with war, and only used her blade and bow for necessary killing—had been not only established but embellished in ballads and tales. Dressing her in fripperies and lace would only raise suspicion.

"A wolf in sheep's clothing," Derian laughed when he was consulted. "I'm glad those days are over. The trauma of lacing Firekeeper into gowns will haunt me to my deathbed. Design something nice-looking with trousers, a shirt that won't bind or drag on the arms, and maybe a waistcoat after the Hawk Haven style. I can't see you in buckled shoes, Firekeeper. Will you wear boots? Going barefoot in the palace would probably be considered impolite."

Firekeeper wriggled her toes in mute protest but agreed. Laria's mother, Ikitata, who had continued with family's cobbling shop after her husband's death, was soon doing a rush order on custom boots.

Laria decided to follow Firekeeper's example, since she was determined to wear Volsyl if at all possible. Everyone knew that Firekeeper had an obsession about not being parted from the garnet-hilted hunting knife she called her Fang. Laria figured she might as well start establishing herself as having similar rights. A partially finished sheath in the shop fit Volsyl nicely, and Laria stamped it with cresting waves, in honor of the rough seas that protected her island home.

How to dress Blind Seer for court raised a great deal of debate, since Ynamynet insisted that his talent for magic should not be hidden any more than that of the others. Blind Seer refused to wear a collar, stating with a growl that Firekeeper did not need to translate that he would not be taken for anyone's dog.

Laria suggested that the great grey wolf be fit for broad leather bands he could wear on his front "wrists." She stamped these with a pattern of curving lines that she tinted in brilliant blue (for Blind Seer's eyes), dark green (for the forests) and gold (because it looked good). The final result was very impressive. Best of all, as Firekeeper put it, Blind Seer could eat the bracers if he got hungry enough. She laughed when she said this, and Laria grinned back.

Loris Ambler's reply came within a few days. It indicated that Queen Anitra would give a private audience to the new arrivals and their escort at their mutual convenience. After that, it was only a matter of finishing the fancy clothes, then making sure that everyone had supplies, since they might need to leave directly from the palace for the ruins. After some debate, Wythcombe decided to bring Rusty the goat along.

"They may speculate that he's my familiar if they wish," he said with one of the grins that had been all too infrequent since they'd discovered that Kabot had vanished, "but I suspect that having him trailing along will simply make me look harmless."

Which I am not, went unspoken.

Loris Ambler met them as they came through the gate into a room that shared the very old, very new, feeling Laria was familiar with from the Nexus Islands. The stone walls were covered with intricate bas-relief carvings in which the dark veining within the white stone accented the figures and symbols. Such art, common where gates had been built, hinted at an ideology that modern spellcasters admitted had been lost in the eruption of anti-magical sentiment after the coming of querinalo. Ancient art was balanced by fresh wood timbers shoring up doorframes, the scent of beeswax used to polish furniture, in the dozens of little ways that the people of Azure Towers had sought to establish their ownership of this barely understood, yet terribly powerful, magic.

Sometimes, Laria thought, *in our efforts to claim ancestral artifacts, we look like children playing dress-up with their parents' cast-off clothing. We imagine it fits and makes us impressive but, deep down inside, we know we're a little ridiculous.*

The people of the continent of Pel tended to pinker skin than anyone else, except maybe for the inhabitants of Tavetch. If, like Derian or Firekeeper, whose ancestors had come from Pel, they spent a great deal of time outside, they darkened to a respectable brown, but if, like Loris Ambler, their livelihood kept them inside, they looked washed-out and pale. Loris's hair was a golden-brown not unlike Laria's own, and her eyes a shade somewhere between blue and grey. She wasn't precisely pretty, but she was well turned-out. Her affect as she greeted them seemed simultaneously relaxed and animated.

Laria liked that Loris Ambler made no attempt to pretend she wasn't interested in the strange ambassadorial group. The diplomat even studied Rusty the goat, flinching a little as the goat returned the favor through those oddly perceptive, split-pupiled eyes, before trotting over to nudge Wythcombe for a treat.

After introductions had been completed, Loris said, "Although I'm sure that it won't be long before rumors spread that the Nexus Islands has made yet another remarkable discovery, Queen Anitra, in her wisdom, has decided that it would be best for all involved if the revelation be handled as diplomatically as possible."

Wythcombe nodded gravely, as if this statement was more than just polite noise. "Absolutely. As Ranz and I explained to the council of the Nexus Islands, Rhinadei is not certain as to whether it would be prudent for us to once again engage in discourse with those lands our ancestors thought best to leave behind."

Laria knew this was perfectly true, but she also knew that Wythcombe had chosen his words to make Loris Ambler eager for Azure Towers to make the best impression possible.

It's one thing when you think you're the one being courted. It's another entirely when the presumed suitor says he may not be interested after all. Wythcombe knows a lot more than just a bunch of spells.

Loris Ambler blinked a few times as she considered what Wythcombe could mean, doubtless adding subtexts of her own. Then she offered a meaningless smile and said, "The meeting will be small: the queen, General Merial, and Trahaene, one of the queen's Once Dead advisors."

"That sounds wonderful," Wythcombe replied with an equally meaningless nod. Laria noticed how the archaic pronunciation he gave to some of the vowels had become more pronounced. Was he nervous or was he subtly reminding the ambassador that he was from elsewhere? Laria couldn't decide. She knew that going after Kabot meant a great deal to the old man—and these were the people who might refuse him permission to do so.

Since there was no need to rest from their journey, Loris Ambler led them from the gate room, along corridors that were cleared even of guards, up several flights of stairs, until they finally emerged in a windowless room that Laria suspected didn't appear on most maps of the palace. For all that the room was without windows, it was well lit by magical glow blocks. Once Laria would have seen these as miraculously bright but, after what she'd encountered in

Rhinadei, they seemed dingy. The air was perfumed with something spicy and floral that made both Blind Seer and Firekeeper sneeze. Rusty glanced around, as if wondering if the source of the odor was something he could eat.

"My goat," Wythcombe said apologetically, "is not house-trained. If you have a place where he could wait without endangering your carpets, that would be wise. You might want to tie him out of reach of any valuable plants, but he won't raise a fuss if he's given something—just about anything—to eat."

Loris Ambler immediately detailed an attendant, who had appeared as soon as they had entered the secret meeting room, to take Rusty to a garden, "not too far away."

Laria wondered why an expression of pleasure flickered across Firekeeper's face. Certainly, the wolf-woman had shown no sign of disliking the goat. Laria would have said Firekeeper actually appreciated Rusty's versatility as a pack animal. Then Laria understood.

With Blind Seer's sense of smell—maybe even Firekeeper's own—tracking Rusty would be easy. The goat was as clean as human ingenuity could make him, but he was still a billy goat and, as such, had a strong odor. That meant that no matter how secret the route along which they had been taken to get to this chamber, Blind Seer could lead them out of the building. A little thing, but one that relieved a feeling of being trapped that Laria hadn't even been aware of to that point.

A fanfare of trumpets broke through Laria's absorption. Fighting an urge to cringe and abase herself as she had been taught to do in the presence of the Spell Wielders, Laria offered a respectful bow as Queen Anitra of Azure Towers swept into the room.

Long before the door opened, Blind Seer heard the armed and armored soldiers approaching. The sounds were muffled by distance and a well-fitting door, but leather did squeak and chainmail did rattle. Nor were those who were marching closer doing anything to muffle the sounds of their approach. For this reason, he perked his ears as a warning to Firekeeper, but did not prepare for a fight. Had threat been intended, surely there would have been some attempt at stealth. Either there was no threat intended or those who were now slowing on the other side of the door believed they were strong enough to overwhelm any threat.

And if that last, they might be surprised, but I do not really think they intend harm. The ramifications for Azure Towers would be very complicated. As we told the Rhinadeians, Firekeeper has made friends in many places, and so have I.

Although sound said that Queen Anitra was not unguarded, when the door to the secret meeting room opened, only three people came through. Blind Seer tried to perceive the three as his human companions would, without losing his wolfish impressions in the process.

Queen Anitra was a woman of middle years. In shades of hair and eye, Blind Seer had found that the Pellanders seemed to be more varied than many humans. Queen Anitra was no exception, although in her case Blind Seer suspected that art was assisting nature. The queen's hair was a soft honey shade, touched with red. Her eyes were a blue nowhere as brilliant as Blind Seer's own. More important than their color was their thoughtful expression, graven into her features with small lines. Queen Anitra was about Firekeeper's height, which was average for a human, but much more roundly built. Her scent—although overlaid with a complex floral medley—said she was healthy. Her dominant emotion was curiosity, sparked with fear when she saw Blind Seer. He took the reaction as his due. It was one thing to hear about a wolf the size of a pony. It was another to encounter one sitting, no matter how politely, in one's home.

General Merial was not a stranger, having been in charge of Azure Tower's forces during the recent war. In appearance, the general was not unlike Queen Anitra, which made sense, since Blind Seer understood they were closely related. However, although the general possessed ample curves, there was no softness to her. Her scent held no fear when she saw the wolves, and her eyes narrowed when she saw that Loris Ambler had admitted several bearing weapons into this private chamber.

Trahaene the Once Dead was so heavily shrouded in elaborately embroidered robes that seeing him as a living creature was almost impossible. He looked more like a yellow and purple fabric cone with a head on top. That head continued the impression that Trahaene was an object, rather than a living thing, by rising to a sharp point. For all his elaborate garb, the Once Dead did his best to efface himself, projecting in many small ways that he was only there in service to his monarch. Despite the heavy musky scent he wore—obviously habitual, since the robes were saturated with it—the odor of his sweat came through. The message it carried was complex. Trahaene was interested, apprehensive, fascinated, and worried.

Blind Seer resigned himself to accepting that he'd never know all the experiences that contributed to this complex blend. Emotionally twisted humans often didn't understand what drove them.

After introductions had been completed, Queen Anitra suggested that they take seats in the assortment of chairs set near the center of the room. Other than selecting an elaborately carved, high-back seat, she did not otherwise set herself above the rest. Judging from the way she settled in against the cushions, that simply might be her favorite chair.

The letter which had been sent to Queen Anitra had only contained the most basic information. Therefore, the first portion of the meeting was occupied with telling her about Rhinadei, then about the Nexans' visit there. There were numerous questions—especially regarding Blind Seer's decision to study spellcasting—but mostly the discussion remained focused. Arasan had the storyteller's gift for vivid detail, and had consulted with Wythcombe as to how to lead up to why it was important that Kabot and his associates be found—and stopped.

After Arasan reached the climax of his tale—their reaching Mount Ambition to find Kabot gone, having left a message for Wythcombe—Queen

Anitra quoted Kabot's words softly: "'Someday we'll come back and let the folks back home know how we did. Sadly, you may be dead by then, having grown old while I didn't age, which is why I'm leaving you this message.' I don't know this Kabot, but that message sounds like a challenge to me. Does it to you, Wythcombe?"

"It does," Wythcombe agreed, rubbing his nose vigorously. "Kabot was rarely sentimental. That bit about me dying from old age before he comes back… That sounds like a hint I should try to catch up. Why? I'm not certain, and there is only one way I can find out."

"Locate him," General Merial said, the two words sword slashes. "You think he came here to Azure Towers. Earlier, you mentioned that one reason you speak a form of Pellish is because most of those who settled Rhinadei had studied at the university. If Kabot was seeking those who would not outright reject him and his interest in blood magic, the university would be a very reasonable place for him to go. Is that it?"

"I could not have stated it better myself," Wythcombe said with deceptive mildness. "The question is, will you sanction my looking for him?"

Trahaene the Once Dead said sternly, "I am certain that my associates and I would be aware of the arrival of a group of alien sorcerers. As do the Nexus Islands, we monitor for indications that a gate has been used."

Wythcombe nodded. "I am certain you do. When I analyzed what remained of Kabot's workings, I came to the conclusion that he did not use a gate, as such, but a transport spell."

"What's the difference?" snapped General Merial.

"A gate is intended to be used more than once. A transportation spell is impermanent, meant only to be used once."

"Very good. Continue."

Wythcombe looked directly at Trahaene and spoke peer to peer—a rank Blind Seer was certain the Once Dead did not merit.

"Depending on how your circle is monitoring, it is possible that you might not detect a transportation spell. You see, unlike a gate, which requires magic on both sides, transportation spells invest most of their magic on the side where the spell begins."

"Ah… I see," Trahaene said, nodding sagely.

"Well, I don't," General Merial said. "Would you clarify?"

To everyone's surprise, Queen Anitra spoke. "I believe that a transportation spell would be akin to a slide. All the energy goes into creating the slide, then pushing off."

Wythcombe beamed at the queen as he sometimes did at Ranz and Blind Seer when they showed they had understood one of his lectures. "Very nice! A slide provides an excellent image because it's meant to carry a person one direction, while a gate permits travel in two. Yes, an excellent analogy."

Not to be left out, General Merial added, "So this spell would be like a snow slide in winter. Impermanent. Leaving no trace after the snow melts."

"Except," Wythcombe said, "perhaps for scuffs on the muddy ground beneath. Those scuffs are what I studied."

"You made that examination very quickly," Merial said suspiciously. "Arasan's tale gave us to understand that your group took many days and dealt with numerous perils to reach Mount Ambition. You then returned nearly immediately via a spell. When did you have time to search for 'scuffs'?"

"Very astute," Wythcombe replied, unruffled, although Blind Seer could smell Ranz starting to bristle at the implication that the old spellcaster was lying. "Before I left Mount Ambition, I placed a recall spell. I knew that my associates would wish to see for themselves that Kabot was gone. They then helped me with my analysis."

"Very clear," the queen said. "Let me consider."

A respectful silence followed as Queen Anitra drew into herself. Laria traced a finger along the hem of her dress tunic, but otherwise the humans might have been statues.

At last, the queen spoke. "Very well. We understand what has brought you to us. While we appreciate your courtesy, and consider ourselves duly warned about this Kabot, if you are hoping for permission to seek him in Azure Towers—especially within the university ruins—I must refuse you. Entry into those ruins has been forbidden even to our own trusted retainers. I cannot make an exception for outsiders."

Her face was stony. Nothing in her scent gave Blind Seer hope the queen could be convinced to change her mind.

"I believe you are being hunted," said the Voice within Kabot's head.

There had been many times since they emerged into the university ruins that Kabot had almost convinced himself that the Voice was nothing more than elaborate wish fulfillment. He missed Phiona; therefore, he talked to himself in her voice as the closest he could come to seeking her counsel. But these words—coming just when he'd been thinking about how isolated he felt—certainly came from some other source.

"What?" Kabot spoke aloud, garnering surprised glances from Daylily and Uaid. He waved a hand at them in reassurance. "Sorry! Pinched my finger on a rock." Then he continued within the confines of his own mind. *"How would you know?"*

"One such as I am does not possess precisely the same senses as you do. I've been concerned for you. As I told you, these ruins are off-limits, and the penalties for trespassing are severe. I've been doing what I can to find if you were in any danger. Today, I sensed—what to call it?—emanations? That will have to do. I traced these and discovered that others are on their way here."

"That doesn't mean we're being pursued," Kabot protested, more out of habit than because he didn't believe what the Voice said. *"Places are not forbidden unless there are those who would desire to enter them."*

"Wise words. Will you forgive me if I anticipated that chain of thought? I

have—call it 'peeked.' Among those who have arrived in Azure Towers is one I recognize from your memories."

"Wythcombe!"

"You have it."

"Here? In the Old Country? How?"

"That I cannot say. But I can swear that I have seen Wythcombe. He is not alone. His companions include several bearing weapons, a monstrous wolf, a falcon, and… a goat."

Kabot shuddered, envisioning this horrific company and, at its head, Wythcombe, his gaze holding no pity as he surged forth to find those he must view as rogues and rebels, to arrest them, to drag them back to Rhinadei where, at the very least, they would meet with censure and, most likely, would be executed. In all his long years of isolation, Kabot had never believed that what Rhinadei would mete out to him and his companions would stop with a few harsh words.

Panic closed his throat so that Kabot struggled to speak, even within the confines of his mind. *"How long do we have?"*

"Several days?" The mental voice lilted with uncertainty. "Wythcombe radiates such power that looking toward him is like looking into the sun. Several of his companions carry ample magic within their auras. The wolf may even be a shapeshifter of some sort, for I read a trace of spellcasting in its aura."

Kabot felt his pulse rising. Shapeshifting was not unknown in Rhinadei, but it was shunned—especially when the shape taken was that of a powerful carnivore. Most of the tales told about beast-shifters dwelt on the insanity that occurred when the bestial impulses overwhelmed the human.

"But you're sure they're coming after us?"

"Why else would they be here—at this place, at this time? You're not a child to fool yourself that it could be otherwise."

"No. You're right. We must take counsel with Uaid and Daylily. Or have you told them already?" Kabot was aware of a splash of irrational jealousy. He hoped the Voice had not noticed.

"I have not. Even when you were all trapped within the webwork of the same spell, I found it easiest to reach you. Now, without the spell, you are the only one I can speak to almost as if I had lips and tongue. Don't tell them this, though. I do consider them my dear friends. I trust you can find an excuse to work the summons I taught you."

"I can."

Kabot felt the Voice recede. As always after an extended mental communication, he had to anchor himself anew in the physical world, and that physical world never failed to be horribly disappointing. When their spell had dropped them into the university ruins, the three rebels had found themselves in what they had later decided must be a test laboratory. Such rooms were usually underground, constructed with thick, often rounded, ceilings and walls, which could be inscribed into a full-coverage protective circle. Since these rooms were usually multipurpose chambers, they were rarely furnished other than with light blocks built into the walls.

The door of their room of emergence had been smashed so that jagged stone fragments jutted from the aperture's edges. When they had ventured without, they had been forced to spend day after day burrowing through rubble-choked corridors. Here Uaid's specialization in earth magics had proven of great worth. Greater, Kabot privately admitted, than his own more esoteric and academic lore had been.

Kabot had come into his own when, after many days of searching, they had found what seemed to be a professor's office, intact behind a concealed door. The tomes and scrolls on the many shelves had been nearly untouched, although they were brittle with age. Since then, they had been carefully examining the ancient writings, but so far there had been no revelations.

As Kabot turned to inspect his companions, Uaid was unrolling a scroll with meticulous patience. Daylily was examining a diagram in a tome about blending mana channels. After so long as phantoms caught within a distorted spell, it still seemed odd to actually see them. Kabot forced himself to study them, to remind himself that they were not just elements within his imagination.

The first thing that struck him was that—although Kabot was accustomed to thinking of the three of them as young—all of them were past their first bloom. Magic was a demanding craft. While someone quite young might become an expert in a single area—as Uaid was with earth magics—versatility took time and considerable study.

Uaid, the youngest, had celebrated his fortieth birthday shortly before they set their plans in action. Physically, Uaid showed his age more than did Daylily, even though she was nearly two decades his senior. Uaid looked very much like an earth mage should: short and stocky, with weathered brown skin. His thick fingers were, despite their apparent clumsiness, astonishingly skillful. If earth magic had not drawn him, Uaid could have become famous as a jeweler. He still might choose a future as an enchanter of arcane items. Uaid's coarse black hair was showing iron grey at the temples and in a few streaks within his tidy spade-shaped beard. His brows were bushy, shadowing eyes the dark brown of freshly turned loam.

Daylily looked about the same age as Uaid: a well-preserved early forty. She was a generalist, not from lack of focus but because what fascinated her were connections, the more disparate the better. Alone of their group, her interest in blood magic probably had less to do with the ready access to mana it provided than with a reluctance to relinquish even one aspect of the arcane arts. Daylily loved to play with cosmetic arts so, at the present moment, her skin appeared a pleasant golden-brown, her hair a shimmering pale pink, and her eyes a clear topaz blue. She was not so much pretty as elegant, every feature well-balanced, her figure rounded without being lush. Many men had fallen hopelessly in love with her, but none had held her heart tightly enough to keep her from this adventure.

But that's true of all of us, Kabot thought. *Except possibly Uaid, and I'm not certain if what he felt for Caidon was love or adoration.*

When he'd been a boy, Kabot's nickname had been "Foxy," not only because his hair was red, but because something about his sharp features—triangular face, pointed chin, expressive brows—had reminded others of a fox. Now in his mid-forties, Kabot's hair, which he usually wore brushed back to display a slight widow's peak, had lost its fire brightness, shading to a pleasant reddish brown. Since their transition, Kabot's hair had grown long enough that he needed to tie it back. As soon as he could find the ingredients to do so, he planned to make a pomade; then he'd ask Daylily to cut his hair to its more usual "just below the ears." As was typical of the descendants of Rhinadei's settlers, Kabot's skin and eyes were variations of brown. Indeed, one of the more startling things they'd found in these ruins was how many of the humans depicted in the fragmentary illustrations were fair-skinned, with light eyes and hair. Kabot doubted that his red hair would have been worthy of comment here, and weirdly felt as if something special had been stolen from him.

Kabot closed the tome he'd been perusing—one on elementals—and shook his head as if something had buzzed in his ear. "Did you two hear that whisper? I think the Voice wants to talk to us."

He knew that neither Uaid nor Daylily would deny that they had heard something. Uaid was very aware that of their original group of five, he had been junior, included as much because Caidon would have refused to leave him than because of his own qualifications. Daylily thought of herself as "sensitive." Part of the appeal of blood magic to her was because she felt that the best route to knowing "other bloods" was by sharing their blood.

After a moment, first Uaid, then Daylily, nodded.

"I think he has a message for us," Daylily said. Her clear topaz eyes clouded. She always referred to the Voice as "he," which irked Kabot. However, since he didn't want to discuss his own impression of the Voice, he kept that annoyance to himself. "Poor soul," Daylily continued. "He must get so very, very lonely. Shall we go back to our room and work a summons?"

"By all means," Kabot said, pleased she had spared him the need to make the suggestion.

"Definitely!" Uaid weighted the scroll so it wouldn't roll up, then shoved himself to his feet.

At their base camp, the two men set up the brazier and selected certain powdered herbs. They were lucky that, although they had lost much equipment during their first failed transition, they had retained many of the basics, including camping gear and apparatus for creating more complex spells. As they had explored the university ruins, they had augmented their supplies in little ways: a cup, mineral powders, a flask, and the like. "Treasure" was indeed relative to situation.

Daylily sang softly to herself as she heated liquid ingredients over a small lamp. Kabot reached out a tendril of awareness, but caught no hint that Daylily was focusing her gift—a reasonable suspicion since, like many others, Daylily often used song to feed mana into her spells. This, however, sounded like a love song. Fleetingly, he wondered if the Voice sounded like some particular person to her.

Although their entire purpose for coming to the Old World had been to seek those who routinely practiced blood magic, nonetheless, they were all intensely aware that each time they worked this spell they were taking an irrevocable step away from repatriation into Rhinadei. As they gathered around the brazier and took out small, razor-sharp knives consecrated to bloodletting, Kabot felt a blending of titillation and fear. Three times three drops of blood went into the fire, three times three more into each of their cups of tea. Words were said, spiced smoke inhaled, and finally the blood-infused tea was swallowed in a single long gulp.

Kabot felt his mana blend with that of Uaid and Daylily, then felt their braided power go forth to link to the Voice. The first time they'd worked this spell, the result had been much like what they had experienced during their inadvertent captivity within the transportation spell. Later, Kabot had experienced an additional visual component. At first it had been little more than the brazier's smoke forming the lines of a face. Now, what shaped above the brazier was the body, from the waist up, of a full-breasted nude woman who bore more than a passing resemblance to Phiona.

Quickly, Phiona briefed them on Wythcombe's probable arrival in Azure Towers, then the smoke form turned a much remembered, much missed, gaze upon him. *"I believe I have discovered the means both for you to defend yourselves against those who might seek to take you captive and, more importantly, to prove your value to the sorcerers whose community you would join. I won't promise that what I suggest will be either easy or without risk but, if you succeed, you will be more than supplicants, you will be hailed for rediscovering an artifact lost for centuries."*

<hr />

"I know the queen forbad us the ruins," Wythcombe said, pacing back and forth, staff in hand. "As a member of Rhinadei, I fully believe in abiding by the law. However, that doesn't change that Queen Anitra has made a bad decision. Kabot must be found."

After their audience with the queen had concluded, rather than returning to the Nexus Islands, they had taken rooms at an inn whose owner—recognizing Firekeeper and Blind Seer—had given them a ground floor suite for what the wolf-woman understood was a very reasonable rate. The son of the inn's owner, it seemed, had been among the troops who had huddled within the shield on the Nexus Islands awaiting morning and probable death. That Firekeeper had led the raid which had taken hostage the commanders of the various armies, thus ending the conflict before it could begin, made her a hero in the innkeeper's eyes.

Firekeeper was pleased, but she didn't have time or energy to luxuriate in this proof of her spreading reputation. Wythcombe was upset enough to do something reckless. She was wondering how she might stop Blind Seer's treasured new teacher without offending either the spellcaster (which only mattered a little) or Blind Seer (which mattered a great deal more).

Arasan threw himself loose-limbed into one of the heavily cushioned chairs, then stretched so his joints audibly popped. "We have requested a second audience with the queen. How do we present our case in a fresh light? Wythcombe, you're a skillful spellcaster– we've seen ample evidence of that.

Can't you—forgive my ignorance—somehow scry for Kabot? If we could confirm he was somewhere in the ruins, maybe we could—I don't know—maybe ask for an escort in?"

"Even if we confirmed Kabot was there," Laria said doubtfully, "it doesn't seem like the queen would do that. I mean, an escort would draw a lot of attention. You're not thinking clearly, Arasan. Are you well?"

"I feel a little out of it," Arasan admitted. "Maybe the gate passage didn't agree with me. If you"—He stared hard at Wythcombe and Ranz—"promise not to do anything impulsive, I'll go rest for a bit."

"Rest," Firekeeper replied. "I will howl if Wythcombe and his apprentices begin running away."

Arasan hauled himself from his chair and vanished into the room he was to share with Ranz. Wythcombe had been allotted a room of his own. Firekeeper was technically sharing one with Laria, although her intention was to see if Blind Seer wanted to go exploring once their more diurnal companions were settled. Now the wolf-woman was reassessing her intention. She didn't trust Wythcombe not to do something against his own best interests.

"Why you so upset, Wythcombe?" Firekeeper asked. "Back in the Nexus Islands, you were told to expect this. Now you act as if it is new to you."

"I also heard that Queen Anitra was considered a wise ruler. I suppose I believed that she would react more proactively to a threat to her people."

"This threat is something I not quite understand, even now," Firekeeper admitted. "I have thought much about what Kabot say. He sound as if he wished to someday show Rhinadei what he had become, but why is that a threat?"

"You wanted to find him," Wythcombe countered. "Wasn't that because you thought he could be a threat?"

"Ignorance is always a threat," Firekeeper replied calmly. "I was very ignorant when I came east of the Iron Mountains. If I had not been lucky in my teachers, I would have made more errors than I did."

"So you just want to find Kabot so you can brief him as to local customs of dress and table etiquette?" Wythcombe's tone was mocking.

Firekeeper grinned at him, a wolf's grin, as much challenge as expression of humor. "If that is what is needed, then, yes. But we—myself and Blind Seer—we have not forgotten that Kabot may have come believing, perhaps, that Old Country is unchanged from what you of Rhinadei tell in your tales."

"Sorcerer monarchs drinking mingled wine and blood from goblets made from the skulls of their enemies," Laria offered softly. "Riding fire-spitting dragons through the skies. The sort of thing that makes a great fireside tale when you're safely away from it—especially since no one who listens to those stories imagines themselves one of the slaves being kept as a source of blood."

"Wait! Not everyone who uses blood magic abuses the power," Ranz objected. "Your own Ynamynet is evidence of that. I think it's stupid to forbid a powerful source of mana simply because it was abused in the past. Maybe Kabot feels the same way. Maybe when he said in his message that he looked forward to coming back to Rhinadei someday, he meant after he'd proven he could use blood magic"—Ranz used the Pellish term deliberately, defiantly—"and become more versatile."

Wythcombe had stopped pacing to listen, now he resumed. "But I can't get away from how Kabot seemed to be challenging me—me personally. When the emergency council came with me to Mount Ambition, we found no sign that Kabot left a message for anyone else."

"And because he left you this message," Firekeeper said, "you feel you must find him."

Whatever Wythcombe might have replied was lost when Farborn, who had been hunting, came soaring in through an open window. *"One comes! Although she wears a cloak with the hood up, I recognize the manner of her walk. It is General Merial. I learned her gait when she was among our captives on the Nexus Islands. If she does not come here to speak with us, then I will never eat another mouse."*

"General Merial comes," Firekeeper translated, then asked the merlin. *"Does she come alone or with her pack?"*

"Alone, best as I can tell, but I will scout." The reply was as much in action as

in what a human would have called words, as Farborn sliced the air on his way out the open window.

Blind Seer rose, ears perked, then padded to where he could sniff the air that whispered beneath the closed door to the suite. *"I think it is too soon for the mice to rejoice. Footsteps approach and, yes, certainly that is Merial's scent."*

"I'll wake Arasan," Laria said, jumping to her feet and opening Arasan's door without pausing to knock. Such formalities had not yet reestablished after their moonspan and more of living together in camps. Wythcombe settled into a chair, and struggled to look relaxed.

There was a sharp rap on the door. Firekeeper let Ranz go to answer it, since that left her and Blind Seer free to attack or flee, whichever seemed the best response. A human might see flight as cowardly, but a wolf knew that living to bring aid later could be the wisest course.

"Yes?" Ranz said, opening the door only enough to see who was without. He sounded a little wary, which was just as he should.

The response was spoken very softly. "I am Merial. We met this afternoon. May I come in?"

"Are you alone?" Ranz asked.

"I am."

"She is!" whistled Farborn from the window and, although Firekeeper didn't translate, Ranz seemed to understand. Closing the door all but the width of a finger, he turned to them. "It's Merial, from earlier. She wants to speak with us."

Wythcombe replied heartily. "Fine with me."

Firekeeper grunted agreement. Arasan, coming sleepily to the door of his room, said, "Give me a minute to brush my hair and I'll join you."

Ranz opened the door and stood politely to one side. "Please, come in."

The general did so, moving with something less than her usual confident stride. Once inside, with the door closed firmly behind her, she scanned the room, noting the open window with Farborn on the sill, Firekeeper and Blind

Seer standing ready, Wythcombe with his hand wrapped around his staff, Laria turning with a poker from the hearth, and, lastly, Arasan, emerging from his room, tugging his clothes into line. His eyes still looked sleep-puffy, but were alight with interest.

Firekeeper took it upon herself to act as hostess. "General Merial, you are welcome. We have a chair here." She indicated the one across from Wythcombe. "We have some tea and some water, I think. We could ask the innkeeper for other food if you wish."

She was very proud of herself for remembering these human social graces, and found the little smile that twitched at the corner of the Meddler's mouth (it was *definitely* him) annoying. But General Merial acted properly, taking the chair Firekeeper offered, then asking for tea, which Laria brought her. Firekeeper settled herself on the floor with Blind Seer, leaving chairs for the humans. Farborn stayed at the window. Firekeeper knew the falcon would periodically dart out to make certain this unanticipated visit wasn't a prelude to some trap.

After tasting the tea and thanking Laria with a small inclination of her head, General Merial studied them thoughtfully. If she had thought her silence would prompt them into asking her why she had come, she had chosen the wrong group. Only Ranz shifted, covering his restlessness by reaching for his own teacup.

"I'm not here to ask you to leave Azure Towers," Merial began, and Firekeeper, who had not even considered such a possibility, was interested that this could have been an assumption. "I'm here as one of the heads of this nation's military with additional questions regarding your account from earlier today, questions that did not occur to me until after we had all left Queen Anitra's presence."

Blind Seer panted laughter. *"Rather, questions she did not wish to ask in front of her queen. But do not challenge her, dear heart."*

Firekeeper rubbed her fingers along the dark line of his spine, and kept her peace.

"If we can answer your questions," Wythcombe replied, all hearty courtesy, none of his earlier anxiety showing, "we would be happy to do so."

"You seemed very concerned about Kabot and his associates," Merial began. "Why do you think he offers any threat?"

Wythcombe replied much as he had earlier, although at greater length. Merial then asked several more questions. What interested Firekeeper more than the questions was that none of them even implied disbelief in Wythcombe's basic premise.

Fingers wrapped around the now empty teacup, the general stared down, as if the pattern on the carpet had somehow become fascinating. When she raised her head, her gaze was resolute.

"Queen Anitra has her priorities. I have mine. Even when we disagree, I believe we are actually in accord, for we both care deeply about the safety of this nation." Merial faced Wythcombe and Ranz. "If you've seen maps of the continent of Pelland, you may have noticed that ours is among the smaller nations—especially if you remember that much of our uplands are mountainous and, therefore, not entirely useful."

"For humans," Blind Seer said, and Firekeeper swallowed a smile.

"There are those—especially our near neighbor Hearthome…"

"And not long ago the Mires," Blind Seer added.

Firekeeper thumped him gently between the ears. General Merial did not seem to notice, but Laria certainly did.

"…that believe we are too small and too unmilitant to defend what many see as the most valuable resource we hold. This is not our mineral wealth, nor the ore and gems from our mines, but the very ruins you have asked to visit."

"Asked," Wythcombe prompted very gently, "and been refused."

"Yes. That refusal is what I wish to discuss. Queen Anitra is very wise to refuse you. If she were to permit you and Ranz—two barely met strangers from another land—in the company of three…"

"Five," chorused Blind Seer and Farborn together.

"Six," thought Firekeeper, thinking of the Meddler and Arasan.

"...from an allied land be the first to enter the ruins with royal sanction, then not only would the requests for similar privileges pour in, but Queen Anitra would be in a very poor position to refuse. For some time, she has been lobbied to permit a small group of carefully chosen scholars, all drawn from our own land, to study the ruins. Each time she comes near to agreeing, she backs away, fearful of the consequences. For that reason, even if you are granted the second audience you have requested, I believe the answer would be the same."

"But you," Arasan said, his tone at its most melodious and insinuating, "while you do not disagree with the queen, you do not fully agree with her either."

"That's about it," General Merial agreed. "Cousin Anitra is correct as far as she has gone, but without proof that Kabot has invaded, she continues to react as if circumstances are unchanged. I keep worrying that he may be within, wondering what he might have found. Before querinalo began to abate, the ruins were just that—ruins. What wealth they contained was of the sort that isn't dangerous of itself—only for what it might buy. Our histories make clear that after the fall of the sorcerer kings the ruins were looted. This doesn't keep people from daydreaming that they'll find a cache of gems or coins. I'll even admit that the force we have on permanent rotation regularly turns back treasure seekers. We don't make a big deal of this because we don't want to encourage others, but we cultivate rumors that the penalties for trespass are very—in some cases, terminally—severe."

The grim expression on her face made clear that the rumors had a solid foundation.

"Now querinalo is abating and a new sort of treasure is being dreamed of. Already there is talk about establishing a new university, both to teach the magical arts and to attempt to instill some ethical code. Some say that Azure Towers would be the best place for such a school for, even when magic was no longer useful, we retained a tradition of scholarship. These suggest that we should systematically search the ruins for texts or diagrams or other, more nebulous, artifacts in anticipation of founding our new academy. Queen Anitra refuses, saying that any magical relics from before querinalo would be tainted, that we would be better to start afresh."

She stopped, looking uncomfortable.

"So," Arasan prompted, "you have good reason to be unhappy about the possibility that Kabot is already within, his actions uninvestigated."

"Correct." Merial's tone was too level. "I asked the queen if we might send a patrol to search for evidence of any new activity, but she remains reluctant. Even if I carefully picked soldiers known for discretion, word might get out. Worse, if something happens to them, we would need to lie, and lies like that tend to twist around and bite you. On the other hand, if something happens and is traced to invaders within the ruins, then all the nations that have argued that Azure Towers is too small to guard such a trust will have a new support for their arguments."

"So?" Wythcombe leaned forward in his chair, knuckles white on the hand wrapped around his staff. "You are in a bind. You can't go in. Yet you fear the consequences if you do nothing."

"Which is why," General Merial said, resolve tightening the lines of her face, "I was considering asking you to go in. Unofficially. Fully aware that if you are caught, I can do nothing to soften whatever penalty the queen hands down."

III

"So why should we take the risk?" Laria heard herself blurt out. "How do we know this isn't some sort of trap? Do you expect Wythcombe to be so eager he's going to do something dumb?"

"Laria!" Wythcombe's tone mingled reproof and amusement, but Laria knew she wasn't wrong. The old man was overeager. If Wythcombe took the bait, then Ranz would trot after him. Firekeeper might be able to convince Blind Seer not to do something foolish, but who would watch out for Ranz?

General Merial looked shocked but Laria held her ground. For the first time, Laria realized her peculiar childhood had its advantages. After surviving the Spell Wielders and their mercurial moods, what did she have to fear from a mere general, even if said general was closely related to a queen?

Laria leveled her gaze at General Merial, daring her not to reply. After a long pause, during which the general studied each of them in turn, Merial shook her head, as if not believing she was required to answer to a mere girl of no particular lineage or position.

"Very well. The simple reason why I wouldn't betray you is that I could not do so without betraying myself."

Arasan shook his head. "That's not enough." His voice brightened and shifted, so Laria recognized the Meddler. "This might actually be some sort of plot concocted by you and the queen. We've already considered what would happen if important members of the Nexus Islands community were discovered breaking the Azure Tower's prohibitions. We decided that we could not impose that risk on our community."

"There are truthsayers," Merial said. "You would be within your rights to insist on one reviewing my testimony. I could not hope to lie."

"That's not the point," Ranz interjected, "as I think you know full well. So you're caught lying. What of it? You admit you did what you did for what you believed was the good of Azure Towers. Few would fault the queen if she gave you a light penalty. Nope. Laria's right. Why should we take this risk?"

Laria wanted to hug Ranz for his support, but she kept her dignity, and only inclined her head in a slight nod.

Firekeeper said in her "Blind Seer" voice. "Your scent is not as disappointed as it should be. There is more, I think. Would you care to discuss it or shall we ask you to leave?"

General Merial shifted uncomfortably when Blind Seer mentioned her scent.

She forgot that we have our own sort of truthsayer with us at all times, Laria thought gleefully.

"Very well. You have made your point. Laria, I apologize. I let myself forget that you have traveled to Rhinadei, served your land in war, and lived under rulers far more difficult than my own queen. Here is why you are secure against my betraying you. What I am going to suggest is that you enter the ruins via a route that is known to only a few people—myself, the queen herself, and her chief counselor. Not even Trahaene, the most trusted of her Once Dead, knows of this route. Therefore, if you are caught, the fact that you knew of this route will show that I was involved."

"That doesn't answer my objection," the Meddler retorted. "You could have made a deal with the queen in advance. In fact, given that you are willing to betray what must be a major state secret, I think it's more likely, not less, that the queen is conniving with you."

General Merial threw her head back, exasperation in every line of her sturdy body. "I have no answer to that objection. Short of bringing you before the queen and making her swear she has not given me immunity from prosecution—which I cannot do—you only have my word."

There was a long silence, then Laria said, "General Merial does have a point. Proving someone hasn't done something is harder than proving they have. Isn't that what you've taught me, Arasan?"

She placed just a little stress on the name, a reminder that the "Two Lives" was coming dangerously close to revealing its dual identity.

"True," Arasan admitted.

"Let's discuss your plan further, shall we, General Merial?" Wythcombe suggested. "There's another way into the ruins? One that bypasses the patrols?"

General Merial nodded stiffly, reminding Laria of a newly enlisted recruit reporting. "Yes. It's a tunnel. Our guess—and that's all we have—is that it was built for some sort of utility—a sewer, perhaps."

Firekeeper groaned and Blind Seer flattened his ears. Farborn whistled with unmistakable amusement.

Merial looked surprised, but when the wolves didn't clarify, she went on. "According to the report left by the patrol who scouted the tunnel, it ends in one of the largest of university buildings—or I should say in the understories of that building's ruins. This structure is located much deeper into the university ruins than the borders where our soldiers patrol. If you were to emerge there, you should be undetected. With Farborn to scan from above, with Blind Seer's sense of smell, with Firekeeper's extraordinary abilities as a scout—as well as whatever other skills you have to offer, my thought was that you could easily discover if there are any traces of fresh human activity."

"Tell us more," Firekeeper prompted before the humans could start raising objections. "Especially about this sewer. We do not much like sewers."

General Merial gave a crisp nod. "If the tunnel was a sewer, it probably hadn't been used for centuries, even before querinalo. The tunnel—shall we call it that instead?—was discovered during the early years of the reign of Queen Anitra's mother, during the clearing of rubble in anticipation of the construction of a road. The new road was diverted from what was thought to be a pit. Later, when studies were made to assess what it would take to fill the pit, it was realized that the 'pit' was actually a segment of a tunnel. Since the tunnel led into the ruins…"

She stopped. Wythcombe smiled sadly and completed her sentence. "And it might be useful someday to be able to access those forbidden areas without anyone knowing, why fill it in? Prudent. What was done so that no one else would accidently intersect it?"

"There was really little chance of anyone digging into it. Most of the tunnel runs through solid rock—it's a remarkable work of engineering. A summer estate for the late queen's mother was built over the opening and the entrance to the tunnel hidden in a subbasement."

"And no one has found it since?" Firekeeper sounded both dubious and interested.

"No one. If we go there, you will understand why." As she spoke these last words, General Merial looked smug.

"So a secret way in to the ruins," Wythcombe mused. "I admit. I am tempted."

Laria nodded, feeling that since she'd been the first to protest, it was her job to show the general had won her over. "Me, too. Anyhow, Blind Seer can smell if anyone has been in the tunnel recently."

Firekeeper grinned one of those unsettling wolf grins. "We"—she gestured to herself, Blind Seer, and Farborn—"can punish Merial if is a trap."

"Oh?" Arasan cocked an eyebrow in one of the Meddler's most mocking expressions.

"Oh," Firekeeper agreed. "What does a queen's word matter to yarimaimalom? If General Merial breaks faith with us, no matter what protection her queen gives her, the Wise Beasts will know the promises Merial gave to us. It may be too late to help us, but they will be sure to take our revenge."

The wolf-woman turned her dark, dark gaze upon General Merial. "Before you go, I should tell you a story about how the Royal Beasts of the Iron Mountains destroyed a human settlement without losing a single creature. Your borders cannot keep Beasts out. Remember that, if you think to break faith with us. Farborn has already gone forth." She motioned to the now empty windowsill. "The warning is already given."

General Merial visibly paled beneath her soldier's tan, then straightened. "Well, then, it's a good thing I don't plan on betraying anyone—not even my queen, although I hope I never need explain that to her."

"An artifact!" Daylily said, her voice high and excited. "Tell us more!"

"Not long ago," the Voice began, "as such things are measured, maybe fifty years before querinalo, there lived a woman who learned how to unweave the world. Why would she decide to learn how to do such a thing? That is a long story, and not really germane to your situation. What does matter is that she learned to do so."

Kabot leaned slightly forward, eager to hear what came next, but Uaid, specialist in earth magics that he was, wasn't content to let this rest.

"When you say 'unweave the world,' do you mean the physical orb? The earth is indeed complex, but I would not use the term 'woven' to describe its structure."

"Uaid," the Voice said gently, "it would be best if I told my tale in my own way."

"I'm sorry, master," Uaid said sulkily. "I simply don't understand how you can talk about the world as something that can be unwoven."

Is that how Uaid sees the Voice? Kabot thought. *As his late master, Caidon?*

I think not. They were more peers, junior and senior, surely, but theirs was a relationship of equals. This attitude seems that of young student reacting to a reprimand from a revered loregiver. Certainly, in matters of earth magic, Uaid had the edge over Caidon.

Kabot tried to remember if he had ever known who Uaid's early teachers had been, but he couldn't recall. He put this puzzle from him, for Phiona was speaking again.

The Voice sighed. "I was going to try to cut out the background, move to my main point, but I can see now that this would be a classic 'haste makes waste' situation. Very well, get comfortable, and I will tell you The Tale of the Unweaver of the World."

Not all that long ago, as such things are measured, maybe fifty years before querinalo, there lived a woman who learned how to unweave the world. Her birth name was Jyanee. She was born in Tishiolo, a small, strange land on the continent of Pelland whose people, language, and customs are nothing like those of the rest of that land mass.

When Jyanee's instructors admitted that she had learned all they could teach her, she applied to a school where the magical arts were taught, only to be rejected by the head of the school—who happened to be her uncle. Some say the uncle rejected Jyanee because he could not see her as other than the little girl he had dandled on his knee. Some say that he and her father, his brother, had unresolved conflicts, and the uncle refused to accept his niece as anything other than her father's daughter. Some said (whispered, more likely) that when the uncle tested his niece, he realized that her raw talent was so tremendous that if given further instruction she would surpass him. Then he would be forgotten except as the uncle of one of the greatest mages of all time.

Jyanee appealed the headmaster's decision. Lest he be accused of unfairness, the headmaster set her a task just this side of completely impossible: to find a unique way of demonstrating her knowledge of the eddies and currents that must be controlled in order to create magic. The headmaster justified this task by saying that if Jyanee was not able to find a unique interpretation, forever after it would be said that her admission had resulted from her being favored by her uncle.

Friends and family alike encouraged Jyanee to seek teaching elsewhere, but she had her own fair share of the confidence (or should it be called egotism?) that had brought her uncle to his high place. She retired to an isolated keep owned by her family in the most remote mountains of Tishiolo. There she set to work studying magical energies, attended by a few retainers who had known her since she was a baby and who loved her more than they loved living in the world.

When Jyanee had not been heard from for a year, her father came to check on her. She sent him away, saying she was immersed in her studies and quite content. When another year passed, her mother came, and received the same answer. So on it went through each sibling, until the boy who had been a toddler when Jyanee went into seclusion was a strapping warrior mage who came to her riding a prancing steed he had taught to run upon the wind.

When Jyanee did not emerge in reply to her brother's summons, this impetuous youth pushed his way past the servants who had grown grey in their faithful service to their mistress, and sought his oldest sister. He found her deep in meditation in a tower carved from a slender mountain peak, so that it was both beneath the earth and yet thrust into the highest reaches of the sky where the air is thin. Jyanee opened her eyes when he burst into her chamber. The warrior mage inadvertently backed away, for he saw that her eyes were of a colorless hue that seemed to see both everything and nothing at all.

Looking upon her brother's fear as if it was a physical thing, Jyanee said, "Thank you for coming so far. Reassure our parents that I am well. If you would be so good, tell my uncle that I will soon speak with him regarding admission to his school."

The warrior mage brought these words back to his uncle (who had accepted the youth without question into his academy, many said because while the nephew had some talent, his gift would never threaten anyone's prominence).

In trepidation, the uncle waited but, when a year passed and then another, yet his niece did not come to petition for entry into his school, he relaxed. Then reports came of strange vibrations within the mysterious foundations upon which the magical arts depended. In time these eddies were traced to the very mountain peak which served as Jyanee's tower.

Prompted by his terrified associates, the headmaster went forth. His niece's servants readily admitted him, saying that he had been expected. Alone he mounted to the tower beneath the earth, above the sky, and found Jyanee sitting cross-legged upon a heap of thick carpets on the stone floor. Before her, on a low table, rested a disk much like a coin, although thicker. The headmaster could barely glimpse the terrestrial materials from which the disk was made, for the mana that radiated from it blinded him.

His niece turned upon him those eyes that saw nothing and everything, noticed how he squinted, and took pity on him. She cupped her hand over the disk, revealing it not so much made as grown from metals and minerals: silver, gold, and copper, interlaced with brilliant sparks of gem.

Jyanee said in a voice that would have been indifferent if it had not held the slightest touch of mockery. "Some years ago, Uncle, you set me to find a unique way of demonstrating that I understand the forces that underlie magic. Through my research, I found not only the roots of magic, but of the very forces that weave together to make up the world. This token connects to four of those threads: four of the greater, for they are associated with the weave of the greater landmasses."

When her uncle would have protested the impossibility of this, Jyanee waved a dismissive hand. "When you—assisted by as many of your associates as you wish—selected from any land, practitioners of any tradition that you choose, can show me that you understand how the world is both thread and weave, then I will acknowledge you as worthy of teaching me."

She continued, "Be warned. The token connects to potent forces. As threads can tangle and knot, as well as be woven, so these can tangle—but the consequences of tying them in a knot would be far worse than a spoiled carpet.

Make sure you understand what you are doing before you put yourselves and, perhaps, all the world, at risk."

Words spoken, Jyanee returned to her meditations, leaving her uncle to gather up the token in a shaking hand and depart.

The headmaster consulted with powerful sorcerers from around the world. Together they were able to confirm what Jyanee had said—that the token was merely the endpoint of something far more complex. Although each secretly wished to command this power, none could deny that incorrect handling of the token could lead to disaster. Therefore, the token was split into four disks, and each disk was consigned to a group from the landmass with which it corresponded.

Destroying the disks, so they learned, would not be as difficult as had been feared. It was almost as if Jyanee, who they now called the Unweaver, was taunting them, saying, in effect, "If you cannot use what I have made, then you may reassure yourself that you and your land are free from any threat misuse might offer by destroying what I have made."

Humans are only human, though, and sorcerers are not known for responding well to being taunted. Therefore, instead of causing the disks to become inert, the sorcerers settled for dampening the disks' potency. When they did this, they stated that they acted not out of fear, but because this dampening would enable them to continue their studies more responsibly. When querinalo came, these studies were still in process. Each of the disks, superficially hardly more than a trinket, escaped destruction. They remain to this day, hidden away, their true power forgotten.

When the Voice finished the story, Kabot, Uaid, and Daylily exchanged excited glances.

Daylily's lips shaped a teasing smile. "Somehow I feel sure that you, dear Voice, know where these disks might be. Perhaps one is here, among the ruins of this university?"

"Your intuitions do you credit, pretty Daylily," the Voice replied caressingly.

"You guess correctly. I do know where one disk is. I believe I can deduce where a second disk might be—and I think that if we have the first and second, we might use their resonance to find a third, even all four. You of Rhinadei are trained from your earliest years in how to subdue potent magics. I believe that you can do what even those powerful thaumaturges of old could not—for they lacked your Rhinadeian training in managing the rawest magical energies. I believe you could control each of these talismans, but possessing even one would certainly gain you admission into the community you left Rhinadei to join."

Blind Seer waited patiently for the humans to finish snapping at each other. When all had had their say, General Merial took command.

"I suggest we make it seem as if you all have returned to the Nexus Islands. Instead, you will go into hiding until I am ready to escort you to the secret route into the ruins."

Blind Seer huffed disapproval, and Firekeeper glanced at him.

"*Tell her,*" Blind Seer said, "*that this will not do. One question after any of us—even something as minor as a request for Arasan to sing at a wedding—will create the need to spin increasingly complex lies. This would be unwise.*"

Firekeeper translated. General Merial looked less than pleased. "I had thought that Derian Carter could give out that you had been sent somewhere else, but I must agree that Blind Seer is correct in pointing out that asking people to create convincing cover stories on the spur of the moment is a dangerous tactic."

"Derian will not be there to make up stories," Firekeeper said. "He is going home to show his new wife to his family. True, there would be others who could speak the lie, but why make our people lie when we do this for you?"

"Harshly put," Arasan added, "but the wolves do have a point. Perhaps we could find an excuse for going into isolation?"

Ranz replied in a manner that, had he been a young wolf, would have been accompanied with drooping ears and tail, just so his elders would not think he was getting above himself. "From what I understand, even though the magical university was destroyed long ago, Azure Towers is still renowned as a place of learning. Why don't we give out that Wythcombe and I are studying with some scholar, learning how the world has changed since our ancestors departed? Arasan is already renowned as a teller of tales, and Laria is his student, so they would reasonably share our interests. As for Firekeeper, Blind Seer, and Farborn—no one will think twice if they vanish. I've caught on that the Old World hasn't really taken to routinely considering the yarimaimalom as 'people.'"

"That could work," General Merial said thoughtfully. "Few enough know you are here or who you are, but the difficulty is that those who do also know of your land of origin. If worded right, we can present your interest to the queen as showing appropriate humility."

"You don't think Queen Anitra might change her mind?" Laria asked anxiously. "I mean, now that we've decided to do what she will have every right to think of as treason on your part, and a sort of invasion on ours."

"I don't," Merial stated confidently. "Both Loris Ambler and I tried to convince her to make an exception, but Anitra's good and bad points meet in this issue. The same care Anitra shows for her people, her consideration of the long-term ramifications of any new policy, can make her very hidebound."

General Merial tapped one neatly trimmed fingernail against her teacup for a long moment, then nodded sharply. "I have it! Nergy, one of my training masters, left active duty last year after an illness. He's known for his interest in recent history, especially the dynamics between nations. I could explain my sending you people to him as a way for him to earn extra coin. Even better, Nergy has a pension as a groundskeeper on some forested land in the general direction we want to go. Perfect for Firekeeper and Blind Seer."

"You sound as if you mean to actually send us there," Wythcombe said with a laugh.

"I am considering doing so," General Merial said. "I think you would like Nergy, you could learn more about Azure Towers from him, and he'd be better supported in any lies if he had actually hosted you."

"I suppose a short delay won't hurt," Wythcombe said, "although I am worried what Kabot will be doing while we lay elaborate intrigues."

"We not know if he is days or weeks ahead of us," Firekeeper reminded. "Even moons."

"Even," General Merial added wistfully, revealing a faint hope that their fears were ungrounded, "if he came to the ruins at all."

Some further arrangements were needed, one of which was sending Laria on a quick trip to the Nexus Islands. Ostensibly Laria was going to ask her mother's permission to stay in Azure Towers but, in reality, she would be briefing the governing council of what was being done—a further precaution against treachery. Then they retired to Nergy's refuge.

Even though Blind Seer knew the delay had been necessary, he was as fidgety as Firekeeper when, many days later, General Merial rendezvoused with them at Nergy's rural retreat. On a crisply chill night, with all the humans riding and Rusty on a lead line, Merial led them via back roads, often through woodlands.

Farborn, Firekeeper, and Blind Seer went ahead to scout the area with eye and ear and nose, but they found no trace either of a trap or—more importantly—of recent activity that could indicate something was being concealed.

The fine, sprawling estate was currently untenanted, having been closed during the winter. The only humans present were a gatekeeper and his family. These must have received orders to ignore the new arrivals for, when General Merial undid the lock on the heavy wrought-iron gate, not even a shadow stirred against the drawn curtains of the small gatehouse built into the surrounding wall.

They crossed the grounds, then went around the house, avoiding the grand entrance that stood protected by a peaked-roof porch. Merial drew to a halt by a no less large, but far less ornamented, entry around the back. This, too, was flanked by a porch with a slanting roof, ample evidence that winter was harsh here in the foothills. Doubtless the ruins of the university, higher up in the white-capped mountains, would be cooler still. Blind Seer didn't mind in the least. Heat, not cold, was his bane.

Idly, Blind Seer wondered why those long-ago mages had established their university in such a difficult place for humans to reach—one so uncomfortable for them with their furless hides. Then he realized that these very difficulties might have had their appeal. Even in days when the magical arts had been more common, the mages would have been all too aware of their vulnerabilities. Perched like falcons in the aerie, the sorcerers of old had pretended at being aloof while—like those very falcons—protecting themselves from those who could do them harm.

When General Merial unlocked the mansion's rear door, the air that came out was only slightly warmer than that outside. Blind Seer had expected it to smell more stale, then realized that the comparative freshness could be explained by Merial coming by—probably earlier that day—to assure all was in order.

Firekeeper gave a slight sniff, meaning, *"Do you smell anything untoward?"*

Since the only scent Blind Seer caught was that of General Merial, mingled with that of her horse, he softly huffed out his breath, then perked his ears forward.

Inside, General Merial led the way along a wide, stone-paved hallway into a large storeroom. One side of this was given over to a set of doors.

"That," General Merial said, indicating a broad, high door meant to slide to one side, rather than swing, "leads to a ramp for moving cases and barrels down to the cellars. We will take the stairs. Let me unlock the door, then light the lanterns."

Although Firekeeper clearly longed to take point, since they didn't know where they were going, she settled for walking just behind the general. Knowing that Merial would become nervous if he were that close, Blind Seer chose to go last. Farborn rode on Firekeeper's shoulder, ready to take flight if anything went amiss.

"When the house was built," Merial explained, her bootsteps echoing within the stone stairway, "the entry to the tunnel was concealed in a sub-basement storeroom that was given over to the sort of things people will keep but don't often need—old jars and vases, bottles, decorations that might be reused someday, and the like."

Blind Seer recognized General Merial's chatter as the sort humans made to cover nervousness. The storeroom was so crowded that only the general, Firekeeper, and Laria stepped inside. Blind Seer lay down, which permitted him to see easily around the humans' legs. From this vantage, he saw Laria press her hand, first against the wall, then against the floor. Each time she closed her eyes and concentrated. Evidently she found nothing that gave her reason for concern, for she got to her feet without comment.

General Merial probably didn't notice Laria's quiet ritual. She was busy removing heavy wooden crates from where they were stacked in front of shelves that lined one section of wall. Blind Seer sneezed at the scent of dust and stale beeswax. Next Merial took a small can from her pocket and dripped oil into what must be a hidden keyhole, for she removed a flat leather folder from where it hung on a thong around her neck and took out a key. This proved to be only the first of a series of keys and locks, but not even Firekeeper complained about the laborious process. Indeed, the very care with which this area had been sealed added to the gravity of the situation.

Only Rusty was restless, straining at his leash, jaws moving as he attempted to chew on the edge of a wooden crate. Wythcombe absently slipped the goat a piece of rubbery old carrot, but his gaze never left General Merial.

"There," she said, at last, straightening upright. "That's the last. Firekeeper, help me slide this section of shelving. Be careful, the jars are heavy."

Firekeeper didn't bother to reply—at least not in a language General Merial would understand. Blind Seer panted laughter at his partner's soft breath of annoyance. Had Firekeeper been speaking Pellish, she doubtless would have said something like, "You step away. I can move this shelf without your help." But Firekeeper had learned to give deference not only to those who deserved it, but to those who thought they deserved it and could be of some use.

Blind Seer was very proud of her.

Moving the shelves revealed a trapdoor concealed in the paving. After heaving it open, General Merial pulled a nondescript sealed jar off the shelf, and pulled out a stout rope ladder.

"Blind Seer and I can jump," Firekeeper said after looking down through the opening. "I will steady the ladder for the rest. Someone can lower Rusty to me."

"I will see you all down," General Merial replied, "then close the door and move the shelf back. Send a message—by Farborn would be best—and I will come to let you out. If you must leave the ruins some other way, it would be wisest to hike into the mountains, then send me a message."

She was repeating plans they had laid out in advance, but Blind Seer understood that not only was the general nervous about letting them in on this secret, she was worried about possibly trapping them. If he were human, he would worry, too, but being a wolf, Blind Seer accepted that once a course of action had been decided upon, one had to follow it through or risk exhausting oneself with false starts.

Wythcombe squeezed into the storeroom. Now he laid what he certainly thought was a reassuring hand on the general's arm. "You forget. Among us we have a curious assortment of resources, magical and otherwise. I am sure we will be fine."

General Merial's verbal reply was noncommittal, but her sweat was suddenly ripe with a complex blend of odors.

Now that reminder, Blind Seer thought as he nudged the humans aside so he could follow Firekeeper into the hidden tunnel, *has frightened General Merial as surely no battle has ever done.*

Firekeeper was relieved when Blind Seer thumped down beside her. The lantern that had been lowered provided enough light for her to see that there was nothing nearby, but she couldn't escape a sensation that they were being watched. Laria shook down the rope ladder, her slim form outlined in the light from above.

"I've hooked it into place up here," she called softly. "I'll come down and take over steadying the ladder so you two can scout."

"Come then," Firekeeper said, kneeling to pull the rope taut. She felt the ladder shift as Laria tested the rungs, then made her way down, brisk as a squirrel.

"Dark, isn't it?" Laria commented, shivering as she took Firekeeper's place.

Firekeeper gave a noncommittal grunt. She'd long ago learned that while she could not see in absolute darkness, she saw much more than most humans did. Sometimes, she thought this had less to do with her actual vision than that she had learned how to interpret what she saw, rather than straining for details that weren't there, as a human would.

What she saw now was a tube of dull grey stone. The tube was easily wide enough for three or even four large men to walk side by side without bumping shoulders. No wonder those who had first discovered this space had thought they had located a cellar. Humans rarely dug tunnels so wide and even water did not cut so smoothly. Firekeeper ran her fingertips over the rise of walls and floor, but could find no seams where tiles or bricks had used.

Old magic again. I am not surprised.

General Merial had told them that one end of the tunnel went into the ruins. The other had collapsed long ago, but the theory was that it may have led to an underground watercourse.

After lowering Rusty, and unhooking the ladder, General Merial wished them well, then dropped the trapdoor. The seal was snug, cutting off light and sound both. Somehow, once the trapdoor had been closed, the world above seemed less real. What was real was the enclosed area, lit only by lanterns held by Laria and Arasan. Rusty bleated querulous complaint, and Firekeeper could only agree with him. She had never suffered from claustrophobia, but this place was entirely too isolated. Blind Seer padded silently back from where he had been investigating the tunnel and leaned against her leg in mute agreement.

"Shall we begin walking?" Wythcombe suggested. "According to the map General Merial supplied, the tunnel goes in more or less a straight line directly to the ruins. We're fresh. Even with rest breaks, perhaps we can reach our destination before noon."

Firekeeper shook her head. "We have already traveled part of the night. We will walk some, then sleep. We will still arrive with much daylight."

Blind Seer and Firekeeper took point. The others arrayed themselves in pairs, taking turns shifting who carried the lanterns so no one would end up with a tired arm. Rusty was given room to wander within the limits of the tether tied to Wythcombe's belt. Initially, the goat strained to go ahead, but soon realized that there was nothing to eat and walked at Wythcombe's side, chewing his cud and leaving a trail of goat droppings to puzzle future explorers.

Initially, the group walked in near silence, the only sounds their own breathing and boots tapping against the stone floor. Firekeeper felt herself lulled by the monotony. There was no scenery. No creatures to provide distractions. No sounds or scents. If this had once been a sewer, it had carried excess rainwater rather than waste.

The journey was beginning to seem like a particularly dull nightmare when Arasan's voice broke the silence. "Anyone care for a song or story? I don't think there's anything here for us to alert."

"Would be very good to hear something," Firekeeper agreed. "This place of nothing makes me uneasy."

"Me, too," Laria agreed. "I've tried reading the walls, but they're as dull as the rest. I can't even guess how long or how far we've walked."

"I lost track of how many steps we've taken ages ago," Ranz agreed.

"The level of oil in the lanterns will mark the passage of time," Arasan suggested. "It won't be a precise measure, but it's something."

"I have no problem with Arasan telling tales," Blind Seer said when Firekeeper glanced over to gauge his response. *"Tell the humans that you and I and Farborn will continue to scout ahead periodically, in case any danger is concealed as the scarlet butterflies concealed themselves."*

Firekeeper translated. This promise of continued watchfulness reassured Wythcombe, who to that point had withheld his agreement.

"First a few songs to liven us up," he suggested. "Let us sing softly and without accompaniment. Then, perhaps, Arasan can tell me and Ranz more of the history of this long-ago university. Later, I can continue my lectures on magical theory. My apprentices have had sufficient holiday."

Arasan's tales and songs, even Wythcombe's lectures, broke the monotony. Firekeeper realized as she translated Blind Seer's questions that she was understanding more about how spellcasting worked, especially how its very versatility and power were also weaknesses. A question from Arasan led to a discussion of mage's tools, such as the staff Wythcombe carried, and even the completely non-magical musical instruments that Arasan used to focus his talent. Ranz was full of questions, so many that Firekeeper suspected the young man was anticipating crafting a staff of his own.

Eventually, even Wythcombe admitted that a few hours' sleep would be useful. When they awoke and had refreshed themselves, Blind Seer suggested he and Firekeeper leave Farborn to mind the humans while they scouted ahead.

Because neither of the wolves could see in complete darkness, Wythcombe conjured a magical glow akin to that of a single candle flame. Firekeeper could hold this in one hand, then cover it by the simple expedient of closing her fist. Wythcombe cautioned them that the light would not last.

"Then if it goes out, we know we are away too long," Firekeeper said, rolling the small bright thing around in her palm. "Twice useful in this place without either light or time. When we turn back, we will see the lanterns. In this darkness, even a little glow carries a great distance."

The wolves padded ahead but, as their surroundings continued changeless, Firekeeper felt she could ask Blind Seer about something that had been increasingly bothering her.

"We went to Rhinadei to find you a teacher, Blue Eyes. We found you Wythcombe, but now we are caught up in his chase. You are not given a chance to pursue your own hunt. Does this trouble you?"

Blind Seer flicked an ear as if trying to hear his own thoughts. "Sometimes. However, I am the one who asked Wythcombe to not give me—and by extension, Ranz—empty exercises. My request was what led Wythcombe to go check on Kabot when he did, so my own will is what set our paws on this trail. When I consider what could have happened if Kabot's being released from the spell that had trapped him for so long had not been discovered, I admit, I tremble. It is enough to make one believe in the deities that humans give so much credit for guiding the course of events."

"Do you think we will find Kabot in the ruins?" Firekeeper asked.

"Find him? Without knowing when first he released himself from the spell? That I can't say. What I do think is that we will learn something to shape further pursuit."

Firekeeper nodded. "If there is trace of Kabot, then we have a trail to follow. If there is no trace, then, well, I would say to Wythcombe that his pack needs to go back to the start of the trail and see if they can find where it leads. Then you can concentrate on your studies."

Blind Seer bumped against her in a wolfish hug. "You are so eager to have me become anathema to our people? An undeniable spellcaster?"

"I am eager," Firekeeper said, stroking along his spine, "to have this magic of yours give you what you desire most: a voice, a means of giving us shapes that match. Selfish, I know, but we have spent many long seasons on hunts that have benefited the packs of others. Is it human of me to wish to put our own hopes first?"

Blind Seer padded on in silent contemplation for long enough that

Firekeeper feared she had indeed shown herself human in his eyes, and felt ashamed.

When he spoke, he huffed a dry laugh. "If you are too human in that, then I am too human as well. In the echoes of my thoughts, I worry that neither you nor I are fully wolves any longer. Then I take a deep breath of this enclosed air, feel how the darkness shrouds my vision, and I must laugh. If we were human in that worst way, we would not be here. We are still wolves, still putting the needs of a pack far greater than many wolves could embrace before our immediate hungers. But that does not mean we cannot satisfy our hunger and that of those who depend on us. The Ones eat first from a kill, not because of status or because the others fear them, but because strong Ones lead a strong pack. I will eat from the results of this hunt to make myself the strong One my pack needs. If at times that seems selfish, well, that is the way of the wolf."

Wythcombe was explaining that, although many mages preferred to carry staffs, these were far from the only option if a personalized magical tool was desired, when Firekeeper ghosted back to join them. When the wolf-woman motioned toward the lanterns, Ranz and Arasan slid the side panels down so only a faint glow remained.

Firekeeper said softly, "We were near turning back, then Blind Seer think sounds have changed, so we go on. Part of the tunnel begins to go up like this." The wolf-woman held up one arm to show a gradual slant. "Farborn scouts up, Blind Seer listens."

Laria glanced over her shoulder, only then noticing that the merlin was no longer perched atop her pack.

"I too go ahead," Firekeeper said, "to watch back and listen to make sure your sounds not carry too far. There will be a time when maybe you will need to go without light. Can you guide yourselves with a hand to the wall?"

Laria saw how Firekeeper's gaze flickered to her in particular, and she nodded firm assent. "I'll take point. If we need to go forward in full darkness, I might be able to use my talent to help me 'see.'"

"Maybe we not need this much dark," Firekeeper reassured her, "but best to be ready. I warn Rusty to be quiet, even if he smells something eatable or is frightened."

Laria knew that although Rusty was what Firekeeper would term "Cousin-kind," and so did not share the yarimaimalom's gift for complex language, nonetheless, Firekeeper could get some concepts across to Cousins. How complex depended on how intelligent the animal itself was. Derian enjoyed telling tales about Grey Patience, the only horse who had ever carried Firekeeper without collapsing into terror, mostly because the horse had resigned itself to its rider's threats.

Without a whisper of sound, the wolf-woman vanished into the dark tunnel. As she moved forward, for the first time in many hours, the sense of timelessness vanished, replaced by an acute awareness of every breath, every anxious step. Laria considered drawing Volsyl, but decided that even with its ability to guide her strikes, carrying a naked blade in near darkness was just plain dumb. She tried counting her paces so she could estimate the distance, but she kept losing count somewhere around fourteen. That was when memories of her childhood intruded.

Laria had believed that she had come to terms with her fear of spellcasters. Hadn't she been traveling with a mage and his two apprentices for several moonspans now? But as she approached when they must emerge into the ruins, possibly to confront spellcasters who craved the opportunity to use blood magic, Laria found herself remembering events best forgotten. Oddly, it was not the great abuses that came back with the most force, but the small, almost casual, cruelties.

Her father's face bruised, his left eye swollen shut, because the boots he'd labored to produce on short notice had been judged inferior, then thrown in his face.

Every child on the Nexus Islands under the age of five being shaved bald for reasons Laria still didn't understand. She remembered how cold she'd been.

Her mother straining to deliver Kitatos while an emaciated Spell Wielder shouted at her to hold still so he could collect the birthing blood.

Other memories, fragmented because she'd forced herself to forget or be forever crippled by fear.

Laria's hand flew to her braid, grasping the ribbon twined within. This one had been worn by Nenean when they'd had their archery competition and held her younger sister's secret excitement that she and Laria could do such a "grown-up" thing together. The memory stabilized Laria enough that when at last Firekeeper appeared before them, Laria dared hope her panic was no longer apparent.

"You can keep light, but low," Firekeeper said, her soft-spoken words husky. "Farborn says that the trail up ends in heavy door. I see if door is locked. When you come to Blind Seer, stop and wait."

Firekeeper gave Laria's shoulder a quick squeeze and said softly, "No matter these others is older. You is in charge."

Laria felt a flash of anger, certain that Firekeeper was patronizing her, then she remembered what her mother had said about the wolf-woman, "In matters of life and death, there is no kindness in her."

When Firekeeper vanished again into the darkness, Laria led the way steadily ahead until Blind Seer stepped into the small halo of light cast by her lantern. The great grey wolf gently nudged Laria so her free hand rested on his head. She let herself stroke his fur, knowing he was offering her reassurance.

There are advantages to being able to smell a companion's mood, Laria thought. *We always think about what his nose tells him in terms of hunting and scouting, but Blind Seer lives in a world where how we feel is as real to him as the color of our hair or eyes—maybe even more real.*

Firekeeper reappeared shortly after. "The door was not locked. I heard nothing, so I opened it. It goes to a great rounded area which has other tunnels going down from it, and many smaller openings above. Farborn watches, just in case, but we three think this sewer has not seen any living creature larger than a rat for a long time."

Something in how Firekeeper tousled Blind Seer's ears made Laria remember that the two apparently had reason to dislike sewers. Asking why would need to wait for another time.

Firekeeper continued, "In this round place are some ladders, going up." She looked abashed. "There is writing, but I cannot read it, nor can Farborn."

The steep ramp they climbed did not end so much in a door as in a hatch, but Laria wasn't about to quibble words with Firekeeper. The hatch was labeled in archaic Pellish, "Emergency Overflow 3." Beside this were carved a series of runes that Wythcombe studied for a long moment before giving a crisp nod.

"This would have been a spell set to activate when the water in the chamber backed up to a certain level. Doubtless, after the university was destroyed, no one was available to recharge the spell, so the tunnel remained sealed these past decades except for the scouts of whom General Merial informed us."

"Spells don't remain active then?" Laria asked.

"Some do; some don't," Wythcombe replied. "This one looks to be the sort that would be routinely recharged—creating such is much less intensive than making an item like Volsyl." He raised one of the lanterns and looked around the chamber. "Arasan, Laria, your Pellish would be closer to that of the time before querinalo. What do you make of the designations near the ladders?"

"Street names or possibly that of districts within the university," Arasan replied promptly. "I'm willing to bet that not all of those access hatches will open, though. See the marks on the underside of the hatches? They're shorthand for 'locked.' I'm guessing those are a lot more modern than the inscriptions on the walls."

"Made by the Azure Tower's scouts," Wythcombe nodded, "to show those who would come after which ports could be opened. That limits our choices a bit. Let's see, among the district names we have 'Doves,' 'Residences,' and 'Herbs' to choose from. Anyone?"

"Herbs," Laria replied, thinking she had been quiet for too long.

Firekeeper flashed her a grin, then darted up a ladder before anyone could make another suggestion. A few moments later, she had the hatch open. She paused, sniffed the air. As she did so, Farborn winged up, turning sideways to pass Firekeeper in midair, and sliced out. Unlike a human, Firekeeper didn't bother to explain that she'd asked the falcon to scout the area.

Really, Laria thought, *I didn't realize how much inane conversation humans make until I met Firekeeper.*

Eventually, Farborn swept back in and Firekeeper started translating. "This goes to a path next to a huge pipe. Farborn says that there is an opening we larger folk can get out through this way if we move rubble. Blind Seer and I could scout ahead, but human things still can trick us. I think is best we stay together."

"Did Farborn see anything to indicate that anyone—anyone human—has been here recently?" Wythcombe asked anxiously.

"No, but he look more," Firekeeper said. "Still, we keep our voices low. Blind Seer will go up next. He will smell what I cannot."

The great grey wolf gathered himself, then climbed neatly up the ladder's metal rungs, followed by the humans. When Firekeeper climbed back down to carry up Rusty, the goat was remarkably cooperative. Laria wondered what the wolf-woman had said to him.

The hatch led into what probably had been some sort of service access, although most of the corridor had collapsed long before. The air that leaked in was mountain chill, refreshing after the long hours in the tunnel. Firekeeper reported that Farborn had not seen any evidence of any human activity. The birds and animals he had glimpsed had been what would be expected in such a place.

"Farborn go to find Sun Diver," Firekeeper explained, "a yarimaimalom eagle he met in City of Towers, who said she would come ahead to see what might be seen while we made our way beneath the ground. You humans who understand this rubble more, show me what to move so we may go out."

To Laria's intense interest, Ranz proved to be the best at assessing which chunks of stone to remove in what order. Building his city of snow and ice had taught him much about how one thing supports another. As the smallest of the humans, Laria was called upon to squeeze in and roll pieces forward. Firekeeper astonished no one by being able to move far heavier blocks of stone than would seem possible for one of her slender build. Before long, they had created an opening that permitted them to climb up to street level. Farborn returned, and reassured them that neither he nor Sun Diver had seen anything that indicated their emergence would be detected.

"But Sun Diver has seen strange activity elsewhere," Firekeeper translated. "A glow of light where she is certain there has been none, a restlessness among the vermin. Farborn knows where to guide us when we are ready."

"I'm ready," Wythcombe said, although Laria thought the old man looked both tired and strained. "Lead on!"

IV

Opalescent fury greeted them when Uaid crumbled into sand a thick stone door high in a ruined tower. This door was the last remaining of many obstacles that had stood between them and the first part of the artifact. The Voice had told them that Jyanee had named her creation Sykavalkay, which was archaic Tishiolan for "Four Threads." The thread they sought had been called "Palvalkay."

The majority of what had obstructed them as they dug through the ruins had been rubble from collapsed buildings. Long-ago conflagrations had raged through the subterranean passages connecting the university's buildings, roaring up once elegant towers transformed into inadvertent chimneys, the heat so intense that building stones had cracked. Floors were memories recalled in drifts of hardened ash. The interior walls of the towers were streaked with soot that seemed to form words in a long-forgotten iconography.

Without the Voice's guidance, Kabot knew they would never have made their way to this particular portion of the ruin so directly. Nor, he admitted to himself, could they have ever gained access without Uaid's earth magic slicing them a tunnel through the rubble. When they had emerged into the proper tower, all that remained was a single chamber high above that took up about half the circumference of the tower. There was a small landing outside of the door that led into it. Kabot surmised that long ago a stairway had led up to that landing, but it was gone now.

Neither the partial floor nor the support beams of the aerie in which they now rested had been made from wood, so these had survived the conflagration. Uaid had softened the stone walls to create the hand and footholds which they had used to scramble up the inner wall to reach the landing. Once they had gained their perch, Uaid examined the door, discovering that it had been grown from stone seeds, much as rock candy could be grown from sugar. The stone proved to be more dense and more solid than granite. Dissolving enough of it that they could creep through had taken many hours and left Uaid panting and trembling.

But the door had not been the only protection for Palvalkay. As they examined the eerie aura of crystalline blue coursed through with flecks of brilliant orange and streaks that shimmered like ice, Kabot tried not to show how impressed he was by this remnant of centuries-old magic.

"A ward," he said, "still active after well over a century. We've come to the right place, eh?"

Crouching low, he backed out of the makeshift doorway and turned to face Daylily, projecting more confidence than he felt. As the rehabilitation teams on Rhinadei had discovered, long-term wards were nearly impossible to break. Even if Uaid dissolved the stone into which the runes and sigils had been carved, the ward would persist. Daylily looked up from nursing a stimulant into Uaid to glare at Kabot, unimpressed by his attempted casualness.

"The Voice would not have misled us," she said tartly. "If you doubt his wisdom, why did you agree to come here? Make yourself useful and figure out how to lower that ward. If you can't, then you and I will need to summon the Voice and ask for his guidance."

Inwardly fuming, Kabot put on his most gentle, compassionate smile. "Do you need help with Uaid?"

Daylily didn't answer immediately. Maybe she was feeling even more uncertain than Kabot himself was. After all, although her abilities were more varied, she must know she could do nothing to lower the ward.

"Deal with the ward," Daylily replied. "I'll take care of Uaid. Save some mana for if we need to summon the Voice. Uaid won't be able to help us with anything arcane for a long while."

That's the second time she's mentioned summoning the Voice, Kabot thought, letting his warm smile drop as soon as he crept back through the hole in the door. *Maybe she's just aching to see 'him' again.*

He felt unwilling empathy. Ever since they had entered this particular tower, his ability to converse with Phiona had ceased. He suspected that that ward blocked spirits along with most other magical emanations.

Now, he thought, talking to himself since he couldn't talk to Phiona, and Daylily clearly didn't want to talk to him, *how do I bring the ward down without asking the Voice? Needing to ask wouldn't do much for my prestige with either Daylily or Uaid—and that's shaky enough right now. I'm not sure who's the leader—me or the Voice.*

He let his mind drift through the abstruse arcane lore that had become his favorite playground when he and Goldfinch had been hardly more than boys seeking to show off for each other by adapting the basic spells they were learning in school. When he was honest with himself, Kabot admitted that Goldfinch had always possessed the finer touch. Kabot had been faster, but his solutions had been messier, had demanded more raw mana to function—which in turn had led him to independently develop techniques that had verged on the anathema arts and had gotten him into repeated trouble with his teachers—which led to his eventual rebellion.

Kabot lost track of time, even of the discomfort of his cramped body. When he finally spoke, his voice rasped unintelligibly. He realized that his mouth was completely dry.

"I've got it!" he croaked, swiveling around and nearly cracking his head against the top of the hole Uaid had put through the door. "I can unlock the ward!"

"You can?" Uaid asked, looking pleased, but not as admiring as Kabot would have expected. Then he realized that more time might have passed than he had realized.

Daylily and Uaid were seated on the floor, leaning against the wall, their feet hanging into the abyss. Their postures showed a degree of comfort that suggested they had been like that for long enough to forget just how far they would fall if they shifted wrong. Smiling her approval, Daylily shoved a canteen over to Kabot. He drank deeply before continuing.

"I can." Without being asked, Kabot went on to explain what he'd figured out about the nature of the ward and the best way to unwork it. He continued after first Daylily's, then Uaid's eyes had glazed over from the effort of following him through complex magical calculations. Finally, Daylily cleared her throat in deferential interruption.

"That's all wonderful, Kabot, but didn't the Voice tell us that we are being pursued? If you really think you can undo this ward, perhaps I should assist you. We need to get away from here before our only achievement is discovering something that our pursuers will certainly try to take from us."

"Good point," Kabot said, able to be gracious now that he was certain his reputation was on the ascendant. "Here's what I need you to do."

Some hours later, the opalescent blue field shimmered, then fell away, giving them access to the forbidden chamber. Kabot wanted to rest but, even more, he didn't want to seem as if channeling the spell had hit him as hard as it had. He forced himself onto his hands and knees, then crawled into the room.

"Come on!" he said, pleased to hear himself sounding so hearty, "Palvalkay awaits us!"

Scanning his surroundings with all his senses, including his ability to "sniff" magic, Blind Seer shook himself heartily when he emerged into the pale spring sunlight. Dark purple and brilliant yellow crocus bloomed in a sheltered hollow. Hardy trees that had pushed roots through fallen stone to thrive on ash and crumbling rock were in full bud, a scattering of newly opened blossoms lightly perfuming the air. Clumps of coarse perennial grasses, showing signs of having been nibbled on by rabbits, were greening up. Despite these attempts by the vegetable world to assert the return of warmer weather, there was little foliage to obstruct the view.

Leaving Firekeeper to help the humans scrabble from the depths, Blind Seer padded to where he could discern what the varying breezes had to tell him about the possible location of their quarry. He found nothing definite, although there did seem to be a faint human scent. The origin of the scent was confused because the breezes that carried it were shunted through the jutting remains of the university towers. The human spoor might even have been created by the guards Queen Anitra had posted, but the character seemed all wrong. This scent held none of the notes of oiled leather and metal Blind Seer would have expected, rather a hint of bodies that had not been properly cleaned for too long, tainted with anxiety.

He tilted back his head and drew in a deep breath, then slowly swiveled his head to better isolate the specific air currents. This time he caught a stronger current carried on the higher breezes. Interesting… Humans did not usually fly, so that would indicate that their quarry—if indeed this was their quarry—had climbed up one of the towers that had not been completely razed when the non-magical humans had risen against their tormentors.

After Firekeeper had carried Rusty from the depths, Blind Seer briefed her, then she briefed the humans.

"But which tower?" Wythcombe asked. "Can Blind Seer tell? And can he tell if it's Kabot? Did he get Kabot's scent back in Rhinadei?"

Blind Seer shook his head, then said to Firekeeper, *Tell him I don't know which tower. The scent is too faint. I didn't really get Kabot's scent back in Rhinadei.*

The rain had taken care of any scent without and even that within was misted. In any case, Kabot and his pack were long gone by the time we arrived."

Firekeeper translated, then pointed to where Farborn showed as a vanishing dot against the sky. "Blind Seer cannot tell which tower, but Farborn has gone to find Sun Diver. He and the eagle may be able to see for us since the walls are so broken."

"We are fortunate to have such allies," Wythcombe said, easing himself to a seat on a large chunk of masonry. "I'd love to check if there is any active magic in use, but that would be a waste of mana. Even I would have trouble getting a reliable result at such a distance."

Ranz was doing his best to hide his restlessness by seeking tufts of grass from among the stones and feeding them to Rusty. Laria sat nearby, trying not to show she was watching Ranz, her hands carefully folded in her lap to make certain she did not accidentally begin to read her surroundings. Arasan leaned against what might have once been the plinth for a statue. From the angle of his head, he could have been studying the skies, but Blind Seer noticed that his eyes were shut and his features curiously slack. Perhaps he was fighting off sleep. After all, other than Wythcombe, Arasan was by far the eldest of their company. Not all that long ago, he had been injured so severely he had almost died.

Blind Seer was about to ask Firekeeper if she thought Arasan might be becoming ill—although he smelled healthy enough—when Farborn plummeted down from above.

"*Sun Diver has found where the humans are!!*" the merlin shrieked, skimming around and through their group in a blur of feathers and sound. "*Look up!! Look up!! She circles where the humans will not see her!!*"

Firekeeper pointed. "There. Where the eagle stands against the sky. That may be where our quarry lies. Before you ask. No. Sun Diver does not know if this is Kabot or some other human pack bold enough to defy Queen Anitra. We need to find out ourselves."

In wolf speech she added to Blind Seer, "*I want to race forth, but something tells me that would be purest puppy foolishness.*"

Blind Seer huffed agreement. "*A wise wolf scouts the prey, knows when to hunt, when to stay away,*" he said, quoting one of his favorite proverbs. "*For this hunt, though, we wolves cannot scout effectively. If this is Wythcombe's Kabot, he is of a people who have never given up the use of magic.*" He paused to consider, then quoted, "'*When first encountering a new type of snake, it is best to assume it is poisonous, rather than learning only after you have been bitten.*'"

Firekeeper scratched gently behind one of his ears as she addressed the others. "Blind Seer and I cannot scout this prey. We will remain with you humans—and Rusty—and assure that you arrive safely at the tower. Farborn, can you go ahead, find a secret place, keep watch, then come warn us if anything odd happens?"

Farborn chuckled. "What isn't odd? The tower may not have fallen, but it is broken in many, many places. One as small as I am can easily find a place to hide and keep watch. I will tell Sun Diver what we are about, ask her to help you chart your way across this broken ground."

"*We would be grateful,*" Firekeeper replied, then briefed the rest.

Arasan rubbed his hands together. "Now, should we try to hide or go for speed?"

Blind Seer quoted, "'*It is too late to take cover after the prey has been flushed.*'"

"But what if they escape while we are picking our way through rubble?" Wythcombe protested after Firekeeper had translated.

"Then we can track them," Firekeeper answered. "Blind Seer is right. We cannot choose to hide once we have been seen, and I do not care to reveal this little pack to those who created storm, thunder, and lightning back on Mount Ambition."

That slowed Wythcombe, who had been about to stride defiantly forth.

Blind Seer added, "*These fallen buildings create a forest of a sort. Let us stay close to them, use their shadows as cover. Remind the humans that the eye sees motion first, so to keep their actions slow and contained.*"

Firekeeper did so, adding, "I ask Sun Diver to show which routes are less visible from above."

With Sun Diver guiding from above, they progressed through the shattered urban landscape, moving quickly when a portion of roof hid them, slowing when they must skulk in the open. The terrain smelled like a peculiar marshland, for the shells of buildings often held dank water, sometimes partially frozen. Doubtless when warmer weather came, these pools and puddles would evaporate, but frozen ground, heavy with crumbled masonry and ash, made a nearly impermeable seal.

The tension of the humans—who kept glancing nervously toward the designated tower—saturated the air with the acrid scents of apprehension and indecision well before their small group reached the base of the structure. Sun Diver departed as soon as they were safely situated near an opening in the tower's shadow—no doubt to hunt, for the wingéd folk needed to eat even more often than did humans. As the eagle departed, Farborn dropped from his chosen cranny, skimming the edge of the tower with consummate skill.

"Three humans remain above," the merlin reported. "For this long time they have simply sat still, two occasionally talking with each other, while the third seemed to sleep, although his eyes remained open. Then the third awakened and spoke with the others. Now they are all busy at something. You should find sneaking up on them very easy... Or you would if you had wings. There is a steep climb from below, for the tower holds no stairs, and all the floors are gone but for the one these humans are perched upon."

"Can we reach them?" Firekeeper asked.

Farborn shrugged, a gesture that came easily to a bird. *"Those other humans did not seem to have wings."*

"Well said," Firekeeper replied. She turned to the humans. "Farborn says that much of the guts of this tower were burned away long ago. High above, one floor remains and that is where the humans are. Wait. I will sneak in just far enough to learn how we may reach them."

Blind Seer went with her. No light came from the opening in the tower's side and he knew that, if they moved slowly, to human eyes the pair of them would hardly show even as shadows. At first inspection, the tower was a hollow shell, its rough stone sides interrupted by the stubs of floor beams, burned and blacked. This tower's shell brought back memories of other such shells and the deaths of dear ones within them. Firekeeper shaped no words to speak of these old sorrows, but the tang of her sweat spoke for her.

Far above was the partial floor of which Farborn had spoken. Between this aerie and the tower's base, there was no stairway. However, on the far side from where the wolves lurked, fresh gouges had been dug into the stonework. Without further comment, Firekeeper withdrew to report. Blind Seer waited, patiently searching for the source of a scent in the air he could not account for.

He flicked one ear back to listen as Firekeeper reported soft-voiced to the humans. "Someone has cut climbing holds, fresh from how they show against the blackened stone. Those are the only way up, so we must climb without stair or ladder. If you do not think you can climb, wait. I will go up and lower a rope when I can."

Blind Seer felt a wash of despair, for although he had learned to climb ladders, upright surfaces and ropes remained beyond him. He considered regrowing his moth wings, but Wythcombe's warning about how mana dug channels caused him to reluctantly decide that he needed to save this option for an emergency or risk having wingéd wolf be the only shape he could create.

But there were ways to lead a pack without surging to the fore. If Blind Seer admitted his weakness, none of the others—he thought particularly of Wythcombe and Arasan—would feel they were shaming themselves if they didn't make the climb. He was about to ask Firekeeper to speak for him when Ranz, silent for most of their hike, spoke.

"No one needs to stay behind," the young man stated firmly. "There is ample water here." He gestured toward the puddles that created a peculiar sort of moat around the tower. "I've mana enough to make a stair of packed snow and ice."

"Excellent!" Firekeeper said. "While I would go up alone, I would rather we ran with the full pack's strength."

Blind Seer had continued to search for the source of the peculiar scent and had located a shadowed place, darker against the tower's shadowed interior. He padded a few paces closer, then drew a deep breath, confirming his suspicion.

"Firekeeper, there is an opening here. From the scent, I suspect it leads to a warren from which this tower jutted up. That may be where those above came from—and they may have left allies behind to cover their back trail."

Firekeeper reported, then said crisply, *"Ranz needs some little time to build his stair. Let you and I examine the depths."*

Upon entering the now unwarded chamber, Kabot, Uaid, and Daylily realized that getting through the ward might be the least of their difficulties. Kabot had thought that they might need to search for Palvalkay, but there was no doubt where it was. To the normal eye, the artifact was merely an ornate gold coin stamped with myriad runes, but to eyes that saw mana, it blazed. The question was, how were they going to get to it?

Palvalkay was suspended within a lattice of crystals that was integral to the surface on which they now stood. None of them doubted that if they were to simply break Palvalkay free, at the very least, the floor would shatter beneath their feet. Doubtless the spellcasters who had created this peculiar safe had known how to release the artifact from its protective matrix, but they had not left any convenient instructions where intruders might find them.

"You must admit," Daylily said hesitantly. "This is a very clever way of keeping Palvalkay secure from theft, while leaving it where it could be easily studied, perhaps even tested."

"Clever, it might be," Kabot replied acidly, "but such cleverness isn't precisely to our advantage."

An argument might have broken out then, but the Voice, no longer barred by wards, shouted within their minds. *"I just felt a mana surge near you, one that doesn't seem associated with you three. Perhaps you should find out what caused it."*

Daylily closed her eyes in concentration, and immediately paled. "It's close! You two figure out how to free Palvalkay. I'll deal with it."

Before either of the men could protest, she ducked through the hole in the wall. Kabot heard the Voice again. From how Uaid didn't react, Kabot was certain she spoke to him alone.

"Now that Daylily is actively looking, I can refine my perceptions. It's Wythcombe and his companions. They're at the base of the tower. A young man in their company is building a staircase—apparently from snow."

"Our retreat's cut off then," Kabot replied, remembering not to speak aloud. There were times that the Voice seemed more real to him than either Uaid or Daylily.

"Maybe physically," the Voice replied, *"but there are options. The Unweaver meant these threads to be woven to each other, so they have an affinity for each other. You can use that affinity to enable you to create a transportation spell far more rapidly than if—say—you wanted to go back to Rhinadei."*

"As if we would," Kabot responded derisively. "Far better to confront Wythcombe and his cronies. But Palvalkay is locked into that lattice."

"I think you will find that Uaid has an idea about how to get it loose. Give your attention to your companions. Daylily is returning to report. Calm her and Uaid, then suggest you have a way to rescue them. Don't mention me."

Kabot sent a feeling of gratitude as he shifted his focus to encompass Daylily and Uaid. Phiona had always understood that a team functioned best when there was a single strong leader.

"What's happening?"

Daylily's report was brief and to the point—and duplicated what Kabot had already learned from Phiona.

When Daylily finished, Kabot favored her with a warm and appreciative smile. "That's not good, but I have an idea how we might leave without needing to confront Wythcombe and his cronies. Let's use Palvalkay to pinpoint the location of another of the threads, then I'll transport us there. It would be best if we could take this one with us, but…"

He trailed off and, as the Voice had anticipated, Uaid filled the gap. "I've had an idea about that. Freeing the artifact from the lattice will take study—their manas are interwoven. However, I believe I can break a chunk of the lattice free, permitting us to take both lattice and artifact with us."

Daylily frowned. "That simple? That implies the lattice is a very weak protection."

Uaid shook his head, his expression both annoyed and smug. "Not at all. It would take someone skilled in crystal dynamics—as I am—to break the lattice without causing the floor to shatter beneath our feet. Even for me, doing so is going to create a great deal of 'noise.' In the days when this was an active university, such noise would doubtless have attracted attention long before the artifact could be stolen. However, since it's too late to be 'quiet,' we don't need to worry about that."

Kabot nodded briskly. "Excellent. You start cutting the lattice. I'll build the transportation spell. Daylily, anything you can do to delay pursuit would be ideal. Try not to kill anyone, if you can help it."

"Of course," Daylily snapped. "After all, we're trying to prove that our interest in blood magic does not automatically make us monsters. However, if they pursue us into dangerous situations, then their blood is on their own hands."

"Precisely!"

Kabot sank to the floor, finding the Voice lighting his way as he prepared to cast his mind into Palvalkay. "Daylily, I'm trusting you with my life and that of Uaid. I know you won't fail us."

Although Laria had seen Ranz both create and build with snow several times during their journey through the ruined lands of Rhinadei, the process had lost none of its wonder. She was trying hard not to stare, because then the Meddler would certainly smirk and ask her oh-so-casually what held her so captivated. Laria's determination to direct her gaze anywhere except where the next tread was taking shape under Ranz's hands meant she was the first to notice that someone was moving far above.

The wolves are right, motion is what you see first, was all Laria had time to think when a rain of fire showered down, centered directly on Ranz and his stair. The young man cried out in pain and surprise. As his creative trance broke, the tread Ranz had been crafting softened into slush. The completed treads hissed wherever a fiery drop hit them, but retained their form.

Wythcombe had been leaning against a segment of the stone wall, resting as Ranz worked. Arasan had been keeping watch outside the tower from the cover of the hole through which they had entered. When he dodged back inside, Wythcombe waved him off.

"I'll protect Ranz! You make sure nothing is sneaking up on us." The rough crystal atop Wythcombe's staff flared, emitting a light that shaped a curving umbrella between Ranz and the rain of fire.

Laria froze, indecisive, until the first of the fiery droplets struck the heavy woolen cloak she wore. She was pulling the hood up to protect her head when a shrill shriek of defiance sounded from above, followed almost immediately by a shocked cry and a reduction in the intensity of the rain of fire. Fierce little Farborn had taken the attack to the enemy. The distance was too great for Laria to discern details, but it looked as if he had grasped something pink and fine—could it be a woman's hair?—with his crystalline talons and was pulling upwards.

Spellcasters are powerful, Laria remembered, *but if you can distract them, you can break their spell.*

Ignoring the scattered gouts of falling fire, Laria ran to where hand and footholds had been cut into the stone. She didn't know how quickly she could climb, but she wasn't going to leave Farborn to fight alone. She was a few bodylengths above the floor when Firekeeper and Blind Seer burst from the tunnel. Without bothering to use the pre-cut hand and footholds, Firekeeper leapt for the rough stone of the wall. Catching one bare foot on an outcropping, then grasping above for a slight jutting protrusion, she began swarming upwards. Laria redoubled her own efforts, and was only a short distance behind when the wolf-woman pulled herself up and onto the landing.

Farborn had been forced to retreat, but his attack had broken the rain of fire. A beautiful woman—her hair *was* pink—gaped at Firekeeper. The wolf-woman was, admittedly, a fairly horrific sight. She had ripped open her right hand while climbing the wall but, ignoring the pain, had drawn her Fang and held the knife, its long blade dripping blood, as she advanced on the sorceress.

A man's voice shouted in heavily accented Pellish, akin to that of Wythcombe and Ranz, "Daylily, get in here!" The woman, presumably this Daylily, ducked through a ragged hole in a still-closed door, then half ran, half rolled toward a light so brilliant that it brought tears to Laria's eyes. She blinked, scrubbing her sleeve over her face to clear her vision. When she could see again, the woman and the brilliant light were both gone, leaving a sense of emptiness behind.

Firekeeper paused to wrap a piece torn from her shirt around her hand. She growled when Laria began to crawl into the adjacent chamber. "We not know if those leave traps. Wait. Wythcombe comes. Ranz builds, even in the fire, and the stair is nearly done."

Laria obeyed, but she didn't move from where she could keep a careful eye on the chamber that, until a handful of breaths before, had held at least two other people. Peering through the opening, she saw neither door nor window, only an intricate crystalline lattice with a hole ripped out of its middle. Laria wondered if the people had somehow crawled through the hole, even though she could see through the lattice and knew there was no one on the other side.

A gust of cold announced when Ranz's stair reached them. Not long after, Wythcombe was kneeling at Laria's side.

"Where did they go?"

Laria shrugged. "There was a bright light. When I could see again, it was like that." She gestured to the empty chamber. "We haven't gone in. Firekeeper thought there might be traps."

"Smart," Wythcombe admitted. He made a few soft murmurs, passing his fingers over his eyes, almost as if he were donning spectacles. "Looks as if they didn't have any time to set traps, but the room radiates a tremendous amount of raw mana. Some of it must be from whatever enchantment they used to escape, but some… It permeates the chamber."

"Permeate?" Firekeeper asked respectfully.

Despite his evident concern, Wythcombe was looking oddly cheerful. "Like the way the smell of an onion sinks into the container that has held it. I've learned something else, too. Kabot was definitely here. I know the signature of his casting. He worked the spell that took them away."

"Where did they go?" Ranz asked eagerly. "Can you take us there?"

Wythcombe's momentary cheer faded. "I have no idea. I recognize the spell. It's one commonly used for one-way transportation. However, that doesn't tell me where they went, only how they went. I'm also astonished that they were able to do the spell so quickly. Usually such spells demand a great deal more preparation and mana."

Arasan's voice startled Laria. She hadn't realized he had come up but, when she looked over her shoulder, she saw that Firekeeper had gone to keep watch below, leaving those with more magical knowledge to consult.

"Could they have drawn power from that 'onion' you caught the reek of?" Arasan asked. "That hole in the crystal lattice looks fresh. If something was encased there and they ripped it loose…"

Wythcombe nodded. "I was getting to that. Either they used that, or they found some other source of mana when they explored the ruins."

"It seems like a weird coincidence," Ranz said tentatively, "just now. I mean, they can't have been up here by chance or for very long. I bet Blind Seer could tell us how long they'd been here by how much scent they left."

"We should ask him," Wythcombe agreed. "As for coincidence—maybe so, maybe not. We approached through areas that may have been warded to alert Kabot if anyone was approaching. They may have decided to grab what they could and get out of here before we caught them. Kabot would be like that."

Ranz's comment about lingering scent gave Laria an idea. She slid into the chamber, delicately extending her perception, centering it on the area where the light had been brightest. No matter what Kabot had used to give power to his spell, surely he would have needed to concentrate on a destination. Maybe she could learn what that had been before the memory faded.

"Laria!" Wythcombe cried out, careful for her safety as he had not been for his own.

Arasan interrupted, preemptory and authoritative as he rarely was. "Let her. She knows the risks and this may be our only chance to trace them. Somehow I don't believe they will have left us a diary or list of possible destinations. Remember, these renegades may be from your land, but they have invaded ours."

He had more to say, but Laria didn't hear it except as a music of encouragement, of belief in her and her abilities. She let her eyes slide closed, seeking, listening, shutting out her own hopes, her desire to be admired, the hint of fear that she would be successful and that once again they would set out after these people who seemed to have lost all sense of proportion in the intensity of their ideals. She felt…

Fear. No. More than fear. Desperation. Coins bright as blood. Coins *of* blood. Piled high. A gambler's stake, rattling in the gambler's hand. The gambler made a tossing gesture, hooked his desire onto something too bright that was elsewhere, yet intertwined with the here.

For a brief moment, Laria saw that elsewhere. She knew it, not from personal experience but from stories told in a woman's voice, deep and sonorous, a voice that for all it held much laughter never lost an undertone of sorrow. Long-trunked trees wearing caps of fronds. Animals that caused the ground underfoot to tremble with their passage. Elegant brown-skinned people. Music.

The image slammed shut. Laria rocked back on her heels, gratefully accepted the canteen of water Ranz held out to her.

"Tey-yo," she said. "They've gone to Tey-yo."

"Tell us what you saw," Arasan urged.

Laria did, reporting as the Meddler had taught her when he was her only teacher, including every detail she could, even when she was pretty certain that they weren't real, just allegorical representations for things that didn't really have shapes or forms.

"So, Wythcombe," she said eagerly when she had finished, "can you take us after them?"

Wythcombe shook his head. "I wish I could, but I don't have enough information to shape a transportation spell. Such spells don't require that you've been to the place yourself, but more is needed than a general—if very vivid—description."

Ranz frowned. "Then how did Kabot work his own spell? I thought the people of Rhinadei had been isolated from the rest of the world for centuries. Certainly, he couldn't have been to Tey-yo."

"A good question—and one for which Laria's description provides a clue as to the answer." Wythcombe gestured toward the gaping hole in the crystal lattice. "I suspect that both how Kabot chose his destination and how he had enough power to manage such a complex working so quickly are related to whatever was there. One shortcut used when working a transportation spell is to use something closely related to the destination as an anchor. Another shortcut is to exploit the bond between two closely related items."

"Like the gem on the pommel of my sword and the sword?" Laria offered.

"Perhaps—especially if the gem is related to the sword's magic. Even better would be the blade and the hilt—two elements so integrally related to each other that one is far less useful without the other. Again, I am oversimplifying. What I suspect is that Kabot somehow discovered that whatever was there"—Wythcombe gestured toward the broken lattice—"was closely related to something else, something located in Tey-yo. He then hooked one end of the transportation spell to that and went where it took him. If—as seems highly likely given the pervasive if generalized aura in this chamber—the item from the lattice was magical, he could have used its stored mana to power the spell."

Ranz looked both impressed and recalcitrant. "But how could Kabot have known that whatever was there was part of something larger?"

Wythcombe raised and lowered his shoulders in a dramatic shrug. "There might have been notes. After all, they may have been searching through these ruins for weeks, even moonspans, since we don't know precisely when they left Mount Ambition. There could have been a visual clue—a mirror without a face, a ring without a setting. Or Kabot might have sensed that whatever was here was part of a larger whole. No matter how I—or my colleagues in Rhinadei—feel about his choice to study the anathema art, no one will deny that Kabot is extraordinarily skilled. Indeed, had he been less so, his interests would have raised less concern."

There was a thoughtful pause, then Arasan said, "Someone should brief Firekeeper and Blind Seer. Do you think there is anything more you can learn here?"

Wythcombe frowned. "If Ranz's stair will last a while longer, I'd like to further inspect this chamber." He directed his gaze at Laria. "I forgot to ask. Where is Tey-yo?"

"I don't know, exactly," Laria said. "A long way away. It's the homeland of some of the Nexans: Skea, Kalyndra, and a few others. What I know about it comes from Kalyndra's stories. There was once a major gate to Tey-yo, but that was blocked right after Kalyndra arrived. I think I heard something about it having been opened again."

Arasan added, "It was. Skea and Kalyndra tried it. They retreated after they encountered something dangerous."

Wythcombe cocked a bushy eyebrow. "Well, dangerous or not, I hope they will let us use that gate to speed our own explorations."

Once again, the Voice was the one who saved them. Kabot's intention had been to create his transport spell to take himself, Uaid, and Daylily directly to Teyvalkay. Phiona's voice, speaking gently but firmly, had chided him as he had begun shaping his spell.

"Remember the ward you found here in Azure Towers," she said. *"Teyvalkay may be equally well-protected. As I recall, a powerful ward will at best interfere with a transportation spell, at worst…"*

Phiona's voice trailed off. Kabot nodded, forgetting she couldn't actually see him. Her words brought back to him the cautionary tales that had been part of his education. He reshaped the spell so that it would take them into the vicinity of Teyvalkay, then added a sigil for concealment.

"Uaid, I'm ready," he said, motioning for Uaid to bring closer the piece of lattice that held the rune-inscribed gold disk. Then he shouted for Daylily.

Kabot pricked the point of his dagger into his right index finger, sheathed the weapon, then swiped his freely bleeding finger across his left palm. Lastly, he touched the finger to Palvalkay, while gripping Daylily's hand with his bloodied left hand. Daylily, in turn, gripped Uaid's free hand. As soon as Kabot felt their manas mesh, he activated the spell, shooting them like arrows toward an unknown prey. They shivered through space where strands, some gossamer fine, some cables like those on a sailing ship, spread out around them, fastened to unimaginable endpoints. Somehow Palvalkay avoided tangling with these as it slung them into green verdure and pervading damp.

Kabot registered first that they were perched on a limb of an enormous tree; next he realized he was hearing drums and flutes, the music growing louder with every breath. Then a crowd of brightly dressed, wildly masked festivalgoers came dancing along the road that ran almost directly under where he, Daylily, and Uaid were hidden by the thick foliage. The colorful throng surged in an ecstatic, intricately choreographed routine which ebbed and flowed around a surpassingly elegant creature that was being carried upon a platform set on long poles. The platform, in turn, rested on the shoulders of four of the most beautiful human beings Kabot had ever seen.

Their dark skin was the deep brownish black of polished ebony. Their eyes flashed like cut jet. Alone among that colorful throng, their faces were unmasked. Although their burden was not light, the four bearers stepped proudly, as might peers of the realm escorting a monarch. Above the waist they wore sleeveless tunics that displayed their muscular arms. Below wide belts that emphasized trim hips, they wore elaborately pleated kilts. The bearers' heads were wrapped in complicated turbans. Jewelry depended from ears, wrists, necks, and ankles. The two in front were women of matchless beauty, the two behind men of equal fineness.

The litter was preceded by some sort of elaborately costumed high priest. With head held high, he led a triumphal song in a language Kabot didn't recognize. Only when they strode beneath the tree in which Kabot and his companions were perched did Kabot realize that what they carried was not actually a creature, but a shrine made in the shape of some fantastical beast.

As colorfully and elaborately garbed as the four bearers were, the shrine was so beautifully made as to cause them to fade into insignificance. The base material must have been wood, else even such magnificent specimens of humanity could not have borne it aloft, but so much of the wood was wrapped in gold leaf, encrusted with gems, hung with small chimes that rang in delicate accompaniment to the bearers' song, that it seemed to be some celestial creature rather than a creation of human hands.

"A dragon?" Daylily mused, her tones hushed and reverent. "No. Perhaps a gryphon. In any case, no common creature. Certainly birthed from legend rather than inspired by natural history."

"What we're looking for," Uaid said, cradling the lattice against him as a bard might a harp, "is close. In the shrine? Or maybe being worn by that priest?"

Kabot felt Palvalkay's yearning. "We'd be fools to try to grab Teyvalkay while it's surrounded by that crowd. We'll follow, keeping to the undergrowth. At least we have one bit of luck. They're making so much noise that we won't be heard."

He spoke bravely but, in reality, even with the mana he'd been able to draw from Palvalkay, he was so exhausted that he wondered if he could walk more than a few steps.

Daylily and Uaid exchanged glances, then Daylily said, "Even if their destination is miles distant, they'll leave a trail we can follow later. Let's rest first."

Kabot managed a rueful smile. "You're right. Why invite detection? Surely, we've shaken Wythcombe and his weirdlings."

The tree in whose wide limbs they had arrived invited resting safely above the ground. Its broad leaves promised a certain amount of concealment. As he drifted off into a soul-healing slumber, Kabot heard Phiona trying to speak to him. He couldn't find the energy to focus on her faint whisper. In any case, he hadn't always listened to her when she was alive. Why should he now that she was dead?

V

Firekeeper waited impatiently while Wythcombe briefed General Merial. She didn't know why such talk could be not undertaken while they were on the road back to the City of Towers and the gate to the Nexus Islands. She'd acutely felt the delay while they retreated through the tunnel. They'd been fortunate that General Merial had decided to wait for a few days in case they found nothing and returned.

"Even if we did not catch Kabot, we consider our journey far from useless," Wythcombe explained to General Merial. "I have now confirmed our suspicions that Kabot's destination was the university at Azure Towers. We know that his group consists of three people: one woman and two men. We have an indication of where they may have fled. Furthermore, Blind Seer will recognize their scents."

"You're certain they're gone?" the general asked for at least the fifth time. Firekeeper growled low in her throat.

"We didn't thoroughly scout the ruins," Arsan replied, "but neither Sun Diver, the eagle, nor Farborn"—he indicated the merlin with an inclination of his head—"detected anyone. Nor did Blind Seer catch a fresh scent. You might want to inspect the ruins yourself, just to be sure. The time has returned when guarding physical borders will not be sufficient to keep out intruders."

"Because," Merial said, her brows furrowing in worry, "as we should have already learned, with the return of magic, the concept of border has now changed. Yes. You are right. I must find a way to bring this to Queen Anitra's attention—without quite confessing what I helped you to do."

Firekeeper laughed. "Remind her how a transportation spell is like but not like a gate. Your queen is stubborn, but not stupid. She will soon enough begin to worry what is happening where her eyes are not."

"I might take your advice," General Merial said thoughtfully. "Although I believe I shall keep your assessment of Queen Anitra to myself. Let's get the horses saddled. We can make at least part of the journey to the City of Towers before dark."

Wythcombe gave a small smile. "I may not be able to craft a transportation spell to where Kabot is, but I can at least take us to the City of Towers—if you will permit. I'd attempt to return us directly to the Nexus Islands, but my understanding is that it is ensorcelled to block such spells."

General Merial looked shocked, then nodded slowly. "Choose a location away from the palace." Then, almost as if to herself, "Firekeeper is right. The concept of a secure border has indeed changed. We counted too much on old spells being forever lost, far too much indeed."

When they returned to the Nexus Islands, they learned that Derian and Isende had departed for Liglim. Elation, the yarimaimalom peregrine falcon, was travelling with them, as was the yarimaimalom stallion Eshinarvash, so their journey would be far easier than it might have been.

As Arasan briefed the Nexus Islands council, Firekeeper couldn't help but think about the mutual friends Derian would soon see: Elise, Doc, Harjeedian, Rahniseeta, perhaps some of the maimalodalum, later many more friends in Hawk Haven. Blind Seer must have scented her distraction, for he nudged her hand to alert her that the discussion had finally reached an interesting point.

"Yes. We've reopened the gate to Tey-yo," Ynamynet said, leaning forward on her elbows and pulling her heavy wool cloak more tightly around her shoulders. Her face grew even more pale as she remembered, "but that doesn't mean it's safe to go through. Skea had to run for his life. He nearly didn't make it back."

"But he did." Wythcombe stated the obvious.

"Not because of any strength of mine," Skea said, moving one arm in a fashion that emphasized the ripple of his muscles beneath his dark skin. "If Ynamynet had not been there, if she had not been a mage of great power, Sunshine would be another of the Nexus Island orphans."

Firekeeper cut in. "But we have a mage of great power, too, more than one. Not all of us have Skea's great strength, but we are not fuzz-furred pups."

"Numbers may not be in your favor," Skea cautioned. "Mother, will you explain?"

Kalyndra pushed a soft coil of her thick grey-streaked black hair back from her face and studied Wythcombe. "Do you know anything of Tey-yo?"

"Not by that name," he admitted. "Although I wonder if it might be a land that is preserved in some of our tales as having a system for studying magic that rivaled that of Azure Towers. As I explained when we first met, the majority of those who united to found Rhinadei were connected in some way to the university of Azure Towers. Those other people were said to be very dark of hair, eyes, and skin, impressively powerful and proud of their traditions. Some joined with Rhinadei's ancestors, but it is said that the majority felt that retreat was a weakling's option."

"That may well be a description of the long-ago people of Tey-yo." Kalyndra's hooded eyes and lazy smile reminded Firekeeper of the slow tap of a great cat's tail. "Let me tell you a little about my homeland. Unlike these rocky islands, or even what here are termed the Old and the New Worlds, which are clement by contrast, Tey-yo is warm all the year round. The seasons are marked by wind and rain, rather than hot and cold. The basic needs for food and shelter are easily met. Indeed, if one chose not to labor more than to pick fruit from a tree or dig tubers from the ground, one could live."

"Sounds like paradise," Laria sighed, looking down at her hands, which were grubby from having helped with the spring planting.

"Nothing is ever that simple," Kalyndra replied sadly. "The same warmth and fecundity that made life so easy for humans, also made life easy for the small creatures that carry disease. Over the generations, it was learned that certain precautions in the disposal of waste, of food, of how water was channeled, would diminish the chance of illness spreading. Living above the ground also helped, whether in trees or on plateaus that dotted the landscape."

Firekeeper, remembering the trials of her childhood among the wolves, how much labor she had expended slogging through tasks her pack had been equipped from birth to perform, rested a hand on Blind Seer's back and said sadly, "So for the good of the pack, then, the easy life could not be. I think, maybe, many did not care for this, any more than every wolf in my birth pack liked giving some of the kill to feed a pathetic Little Two-legs. There was unhappiness, yes?"

Kalndra nodded. "So our tales tell. Over time, magics to aid health were developed, but those who could work magic did not see why they should use their spells to preserve those who could not even bother to dig latrines or take basic precautions to preserve their health. Moreover, the mages expected financial support in return for magic. Eventually, a stratified society developed. On top, as in the Old World, were those who used magic. Next were those who supported the users of magic and who, in turn, benefited from magic. At the bottom were those who preferred to live a subsistence existence and so largely did without magic. These last called themselves the 'Mrrettm,' which roughly translates as 'Acceptors'—by which they meant that the price they accepted for Tey-yo's warmth, generous food, and essentially easy life would sometimes be paid in early death and disease. They called everyone else the 'Kleefm,' 'the

Selfish' for taking all that Tey-yo offered and fighting so hard to avoid paying the price."

"What did the Selfish call themselves?" Ranz asked. "Because I'm guessing they didn't see themselves as selfish any more than the traditionalists in Rhinadei see themselves as close-minded."

"In reaction to the Mrrettm," Kalyndra replied, "they called themselves the 'Rrrteerim,' which roughly means 'the Grateful,' because they said they were grateful for Tey-yo's generously providing the basic needs of life to encourage them to find ways to defeat disease and other life challenges that Tey-yo presented."

Kalyndra waved down further questions. "Let me be brutally honest. I believe the tales that tell how when disease struck the Mrrettm, the Rrrteerim made no effort to cure the sufferers. Because of this, numerous Mrrettm communities were wiped out, from the wisest elder to the youngest infant. Some of the Rrrteerim held the belief that in time all of the Mrrettm would die off, leaving only those who practiced magic—for the good of the community in many cases—and those who supported them. But then…"

She took a deep breath and drank deeply from a tall glass of cold tea as if to wash a bad taste from her mouth.

"Let me tell the next part for you, Kalyndra," Arasan said gently. "You've put yourself through it often enough." He put on his storyteller voice. "When querinalo came, the established order was overturned practically overnight. Worse, because maintaining the health of their followers was the foundation of the rule of magic, when the magic users fell ill, this sent Tey-yo's society into chaos, not just on a social level as in the Old World, but right down to moral and ethical considerations.

"What followed was death on a massive scale—on a much greater level than was experienced in the Old World. Not only did most of the magic users die either from querinalo or by being murdered, so did enormous numbers of the population that had benefited from their patronage. When disease was no longer held at bay by magical precautions and cures, the most vulnerable populations were those who had never developed physical resistance. Suddenly the despised Mrrettm had the advantage, for a portion of their population had developed resistances to the many illnesses and parasites that plagued Tey-yo. I'm sure your imaginations are up to envisioning what happened."

Firekeeper had heard the yarimaimalom's tales of what human did to human once magical control was removed—and that had been in the New World where the mages had been comparatively mild in their rule, because they needed the cooperation of the colonists. She shivered and snugged herself into Blind Seer's side as if his fur could warm them both against the horrors that roamed freely through her mind.

Laria looked ill, and Wythcombe very serious. Ranz, however, only looked interested. Firekeeper wondered if the fact that Rhinadei had been spared the worst of the social collapse after querinalo meant he had no idea how terrible such wholesale destruction could be.

"But what happened later?" Ranz asked. "When querinalo began to weaken? I mean, you're trained in blood magic. My understanding is that Skea had a magical gift as well, although it did not survive querinalo. So some magical traditions must have survived."

"Some," Kalyndra admitted, "although not as many as in the Old World. Most of the traditions that survived were empty superstitions: chants and charms that were used in conjunction with medicines and physical remedies for fevers, chills, diarrhea, and other maladies. Perhaps you can understand why those who suspected, as I did, that the charms were more effective when I said them and infused them with a power I felt within me, were careful with whom they shared this knowledge.

"Contact with the world outside of Tey-yo came when King Veztressidan's Once Dead rediscovered the Nexus Islands and began to explore where the gates led." Kalyndra sighed deeply. "What happened then is an epic in itself. I will simply say that King Veztressidan's Once Dead sought allies, provided education, and eventually incorporated us into their structure. Some of us lived dual lives, part here on the Nexus Islands or the Mires, part attempting to re-establish a small magical presence in Tey-yo. However, our attempts to reintroduce magic to Tey-yo ended just last year."

Her rich brown eyes flooded with tears. "The Mrrettm discovered what we were doing and wiped our small enclaves. My husband—Skea's father—was killed defending us. I escaped with a very few of our people. Skea was already here on the Nexus Islands. When we tried to return to Tey-yo, we learned the gate had been blockaded against us. Only a few moonspans ago, we managed to get the gate working again but, as Skea has already said, what we found was nothing to encourage us to return."

"So," Wythcombe said, "what should we expect? Because I'll tell you this, I'll try to make our way to Tey-yo whether or not you let me use the gate. It will definitely take me longer, and who knows if Kabot will even be there when I arrive, but I'm not giving up."

"And as Wythcombe is Blind Seer's teacher," Firekeeper added, "so we will be going with him. Blind Seer say he asked to be taught by doing, so he will not abandon Wythcombe mid-hunt."

Ynamynet gave a thin smile. "Firekeeper, we all owe you and Blind Seer so much that any gate we can open will be available to you, even if we think it unwise. Let us consider that argument settled. Skea, I suggest you be brutally honest. That's the best way to help them come home alive."

Skea folded his arms across his chest, leaned back in his chair, and furrowed his brows. Then he began speaking in the same detached manner Firekeeper had seen him use when he had to report the deaths of friends old and new as if they were nothing more than pieces pulled from play in a board game.

"After we established control of the Nexus Islands, the council agreed that we must learn as much as we could about the gates. Our primary goal, as you know, was to locate all active gates and learn, if possible, where they led. A secondary goal was to discover if we could repair or reactivate gates that had been put out of commission. Since we knew precisely when the gate into Tey-yo had been sabotaged, it was a logical one to use as a test."

Also, Firekeeper thought, *because we all knew how you and your family never stopped wondering what had happened to those you had been forced to leave behind. Why do humans feel that admitting to one love will cheapen another?*

"If you're interested in the details," Skea said, directing this next comment to Wythcombe and Ranz, "we can direct you to the team who did the work. However, I suspect you're more interested in knowing what we found when we managed to get the gate open. Our first scouts were some of the yarimaimalom. They reported that the entire plateau which had housed the community of Nalrmyna was no longer occupied by humans."

"How did you manage to talk to the yarimaimalom?" Ranz interjected. "I gathered Firekeeper wasn't there."

"She wasn't," Skea agreed. "But Derian Counselor can talk to Eshinarvash, and Eshinarvash to the other yarimaimalom. Plik can also talk to the yarimaimalom. There can be translation problems when sharing perceptions between species, but whether or not humans were living in the vicinity of the gate seemed a fairly basic question. Indeed, the yarimaimalom scouts were correct. There were no humans in Nalrmyna, but that did not mean they had abandoned the area, as we learned when we sent a team of humans through."

Kabot awoke stiff from sleeping in a mostly upright position, but with his head far clearer than it had been. Early morning light filtered through the thick green leaves, which must mean he had slept through the night. Well, he guessed he must have needed the rest.

Daylily was still asleep, but Uaid was awake. The younger man was seated on a tree limb, his back against the trunk and his legs stretched out in front of him. He held the remnants of the stone lattice braced on his lap. He'd screwed a jeweler's glass into his right eye and was closely examining the area where the lattice merged with Palvalkay. When Kabot shifted to grope for his water bottle, Uaid looked over and nodded greeting.

"Good morning. Turns out that this tree has a fruit that the birds were eating. Daylily checked it over before she went back to sleep. She said it should be edible as long as we don't eat too much all at once. You'll find some just overhead."

Kabot nodded thanks, hauled himself upright, tested his balance, then inspected what was apparently breakfast. The fruit reminded him of large figs, although the pulp shaded from deep green into yellow and had fewer seeds. Weird figs, overripe and sampled by birds, wouldn't have been Kabot's first choice for breakfast, but since the Voice wasn't whispering warning, he decided to give them a try. While Kabot was searching for a fig that wasn't too bird-pecked, Uaid went on.

"I've been thinking. If our having Palvalkay will make it easier for us to detect the thread we followed here, the reverse may be true. Best as I can tell, the lattice isn't providing any ward. If I can safely break the artifact free, can you could work something to shield it?"

Kabot wished he'd thought of the possibility that they could be tracked via Palvalkay, but he *had* been bone-weary. Anyhow, what good were allies if you had to do all the thinking? Instead of saying the first snippy thing that came to mind, he made himself be polite.

"You have a good point. Although, if I shield the artifact, we're going to have a harder time using Palvalkay to find the next one."

"Teyvalkay," Uaid interrupted. "That's what you called it earlier."

"Yes," Kabot said. "I'm not sure where I got that name." Uaid looked at him suspiciously, but didn't press the point, so Kabot continued. "As I was saying, if I build a ward, it's going to make it harder for us to use the resonance between the artifacts as a guide."

This time Uaid didn't speak, but something in how tightly he pressed his lips together made Kabot realize that the younger mage was debating between speaking out and risking annoying Kabot. He was obscurely pleased by this indication of deference.

"You have a suggestion?"

Uaid shrugged. "Just a thought. It might be smart to follow them, then see what we can learn without using magic. We don't know anything about the abilities of Teyvalkay's current custodians. They may be only lightly talented. However, they could be nearly as powerful as you."

Was there a veiled insult in the comment? Kabot studied Uaid, but he decided no offense had been intended. Uaid possessed considerable ability, but his nature had always been that of a follower. Caidon had done nothing to encourage him to be otherwise. Now that Caidon was dead, Uaid needed someone else to follow. Kabot had been the leader of their rebel cabal. The progression was perfectly logical.

"You've been thinking things through," Kabot said approvingly, letting his tone imply that he'd had many of the same thoughts.

"Well, you and Daylily were resting," Uaid said. He turned the jeweler's glass restlessly between his fingers. "She stayed awake through the darkest hours, and only let herself sleep when I came around. She said to let you rest, that you'd spent the most mana of any of us."

"Daylily has always been a generous soul," Kabot said, "as well as proof that versatility is as valuable as specialization. We're lucky to have her with us. Let's let her continue to sleep while we proof Palvalkay against detection. Can you shield me so that my workings won't provide a beacon?"

Uaid nodded. "I couldn't if this were going to be a large working, but my master made certain all his students could provide a small barrier."

"Good. I'll eat another one of these interesting figs while you finish getting Palvalkay out of that lattice. Then we'll get to work."

By the time Daylily was fully rested, not only had Uaid and Kabot released Palvalkay from the lattice and resecured it within a neatly woven ward, they had a much better sense of their new surroundings. The surrounding forested environment was tropical, the plants adapted to a hotter, wetter climate. From their arboreal perch they recognized many brightly colored birds they knew from similar regions in Rhinadei. The ground-dwelling animals they glimpsed included various rodents and lizards; long-limbed, long-tailed monkeys, and a variety of smaller predators, some more feline, others long-bodied and sinuous after the fashion of weasels. At one point a moderate herd of elephants, surprisingly quiet on their enormous feet, passed along the trail, sampling foliage that had been bruised by the humans in their festival procession.

None of the creatures they had seen were completely unfamiliar. In those long-ago days when powerful magic had ruled, exotic animals were routinely transported from one part of the world to another. Some had not survived the departure of their human caretakers. Others had adapted astonishing well, even threatening creatures originally native to the land. The same was true of vegetation. Some plants and animals had adapted in peculiar ways. Rhinadei boasted several populations of elephants—including one subgroup that, while mostly the usual shades of grey, also had members whose hides were dusty blue, purple, and maroon.

After Daylily awoke and "freshened up," which included turning her hair and eyes from pink and blue to hues of rich green, she examined their surroundings, locating various plants that should be safe for them to eat. With profuse apologies, she stole eggs from the nest of a duck-like creature that fled from her approach. She then found flint and, with the steel of her knife blade, kindled a fire so they could bake the eggs.

So fortified, the trio set out to find where the procession had taken Teyvalkay. Hours passed, but something—maybe their alien odor—kept the native creatures at a distance. Occasionally, a monkey mocked them. Some of the bird whistles seemed distinctly derisive, but other than these reactions they might have been alone beneath the overarching green canopy.

They caught the scent of wood smoke before they saw the village. They took to the trees, climbing carefully until they caught a glimpse of a still-distant settlement. Broad stretches of tended fields, liberally interspersed with enormous trees, surrounded a community defined by a wooden palisade. Dark-skinned people moved purposely about tending the fields; herding cattle with long, twisting horns; working at looms; stirring what might have been dye pots; fishing in a nearby river; all busy despite the damp warmth that made Kabot want to curl up and sleep. There was even a group of men moving some trimmed timber with the assistance of a team of elephants.

Judging the size of the population was difficult because structures were built in the trees in addition to those on the ground. Even the trees out in the fields boasted neat little cottages, although these might have been temporary dwellings for the convenience and safety of the farmers. The wall around the town proper seemed to indicate apprehension regarding the community's safety, but whether the danger was from other humans or from the abundant wildlife was an open question. Kabot did notice that, as far as he could tell, none of the tree limbs crossed the palisade.

"It looks like a pleasant enough place," Daylily said. "I'd bet a tidy sum that the trail we've been following ends there. The question is whether or not the artifact is there as well."

"We're definitely going to need to investigate further," Kabot agreed, "and that's not going to be easy. We certainly can't hope to blend into the local population. Even if we worked some sort of disguise spell, I didn't recognize the language the people were using."

"Still," Daylily said, "we aren't without resources. Let's watch for a day or so. Maybe we can find a way to get in without being noticed. Maybe we'll see the procession leave and can waylay them when they reach somewhere isolated."

With her green hair and green eyes, she looked so much like the gentler sort of woodland spirit that her ruthlessness shocked by contrast.

But she, like you, is a practitioner of the anathema art. Of blood magic. Never forget that, in Daylily, practicality and brutality walk as one.

The pack that Blind Seer and Firekeeper would be leading into Tey-yo differed slightly from the one they had brought out of Azure Towers. Arasan had confessed that he hadn't been feeling well for several days, and asked if they would mind if he stayed behind. He assured them that he intended to rejoin their number but "My strengths are in song and ready wit. Neither of these seem as if they will be of much use in the situation Skea and Kalyndra have related."

Blind Seer felt relieved. He had been aware for some days that Arasan had been acting oddly—and he hadn't been able to rid himself of a suspicion that the Meddler might be up to something. This purely physical explanation provided an alternate excuse. Doubtless the trip into Rhinadei had been more difficult for Arasan than he had wanted to admit.

Arasan's replacement was to be Kalyndra. Apparently, the humans in Tey-yo spoke yet another language than the ones Blind Seer already understood. Everyone agreed that, if they needed to interact with the local population, resorting to gestures and mime was not the wisest choice. There was also the question of how the local community remembered lighter-skinned peoples, for Tey-yo had held itself somewhat apart from the Old World nations. While there had been trade, there had also been conflict. Kalyndra thought that it would be wise to have at least one of their number be able to blend into the local community. Firekeeper agreed, but took care to caution Kalyndra.

"Remember, the last time you went into Tey-yo," Firekeeper said, "it not matter that you and Skea were like to the local packs. You were different enough for them to attack, to try to kill."

Kalyndra shrugged agreement. "That's impossible to deny. However, we believe that someone detected us coming through the gate. The plan we now have, where you and Blind Seer will cross after dark to scout, then return for the rest of us if no one is around, may avoid that difficulty."

Blind Seer huffed agreement. This travelling by means of gates reminded him too much of when the One Female was denned with pups. No matter how carefully the pack planned, the most securely placed den was vulnerable at its openings. Ranz had asked Wythcombe if there wasn't a way that he could draw on Kalyndra's knowledge of Tey-yo to design a transportation spell so they could avoid the gate entirely, maybe even get closer to where Kabot had gone, but the old sorcerer had shaken his head.

"Even if Kalyndra and I worked in concert, she is as ignorant of the transportation spell as I am of Tey-yo. Additionally, there is the issue of distance. From what I understand, Tey-yo is a tremendous distance from the Nexus Islands. I was wearied enough by creating the spell that took us from where General Merial awaited us to the City of Towers. Even if I did know where we were going, I could not take us from here to Tey-yo, not without a great deal more mana than I have at my disposal."

Ranz looked as if he was going to ask if Wythcombe could teach him the transportation spell, but thought the better of it. He'd asked once already, and had been told very firmly that even though he was remarkably skilled for one of his age and education, the spell was far beyond him. Still heady with the praise he'd garnered from construction of the stairway of ice and snow, Ranz had not looked pleased at being reminded that, as of yet, his new teacher considered him a very young hunter.

Blind Seer was worried about Ranz's shifting attitudes. When they'd left Wythcombe's mountain home, the youth had smelled of bright optimism. He'd finally gained the attention of the One of his dreams, attention which he believed would redeem not only him but his disgraced sire. Nor had Laria's obvious admiration hurt. Although Ranz had not given the least sign of returning Laria's affections, he was very aware that he was admired and strove to live up to that admiration.

Their arduous journey across the ruined lands of Rhinadei—a journey made more difficult because Wythcombe refused to use magic to ease the way as long as there were other alternatives—had apparently made Ranz begin to doubt his choice of a teacher. Wythcombe's superb ability in keeping back the ensorcelled storm that had been set to attack any who climbed Mount Ambition had eased that doubt some. Nonetheless, each time Wythcombe refused to produce some dramatic magic as the solution to a difficulty, Ranz's scent further shaded with doubt. Had he been a young wolf, doubtless the One would have given the young man a solid drubbing to remind him that he was not yet ready to lead the hunt. Wythcombe did nothing.

Indeed, Blind Seer didn't know if Wythcombe was aware of Ranz's changing attitude. Or was he aware and this ignoring was part of his instruction of the young sorcerer? Or was the old man simply so focused on his need to find and stop Kabot that he had no attention for anything else? Blind Seer had discussed his impressions with Firekeeper, but she didn't have any better idea how to deal with Ranz—or Wythcombe—than Blind Seer did. In the end, both wolves had decided that they would watch and wait—and hope that humans knew best how to deal with their own kind.

When Firekeeper and Blind Seer emerged from the gate into Tey-yo, the first thing that Blind Seer was aware of was how heavily the air smelled of both rotting vegetation and a variety of creatures whose odors were not immediately familiar to him. Amid these strange odors was one that dominated the rest. After several deep breaths, he realized that this "odor" was not like the others, but tied into his ability to scent magic.

"It is not new magic," he explained to Firekeeper, who stood next to him, scanning the darkness with her night-seeing eyes, "such as when a new working has just been done. This is older, a deep scent like that which lingers even in midsummer in a den where bears slept all the winter before."

"I am nose dead," Firekeeper stated with her usual resignation, "twice so when the scent is that of magic, old or new, but I will admit to being curious. Shall we look for its source before we go back? I neither see nor hear nor—even, as best as I can—smell any fresh human scent. I think we are safe to prowl, especially if we are very careful."

Blind Seer took a deep sniff of the warm, damp air. The only human scent he caught was stale, nor did there seem to be any large creatures about. That didn't mean this place was "safe," but it should mean that he and his Firekeeper could scout further without fearing immediate attack.

"Why not? The others were told a quick return would mean we were fleeing some danger, that if we found no immediate threat, we would go further afield."

This was not said so much in words, but in his tossing his head up to catch the air-carried scents, down to find those that lingered in the soil. Firekeeper understood him, as she had from when he was a chubby pup and she a lanky starveling Little Two-Legs. Unlike humans, neither felt the need to remind the other to be careful. Taking care was not second nature to them, but the reason they remained alive.

They also did not need to discuss how Firekeeper would be alert to their more general environment, permitting Blind Seer to focus both on his ability to trail magic and to use his sharper senses. Wolves automatically divided tasks. Why else bother hunting in a pack?

As Blind Seer gave his attention to finding the source of the magical scent that had so permeated the area, he was aware of another unfamiliar sensation, touching lightly on the edges of his awareness. Faint and distant, it seemed neither urgent nor threatening, so he put it aside to investigate later. There was only so much a pack of two could do. As the proverb said, "Winter packs are larger for a reason." He only hoped that he was correct in feeling that they remained in summer and had not, despite the heat and damp, crossed to where winter rules should be abided by.

Firekeeper was unsurprised that the place the gate had brought them reminded her in many ways of the ruins of the university in Azure Towers. One of the first things they had learned about gates was that they were expensive to build—requiring a huge amount of mana, as well as enchanters skilled in all manner of abstruse spells. Even after the gates were built, an ability to use magic was required to operate them. For this reason, most gates had been constructed in locations that were both central to a population and associated with the use of magic. When asked, Kalyndra had said that this Nalrmyna had not been a university—quite—more a place for those who were already advanced in their skills and desired a place where they could research further developments.

Nalrmyna was special for another reason. Since Tey-yo's warm, damp climate bred disease and parasites, higher ground was coveted, even by those who had access to the best protections from sickness, protections Kalyndra had already placed upon the exploration team. Higher ground was also often more comfortable, less inclined toward flooding, and offered other benefits that Firekeeper didn't quite understand. She did understand one that Kalyndra had not mentioned: high ground permitted one to see a great distance and was easier to defend. However, if the enemy was strong enough, it could also mean the defenders would find themselves trapped.

This had been the fate of Tey-yo's elite sorcerers when querinalo came. As in Azure Towers, in Nalrmyna everywhere one looked there remained evidence of the violence that had taken place. Unlike in Azure Towers, here a riot of green growing things had covered much of the destruction. Firekeeper was reminded somewhat of the islands of Misheemnekuru, off the coast of the land of Liglim, and took great care lest she and Blind Seer tumble into a cellar or other subterranean remnant of the dwellings that had been here.

Another way in which Nalrmyna differed from Azure Towers was that there was evidence that the ruins had been not so much rebuilt as repurposed by later residents. Sometimes one or more walls that had not completely collapsed had been used as the basis for a new structure, making for some very oddly shaped dwellings. The young trees that had thrust up from among the ruins had been cut back, their trunks and limbs used to make roofs. Firekeeper thought that some of these rebuilt dwellings were still occasionally used but, from the new growth sprouting along paths, even draped across doorways and windows, she knew they had been vacant for some time.

As the two wolves moved across the cluttered landscape, Firekeeper caught glimpses of several possibly dangerous beasts, including a spotted wild cat and a very alert reptile with impressive teeth, but not even these little rulers of the wilderness chose to challenge the intruding wolves.

And that shows how very sensible they are, Firekeeper thought with satisfaction.

Aware that the little poisoners—snakes and insects—would lurk among the buildings, Blind Seer kept them to the curved paths. This made their progress anything but direct. Nonetheless, each time he had a choice of turnings, he chose the way that would take them closer to something that bulked large enough to block the view of the stars. Eventually, Firekeeper's night-adapted eyes discerned that this was not a cluster of boulders or a hillside, but rather a structure far less ruined than the majority that had once crowded this plateau.

When the wolves were a handful of paces away, they stopped in wordless accord. Broad, shallow steps led up to a columned portico that supported a triangular façade. Behind this, the building proper extended long and flat, without windows, and only one large door. Although the façade made it difficult to judge for certain, Firekeeper thought the structure was several stories high—and there was no way to tell how far it went underground. She sniffed, but to her nose it smelled no more alive than any of the other buildings, and she wondered why none of the local creatures had taken up residence within. She also wondered what purpose it might have served for the humans who had built it.

"A temple, perhaps?" Firekeeper suggested, tilting her head to one side to study the building's façade. Heavily inscribed with a host of intertwined, highly stylized carvings, it recalled to her the temples she had seen in other lands.

Temples and the religions they stood for were a concept Firekeeper still had to work her mind around. Neither the wolves who had raised her, nor the Beasts who had been their neighbors, had the concept of deities. There was a wolf proverb that stated how wolves felt about expecting help from someone other than oneself or one's pack: "Ask the wind. Ask the rain. Empty howling and wet fur are all you earn for your pain." It had definitely been Firekeeper's great good fortune that the first humans she had met had been from Hawk Haven, where religious intervention was requested of somewhat nebulous divine forces through the intermediary of a person's ancestors. It had been a while before she realized that the people Derian, Elise, and other of her new human friends spoke about asking for help were dead—and, to the wolf way of thinking—gone.

However, Firekeeper had learned a great deal about temples, religion, and related matters during her, initially involuntary, residence in Liglim, where every aspect of life was centered around a complicated pantheon. She had come to accept this aspect of human culture. There were even times she thought it might be restful to believe there were divine forces who, if asked just right, would provide solutions for life's more complicated problems. However, in Firekeeper's deepest heart, the wolf way, even if humans thought it cold and disheartening, was the only one that spoke to her.

"Temple?" Blind Seer sniffed the air. "Perhaps. Certainly, there was something about this place that caused those who wrecked the rest of the settlement to leave this one building intact. What damage has been done to it has been done by the passing of time and lack of caretaking, not through intent. More interesting, the 'scent' I told you about is strongest here—as are various human odors. Shall we see what is inside?"

Firekeeper dropped her hand onto his back by way of answer. Side by side, they mounted the wide, shallow staircase that led to an enormous door. This, from a distance, appeared to be closed but, close up, proved to stand open wide enough for them to slip through one at a time. Blind Seer went first. Firekeeper followed only after a slight swish of his tail told her the way was clear. Once inside, they found themselves in a large open room shaped like an elongated oval. The floor was mostly covered in dead leaves and other wind-carried detritus, damp enough to be softly rotted but not unpleasant.

Staircases leading both up and down radiated off of this central area. Other than these, there were no exits. A rounded counter stood in the center of the room, where the pupil would have been in an eye. Blind Seer ignored this, so Firekeeper did as well, trusting that his nose for scents natural and supernatural would be their best guide.

After a brief pause during which Blind Seer cast around for scents, and

Firekeeper studied their surroundings, Blind Seer huffed softly and led the way to the staircase going up, to the left and more to the rear of the chamber. The treads were made of stone and seemed solid, although weather-stained on the lowest reaches. They trotted up, neither feet nor paws making any sound to break the silence. At the top of the staircase, the stone tiles of the floor were hardly littered, nor was there evidence that even a small songbird had nested in this sheltered place. This made Firekeeper uneasy, but as Blind Seer continued to move briskly along she followed, slowing when he did not check for possible traps or weak parts in the floor.

"I think this should be a safe trail," the blue-eyed wolf replied, her hesitation like words to him. "Not because I boast upon myself for my wisdom or think that I know each and every one of the myriad ways traps can be laid for the unwary. Not that. We have a more interesting guide. I have found a faint scent trail, protected by the building although it is not new: Kalyndra, Skea, and Ynamynet. I think it will be interesting to be guided by how straight and directly they made their way. I think they came to Nalrmyna not only to seek others of their kind, but for another reason. Shall we see if we can guess what brought them here, hotfoot and without concern for their safety?"

Firekeeper grunted soft acknowledgement. So Kalyndra had not told them the entire truth about that previous, disastrous visit to Tey-yo. Unlike a human, Firekeeper did not speculate aloud, but waited until Blind Seer had guided them along corridor and cross corridor, through doors that certainly had been kept closed until recently but now stood open, as if whatever they had protected no longer needed protection. Glancing at these portals as they passed through, she thought that at least one would have been very hard to detect if it had been properly closed.

Eventually, their trail ended in a small, windowless room, unfurnished except for a deep hole set into the floor. The tile that would have covered the hole had been pulled to one side, revealing that the compartment was completely empty.

"So I expected," Blind Seer said. "As a rabbit's den can still reek of rabbit after the rabbit has fled, so this place continued to reek of whatever this was long after it was gone."

"The source of that magical aura you sensed was here?" Firekeeper asked, surprised. The hole seemed very small and insignificant.

"It was but…" Blind Seer shook himself hard. "Why ask questions of the air when there is someone who knows far more than she is telling?"

"Yes," Firekeeper agreed. "Let us go back to the Nexus Islands and speak with Kalyndra."

Laria jumped to her feet when Firekeeper and Blind Seer transitioned back from Tey-yo. She'd been waiting with Wythcombe, Ranz, and Kalyndra near the gate, and they were just beginning to speculate whether something might have happened to the wolves. When the wolves returned, Laria had anticipated varied possibilities, from Firekeeper motioning for them to pick up their gear and depart, to one of several reasons for delay. What she didn't expect was for Firekeeper to turn her dark eyes squarely upon Kalyndra, her gaze accusing, her voice huskier than usual.

"So. Why you not tell us about the magical thing—the artifact? The one you went back to check on at Nalrmyna? What was it? And who you think took it?"

Kalyndra's initial expression of astonishment changed to one that might even have been amused. "I knew that Blind Seer had a keen nose for magic, but to scent a magical item that is no longer there? I am impressed."

"Blind Seer say," Firekeeper translated, "that this artifact have a strong scent, much stronger than the one in the stone lattice in Azure Towers. He asks if you know why this would be."

Blind Seer tilted his head to one side, his ears flickering back. Laria didn't need to have Firekeeper's gift for speaking to the Beasts to know that he was adding, "And don't try to pretend you don't know what I'm talking about."

Kalyndra didn't. "From what Wythcombe has speculated about the artifact Kabot stole before he vanished, the stone lattice probably served to contain the artifact's power. That would mean that its aura would have been kept close, as the scent of cut garlic can be contained within a tightly sealed container. The artifact that was kept at Nalrmyna may once have been shielded, but by the time I knew of it, those shields had long been broken."

Firekeeper nodded. "Ah… Blind Seer says this explains why the entire plateau stank of it. Not a bad smell, although one very hard to explain. But garlic dries out and stops smelling after a time. Did this not dry out, then?"

Kalyndra looked uneasy. "It did and then it was—to use the garlic metaphor, although we are stretching it to the point of distorting the meaning—rehydrated. I'd guess, although my gifts do not incline that way, that this may have caused it to 'stink' again."

"What was it?" Ranz asked, deeply interested. "And who has it now?"

Kalyndra sighed. "It's a complicated story. Wythcombe wants to get on Kabot's trail. Do we delay for a story or shall I tell it when we have more time?"

"Is not knowing likely to increase our danger?" Wythcombe asked.

Kalyndra considered. "I don't think so. Actually, I think that we'd be in greater danger if Kabot gets his hands on the artifact first."

"Then we go," Firekeeper said, "but I wish to hear this story—and I wish to know why you not tell us, and the Nexans, the truth sooner."

Laria's hand rested on the hilt of Volsyl as she walked through the gate, but the ruins remained empty of any human threat. Once their group was through, Kalyndra indicated a broad roadway that was mostly clear, although the gaps between the paving stones were interrupted with tufts of grass and the occasional small shrub.

Wythcombe murmured a few words, creating a light that flew in front of them, its glow soft and hooded so that it illuminated where they walked without creating a beacon that would draw attention. The wolves took point, clearly not wishing to have their night vision spoiled even a little. Laria and Ranz dropped to the rear, Farborn riding on Laria's pack so he could watch behind them. Kalyndra had warned them that there were night predators who would find even as fierce a merlin as Farborn a tasty morsel.

"The trail down from the plateau begins at the end of this road," Kalyndra said. "Since the wolves did not sense any humans here, nor any large predators, I suggest we descend while we have darkness for cover. Come daylight, we would be quite visible."

No one disagreed, but there was something in Firekeeper's silence that prompted Kalyndra to begin speaking again, "And while we walk, I can tell you more about what happened, both when we made our return here, and before that."

"Good," Firekeeper said. "If you keep your voice low, we wolves will hear, both you and anything that may come after us—although this place is strangely without the larger predators. I would think at least one of the solitary big cats would find enough hunting here."

"It would," Kalyndra agreed, "but when querinalo began to first release its grip, and those with magical talent drifted to Nalrmyna, hoping to find others of their kind, one of the first things that was done was to awaken old wards that kept the larger, more dangerous, wild things away. Tell me, does Blind Seer feel any uneasiness about remaining here?"

Firekeeper paused, then translated, "He says 'I do not, but then I may be large and dangerous, but I am not precisely wild.'" She shifted her tone and added, "But do not think this means he is 'tame.' What it means is that wild things run first, then think. Blind Seer always thinks, even when he is running. So you were telling…"

Kalyndra strode a few paces, then began speaking in the same voice she used to tell the children stories. Laria felt as if somehow their surroundings spoke with Kalyndra so that, even though Laria did not attempt to use her talent, she could see what had happened all those long years ago.

"The first ones who returned to the plateau where Nalrmyna had stood before it was destroyed by querinalo and envy, were the descendants of one of the chief researchers: Aroxol, who had been renowned for his bright and inquisitive mind. In his deathbed ravings, Aroxol swore that what he had left undone when death took him would make him too restless to remain within the Realms of Just Reward. Therefore, to honor Aroxol and his promise to return, his name was passed to his descendants.

"The first to bear his name was the child his daughter had been carrying when he died. What task Aroxol had left undone, his daughter did not precisely know, not being magically gifted herself. From deciphering her father's deliberately cryptic notes, she gathered enough to weave a tale for her daughter, the second Aroxol."

Kalyndra paused and said in her more usual voice, "In the language spoken by Aroxol's family, prefixes were used to indicate one who bore the same name in honor of a progenitor, so this granddaughter was called Do-Aroxol."

"Do-Aroxol preserved her grandfather's writing in a journal she never let leave her, appending her own dream visions and drawing beautiful pictures. This journal was given her nephew, who was born after her death, and became Wa-Aroxol. When Wa-Aroxol grew to the age of reason, he felt stirrings of true magic awakening in him. He did not immediately return to Nalrmyna, but devoted himself to learning everything he could that would help him to survive and to protect the expedition he eventually planned to lead to a place that had been shunned for generations.

"I do not need to tell you what Wa-Aroxol found, for you can see it all around you. Actually, the destruction was worse and the area far more dangerous, because after the Mrrettem had burned and pillaged, they had abandoned the plateau. Without the wards, the wild creatures hunted where humans had lived in their pride. There were no cleared roads then, no little houses, but one building remained untouched. This was Nalrmyna, the research center that had given the town its name, a facility had been used by the elite of Tey-yo's magic users, of whom the first Aroxol had been considered a leader and an exemplar."

At least according to his descendants, Laria thought. They were leaving the plateau now, descending along a path much more overgrown, for in places the paving had been ripped up and trees had taken root.

"Nalrmyna was locked then, but the writings of Aroxol led Wa-Aroxol to where a key could be found. Those same writings also discussed the wards that had protected the place, and Wa-Aroxol found that he had the gift that would awaken them to life. So a new community gradually began to take form.

"I will skip much of what happened over the next several decades, but for two crucial elements. One is that Wa-Aroxol eventually located what had so obsessed Aroxol—a powerful but peculiar artifact that, based on what I have learned from you, I now suspect may be related to what you believe Kabot found in Azure Towers."

"Interesting," Wythcombe said savoring the word.

Firekeeper prompted, "The second? Tell. Blind Seer says I am to be patient, but truly, I also wish to know."

Kalyndra chuckled. Firekeeper's impatience was legendary among the Nexus Islanders. Laria knew the senior spellcaster would have been touched by Firekeeper's reassurance.

"I will tell," Kalyndra said. "At first, what I am telling you may not seem to pertain to our situation, but it is directly related to why the community Wa-Aroxol founded was wiped out, and why the fragment of the artifact is no longer here."

Blind Seer could smell the apprehension in Kalyndra's sweat as, after taking a swig from her water bottle, she began the next part of her tale.

"As he grew older, Wa-Aroxol trained Xera, one of his most promising assistants, to take over as leader of the community, supported by a team of researchers, for the community had grown beyond its small, familial origins. From Wa-Aroxol's day, the Rrrteerim of Nalrmyna had been keeping an eye on the local communities of Mrrettm for the onset of querinalo or other indications that someone possessed a magical gift.

"They then trained and educated as many of these as they could. Wa-Aroxol and Xera had a special interest in spellcasters or those whose gifts would aid in research. (They would have loved Laria, for example.) Those whose abilities did not fit these categories, as well as those who simply did not want to settle on the plateau, were permitted to go home. When Wa-Aroxol died, he left a thriving, stable community of somewhat isolated, magically gifted intellectuals.

"Xera proved to be a good leader. She was not the most talented of the researchers, but she knew enough of each area of specialization to be able to respond to needs and complaints. She strengthened ties to the Mrrettm communities in the jungles below the plateau. When the Nexus Islands were repopulated under the rule of King Veztressidan, and contacted Tey-yo, Xera handled this well, keeping Nalrmyna independent but using the contact as a means of expanding influence and providing outlets for those who had been born into the Nalrmyna community, but did not quite fit either there or in the Mrrettm communities below."

Ranz asked, "Were you a researcher?"

Kalyndra nodded. "I had been recruited from one of the villages. After I showed a gift for alchemical magics, I was assured of a home. I met my late husband, who had been born in Nalrmyna and had no desire to leave. Although our son, Skea, survived querinalo, it was as Twice Dead—that is, with no magical gift remaining. Contact with the Nexus Islands gave Skea a place where his non-magical talents, combined with his sophistication in the ways and traditions of magic, were valued."

Blind Seer heard Ranz draw breath, doubtless to ask more questions, and growled softly. Firekeeper translated, "Later for that. We must know more about this hunt."

The wolf heard the chime of the beads in Kalyndra's hair as she nodded agreement. "Trouble came in a form no one would have anticipated. Hohdoymin was one of those who had been given a basic education, then sent home when his talent, in the end, proved to be nothing more than a gift for being liked. Hohdoymin and I were much of an age, and I remember very well how he could charm our instructors. I think he was genuinely shocked when he was told his services would not be needed. I think he had envisioned himself as inheriting Xera's position, using his gift to smooth ruffled feelings, traveling the world via the gates, and becoming a power.

"After Hohdoymin was sent home, he moved into trade. This meant he was a frequent visitor to Nalrmyna, and a valued liaison. What those of us who had known him from a boy slightly younger than Laria did not realize was how, as he matured, Hohdoymin had developed his initial talent into a blinding charisma. This was not wholly magical. Hohdoymin genuinely liked people and—even more importantly—he wanted them to like him. He studied the arts of personal contact and manipulation as I studied alchemy.

"We also did not realize just how much Hohdoymin resented having been sent home, and wanted to prove that he would have been the best choice as Xera's successor. When Hohdoymin learned that the Nexus Islands had changed hands, he had the rallying point he needed to bring his Mrrettm followers to rise against Nalrmyna. I don't know precisely what he said. I suspect he cultivated fears that the new rulers of the Nexus Islands would try to invade Tey-yo as they had invaded the Islands.

"You must understand, although my husband and I were still living in Nalrmyna when the conflict finally broke out, we were absorbed in our projects, enjoying visits to Skea and Ynamynet. Then one morning we awoke to chaos. As you know, I managed to escape, along with a few others. My husband, our extended family, and the close community we had lived in for so long were not so lucky."

Blind Seer thought what a mixed blessing that escape must have seemed, for at that time the Nexus Islands themselves had been under siege—if not yet actively at war. Kalyndra's husband had died shortly after the transit, and it must have seemed that she was likely to lose her remaining pack: her son, his wife, and their daughter, as well.

"Then, when you try to go back, the gate is blocked," Firekeeper finished for Kalyndra, her tone heavy with sympathy. "But when the gate was opened again—I think you go to find not only what happened to the people, but also to this artifact. Why you not tell us this?"

The words were phrased as a question, but there was no doubt they were more like an order. Kalyndra paused to wipe sweat off her face—the air near the base of the plateau was hot and sticky—before she replied.

"Honestly, I didn't know what good the knowledge would do anyone. Ynamynet knew what we were doing, so it wasn't precisely a secret, but we didn't have the resources to pursue an artifact that had refused to reveal its full secrets after decades of probing. Also, there was the likelihood that anyone with enough magical ability to use it was probably dead."

VI

"You probably don't want to hear this," the Voice said, "*but you're being pursued again.*"

"*What!*" Kabot barely managed not to exclaim aloud. Uaid squeaked in shock, but fortunately the sound blended into the riot of small bird and animal noises that had started up once the creatures had decided that these new arboreal tenants intended no harm. Daylily pressed a gentle finger to Uaid's lips to remind him of the need for silence. Thus far, no one in the village seemed to have noticed that they were being observed, but it wouldn't do to give them reason to suspect.

The three rebels had set up camp in a blind Daylily had created in a large tree that was off the road, but still offered a good view of both the road and of the village with its surrounding fields. The tree wasn't the most comfortable place to spend long hours, but the limbs were wide and thick enough to permit them to move without shaking foliage giving them away. There was fresh water nearby, and Daylily had shown herself a nearly miraculous forager. After making sure that the smoke would be filtered by the boughs, they risked a small fire during the day for cooking. At night, they did without a fire, and trusted to their own alertness and the fact that the more dangerous of the local wildlife seemed to give the village and its environs a wide berth.

Despite having food, water, and other creature comforts, theirs had been a depressing vigil. They had unwarded Palvalkay long enough to confirm that Teyvalkay was within the palisade. The longer they watched, the more there didn't seem to be any way for three peculiar-looking strangers to sneak past the palisade, into the village, in order to loot what appeared to be a highly restricted area. Some visitors came in by the road or river, but all were of the dark-skinned local type. Other than in that initial procession, none had worn convenient masks or peculiar costumes.

Really, Kabot thought, *if we'd realized what we would be up against, we would have taken our chances and raided the festival parade.*

But he knew that he was being petty. He'd been so exhausted that he'd been useless. Uaid hadn't been much better off.

"Wythcombe again?" Kabot asked. "How? We left no trail he could follow."

The Voice gave the impression of shrugging. "*I can't say, but you may trust the accuracy of my report. Wythcombe and his companions are in Tey-yo. Perhaps they won't be able to find you amid this riot of greenery but...*"

The Voice trailed off. Daylily picked up the thought, speaking softly, "But we dare not take the risk. Somehow, Wythcombe discovered where we went after Azure Towers. It would be foolish to trust in leaves and vines to hide us."

"Perhaps we give up on Teyvalkay?" Uaid suggested. "Jyanee created four threads. Perhaps we should seek another."

"And leave Wythcombe to seize this one?" Kabot snarled. "Then doubtless come after us again? Oh, that would be wonderful—to lead him directly to a part of Sykavalkay. No. We must take Teyvalkay, then pursue the next thread. It may be a fluke that Wythcombe was able to track us."

"But how are we going to get Teyvalkay?" Uaid pressed. He waved an arm in the direction of the town and its surrounding fields. "Waiting until dark and sneaking in seems like our only option, but none of our abilities particularly run in that direction. I suppose I could try to create a localized earth tremor of some sort, but in a community where all the buildings are wood… That's asking for fires. People would certainly be injured, maybe killed—and we still might not get Teyvalkay."

Daylily's lips were parting, but whatever suggestion she had been about to make was forestalled by the Voice speaking into their minds.

"I didn't want to suggest this but…" The Voice paused, the degree of apprehension permeating her mental voice making her seem very unlike Phiona. Phiona had been very direct in expressing her views.

"Go on," Kabot replied roughly.

"If you unward Palvalkay, then awaken its potential, Teyvalkay should react. There's a good chance that the holder would then come to investigate. You could choose a location advantageous to you and…"

"Seize Teyvalkay!" Kabot completed. "Yes. We discussed this option already and dismissed it because the holder might bring an army. Now that we know Wythcombe is after us, and we've run out of time for waiting, maybe we should consider it again."

"I think the chance that Teyvalkay's holder will bring an army is small," the Voice said, sounding more confident. *"There is little evidence that magic is in common use here. Even the procession we followed, although centered on the palanquin that carried the artifact, was devoid of any but passive magics. That would argue that, as in so much of the world outside of Rhinadei, magic ceased to work here and has been slow to recover favor. I would guess the holder walks a very thin line between being worshipped and being assaulted. But, odd as it may seem to you, armies were not the reason I was reluctant to suggest that plan."*

She paused for so long that Kabot prompted with a small, "Hmm…" from deep in his throat.

"There is a risk involved in your awakening Palvalkay. I told you that each thread of Sykavalkay has the potential for great power. You saw how carefully the fragment was contained at Azure Towers. I believe the lattice was not merely prevention against theft, but prevention against misuse. Think of the artifact as a powerful wild horse. Even the best rider may be thrown and trampled."

"We're taking one risk if we don't use it," Kabot replied, trying to project confidence, "and another risk if we do. I think we should try. Uaid? Daylily?"

After a pause, both nodded. Daylily added, "We stand to lose everything, even our freedom. To avoid capture, I think that some risk is in order."

Her tone was very dry, and Kabot heard accusation within it. "You're blaming me! Why?"

"Because," Daylily replied, her voice soft with the softness that is worse than screams, "if you hadn't taunted Wythcombe, maybe he would have let others lead the search for us. Maybe we would have been lucky and they would have decided to leave well enough alone, since we were gone."

Uaid tugged nervously at his beard. Something about his body language told Kabot that Uaid and Daylily had discussed this, probably more than once.

"Why did you do it?" Uaid asked, his tone pleading for some comforting, rational explanation.

Kabot said slowly, "I guess I was angry that all Wythcombe did was come and stare at us, that even as decades passed and he evidently grew in power and prestige, still he did nothing to save us."

And, he thought, *as angry I was, I was grateful, too. Grateful that he never stopped caring.*

The jungle was a sensory nightmare, the thick, moist air overflowing with a wealth of unfamiliar sounds and smells. Firekeeper did her best to sort the information and wished, for one brief moment, that like her human companions she could simply dismiss it all as part of the background. Blind Seer shook out his coat, then shook again. Their travels had taken them from early spring on the Nexus Islands to autumn in Rhinadei, so his coat had kept much of its winter thickness. If they were here long, the heat would become onerous. Unlike the humans, he could not simply strip down, and shaving him would cause its own suite of problems.

This made Firekeeper consider that the ability to adjust the density of his coat would be at least as useful to Blind Seer as growing moth wings, and she made a note to discuss the matter with him when they had a moment to themselves. For now, there were other things to deal with. Wythcombe was casting about anxiously, as if by looking here and there he could somehow spot Kabot. Kalyndra was inspecting the road—actually, it was little more than a trail—that led from the jungle to the plateau. As if she felt Firekeeper's gaze, the spellcaster turned to her.

"Can you and Blind Seer tell if any humans have been near here recently? I'm worried. After Skea, Ynamynet, and I were attacked, we assumed that someone was keeping watch on the gate. You said you found no fresh spoor above, but it is possible that someone is keeping watch from a distance."

"Or magically?" Wythcombe suggested.

"It's possible. Anything is possible. That's the problem. The rules are changing so fast I don't know what to omit. Just because we"—the term clearly was meant to embrace all the cultures the Nexus Islands had encountered—"haven't found an easy way to observe from a distance doesn't mean someone here hasn't. Or someone could have a talent. Or there could be yarimaimalom here, allied with some local Firekeeper."

Blind Seer's grumbling growl made quite clear without need for translation that in his opinion it was unlikely that there was another like Firekeeper anywhere. He then dropped his nose to the ground and began analyzing scents, beginning with those closest to the trail they had taken down from the plateau and radiating outwards. Firekeeper knew that he had not found any fresh spoor either magical or human, so was seeking older signs.

She said as much to the others, then went on, "What you say is wise, Kalyndra. Farborn will go above time to time to see if there are signs that many humans—you said you were attacked by many—are coming this way. The trees are so thick here, we cannot be certain he will see even from above, but when humans move fast, the birds and small creatures tend to flee. Farborn would see that."

She turned to Wythcombe. "Can you sniff out Kabot or the thing he took from Azure Towers?"

Wythcombe ran a knobby hand along the polished shaft of his staff. "I think it would be best if I sought Kabot. That artifact makes me a touch apprehensive. Even warded as it was, it was very powerful. If, as Kalyndra has speculated, it is indeed related to the one Nalrmyna was studying, then…" He shook his head as if the physical act could clear his head of uncomfortable speculations. "Before I left Mount Ambition, I broke loose a fragment of the stone in which Kabot inscribed the spell containing his farewell message to me. I may be able to use the latent mana in the runes as a focus."

"What can I do to help?" Ranz asked eagerly.

"Protect the others," Wythcombe said, "but be warned. Your magic for cold and ice may be difficult to maintain in these warmer surroundings. You will not want for moisture, though."

Kalyndra put a hand on Wythcombe's arm. "If you wish, Wythcombe, I can channel mana for you—without using blood magic, although I admit that would be easier. As an alchemist, I had to study how the energies of various things that lack blood can be intertwined."

Wythcombe gave her a short, respectful bow. "I would be grateful."

Ranz shot Kalyndra an envious look that Firekeeper completely understood. Clearly, he wished he had thought to offer. Wythcombe had raised the young man's self-esteem by asking him to protect the rest, then immediately shot him down by reminding Ranz that his abilities would likely be limited.

"*Really,*" Firekeeper said to Blind Seer who had drifted some distance and was now sniffing the base of a wide-trunked tree, "*that old man has been a One unchallenged for too long. He has forgotten how strong wolves must be carefully led.*"

Blind Seer coughed laughter. "*Wythcombe is not a One. The problem is, his power is so great he is treated as such. Leave him be for now. The scent trails here confirm Kalyndrya's account of how the plateau makes the great predators uncomfortable. There is one great cat whose regular hunting route avoids the* plateau, but he pisses here regularly, seeking to claim it. I may need to range farther to seek human spoor. Can you mind the pack?"

"With Ranz and Laria? I can try. Take Farborn with you."

Blind Seer didn't argue that he didn't need the help of a mouthful of bird. They'd both learned to value the wingéd folk's aid.

Wythcombe had taken advantage of the relative openness near the base of the trail and was using the butt of his staff to make a complicated drawing in the dirt. Kalyndra was watching with interest. Ranz, in contrast, was trying not to watch.

Firekeeper swallowed a sigh. Years ago, Derian had been uncertain that he should associate with—much less befriend—the many noble-born people he had been forced into contact with. He had grown more sensible with time. Perhaps Ranz would too become sensible, although at this moment she wanted to trounce him as she had never wanted to trounce Derian.

But then I am so much wiser than that Little Two-legs I was, for all I sneered at human ways. I have called myself a One of wolves. Let me see what I can do with our two fine human pups.

"Laria? Ranz?"

Ranz looked startled at being spoken to. Laria, who had been holding Rusty's leash and watching idly as the billy goat sampled any plant within reach, jumped. Firekeeper swallowed another sigh.

Here we are in a strange place. Kalyndra has warned us that enemies may come at any moment, and these two are caught in daydreams. Humans!

But she let none of her bemused irritation show. "Blind Seer must cast further afield to see if he can learn from which direction came those who tried to kill Kalyndra and the others not so long ago." *That got them! Hah!* "I cannot watch all the directions and, until we know more, we must stand like a tethered bird right where the mountain cat is expected to strike. From this place there are many trails. I would set you to guard."

Ranz looked puzzled. "Trails? Many? The greenery is like a wall!"

Laria tethered Rusty to a sapling that was hopefully too thick for him to chew through, then drew Volsyl. "I don't see any either trails either. Firekeeper, remember, I grew up on an island where most of the trees were widely scattered and not very tall. You saw the forest where we found Ranz—tall trees with lots of open space beneath. This place is as strange to us as the ocean was to you."

Firekeeper dipped her head at the justice of Laria's reminder. "True. I will show you how to find trails. Look at the green not as a wall, but as something of parts: leaves, vines, tree trunks, these last both big and small."

Unlike a human, she didn't insult them by asking if they could do this. She could see by the bright interest in their eyes that they were trying. Laria was even starting to smile.

Firekeeper continued, "Now, among plants there are the fast growers, the slow growers. Trees are the slowest growers, especially in trunks and limbs. Grass is a fast grower, sometimes springing back within a few breaths. Between these are the vines, the small leafy herbs. Remember, too, that plants take advantage where there is sun, where there is rain. A trail, especially made by humans or larger animals, who may tear off tree limbs or even remove entire trees to ease their passage, may quickly fill with these little fast growers. Now, tell me, where are there trails?"

She made this last a question, a game, not a command. Ranz, in particular, was chaffing from being ordered about. She let her gaze rest on him, silently offering him the first guess, not because he was older and wiser than Laria, but precisely because he was not wiser, and was the more likely to be offended at being wrong. However, Ranz had shed his earlier pique because of her self-evident respect for his intelligence, and was trying hard. He pointed to where stood two fine grandmothers of a type of tree Firekeeper did not know, but suspected were a foundation of this hot, damp forest.

"There! Looking at it your way, they're like pillars marking a city gate. You could ride two horses side by side through there with room to spare. Their limbs even make a sort of arch."

Kalyndra glanced over and grinned. "Elephants, one at a time, but you have

Kalyndra, you said that this route leads to the closest town. Is that where the man you mentioned—Hohdoymin—had his base?"

Kalyndra shook her head. "No. He was from another village, closer to the lake, but I have no idea how far his influence may have spread."

"We'll be careful, then," Wythcombe said, "but maybe we'll be lucky and, if anyone is coming to check Nalrmyna, we'll be able to avoid them."

Avoid, yes, Firekeeper thought, *but not avoid being tracked, not with you heavy-feet humans.*

Since Firekeeper felt that they should move in Kabot's direction before the sorcerer got wind of them and vanished again, she didn't feel like wasting time explaining this. She would simply stay alert.

"I will howl," she said simply, and followed words with action before anyone could start arguing that this was a bad idea. The jungle around them fell momentarily still as the high notes of a wolf's hunting call cut through the steamy air, then almost immediately resumed as the local wildlife concluded that whatever the noise was, it wasn't the call of any danger *they* knew. Firekeeper found this interesting. Although she had yet to meet any, she had heard tales of wolves less heavy of coat than her people that actually *liked* living in such places.

Maybe Blind Seer can meet one of these and learn how to take that shape, she mused as she padded over to inspect their prospective route.

"Firekeeper," Laria said hesitantly. "Blind Seer didn't answer. Are you sure he's not in trouble?"

Firekeeper grinned at her. "One howl is enough. He would not make noise for no reason. That is why I am sure he is fine. He would call if in a trap. Anything that can take him and Farborn both…" She shrugged to show how unlikely that would be. She didn't bother to explain that if something dangerous enough to harm Blind Seer was out there in the tangled green, she couldn't abandon these weaker members of her pack even to seek Blind Seer. "Our scent will be enough for him to find us. Let us move along quickfoot before Wythcombe decides to lead."

Wythcombe had done nothing so foolish. He had untied Rusty and led the protesting goat over to join them. "Firekeeper, shall you and Kalyndra take point? She knows something of the local plants and animals, and can advise you. The rest of us will come after, at whatever distance you advise."

"Fine," Firekeeper said, knowing it was anything but, but also aware that there were few choices. Laria would remember to watch their back trail. Until Blind Seer and Farborn rejoined them, that was as much as she could hope for. "We will use the trade road."

With no further discussion, Firekeeper parted the foliage and led the way. A few long paces from the clearing at the base of the plateau where the sunlight could not penetrate as easily, the former road was much easier to find. An elephant might not pass without crushing and bruising the vegetation, but five humans and a goat managed well enough. Before long, the trail they followed intersected another, much more frequently used one. After that intersection, their own road also showed more evidence of use.

Without being asked, Kalyndra said, "We're still a fair distance from Glesteero, but close enough that we should take care. From this point on, we'll find more clearings and might encounter woodcutters, hunters, or foragers."

Firekeeper nodded and was about to move on when Blind Seer soundlessly melted from a clump of broad-leafed shrubs. Her first impulse to throw her arms around him and hug him close to her was instantly halted when she saw that his hackles were up.

"Ask Kalyndra what sort of hunters move in great packs of maybe some fifty, armed with long spears, clubs, and swords. I think their prey might well be us."

"Kabot!" Tension in Uaid's voice alerted Kabot that this was not the first time Uaid had tried to get his attention.

Reluctantly, Kabot drew his thoughts from the arcane intricacies he had been devising in anticipation of awakening Palvalkay. Even before he opened his eyes, he was aware of the rhythmic clanging of a distant bell. They'd heard the bell before, signaling daily gatherings, but this peal was different: strident and urgent.

"What?" Kabot hissed, remembering that this was not the place to shout, no matter how irritated he felt.

In reply, Uaid pointed. Based on their previous days of observation, at midday the village should be quietly busy. Now it stirred like a nest of ants that had discovered a pool of spilled honey. Fieldworkers were streaming in from their labors. More were running in from the timber-cutting operation. Kabot noticed that everyone responding to the bell was strong and athletic. It didn't take a great leap of imagination to deduce that the militia was being called up.

"Have they sent out scouts?" Kabot asked.

Uaid shook his head, not in negation, but rather in confusion. "Daylily's climbed to where she can get a better look."

By the time Daylily returned, very few new arrivals were coming to the village and the gates had been closed.

"I found a place where I could see the temple square better, near where we saw them take the palanquin. The man who walked in front of the palanquin is in charge; he's very impressively garbed and giving orders. The militia are getting their weapons, then mustering in the temple square."

"Looks as if they're preparing an armed excursion," Uaid said.

Kabot nodded. "The question is, are they after us or is this unrelated?"

"Could this have something to do with Wythcombe?" Daylily suggested. "We've been perched here for several days. The only ones to take notice of us have been monkeys and birds. The Voice warned us of Wythcombe's arrival a short while ago, then this… I think we'd be unwise to rule out a connection."

"Good point!" Kabot replied, his mind racing. "Whatever the reason, this will work to our advantage. If the militia departs and leave Teyvalkay behind, this may be our chance to seize it. If they bring Teyvalkay out, we can follow them and make our move—possibly when they're busy with whatever they're after."

"If we follow, we won't have our choice of terrain," Uaid mused, "but you're right, we can't risk losing sight of Teyvalkay."

When the militia departed the village and headed in their general direction, Kabot was astonished to realize that his main reaction was relief. During the time that it had taken for the villagers to assemble, arm themselves, set up their home defenses, and actually depart, his mind had swirled with speculation. What would they do if the villagers carried Teyvalkay off in another direction? What if they took boats on the river? What if they stayed in the village, highly armed and on alert?

The militia wasn't huge: maybe fifty men and women, all muscular and in fine condition. Most were armed with long spears, machete-like swords or elegant maces, and full-body shields. Many carried one or more short throwing spears. Body armor was light to nonexistent, probably a concession to the warm climate. As soon as the militia was clear of the town, Kabot closed his eyes and released the spell he'd prepared to let him detect Teyvalkay. He sagged in relief when he saw it was with the departing group. Not surprisingly, it was being carried by the same man who had coordinated the muster. He marched in the center of the band, flanked front and back, as well as on either side, by warriors who wore helmets, gorgets, light back and breast protection, and greaves.

The leader was one of the few who did not carry spear, shield, or machete. He bore a sort of mace or flail, that looked as much ceremonial as practical. Kabot guessed that the leader trusted in his bodyguards, and, possibly, in Teyvalkay. This hung around his neck, one part of an elaborate necklace.

Kabot intensified his focus as much as he dared without risking being detected himself. After careful examination, he decided that most of the necklace's various beads, charms, and carved fetishes were only decorations. The strongest magical aura came from twin gold coins joined along one edge. Each coin was somewhat smaller than Palvalkay but, to Kabot's magically enhanced vision, they blazed like eyes of fire. To normal vision, in contrast to the beads that made up the rest of the necklace, the coins were rather drab.

They weren't even the centerpiece of the necklace, but hung off to one side, slightly lower than the man's left collarbone.

Clever misdirection, Kabot thought. *Or maybe I'm giving him too much credit. Maybe he himself doesn't know what element holds the necklace's magic. He certainly hasn't been using it.*

The three rebels waited in absolute stillness in their blind, dreading being seen. However, although the militia members were admirably alert, they did not seem to expect trouble so close to home. They trotted briskly along, not in complete silence, but certainly not with the festival atmosphere of that earlier procession.

"So what does that tell us?" Kabot asked his companions through a temporary link created through their mingled blood.

Uaid replied, *"They know where they're going. While they're not stupid enough to leave their town unguarded, the home guard's a formality. The real question is shall we follow closely or wait?"*

"Wait," Daylily responded promptly. *"They may not be looking behind every tree, but they're not careless. Once they're away from safe territory, they're going to be considerably more alert. I would guess that part of the reason for all that singing and dancing and music during the festival was to keep the wildlife at bay. This group—especially if they're after someone—can't risk making that much noise. Let's trail them, keeping sufficient distance that we're unlikely to be detected, but close enough that the predators will perceive us as part of the crowd."*

Kabot agreed, thinking that Daylily's obsession with appearing both younger than she was and like a storybook idea of a sorceress made it easy to overlook that she was his senior by a good many years and far from frivolous. If she had wanted, she could have taken over leading the group. Lucky for him that while she was passionate about gaining knowledge, that passion was unfocused.

Somewhat stiffly, they climbed down from their tree and trailed the militia. Nerves already stretched nearly to breaking couldn't maintain that pitch for long, so Kabot found himself calming. The uncertainty was over. They were doing something. When the militia met up with whoever it was they intended to attack—Kabot didn't believe for a moment that this was merely an escort for a trade caravan or some visiting dignitary—then his group would take advantage of the confusion to make a strike of their own. Fifty armed warriors was more than Kabot wanted to confront, but the man wearing the necklace was lightly armed and surrounded by only six guards. Kabot would put himself and his allies up against six warriors anytime.

Funny to think that these people might be planning to take on Wythcombe and his peculiar companions. They were doing Kabot another favor there. They'd supply him with Teyvalkay and, if he was lucky, remove Wythcombe from contention as well.

If I'm lucky, Kabot thought. *Well, I'm a firm believer in making my own luck.*

Laria was relieved beyond belief when Blind Seer, followed shortly thereafter by Farborn, emerged from the jungle to one side of the trail. She could tell that Firekeeper was, too, but the wolf-woman pulled up short halfway into one of those enthusiastic pounces with which she commonly greeted the enormous wolf. Firekeeper didn't have ears to prick nor hackles to raise, but somehow she managed to give the impression of doing both.

"Blind Seer say," she began, holding up one hand to halt them in mid-step, "that hunters come. Or maybe these are not hunters but warriors, for they carry no bows or nets, but rather spears and swords. He asks, Kalyndra, if you know who they may be and if they might hunt us."

"Not without seeing them. Is there a way we might get a glimpse without them seeing us first?"

Firekeeper shrugged. "Perhaps hide up in some of these great trees. If warriors go to Nalrmyna then we know along which trail they will come."

Kalyndra nodded briskly. "I know the sort of tree we want, a broadleaf whose foliage will conceal us from those below. We can choose one that offers a line of sight on the trail, but not right over it."

This was quickly done. Laria and Ranz assisted Kalyndra and Wythcombe up into the tree Kalyndra selected. Laria thought she had seen large trees during their journey through the mountains in which Wythcombe had retired into his hermitage, but those sky-reaching giants seemed spindly compared to these solid, wide-leaved jungle trees, some of which had limbs wide enough that she could have slept stretched out on them. Rusty was perfectly content to join them aloft, especially after Firekeeper handed up a few leaf-heavy boughs.

"So he can eat but not shake the branches. Farborn says the warriors be here soon, so stay quiet. No matter what you see, do not stir until they have passed by and I give sign."

Laria frowned. "But Firekeeper, what about you and Blind Seer?"

Firekeeper grinned wickedly. "We hide down here, so we can follow. If they see us, we vanish into jungle—away from where you hide, no fear. Farborn will perch where he can keep sharp watch over."

Laria had to be content with that. She found herself wishing that Arasan and the Meddler were there. The one would say something soothing, the other obnoxious. Either would be better than this slowly building, silent tension. Even Rusty seemed to sense it, and stopped tearing at the leaves, contenting himself with chewing his cud.

They heard the footsteps first, audible more because of their number than because the approaching humans were being particularly noisy. Then they heard a few voices, again not raised, but whoever was speaking apparently felt no need to keep silent. When the source of the voices came into sight, Laria felt no doubt that these were warriors, not hunters. She couldn't have said why, since long spears were a good choice when attacking a creature much larger than a human, but she knew. The beginning of the column walked in pairs, but toward the middle the band widened so that a single man could walk flanked by two others.

These two were more heavily armed and armored than the rest, as were the two in the pair ahead, and the two in the pair behind. Clearly these were elite warriors. The one these elites guarded was a man who, in vivid contrast, was the most lightly armed of the entire company. His only weapon was a mace whose ornate embellishments showed it was meant for ceremony, rather than hitting anything, but Laria wasn't fooled into thinking him harmless. She had grown up surrounded by spellcasters, and she fancied that the ornate necklace the man wore must be his focus.

She glanced over at Kalyndra, shocked to see that older woman's usually tranquil expression was distorted by a teeth-bared snarl of barely contained rage. When Kalyndra saw Laria looking at her, Kalyndra mouthed: "Hohdoymin." Laria squeezed her features into a grimace of sympathy. So that man walking so calmly along, surrounded by his guards, was the man responsible for the deaths of the community that had taken him in, given him an education, and believed him a friend.

Wythcombe frowned deeply as he studied Hohdoymin. There was no rage in his expression, as there had been in Kalyndra's, rather the intense thoughtfulness that Laria had seen when he faced a particular arcane puzzle. Something about Hohdoymin, perhaps?

As the war band passed, Laria tried to locate Firekeeper and Blind Seer, wondering what she would do if someone spotted the wolves. Should she try an arrow shot, or should she trust Firekeeper's brag that she and Blind Seer could vanish into the jungle? Holding still might be best. After all, what good would Laria do anyone if she gave away that there were four humans and a goat hiding close by? But if the wolves were overconfident and got into serious trouble, well then, all bets were off.

The war band went by, vanishing down the trail without realizing how closely they were observed. Laria was getting edgy, wondering why Firekeeper and Blind Seer hadn't come for them, when two men and a woman trotted cautiously down the trail, clearly following the warriors. Laria had never seen the men in person, but she recognized the taller of the two from the message he had left for Wythcombe. This was Kabot, in the flesh and looking a lot less confident and dashing than he had in that arcane image. The woman was the same who had rained fire on them back at the ruined tower in Azure Towers. Her hair was green now, but there was no mistaking her. The other man had a strong, stocky build, black hair shading to iron grey at the temples and a spade-shaped beard, also streaked with grey. All three possessed the ragged look of people who had been living rough, but they were stalking Hohdoymin's war band with the careful confidence of predators.

Laria looked anxiously over at Wythcombe, worried that he would forget they couldn't confront Kabot without alerting Hohdoymin's warriors. To her relief, although the old man's expression was fearsomely alert, he showed no sign he was about to do anything impulsive. Ranz was holding Rusty's tether, his gaze locked on the three rebels, his expression one of fixed fascination. Kalyndra was so intently focused on where Hohdoymin and his band had vanished down the trail that she visibly started when the new arrivals crossed into her field of vision.

Laria put a hand out to steady her, and Kalyndra patted her hand reassuringly. Everyone froze as Kabot and his two associates approached, came abreast, then continued on without noticing that they had been seen.

"What…" Ranz was beginning, the word more a shape on his lips than a sound, when shouting came from the direction where Hohdoymin's band had vanished, followed by a wolf's howl cutting through the hot, still afternoon.

Blind Seer smelled excitement and aggression rising from the warriors, but very little fear. He had caught similar scents from human soldiers who knew they were going into danger, but felt equipped to deal with it. This seemed an argument in favor of their being the same group that had attacked Nalrmyna at least twice before. These men and women were confident that whatever challenge awaited them was something they could handle.

When he and Farborn had first seen this armed band coming down the trail, Blind Seer's first duty had been to warn his pack. Now he had the leisure to more carefully analyze these probable opponents.

Humans were like wolves in that they usually had a leader, but a human leader did not always physically lead. Even if the presence of bodyguards hadn't indicated who this pack's One was, Blind Seer's ability to scent magic would have directed him to the man who walked with easy confidence at the center, protected as a herd of elk protects their calves. As Blind Seer sought to isolate the leader's scent, he discovered something very interesting. Although the man did have some magic of his own, the far stronger magical odor rose from the complex necklace that spread over his neck and shoulders. Something about its scent seemed familiar, even though Blind Seer felt certain he had never smelled this specific odor before.

Had Blind Seer not been analyzing the scent trails so carefully, the spellcaster wolf might have taken longer to catch the fresh scent of the three humans who stalked the warriors. As it was, with his senses open to catch every detail, he was almost rocked back by the strength of four magical auras, all different, all so powerful as to nearly overwash that of the necklace the war band's leader wore. He knew three of them at once: Kabot, the woman who rained fire, and the unknown man. No surprise, these, but the last…

Blind Seer stiffened when he realized why the scent of the necklace had been somehow familiar. It was that which had had lingered in Nalrmyna. Between one breath and the next, Blind Seer knew what he and Firekeeper must do. Quickly he summarized what he had learned, then continued.

"Firekeeper, I want that necklace."

A human might have asked why he felt so strongly about this, but Firekeeper accepted that in this hunt for things of magic he was the One and she his first hunter.

"Then we must take it before Kabot and his pack decide to attack. Now?"

Blind Seer considered. There were advantages to waiting until dark, but the humans would also know that they were handicapped by darkness. For that reason, he doubted that Kabot would wait until then. The war band—Hohdoymin's until they learned otherwise—would reach the plateau long before night. Nalrmyna was human-built, so humans would be at an advantage. Neither the clearing at the base of the trail, nor the trail itself would be as much in the wolves' favor as this thick jungle. Moreover, when Blind Seer and Farborn had scouted, there had been no scent of Kabot's pack. Therefore, this was unfamiliar terrain to them.

He decided. *"Firekeeper, I do not want Kabot's pack to close the distance between them and these warriors. With Farborn's help, I should be able to startle these humans for long enough that I can tear the necklace from the leader's neck, then reach cover."*

Firekeeper touched her bow and pointed at the war band, effectively saying, "I have my bow. I could shoot a few of the warriors and still be in place to keep Kabot's pack away."

"No. These warriors are prepared for human-style attack. Surprise is better. Here is what I have in mind..."

He told her. From the branches above, Farborn chuckled. *"I like it, Blue Eyes. I will fly with you in this."*

"I don't like it," Firekeeper countered, "but given what we know and what you wish, this seems best. I warn you. As soon as Kabot is dealt with, I will be back to you."

"I expected no less, beloved. Keep yourself safe. Remember that at least Kabot's female packmate can use her magic to fight."

Firekeeper squeezed him tightly, then vanished to intercept Kabot's pack. Farborn bounced excitedly from crystal-sheathed leg to crystal-sheathed leg, then glided from branch to branch as the great grey wolf moved like a shadow through the undergrowth. They paced Hohdoymin's war band until Blind Seer had a sense for their rhythm, who was edgy (not really anyone), who was alert (the two on point, the two to the rear, the rest were secure in the security of their herd). When the band came to where the trail widened slightly so that, without realizing they were doing it, the humans spread out just a little, Blind Seer gave Farborn the signal to strike.

He didn't wait to see if the little merlin did as he had promised, for Farborn was still intensely eager to prove himself. If anything, he would be likely to do more, rather than less, than had been requested. Blind Seer knew that the best way to keep the merlin from foolishness was to give him no opportunity.

Farborn skimmed across in front of the war band, just close enough to distract. The pair of warriors on point jumped, but here Farborn's small size was all to the advantage. The warriors were beginning to chuckle, ready to laugh about having been startled by such a small bird, when Blind Seer made his leap. The warriors all carried their spears in their hands, machetes or maces at their belts. Therefore, in close combat, the wolf had the advantage. Nonetheless, if he could, Blind Seer didn't plan on harming anyone. Instead, he dove into the gap between two who walked along the edge, then between the two bodyguards. Lastly, he crashed his not inconsiderable weight directly into Hohdoymin's legs, knocking the man flat onto his back.

Hohdoymin hadn't even fully landed on the soft earth when Blind Seer seized the necklace. The wolf had already noticed that the magical odor came most strongly from one side, while the other was no more magical than any other strand of beads and gewgaws. The cord was heavy as such things went, but nothing to the fangs of a wolf. He sliced through it as neatly as if he had used a dagger, grabbed both sides of the necklace in his mouth so as to not spill the beads. Then, while the disoriented humans were still recovering from this unexpected invasion, Blind Seer slipped into the thick greenery on the other side of the trail. It was done so quickly that he was still putting distance between himself and the war band when he heard Firekeeper howl.

Firekeeper waited in the deep shadows near the trail for Kabot's pack to close the distance between themselves and Hohdoymin's war band. Her considerable respect for how dangerous spellcasters could be had been enhanced during the days they had travelled with Wythcombe and Ranz through the ruined lands of Rhinadei. Given that they were stalking Hohdoymin's group, surely Kabot's pack would be ready to attack.

Moving slowly to brush a particularly annoying multi-legged insect from where it was crawling over her bare forearm, Firekeeper eased to where she could see the approaching trio. As she did so, she realized that her pack knew very little about the abilities of Kabot's companions, and really very little about what Kabot himself could do. That was strange, since surely Wythcombe and the elders of Rhinadei must have collected information about these rebels. Was the one who had drawn that horrific thunderstorm to hover over Mount Ambition among the three who now made their way so noisily along the trail?

Ah well, the wolf-woman thought. *Too late to ask now. Surely we will be done with these three quickly, now that Wythcombe has them in his reach. He will take them back to Rhinadei, so their own pack can deal with these dangerous outliers.*

Firekeeper smiled when she heard Farborn set the first part of Blind Seer's plan into action, quickly followed by shouts of consternation when Blind Seer in all his lean, shadow-with-fangs magnificence leapt into the midst of the armed band. But Firekeeper's pleasure at the fearsome impression her partner was certainly making did not make her less alert. She knew to the breath when Kabot's pack realized that the situation had altered. Now one of two things would happen: either they would flee for cover or they would try to take advantage of Hohdoymin's war band being distracted. She watched as they came to a quick halt, peering ahead with wide eyes.

Kabot snapped in his Rhinadei-accented Pellish, "Quick! The villagers must have caught up to Wythcombe and his gang. Cover me. Necklace and out."

Wythcombe? Firekeeper thought in astonishment. *How do these noseless ones know he is here? Did they catch his scent as Blind Seer did theirs? I think not. This has the sound of a plan made in advance and often refined.*

Indeed, after Kabot spoke, there had been no pause among the trio. Without completely abandoning caution, the three began to walk more quickly, alert for their first sight of what had so alarmed Hohdoymin's band. Firekeeper noted how fingers were crooked or hands rested on items strung on belts or around necks. She suspected that even though none of Kabot's trio carried a staff like Wythcombe's, this did not mean they did not have some means of focusing their magic. Leaping out in front of them would be purest puppy foolishness, so instead Firekeeper tilted back her head and howled.

The sound was clear and chilling, meant to freeze the prey in its tracks, and Firekeeper was not disappointed. The jungle, already stilled from the passage of so many humans, grew even quieter, as if the very wind amid the leaves was holding its breath. The upheaval among the members of Hohdoymin's band ceased for a long moment, the warriors paralyzed by purest fear. Firekeeper did not intend to rely only on sound alone, however. Her bow was strung. Swift as thought, she sent an arrow to bury itself as threat and warning in the trail at Kabot's feet.

The spellcaster stared at the arrow not so much in the panic Firekeeper had hoped for, as with calculation. But Kabot learned almost immediately that time to calculate was not among the resources at his command. From where Wythcombe and the others had waited in the trees came the sound of four humans and a goat descending in haste. Kabot was not a fool. He knew that he and his companions were caught between two dangers: ahead, some fifty or so, armed and angry; behind, some unknown threat.

Or maybe not completely unknown, Firekeeper thought. *That is worrisome.*

Farborn flashed overhead, shrieking that he would check on the humans and Rusty. A breath later, Blind Seer's head bumped against Firekeeper's arm. The great grey wolf carried Hohdoymin's necklace in his mouth. The cant of Blind Seer's ears told Firekeeper that it was not the best-tasting prey he had ever hunted, even as his tail expressed pride at a successful hunt.

Since no beads were dropping from the strand, Firekeeper guessed that

Blind Seer held the broken ends in his mouth. She reached down, and took the strands.

"*Can you knot it off and put the thing around my neck?* Blind Seer asked.

Firekeeper replied by doing as he requested, then tapped her canteen in mute offer of water with which to rinse his mouth. Blind Seer shook his head, then tossed it back to howl the cry that the One gives when summoning the full pack to the hunt. Firekeeper flung her own head back, adding her voice to his. The pair had practiced making two sound like many more, and she delighted in mixing in a descant of yaps and barks to Blind Seer's deeper, rhythmic call. For good measure she threw in a jaguar's near roar and the eerie scream of a panther. They had seen wildcat tracks. If Hohdoymin's people did not know to fear the wolf, they would know to dread the great cat that drops from above to take its prey.

Hearing the wild song, Kabot and his two companions began to back away. One howl and a single arrow was nothing to the possibility that something with many voices lurked among the tangled vines and broad-leafed trees. Firekeeper tilted her head, asking Blind Seer if they should give chase.

"*Let Wythcombe fight with them,*" Blind Seer said. "*You and I must make sure that Hohdoymin's band does not retreat this way. Didn't Kalyndra say that Hohdoymin originally lived in a village near a lake closer to the plateau? Let us give him reason to tuck his tail and run home.*"

Firekeeper agreed. She did not think Kabot's trio would surrender meekly just because Wythcombe demanded it. If Hohdoymin's warriors came upon the two groups while they were fighting, then it might go badly for them all. Better to drive these warriors toward what they would surely believe was safety. Besides, such singing was a great deal of fun. Wolves, like most wild hunters, enjoyed chasing what ran.

"*Take cover, dear heart,*" Blind Seer ordered. "*You do not look like the local humans. Best we not remind these that they set out to hunt those from the plateau.*"

Firekeeper melted into the cover of the jungle, while Blind Seer ran openly down the path, every line in his lean, muscular body a challenge. Blind Seer stopped outside of the range of the long spears, and waited to be noticed. The war band had recovered from its initial shock, but had not reassembled into a coherent pack. Instead they shouted and argued in small clumps. Firekeeper and Blind Seer didn't need to be able to understand their language to tell that some were urging a return home, while others were determined to fulfill their mission.

Hohdoymin sat on his backside in the middle of the trail, legs splayed, poise vanished. He may have had a magical gift for making himself liked, but doubtless having been knocked over by an enormous creature and having his necklace ripped from him had been disorienting. Two of his six bodyguards were offering comfort. The other four were trying to restore some sort of order.

Astonishingly, none noticed the great grey wolf that stood between them and their retreat until he howled a sharp command for attention. Perhaps it was because Blind Seer was wearing their leader's necklace over his own proud ruff, but no one as much as shifted from leg to leg, much less raised a weapon or reached for a throwing spear. Blind Seer bared his fangs in both threat and smile, then carefully raised one foreleg and pointed. The point was a gesture he had learned from hunting dogs, but there was nothing doggy about it now. Combined with those gleaming fangs, the motion communicated both threat and command. The nerve-shattered war band obeyed. First in ones and twos, then in a panicked rout, they tore down the trail away from what must have seemed like the wilderness incarnate.

Only Hohdoymin refused to join the flight. Hands outstretched, fingers bent into claws, he bounded to his feet. He would have run at Blind Seer and tried to wrest the necklace from him if his bodyguards had not prevented him. Hohdoymin screamed at them, but they dragged him after the rest.

Blind Seer and Firekeeper might have followed to make sure that the retreat was complete, but Farborn dove from the sky and circled them with tight-winged eagerness.

"Hurry back! You are needed! I will watch these warriors and bring warning if they find their hearts and return."

As one, Firekeeper and Blind Seer let the fear song they had been building die in their throats. Fading into the thick undergrowth, they raced back toward where voices angry and shrill promised that they were indeed, as Farborn had said, needed.

VII

Kabot had barely given Uaid and Daylily the command to move ahead when a piercing wolf's howl broke though the jungle's stillness. His hair prickled up along the back of his neck at that call of the primeval night sounding in broad daylight. A moment later, an arrow buried itself in the path, promising that whoever howled had more than sound to offer.

Daylily whispered, "Do we go forward or back? Something has the militia in a turmoil. The arrow seems to want us to back up."

Uaid was listening along the way they had come. "I just heard a crack, like a branch breaking or something."

"So we're caught between two threats," Kabot began. He would have said more, but a riot of wild howling and barking, seeming to come from all directions, made speech nearly impossible. Daylily's now-green eyes widened and she began to edge back the way they had come. Unwilling to split their tiny group, Kabot motioned to Uaid, and they hurried after Daylily.

They nearly collided with a group of people who had been running up the trail toward them. Daylily practically ran into the arms of a stately older woman with the dark skin of the locals, whose ropes of woolly hair were streaked with grey and ornamented with a variety of charms. Wythcombe stood nose to nose with Uaid. Seeing his pursuer, Kabot leapt to one side and found himself alongside a young woman who was struggling to keep a very large goat wearing saddlebags from dashing away in panicked flight. Slightly behind these first three stood a handsome young man whose dark hair was kept out of his grey eyes with a wide band of dark-blue fabric.

In memory, the Voice spoke, *"His companions include several bearing weapons, a monstrous wolf, falcon, and... a goat."*

"Kabot!" Wythcombe's initial expression of honest relief was replaced with one far less friendly. "We're here to take you back to Rhinadei."

Kabot acted more quickly than he would have thought possible. With his left hand, he grabbed the young woman by one shoulder. Hauling her back against him as a shield, he drew his long belt knife with his right hand.

Startled, the girl released the goat and kicked back at Kabot with one foot, catching Kabot solidly below the knee. He winced, but maintained his hold, pulling the girl closer to him and resting his naked blade against her throat in a promise of violence. To his surprise—especially given that the girl wore a sword and had been so quick to counterattack—his captive began to shake, the fight draining from her in an instant.

When Kabot grabbed for the girl, Daylily shoved the woman in front of her so hard that she stumbled. Then Daylily jumped back so she was behind Kabot and his prisoner. Uaid backed away from Wythcombe. As he did so, he shot Kabot a look that said as clearly as words: "Are you really sure this is a good idea?"

Kabot had no doubt. "We're not going back to Rhinadei, Goldfinch. And Rhinadei doesn't want us, not really, not except as another object lesson. Leave us to find our way in these new lands."

"Not new," objected the dark-skinned woman. "Not yours to conquer. You will find no welcome if you begin your sojourn outside Rhinadei by taking hostages."

She spoke the language of Rhinadei, although with an odd accent. In contrast, the dark-haired young man who spoke next had a solidly Rhinadeian accent.

"Let Laria go," he pleaded. "You're terrifying her. Let her go and I promise, I'll make Wythcombe talk to you about other options. The world outside of Rhinadei is different from what we were taught. Rhinadei has lost touch."

There was sincerity in the young man's words, but something else too, something that didn't seem right. Again, Kabot remembered what the Voice had said: "*His companions include several bearing weapons, a monstrous wolf, a falcon, and… a goat.*"

He'd seen only one person bearing weapons—this girl. He'd seen the goat. But the wolf? The falcon? Was the young man trying to buy time for someone else? Someone who had howled in the jungle? Someone who shot a bow?

Panic rose. Kabot pressed his knife into the soft skin of the girl's throat, felt the blood bead forth, then begin to course over where his arm, bare in this horribly hot climate, wrapped around the girl. He was vaguely aware of the softness of her young breasts, of her panicked breathing as she tried to stifle her sobs, but what he felt more acutely than either was the blood: so hot, so full of mana. This girl had a magical gift—a talent he thought—untapped for some time, rich with potential. Something close to Kabot began to respond to this source of fresh power, to his desperate need. Kabot struggled to focus. This of all times was not the time to lose control.

Wythcombe was staring at him, those familiar eyes in that unfamiliarly aged face alive with pity and horror. The young man had stopped talking and, with his newly acute senses, Kabot could tell he was shaping his mana for some sort of working.

"Don't try anything," Kabot said, his voice thick, as if he'd hit the not quite drunk state of intoxication. "I mean it. Anything happens to me, and I can't help but damage this girl, this, what did you call her, Laria?"

"Yes. Laria."

The voice that answered didn't come from any of the three who stood facing Kabot, nor from the goat, who had wandered back and was idly nibbling at the edge of Wythcombe's sleeve. This voice was husky, just a little deep, possibly female, but right now Kabot would not have been surprised to find it was not human. The husky voice spoke on, simultaneously tight and preternaturally calm.

"If you kill Laria, you will die. That is the problem with hostage taking. Hostages are only good as long as they live. If Laria dies or is even so badly hurt, then you will wish for a clean death. We promise."

The words were underlaid with a growl so deep and resonant that Kabot wondered that the speaker's throat could both shape words and emit that sound. Then Uaid spoke, his voice so mincingly precise that Kabot knew he was very, very nervous.

"Kabot. We're surrounded. There's a… woman and next to her is a wolf the size of a horse and it's wearing that necklace. They don't look at all happy."

"Surrounded," the husky voice echoed. "Yes. Wythcombe may have old fondness for you, but Ranz? I think no. People like you have maked his life not so pleasant. And me and Blind Seer have a trust for Laria. Release her to us now, and we will let Wythcombe have you. Do not release her and, for a little, we have what is called a stalemate. But only for a little and after that little, you die."

Kabot believed what that voice said. He really did. In another situation, he would have surrendered, hoped that he could talk his way around Wythcombe. He'd done that so many times when they were young. But something else was pounding through his system and now he recognized what it was. In anticipation of using Palvalkay to draw Teyvalkay from the village, he had immersed himself in its aura. When the villagers had begun their unexpected exodus, he had dropped Palvalkay into a little bag that he had hung around his neck. It lay there now, and he could sense it licking at the girl Laria's mana-rich blood.

Kabot fought to concentrate. Daylily was speaking now, arguing that they needed some sort of promise before they could trust what that rough-voiced woman—Firekeeper, it seemed she was called—to keep her promise. Kabot didn't pay any attention to the byplay. In the confines of his mind the Voice was speaking to him as Phiona might have done.

"You don't need to surrender. Can you feel it? Yes. Fresh blood makes it easier, doesn't it? You're learning fast. Now. Open your mind. Tap into Palvalkay. You don't need to invent an elaborate transportation rote. You've done it before. Find the channel, then ride it. Good. Now, see? There are three lines going out. One goes to Teyvalkay. So close, alas, but too far. That wolf would let the girl Laria die rather than surrender it. He's no fool.

"Two lines remain. One is shorter, stronger. That's right. Closer. But I'll let you in on a secret. You don't want to go that way, not until you have at least one additional thread. I'll tell you why when we're not so pressed for time. So that leaves the other. It's thinner, more tenuous, but you're well-rested and have been storing mana. You can do it! I'll whisper to Daylily and Uaid. We're not the sort to abandon old friends. Not like Wythcombe, are we? Good. You have it? Then a deep breath, focus on the spell you're building. Keep a tight hold on the girl. She truly is your shield—as well as a wellspring you can tap again. Now. Daylily. Uaid. Ready? We're off! Imagine their faces when they see what you've done. I could just die laughing."

And to the sound of disembodied laughter, aware of Daylily and Uaid linked to him, of the mana-rich weight of the sobbing girl in his arms, Kabot launched into the current that connected Palvalkay to another thread, one so, so very, very far away.

He heard the girl scream "Firekeeper, help me!" and then he heard nothing at all.

The scent of Laria's terror nearly overwhelmed the scent of her freshly shed blood as it trickled over Kabot's hand and mingled with his sweat. That sweat told Blind Seer its own story: defiance and excitement blending with something very human—the awareness that Kabot knew what he was doing was irrevocably foolish, but that he was going to do it anyhow. The other two humans were shocked more than anything else. Clearly, they had no advance warning as to what Kabot intended to do.

Firekeeper had stood taut and tense beside Blind Seer, miserable that she could not do more, but also confident that she would be able to rescue Laria. Indeed, Firekeeper's main concern had been that she might need to wait for nightfall when the advantage would be hers and Blind Seer's. Now, between one breath and the next, the option of rescue had vanished along with four humans: Kabot's three and Laria.

Blind Seer bared his teeth in a smile that was very nearly a snarl. *No. Correct that. The option of an immediate rescue has vanished. I know my Firekeeper. Laria will be rescued. Let us hope that the girl is in a condition to appreciate being saved.*

Ranz raced into the newly vacated space, as if he could somehow catch up with the kidnappers. Kalyndra didn't move from where she had been standing, but looked at Wythcombe.

"Earlier, you told us how Kabot and his associates had simply vanished from the university towers. Was it like that?"

Wythcombe leaned his forehead against the polished wood of his staff. "We don't know for certain what they did last time, since they vanished before we reached them. We only saw that they were no longer where they had been, and knew they had not passed us when making their departure. However, I believe Blind Seer would have reported if he had smelled quantities of fresh blood." He glanced at the wolf, who nodded. "Now, as then, I suspect that the artifact they have is somehow assisting them."

"This time we have artifact, too," Firekeeper said, pointing to the necklace that Blind Seer wore. "Use it to take us after them."

Wythcombe shook his head. "I can't. Kabot was attuned to the artifact he used. Achieving such attunement takes time. I can't help but feel that there is something we're missing. Kabot was always talented, but he has spent the last several decades in a magical hiatus. How did he learn these techniques? How did he become so much more powerful? The theories say…"

Trembling with fury, Ranz interrupted. "A girl has just had her throat slit open, then was dragged off by a madman! How can you stand here calmly discussing theory? We must go after them before they do Laria more harm."

Blind Seer growled, and Firekeeper translated. "Ranz, if you know how to sniff out her trail, then lead the hunt and we will run at your heels. Otherwise, we must give Wythcombe his say. You don't think he's worried about Laria?"

"I am," Wythcombe said, straightening and extending a hand placatingly toward Ranz. "I'm shocked and horrified. I have seen two things that I never thought I would—Kabot awash in human blood, and a transportation spell worked without any previous preparation. I'm sorry if I focus on logistics and theory. And I apologize for failing your expectations as to what a great mage should be able to do."

Kalyndra cut in before Ranz could speak. "Wythcombe, you may not have seen anything like how Kabot behaved, but I have, many times. That look on Kabot's face was terribly, terribly familiar. Although you of Rhinadei may not believe this, not all of us who use blood magic are the same. Many of us use very little blood in our workings, and most of that from willing donors. Much of our blood magic takes the form of using blood as a means of blending our mana with another's. Stealing blood from an unwilling donor is supposed to provide a unique, heady sensation, one that can drive a spellcaster to near madness. That's what I saw on Kabot's face."

Wythcombe looked sorrowful. "I wondered if that was so. Although I have not practiced any form of blood magic, I have shared mana with other mages when doing collaborative workings. Even that provides a peculiar sensation that takes time to grow accustomed to." He shook his head as if to physically banish distracting thoughts. "However, Ranz is right. This is not the time nor place for theories—at least until we discover what theories we need to take us to Laria."

"And," Blind Seer added, "although we have chased Hohdoymin and his people away, they will return, and he will want to retrieve this necklace. Best we make that last, at least, impossible. Let us return to the gate and from there to the Nexus Islands. While we are returning, you should tell us everything you know about Kabot and his companions."

Firekeeper translated, adding, "Because you must have learned something about them when you were with the elders of Rhinadei."

Wythcombe nodded, then whistled for Rusty. The goat seemed relieved to have someone take responsibility for him. "I would have done so before, but there didn't seem a need. Very well, originally, the group consisted of at least five."

Blind Seer set himself on point, while Farborn winged ahead to make sure no one was lurking near the plateau. Firekeeper dropped back to cover the rear, snorting in frustration at the human fascination with unnecessary detail.

"Old man, originally later. Tell us first about those who remain."

The awareness that the cut on her throat had been cleaned and bandaged gave Laria very little comfort. The Spell Wielders had never been wasteful of the lives of their slaves. They had too few and were too aware how vulnerable that made them. The situation must be worse for Kabot and his allies. At least the Spell Wielders could periodically trade for new slaves. Kabot and his two companions had only her.

Laria remembered hardly anything after the moment when Kabot had put his knife to her throat and she had realized that the warmth she felt against her skin was her own blood. At some point, she had passed out… Or maybe that had been the spell draining her? Now, as she came back to awareness of herself and her surroundings, Laria kept her eyes closed and her breathing even. Two people were talking, their voices unfamiliar, but their Pellish recognizable by its distinctive Rhinadeian accent.

"Kabot's still out," came a deep male voice. "The girl, too. She seems to be resting normally. He looks a wreck."

"Laria," a woman's voice said firmly, and Laria had to stop herself from replying. "The girl has a name. Remember, Uaid, from the start we resolved we would not dehumanize those whose blood we used. Kabot seems to have forgotten that, but I have not."

"I'm sorry, Daylily," the deep voice—Uaid's—responded deferentially, even gratefully.

Laria made a mental note of this. Hierarchy was important. Uaid was junior here, and apparently had no desire to take over. Kabot was not as firmly in charge as Wythcombe had assumed. Both Daylily and Uaid seemed less than delighted with his recent actions.

"Where in the name of the seven acceptable rites are we?" Uaid said plaintively. "We're fairly deep underground. I can tell that much. However, where…"

"A ruin of some sort," Daylily added. "Could Kabot have brought us back to Azure Towers?"

Laria's momentary spark of hope faded with Uaid's reply.

"No. There's nothing familiar about the feel of these ruins. Different soil. Not as much burned matter. Nowhere near as much latent mana. I suppose it's possible that we're in a section of the university a fair distance from where we were before, but my guess is that we're somewhere completely different."

Daylily didn't argue. This told Laria that, at least where Uaid's presumed specialization was concerned, he was definitely an expert. Not good. She might have appealed to an apprentice, especially one who doubted his teachers.

When Daylily next spoke her tone was hesitant, tentative. "Have you heard anything from the Voice? I've sort of reached out a few times, but I'm not feeling anything. I thought he might know where we are."

Uaid didn't reply verbally, which Laria figured meant he'd indicated a negative. If he knew, he'd have said something, wouldn't he?

But something Daylily had said had set Laria's heart racing. The Voice? By that could she mean the Meddler?

Like everyone on the Nexus Islands, Laria had heard the tales of how the Meddler had contacted the jaguar Truth, as well as others he had sought to manipulate for his own ends. Truth always spoke of this as hearing a voice, so had Firekeeper. Was this the same Voice? Her teacher? The Meddler? Had he allied himself with the rebels? That wasn't at all impossible. Many of the Meddler tales that Urgana had told involved the Meddler trying to help the underdog in some particular situation—often to the detriment of those he tried to help.

But the Meddler had been kind to Laria, teaching her how to cope with her newly awakened talent. He also seemed to have taken a fancy to the Nexus Islanders. Then Laria remembered how oddly Arasan had been acting lately. And he had chosen not to come with them to Tey-yo. Was that because he needed to concentrate on helping the three rebels? Rebels appealed to the Meddler. At least that's what Urgana's stories all seemed to say. The Meddler helped the underdog, but did the Nexus Islanders still qualify as underdogs? They controlled the Nexus, after all. Maybe the Meddler had decided to move on, find himself a new project.

Oddly enough, thinking about the Meddler and how he'd taught her, gave Laria a fresh sense of purpose to counter the hopeless dread she'd felt upon awakening. If she stayed here like a drooping flower, everything she feared was going to happen. So she needed to do something. But what?

Well, first, maybe she should let on that she was awake. Stories were the only places where captors discussed all their plans and vulnerabilities in front of the clever heroine. If she "woke up," she could at least learn something about her surroundings—maybe even escape. Sure, she was scared, but that wasn't going to change if she played dead.

Before she could think herself out of it, Laria tried to shove herself into a sitting position. Volsyl had been taken from her, but she hadn't been restrained.

She didn't know whether to feel relieved or insulted. Then, she opened her eyes and understood. She hadn't been restrained because even if she managed to escape, there was nowhere for her to go.

Firekeeper almost wished for an encounter with Hohdoymin's band or, lacking that, a clash with one of the wild denizens of the Tey-yo jungle. These were problems she could fight or intimidate or, at a last resort, outrun. Any of these were preferable to what she would face when they returned to the Nexus Islands and she had to tell Ikitata that she had lost the cobbler's elder daughter.

However, doubtless because of the amount of human activity, the jungle offered them no threats larger than insect bites, and Kalyndra had an ointment to deal with those. Farborn winged back to report that Hohdoymin and his associates had not, in fact, gone as far as the village by the lake. Instead, they had turned down a side trail and seemed to be heading for a large village. Hohdoymin was in disgrace but, in light of everything else that had happened, even Kalyndra couldn't take too much delight in this.

"If matters were different," she said with a fierceness that delighted Firekeeper, "I would seek reparations for what was done to Nalrmyna, but revenge for the dead must wait upon rescuing the living."

After they had transitioned through the gate, the others went to brief a hastily assembled council. Firekeeper and Blind Seer sought Ikitata at the workshop where she had once labored with her husband. By great good luck, Ikitata was alone when they arrived. She looked up from the heavy boot she was resoling, looked side to side then, and not seeing her daughter with them, seemed to understand what they had come to tell her even before they spoke.

"Is Laria dead?" The words were spoken with the calm Firekeeper had learned meant that the speaker was actually screaming inside.

"We do not think so," Firekeeper said and pretended not to see the tears that flooded Ikitata's eyes. Humans were strangely sensitive about such things.

"Nor was she badly hurt, when last we have seen her, but we have lost her. She has been taken from us."

Ikitata listened without a single word as Firekeeper explained how Laria had been kidnapped. When the wolf-woman finished, the cobbler raised her hammer and drove a nail into the boot's sole with a precision that was worse than any sort of violence.

"You will find her," Ikitata stated.

"I will. We will."

"That's a promise."

"On my life."

Ikitata nodded. "Good. I believe you. Go find her. Bring Laria back or word of her. Do many know of this?"

"No. We bring ourselves through the gate and the only one near was Enigma, who is no one's gossip."

"Then tell them to keep the news to as few people as possible. Kitatos and Nenean have been very brave but, although they show it less openly than Laria, they are still suffering from their father's death. Best they not worry that they may have also lost their big sister."

"But you?"

Ikitata forced a thin smile. "I am One of my little pack, Firekeeper. For them I can brave my fears. Now go, before the word gets out and I have two frightened pups."

Gratefully, Firekeeper turned and fled. Loping beside her, Blind Seer said, *"That one believes Laria may be dead. But I do not think so. Dead blood is of no use to these would-be blood mages."*

Firekeeper shook her head. *"I think rather, Ikitata fears that Laria lives, but will be driven mad. We must find her before Laria is taken to places from where she may never return."*

The council meeting was so secret that the door wasn't even guarded. Firekeeper and Blind Seer walked in to hear Wythcombe and Kalyndra answering questions from Ynamynet, Skea, and Urgana. Ranz sat leaning against the wall, his expression flat with shock. Firekeeper didn't fool herself that this was because Ranz was suddenly aware that he was in love with Laria. Rather, from the time Ranz had learned of what his father had done to save him and his mother, Ranz had privately romanticized blood magic. Not even the ruined landscape of Rhinadei had brought home to him the reality of the horrid abuses that could arise. He might even have begun to idolize the unseen Kabot as a hero who was speaking out for what Ranz wanted to believe.

But bright blood over the shining steel of a sharp blade had washed those dreams away, and Ranz was trying to accept the reality revealed in the eyes of a spellcaster drunk on access to the mana that lingered just below a victim's skin.

Firekeeper waited for Wythcombe to finish, then said, "I have told Ikitata. She says, please, do not tell that Laria is taken, so that Kitatos and Nenean not worry."

"Sensible," Ynamynet said. "I think we can keep this secret—especially if the rest of you depart as quickly as possible, so Laria's absence will not be noted."

"Depart," Kalyndra said, "but to where? We assume that the rebels were using the artifact they took from Azure Towers, but that isn't enough to tell us where they went."

The door opened and Arasan entered, closing the door behind him. He leaned back against it as if to make a further barrier with his body. "It isn't. However, I may know how to trace their general location. Then, if we're lucky, there will be a gate nearby that we can use to reach them before Laria is harmed. Up to this point, the artifacts have been close to where there were gates—the university in Azure Towers, Nalrmyna in Tey-yo. We can hope the same is true for this one as well."

The room fell silent with the sort of stillness that isn't just no one speaking, but occurs when everyone has frozen because they have too much to say. Ynamynet was the first to recover.

"Arasan, I can't believe you were listening at the door all this time. Even if you were, I think I would have known if you penetrated the silence I put around us. How is it that you know so much?"

When Arasan met Ynamynet's gaze, the Meddler looked out of his eyes. "I have some very peculiar sources of information. And, even though we're all worried about Laria and want to rescue her as quickly as possible, I think I'd better tell you about them."

"If listening will get us fast to Laria," Firekeeper said, "talk."

"All I ask is that you don't argue with me until I'm done," the Meddler said, moving from where he had slouched against the door to a seat at the table. "Then you can all tell me what I'm telling you is impossible as much as you want."

"That seems fair," Wythcombe agreed mildly.

Nods from the rest encouraged the Meddler to begin.

"As most of you know and some of you suspect," the Meddler began, "there are two of us in this body. The one is Arasan. The other is someone all of you persist in calling *the* Meddler. I'm stressing this point because, practically from the first time I met any of you, I kept saying that while I may be *a* Meddler, I am hardly the only one. My long-ago friends called me Chsss."

He looked at Urgana, who had made it her passion—although she would have likely termed it her religious duty—to make sure everyone heard at least one of the many Meddler tales in her repertoire. That her storytelling had been popular among some segments of the community had been an unexpected bonus, one that had assured that the stories would be retold.

"Chsss," the archivist repeated. "An archaic word in the language of the Liglim meaning a light that conceals as much as reveals. Sometimes it's translated, 'twilight' or 'dusk,' but 'half-light' is better, because 'chsss' contains no reference to time of day. Go on, Chsss."

So acknowledged, Chsss continued. "Some Meddlers were murdered. Others, like myself, were imprisoned beyond death. None of those who hunted *the* Meddler ever seemed to ask themselves the obvious question why, if they had killed *the* Meddler, new Meddlers always appeared. Or if they did ask, they took this as reinforcement of the belief that the Meddler was a sort of deity."

Firekeeper shifted to lean more comfortably against Blind Seer, but Chsss took her movement as an unvoiced criticism.

"I am not getting off the point, dear Firekeeper. My point is twofold. One, there has never been *the* Meddler, but rather a loose association of those who acted where others refused to take a stand. Two, I was not the only Meddler to be sealed away. Nor was I the only one to survive long after my death."

"Wait," Ranz interrupted. "I know we're not supposed to ask questions, but this isn't a question. It's a request for clarification. Are you saying there was a sodality of those who liked to meddle? A sort of formal organization? Why?"

Chsss gave Ranz an irreverent grin. "Short answer—which means it has all sorts of holes in it—the reason for our 'sodality,' as you call it, was mana. As I just mentioned, there were places, cultures, where the Meddler was worshipped as a deity. Organized worship funnels mana. Creating a sodality to make certain such worship was encouraged was a very Meddler thing to do. There's another reason but, before Firekeeper starts growling, let me get back to why I might be able to trace Laria."

Ranz nodded. Chsss's grin vanished as he continued.

"Until Firekeeper accidentally freed me, I was very effectively sealed away. After that, I was not at my best—again, if you want details, ask me later. Joining with Arasan gave me a body, but it also meant that I lost a lot of my magical abilities—ask later. That meant that I wasn't aware that when Wythcombe set us on Kabot's trail, he had also, inadvertently, put us on the trail of another Meddler."

"What!" the chorus was general. Even Farborn shrieked. Firekeeper felt Blind Seer rumble a low, throaty growl that meant, "We need to deal with more than one of them?" She wondered if Chsss would be flattered to know that Blind Seer, at least, believed his claim of belonging to a pack. She wondered if she believed. After all, having another Meddler to blame would be a very Meddler sort of thing to do. However, confirming Chsss's assertions could wait until they had rescued Laria, for Firekeeper did believe that Chsss wanted his protégé out of Kabot's hands. He had always shown a capacity for attachment that bordered on obsession.

"Kabot is the sort who attracts Meddlers," Chsss went on. "He's an idealist who, even if he knows other people may get hurt, doesn't let that stop him from pursuing his ideals. He's smart. He gathers followers. And he's not the type to be satisfied with just one lofty goal. Even if Kabot had found the university at Azure Towers active and learned how to use blood magic, he wouldn't have settled down, taken a teaching position or opened a shop. No, he'd have gone back to Rhinadei, recruited others, fought—possibly literally—to have blood magic accepted."

"True." Wythcombe spoke as if he had been asked a question. "That's Kabot. So you think a Meddler detected this passion, this idealization, and somehow attached himself to Kabot?"

"Attached? Hmm… Not exactly the word I'd use. Insinuated is better. This Meddler lacks a physical form. In many ways, this makes him—or her—I can't really say which, but don't fall into the trap of thinking of a Meddler as an 'it,' because if we all share a single trait, it's that we're anything but impersonal. We're the opposite—personality distilled."

He shook his head, much as a horse would to shoo off a fly, and Arasan spoke, "Trust me on that. Chsss saved my life, but it's been a little like saving a drowning person by pulling them under until they can't struggle anymore. Sometimes I wonder if the only reason I 'surfaced' again was because, without me, Chsss can't tap my magical abilities, limited as they are."

The facial expression shifted and Chsss looked hurt. "I like you, Arasan. I like sharing a body with you. I wish you'd believe that. I just… but I am not going to get off the point."

Wythcombe interrupted the peculiar conversation. "So you're saying that Kabot may have been taken over by this Meddler?" Wythcombe sounded hopeful, and no wonder. If Kabot had been taken over, then he wasn't to be blamed for his more extreme actions, including the attack on Laria.

"I wish I could agree with that," Chsss said, his tones rich with compassion, "but I can't. If Kabot's associate 'took him over'—which isn't as easy to do as all of you seem to think—then he'd be restricting himself. However, if he advises Kabot, and then Kabot comes to rely on him, to call on him, that's the first step to worship, to mana, to becoming first a demi-deity, then, depending on the size of Kabot's following, a deity not so demi."

Firekeeper found herself thinking that it was a good thing that Harjeedian, the aridisdu of Liglim who had first told them Meddler tales, was back in his homeland. If he heard this, he'd be spitting sparks, not only because of the idea that a Meddler could become a deity, but because of the doubt this would shed on the divinity of those forces Harjeedian worshipped.

Chsss continued, "So, while I can't trace Laria—although I've tried—I can... Well, I think I can... trace Kabot by tracing his Meddler."

"Will this Meddler be able to scent you on his trail?" Blind Seer asked.

Chsss shrugged. "Possibly. Thing is, this is one time when his being so much more powerful than me will work in my favor. As Meddlers we share access to the mana of our sodality. I suspect that I've been getting so tired because Kabot's friend is drawing hard on that common pool. He's probably already aware of me, not as a person, just as minor competition. Even if he notices my actions, he may think it's me trying to reestablish my mana flow."

Ynamynet had listened with even more of her characteristic icy stillness. Now she nodded crisply. "I understand why you felt you needed to explain the background. I suppose you could have simply told us you could trace Laria and leave it at that, but if there's one thing I've learned from listening to Meddler tales"—her face broke into an uncharacteristically brilliant smile—"which my little girl loves, by the way, is that Meddlers rarely hide what they're doing. Leading their chosen—well, Urgana always says 'victims,' but that's probably insulting to you, so I won't—leading their 'chosen' with full knowledge that they're being influenced is part of the fun. I accept that. How long will it take you to narrow down where Laria is?"

Chsss gave a wide, slightly insincere, smile. "Not long. This one is pulling hard at the pool. I only need to follow the current."

Something was wrong. Kabot knew it as soon as he awoke. He should feel horrible, aching in every muscle, including some so small that most of the time he would have sworn they didn't exist. His head should be throbbing, and the very idea of any but the dimmest light should make him want to vomit. "Worse than a hangover after a three-day binge." That was what Caidon had once said about the effect of overextension. Kabot, more abstemious by nature, had agreed as if he knew what he was talking about.

What was wrong was that Kabot felt none of these ill effects. He didn't feel exactly good, but he didn't feel particularly sick or weak or wrung out. His stiffness was from sleeping on a blanket spread over an uneven floor, his nausea from lack of food or water. As he was marveling over this miracle, he heard people talking softly.

Daylily and Uaid were discussing the best way to prepare cave crickets and water bugs for eating. Kabot wondered if he was hallucinating but, after a few more sentences, he decided they were perfectly sincere. Slowly, intellectually aware that light should hurt, Kabot opened his eyes a slit, discovering that he lay on his back near a wall. By tilting his head slightly, he could examine the rest of the room.

The area was irregularly shaped and maybe fifteen paces across. There were no windows or doors. What light there was came from some strategically placed lantern spells—Daylily's work. At first, Kabot thought this must be some sort of natural cavern. Then he revised his assessment. Surely this had originally been an artificial chamber whose doors and windows were now filled with rubble. Some of the walls had either partially collapsed or were hidden behind detritus. The air wasn't exactly fresh, but it wasn't stale, so there was some connection to an outer area.

Uaid and Daylily stopped arguing—they'd pretty much decided on "steamed"—alerted by the slight movement of his head.

Daylily crouched down next to Kabot and held a canteen to his lips. "Slowly... You've been unconscious for a long while, so you doubtless have both a dry mouth and a dehydration headache. We can't waste water, so we'd prefer if you didn't start throwing up. There's water here, but gathering it takes effort."

As Kabot sipped, careful more because of the awkward angle then because he felt terribly nauseous, Daylily continued with forced casualness, "And, speaking of 'here,' do you have any idea where you've taken us?"

She was trying very hard to be polite, but Kabot could see the anxiety in her still-green eyes, and knew that if her anxiety made her too agitated to work spells, they would be in more trouble than they apparently were already. Daylily's eclectic magics would be necessary to keep them alive while they figured out how to escape. Of course, this time they had a source of mana they had lacked in that dripping jungle. Kabot let Daylily take the canteen away and help him to sit up. He slowly craned his stiff neck, until he located the girl, Laria. She sat huddled in front of one of the larger rubble heaps, about equidistant between where he had been sleeping and where the other two had set up a makeshift camp.

Or, another way to see it, she's sitting as far from any of us as she can get.

The wound Kabot had inflicted on Laria's throat had been neatly bandaged. Although her face still showed tear tracks, she was no longer crying. Instead, her expression had hardened into what looked like a well-practiced neutrality that didn't change even when Kabot was sure she knew he was looking at her. This calculated indifference bothered Kabot far more than outright terror or loathing would have done, and he wasn't certain why.

Since Kabot actually didn't know where they were—except that this was supposed to be where another part of Sykavalkay could be found—he decided to take refuge in his perceived infirmity. He opened his mouth as if to speak, then squeezed his eyes shut. He was rewarded by Daylily pressing the canteen to his lips. He swallowed tepid water, registering that it tasted strongly of dirt and was faintly gritty, then swayed. Daylily put a strong arm around him, then lowered him back onto his bedroll.

"Can't talk yet? I understand," she murmured soothingly. "When we arrived here—wherever here is—both you and Laria were unconscious. I wasn't feeling very strong myself, but I managed to make enough light so that Uaid and I could investigate. When we realized we were trapped underground, Uaid managed to reshape the stone floor to gather water from a seep. I've put a purification charm on one of the canteens. So far we've collected enough for our needs. So the good news is we're not likely to die from lack of water. The bad news is pretty much everything else. We don't know where we are—although we're pretty sure we're not in Rhinadei, Azure Towers, or that jungle. Our food supplies are limited to what I happened to have in my pack when we took off after the villagers. We might be able to augment that with insects and fungi, although the latter is always a chancy proposition."

"Therefore," Uaid put in, his tone much less conciliatory, "if you can get us out of here the way you got us in here, that would be helpful. Also, Daylily forgot to mention that we've not been able to contact a certain advisor who, in times of past trials, has been of great assistance to us."

The Voice, Kabot thought. *Uaid's being careful not to mention just who our 'advisor' is because of Laria. That's prudent. Who knows what she would think if she knew we all hear voices? That's usually considered a sign of insanity. Of course, if Laria knows anything about magical communication, she's already going to wonder who we think we can contact. Contacting someone over a distance is not as easy as the grandmother tales make it seem.*

Uaid continued, "Perhaps when you're feeling stronger, we could attempt to reach our advisor. At this point, I'm willing to try anything." His gaze flickered in the direction of Laria. "I'm done with being entombed—and this entrapment is not likely to be nearly as painless as the last…"

"As the last time you got us stuck somewhere," Kabot mentally filled in the words Uaid would certainly have said, might have already said to Daylily,

but wouldn't speak in front of their captive. Kabot stifled an urge to laugh hysterically. He really was developing a track record for transporting them into untenable situations, wasn't he?

Kabot raised an arm to rub the back his hand across a forehead that should ache abominably. When he dropped his hand back on his chest, he felt how the fabric of his shirt remained stiff with Laria's blood. Beneath that lay Palvalkay, humming faintly as it continued to feed a trickle of mana into him. Somehow, it seemed excited. Kabot wondered what would excite an artifact. He wondered a lot of things. While he worked them out, he might as well take advantage of his perceived infirmity to think. His only regret was that he couldn't ask for something to eat. That would be completely out of character.

"Gotta rest..." he muttered, easing himself into a meditative state that would look much like sleep. Neither Daylily nor Uaid protested.

"*Phiona,*" Kabot thought reaching out, "*please help us. You got us into this, right? Now you'd better get us out.*"

"*Sweet Firekeeper,*" Blind Seer said, "*have you forgotten the proverb? 'Hunt when hungry, sleep when not, for hunger always returns.'*"

He knew that to their companions, it would appear that both he and Firekeeper were asleep, curled beneath an open window at one side of the large conference room in which, out of respect for Ikitata's request that her children not learn that Laria had not returned with the rest from Tey-yo, they were camping. Ranz and Wythcombe could have had their own spaces but, like a true pack, stayed close. Even Rusty waited with them, drowsing and chewing his cud in a makeshift pen to one side of the room. His strong odor was why the windows were open, even though the spring nights were not at all warm.

Kalyndra and Farborn were not with them. Kalyndra was helping Chsss prepare his spell. Farborn was small enough that he could leave without risking being recognized.

"I am *hungry*," Firekeeper grumbled. "*Not for food, but to go after Laria. She must be so very frightened.*"

Blind Seer considered reciting any of a number of appropriate proverbs, but settled for nuzzling Firekeeper instead. "*And what good will you do her, coming after exhausted? We have been in constant motion these last few days. Rest now. This may be your last chance to sleep safely for days to come.*"

Firekeeper's breathing told him when her pretense became reality. Soon after, he slept as well. His dreams were troubled by spiders with legs like human fingers.

The next morning, they wordlessly gathered to watch Chsss as he drew a complicated pattern by dipping his fingertips in oil, then moving them over a sheet of glass set upon the tabletop. Although Blind Seer could scent the magical currents Chsss was using, the wolf could make no more sense of these arcane breezes than a newborn pup would make of light, sound, and odor upon first creeping forth from the den. He lacked reference, even as a pup's nearly blind eyes perceived light as an overwhelming, but meaningless, reality.

The wolf-mage's only comfort was that neither Kalyndra nor Ynamynet seemed to understand what Chsss was doing any more than he did. Even Wythcombe's expression was mildly perplexed. But none of them believed that Chsss was putting on a show meant to impress them with his earnestness. He had made no effort to shield his workings from even the most senior spellcasters. Kalyndra reported that he had even asked for assistance—although never mana—a time or two.

Finally, Chsss leaned forward on his elbows to better view the complicated pattern. His completed drawing resembled a spider's web—if said spider had possessed far more than eight legs and a very different conception of how many dimensions in which it could weave. Chsss scrubbed his ears with his palms as if to rub away some music the rest of them could not hear. He accepted the glass of mulled wine Kalyndra offered him, not even wrinkling his nose at the odor of various fortifying herbs and spices with which she had enriched it.

"I have a location," he said, without any of his usual theatricality or sly humor. "If someone would bring the globe?"

What Chsss did next gave the lie to his claims to have lost much of his magical ability. Flexing Arasan's long-fingered and sensitive musician's fingers, he peeled the design he had drawn from the glass. While all of them except for Wythcombe were goggling at the impossibility, he draped it over the globe.

The globe had been crafted from quartz crystal in the days before querinalo, rediscovered by Urgana in one of the archive's supply closets. The oceans had been left clear, while the landmasses were etched so that they were nearly opaque, although still sufficiently translucent that the orb below them could be seen.

Wythcombe leaned forward, fascinated. "Is that globe accurate? In Rhinadei, we have maps, but they are by no means this detailed."

Urgana replied, "We haven't had an opportunity to check every detail, but we asked King Hurwin the Hammer to take a look in reference to the parts of the world he knows. The Tavetchians are seafarers, and, for a portion of the world, their maps are as good as we get. We also asked some of the yarimaimalom gulls to look at it—the aerial perspective, you understand? As best as we can tell, the globe is fairly accurate. The avians had less to offer than you might imagine. They do see things from above, but they navigate by far more than sight. Interestingly, there is one region that is indistinct even on this globe—and the yarimaimalom avians didn't know anything about it. "

She tapped an area in the southern hemisphere. "Rhinadei, I suspect."

While Urgana had been answering Wythcombe's question, Chsss shifted his pattern over the globe. Blind Seer could—not so much "see"—although he was certain this was how his humans would perceive the eldritch energies—but "hear" how Chsss shifted the complex artistry of his webwork until it covered the globe in the only fashion that did not create a jangling misfit. Many of the web strands went through the globe, crisscrossing in a fashion that hinted at geomantic mysteries. When the web was in place, Chsss flopped back into his chair, wiped away the sweat that beaded his forehead, then waved a hand toward the globe.

"Wythcombe, will you do the honors? I think you should be able to trace what region in which the other Meddler has shown an interest in of late. If I do the interpreting, someone"—he gave Firekeeper an affectionate glower—"is likely to start accusing me of deception."

"I would be honored," Wythcombe replied. "I'm curious. How far back does your tracing go?"

"Theoretically, into infinity. In reality, since I was most interested in the present, I focused on getting a clear view of the last year or so."

Wythcombe nodded, then closed his eyes in concentration. After a few slow breaths, he confidently placed one finger over a point on the globe, then began to trace portions of Chsss's web. As he did so, a jagged line that moved not only over the globe, but at times through the surface, took brilliant shape. When he was finished, Wythcombe open his eyes and leaned to inspect his work.

"I don't know the geography of the entire world," he said apologetically. "We of Rhinadei have been insular for centuries. Ynamynet, could you tell us where the line I have drawn takes us? The tracery starts here"—he pointed—"in what we suspect is Rhinadei."

Ynamynet joined Wythcombe, who moved aside, perhaps as much because of the chill she radiated as out of manners.

Her tone was analytical, but Blind Seer could smell her excitement. "From Rhinadei, the path goes to Pelland, and, no surprise, to the coast, where the ruins of the university of Azure Towers are. From there it goes all the way down to Tey-yo." She moved the globe on the complicated stand that enabled it to be tilted side to side as well as spun around. "Yes. This is the general location of Nalrmyna. From there…" Her fingers angled the globe with swift precision, seeking the endpoint where they would find Laria. "From there, it goes to the New World, north of our mainland gate in the Setting Sun Stronghold, past Liglim, past the inland channel, up…"

She halted and looked at Firekeeper for confirmation. Although Firekeeper was not much for reading, she had learned to appreciate maps, and now she nodded stiffly.

"Yes. That is Hawk Haven. Inland. Near the city called Eagle's Nest."

Ynamynet shook her head in consternation. "I was afraid of that. There is no active gate in Hawk Haven."

Firekeeper's dark-brown eyes met Blind Seer's blue, not so much to ask his advice, as to tell him what she planned to do before she did it. When he did not growl, Firekeeper breathed out a deep sigh.

"There is a gate. A gate that works. We found it some moonspans back, but we did not tell you what we had found."

VIII

If there's a way out of here, Laria thought, *it's going to be where the wreckage is the worst. That's where there would have been windows. That's where there would have been doors. Kabot's people aren't thinking straight. Or maybe they don't really care about getting out. Maybe all they care about is finding whatever it is they're after. Then they'll just magic themselves away. If I don't want to be magicked away with them, then I need a door or a window. I could probably find where one was with my talent, but then what?*

Laria realized that even if she did figure out where a door or window was located, she probably couldn't burrow her way out. Who knew how deeply underground they were? Hopelessness started to creep up on her again. If she were Firekeeper, she'd take down all three of these, sorcerers or not, then probably dig her way out through solid rock.

No. Not even Firekeeper could do that. Not really. Oh, the Rhinadeians might not be a problem for her, but Firekeeper would be just as trapped as Laria was. The difference was, Firekeeper could at least put the sorcerers on the defensive, and Laria couldn't. She looked longingly over to where Volsyl was heaped with the rest of the sparse equipment, but she knew that even a magical sword wouldn't solve her problems.

Am I really so pathetic that I'm just going to sit here and let myself be used as a blood source? I can't fight them, not like Firekeeper would, but surely I can do something.

As she nervously twisted her fingers through the leather lacing of her boot, a memory spoke in Laria's head: her mother, Ikitata, telling Laria the hard, cold truths of being a slave on the Nexus Islands.

"*You're of an age now, Laria, when one of the Spell Wielders is likely to take notice of you. You won't have a choice about that. What you will have is a choice as to how you'll handle it. They're powerful. Yes. They hold us captive. Yes. But never forget, no matter how horrific some of them look, they're human, too. You can use that humanity not so much against them as for you. If you can make them see you as another person, that may protect you, especially if you're lucky enough to be adopted by one of those who wants to be liked.*"

Laria felt the beginnings of hope. She'd been so lost in past terrors that she'd forgotten how very different her situation was from what she had faced in her childhood. Kabot scared her but, the other two… She forced herself to shove aside the words she'd let cover them with an intimidating aura—spellcasters, powerful, captors—and look at what else they were. Rhinadeians. Rebels. Refugees. They might be her captors, but they were being hunted by people who wouldn't stop. Deep down, Daylily and Uaid had to know that when Kabot had taken Laria prisoner, he'd sealed their fate. If Laria didn't want to find herself once again a hostage with a knife at her throat, then she had to do what she could to make the concept repugnant to Uaid or Daylily—both if possible. And soon. Kabot had awakened briefly, then collapsed again, but Laria had a feeling that the next time he came around, he'd be asserting himself more.

Laria shoved herself onto her feet. Uaid and Daylily looked over from where they'd been focusing on some aspect of cookery. Now that she had put her own fear aside, Laria saw how worried they were. She could use that.

"I'm hungry," she said. Not whining. Just stating a fact. She walked over to where they'd set up camp. "I'm really, really hungry."

Uaid looked guilty. Daylily swiveled, reached into her pack, and took out a large fruit, somewhat like a fig, overly ripe and definitely bruised.

"Eat it slowly," Daylily said. "We don't have much."

Laria took the fig from Daylily's hand, trying to look trusting, although every nerve she possessed screamed for her to run. "Thank you." She looked down at her feet, then began to slowly back away. She stopped mid-shuffle.

"Water? Please?"

This time Uaid responded, reaching for a tin camping cup and filling it, not from the seep, but from a canteen. "This has been purified. It's safe to drink."

Laria accepted the cup, shuffled back a couple more steps, then hunkered down. After she had eaten a few bites of the fruit and washed it down with water, she said, very softly, "Are we stuck here? Can he"—she looked over at Kabot and shivered—"get us out?"

The "we" and "us" had been carefully chosen to make a connection between herself and the other two, while separating Kabot into his own group. These were Rhinadeian. Rebels or not, from what she'd overheard when she'd first awakened, Daylily at least wasn't pleased with how Kabot had used Laria.

There was a long silence during which Laria nibbled more of the overripe fig. Eventually, Daylily said, "We'll get out of here. I'm certain."

Laria looked around. Young and helpless was one thing, but stupid. No. She didn't want to be taken for stupid.

"I think the door must be there, don't you?" She pointed to the largest heap of dirt. "Where I grew up, there are lots of ruins. You get to know the look. Since the ceilings are fine, there has to be some other reason for all the dirt, right? A weak spot, like a door that was pushed open by a collapse."

She let her momentary enthusiasm ebb to embarrassment. "Uh… I mean, sorry. Just because I think the door is there doesn't mean it goes anywhere. Sorry."

Uaid rose from where he'd been sitting and stretched his fingers. Laria froze, wondering if she'd overestimated how guilty these Rhinadeians felt about how she'd been treated, and she was about to be hit, but Uaid all but ignored her as he strode over to the largest mound of dirt.

"It can't hurt to check," he said, his tone so deliberately casual that Laria realized that she'd embarrassed him.

Careful. Careful. Embarrassed people are dangerous.

Laria had already gathered that Uaid's magic was centered on earth and stone. She'd heard about such magics—Urgana's deceased sister, Ellabrana, had been an earth mage, and her work was ubiquitous on the Nexus Islands—but she'd never seen an earth mage at work. She decided it was all right to seem interested, as long as she seemed awed as well.

Uaid began by burying his hands up to the wrists in the pile of dirt and rubble. He closed his eyes and began to murmur. Laria knew he was vulnerable now and Daylily was distracted, but she made no move. What good would attacking them do her? Even if she was successful, that would just leave her trapped here, with no one to stand between her and Kabot. And if she managed to… eliminate… Kabot? She'd still be trapped. Laria believed with all her heart that Firekeeper and the rest would try to find her, but she'd seen how hard it was to trace the rebels. Finding her could take days. Or longer. After all, this time they wouldn't have her to read the surroundings for clues.

Laria watched in unfeigned fascination as Uaid began moving his hands through the rubble and dirt, something he did as easily as if it were water. Even when he pushed his arm in up to the shoulder, moved it back and forth, up and down, only a few little bits of dirt were shaken loose. Then his expression changed. He began to move his arm lower and lower in the pile, obviously homing in on something.

But if it's the door, why so low? Maybe it was shut when the building collapsed and part broke?

"Daylily," Uaid said, his tone so deliberately nonchalant that he might as well have been shouting, "I'd like your opinion on something. Come here, tell me… Well, just tell me."

Looking distinctly puzzled, Daylily trotted over to where Uaid was. She waited until Uaid had pulled his arm free, stood up, and was in a position to keep an eye on Laria. Then, humming a few bars of something Laria thought Arasan would immediately want to set lyrics to, she began making shapes in the air over and around the pile of rubble and dirt. She started at eye level but, like Uaid, ended up sinking down until her examination was focused on an area close to floor level. When she rose to her feet, her leaf-green eyes were shining.

"I felt it, too! The next thread is there, buried under all that rubble."

"I think there's a door, too," Uaid said, giving Laria a polite nod of acknowledgement. "Should we wait for Kabot to come around?"

The reply came from a voice thick and rusty with sleep, but far more powerful than it had been before.

"No need. I'm awake."

"A gate to Hawk Haven!"

"Are you certain?"

"You didn't tell any of us? Not even Derian?"

The outcry was general. Firekeeper waited until it stilled before speaking.

"Truth showed us and only us, and when Truth does this, perhaps telling is not the best thing. Now, we can wait and chatter, or we can go find Laria."

"Where is the gate?" Ynamynet asked.

Firekeeper replied, "On the mainland, not too far from the Setting Sun Stronghold, but not part of it. Come with us, if you wish, and see it. We told King Tedric we would keep it a secret, but I think he would understand that now, with a pack member taken by blood mages, we cannot keep the secret entirely."

"King Tedric?" Like all the Nexus Islanders, Ynamynet had heard many stories about the elderly king of Hawk Haven, Derian's homeland, as well as the first human land Firekeeper had visited. "He asked you to keep it a secret?"

Blind Seer rose and padded over to the conference room door. He reared up on his hind legs, pushed down on the lever, then shoved the door open. Firekeeper didn't feel she needed to translate.

"We go. If you want to see, to know, then come with us."

They did, of course, stopping only to gather up their packs, say quick good-byes, and, in Firekeeper's case, make a quick dash over to the blacksmith. For this trip they left Rusty behind because, if all went well, they would not need their foodstuffs and camping gear. If something went wrong, they did not want to strand the goat.

At the Setting Sun Stronghold, Firekeeper ducked into a storeroom and returned with a long ladder. Ynamynet raised an eyebrow, but otherwise didn't comment. Although Wythcombe and Kalyndra both had questions, Firekeeper refused to go into any details until they were hiking through the forest toward where the gate was hidden. Then, trusting to Blind Seer's and Farborn's sharper senses to detect any predators crazed enough to attack such a large group at midday, she launched into her account.

When Firekeeper finished relating how she and Blind Seer had found the gate, and how it had taken them to the ruins of what appeared to be a school of some sort, she paused. There had been surprisingly few questions, which didn't mean there wouldn't be. After all, she'd left out the complicated part.

"*Do I tell them about the statue?*" she asked Blind Seer.

"*Yes. And not for the reasons you think you should,*" the great grey wolf responded. "*I think I know why it acted the way it did. And I think it may still be a problem.*"

A human would have asked why, but wolf speech was as much gesture as it was sound or scent. As he had spoken, Blind Seer had moved his shoulders in a fashion that drew her attention to Hohdoymin's necklace, which he still wore. Maybe because the many little charms and beads dispersed its weight, maybe because it was as much woven as strung, the necklace did not sink through his scruff and hackles, but rested slightly atop the dense fur, as if borne up on the lightest of breezes. When Blind Seer shrugged, Firekeeper realized what he meant. Though her breath came short, she began to explain.

"Once through the gate, we went through several doors. Outside of one we found a rounded room with some doors off of it, and a stairway going up. There was also much rubble and places where ceilings or walls had given way. But time had made the unstable stable, so we explore. You see, then we did not yet know where the gate had taken us, and we thinked we should learn this. While we were checking the nearest room, making sure our backs were safe before we went up the stair, we were attacked."

"Attacked?" Ranz blurted out. "But you said the place seemed deserted."

"And so it was," Firekeeper replied, hearing not disbelief but how caught up in those moonspans-old events the young man had become. "What attacked us was a statue that came to life and tried to make us dead. In the end, we did not so much make it dead as make it weak. When it was down and Blind Seer held it with his weight, I tied it with both ropes and with wire. Then we buried it beneath the largest of the heaps of rubble and piled both stones and timbers on top of it. We telled King Tedric, too, and his bodyguard, and we all think that this is enough."

Blind Seer said, *"Translate for me, dearest,"* and continued, Firekeeper speaking his words nearly as quickly as he shaped them. *"At the time, I only recognized the scent as that of old magic, sleeping until wakened by whatever need had been set to direct it. Now"*—here he shook slightly, so that the charms and beads of Hohdoymin's necklace caught the light—*"as a pup learns how an elk and a deer may smell alike but not be the same, I know what that scent is like. It is close kin to the coins hidden within this necklace, to the charm Kabot took from Azure Towers."*

"So you believe," Wythcombe said slowly, "that not only will this gate take us to Hawk Haven, it will take us to where Kabot and the others went."

"And," Firekeeper agreed somberly, "if they have traveled as they did from

Azure Towers to Tey-yo, following the scent trail of the artifact they found, then they will have grabbed the scent of the artifact and be there ahead of us."

"I was getting to that," Wythcombe said, his tone calm but his scent as sour as that of an old snapping turtle disturbed when enjoying a warm mud bath. "Blind Seer, because we've all been so worried about Laria, I have not asked you for the charm you took from Hohdoymin. Now, especially that we're closing on Kabot, I think it would be wise for you to give it to me."

Blind Seer panted what those closest to him knew as laughter, but the way he pinned his ears back also gave warning. *"I think not,"* he was saying, and Firekeeper translated for him, although she thought any but a blind idiot would understand the meaning. *"I won this prize, and I will keep it. Unless you think you can take it from me."*

He growled then, deep in his throat, and this time Firekeeper did not bother to translate.

Let Daylily and Uaid waste time trying to figure out how to cook cave crickets and what fungi might be safe to eat, Kabot thought derisively as he sank deep into meditation. *That just shows they're already beaten, trapped within the limits of their own imaginations. Who cares if we have enough to eat? We're not staying here long enough to starve.*

"Yours," said the Voice, "are the thoughts of those who have the capacity to change the future. There are reasons you were the first among your company to whom I was drawn. The others, yes. They have vision, but it's more limited, and so more easily defeated."

Kabot grinned what Wythcombe had always called his "fox in the henhouse" grin. The phrase hadn't been precisely meant as a compliment, but they'd been parting ways even then.

"Uaid and Daylily said they hadn't been able to reach you," he said, not precisely asking a question, but the Voice replied as if it had been one nonetheless.

"I was less available than I am now, and, as I said, I have always found it easier to talk with you. I'm not sure what they would have asked me."

"Almost certainly where we are," Kabot responded, trying to seem as if he didn't care. "That's the first thing Daylily asked me. The second would probably have been if there was a way out. I haven't examined the room closely, but we seem to be in yet another set of ruins."

"Are you surprised? I told you that Sykavalkay had been separated into parts and those parts taken to different lands to be studied. This was before the curse. As I told you, all facilities dedicated to the practice of magic, up to and including the homes of many sorcerers, were destroyed in the upheaval that followed the curse. Surely you don't expect to find yourself in a tidy palace."

"That might be nice," Kabot retorted, then sighed. "Or not, because it would mean that one of the newly reawakening sorcerers in this post-curse age might have found one of the threads. How could a wolf have realized what Teyvalkay was? I suppose it's too much to hope that he was just wearing that necklace on some whim of his mistress—Firekeeper, I think I heard her called."

"Don't underestimate Blind Seer," the Voice chided. "I have heard it said that he may be among the most rawly gifted of the post-curse spellcasters. He lacks training, though, and that is to your advantage."

"I'm glad we have some advantage," Kabot countered. "They have Teyvalkay. We have Palvalkay, so we're even there."

"Not even," the Voice assured him. "As I said, Blind Seer lacks training. He also has—peculiar as this may seem to you—an aversion to blood magic. Since Sykavalkay was created by one who accepted the use of blood magic, the threads respond most rapidly when blood magic is employed."

"I wondered if that's why I don't have the usual post-overextension hangover," Kabot mused. "Did I bring us where the next thread is?"

"Xixavalkay," the Voice said. "Named using an abbreviation for the Tishiolan name of the third major landmass. Why don't you check? You have Palvalkay, and you have learned a great deal about how to detect other threads by the resonance between them."

Kabot reached. Xixavalkay was so close that its aura struck him like a blow. Indeed, he was looking so hard that he sensed something else.

"Teyvalkay?" he said. "Xixavalkay is indeed very close, but I seem to sense Teyvalkay as well."

"Let me see," the Voice said, and when she next spoke, she sounded astonished. "That is indeed Teyvalkay. Still distant, but I suspect, I fear…"

"Wythcombe? Again?" Kabot moaned. Because he felt the moan in his chest, he knew that he was waking up. "But how did they find us so quickly?"

Phiona's voice laughed softly, mockingly. "*I can't say…*"

Kabot was about to try coaxing her when excited conversation broke through his awareness and dragged him close enough to the waking world that he lost the sense of her presence. Uaid's voice…

"Daylily," Uaid said, trying to sound calm and matter-of-fact and completely failing, "I'd like your opinion on something. Come here, tell me… Well, just tell me."

Daylily's footsteps crossing the gritty floor, away from where Kabot lay. Silence, then.

"I felt it, too! The next thread is there, buried in all that rubble."

"I think there's a door, too," Uaid went on, no longer bothering to hide his excitement. "Should we wait for Kabot to come around?"

Kabot forced his sleep-numbed vocal cords to shape words. "No need. I'm awake."

Three heads turned to look his way. Uaid looked slightly annoyed. Daylily seemed pleased, but the girl, Laria, took an unconscious step away from him. While Kabot himself remained on a blanket to one side of the makeshift camp, the others had moved closer to one of the larger heaps of dirt. Kabot put this together with what he had heard, and understood.

He shoved himself up onto one elbow, then to a sitting position. Palvalkay tingled slightly, as if greeting him.

"So I got us about as close to where we wanted to be as was physically possible," Kabot said. "We wouldn't have wanted to arrive underneath all of that." He waved a hand toward the rubble heap and grinned impishly, inviting them to share the joke. "Right? Uaid, how do you advise we go after the thread?"

Uaid's expression was extremely neutral, but whether this meant Kabot had offended him by asking him to "advise" rather than take charge, or if he was mentally reviewing his detailed knowledge of earth magics, Kabot couldn't be sure. The only thing he was sure of was that he couldn't reassume command sitting on his butt. He pushed himself to his feet, and strode authoritatively over.

"Uaid? Thoughts?"

The earth mage rubbed his fingers in his beard. "From what I felt, the rubble on this side has had a long time to settle, but further in it has been disturbed, perhaps as recently as within the last half year. If we're not careful, we could bring the ceiling down. My suggestion would be for me to fuse, say, about this much"—he held up a thick forearm and indicated the space between wrist and elbow—"on the top and sides to create a substitute door lintel. Then we can remove the rest of the detritus without worrying we're going to bring down the ceiling."

Kabot fought an urge to look up. "You said you thought the farther side of this heap had been disturbed recently. Wouldn't that have brought this ceiling down?"

"Not necessarily," Uaid replied pedantically. "From what I can sense, this area"—he swept an arm to indicate the mound of dirt and rubble in front of him, then to the left and back, where there were other, smaller mounds—"are where parts of the upper structure of the building gave. There"—he pointed to the unseen area on the far side of the largest rubble heap—"seems to have maintained integrity. Don't ask me why. I haven't had a chance to investigate. If you think it's wise, I can expend the mana to do so, but…"

He trailed off, almost but not quite, insolent. Kabot wasn't pleased, but he didn't dare show it. For some reason, even though Kabot had been the only one of their remaining company with the esoteric knowledge necessary to work a complex transportation spell, Uaid was acting as if Kabot was the least useful of them all.

"And maybe in the present situation that's true, but this won't last. Let Uaid get you to Xixavalkay; then you can get the lot of you out of this room before it become a tomb—or a trap. Remember, pursuit is closing."

Kabot wasn't certain if the words were his own thoughts or faint whispers from Phiona, but either way, there was no doubting their wisdom.

When they arrived at the low hill beneath which the Hawk Haven gate had been hidden, Firekeeper cleared away the artistic arrangement of stones and deadfall that she had constructed to conceal an opening in the hillside, then lowered the ladder.

"I go first," she said, "with a lantern. Come down one by one. Blind Seer will guard and come last with Farborn."

Ynamynet and Kalyndra, who had accompanied them, were among the first down. They stood, eyes wide, examining their surroundings. Even Firekeeper had to admit the room was impossibly lovely. Floor, walls, and ceiling were covered with colorful ornamented tiles that refused to shape any recognizable pattern, yet were somehow all the more lovely for that refusal. The colors were bright: blue, red, yellow, green, orange, just enough black for outlines, just enough white to make the other colors seem more themselves. The gate was invisible within this riot of apparently random color.

"You say that Truth showed you this?" Yanamynet said.

"Truth showed us the hill," Firekeeper corrected patiently, "and we finded—found—the rest. You know Truth. She is insane, but very wise in some things. "

The two spellcasters nodded. Kalyndra was turning slowly, inspecting the tile with an appreciative eye.

"I'd love to know the story behind this place," she said. "This close to the Setting Sun Stronghold's gate, but separate and hidden. There must be a reason."

Arasan might be shaky on his legs, but his mind was sharp as ever. Once he was off the ladder, he turned to Ynamynet. "I—we—have been thinking about the facility on the other side of this gate. Given that the Old World sorcerers' public policy was to refuse teaching of any form of magic to the New World colonists unless those with ability returned to the Old World for their education, our theory is that this gate may lead to what was once a secret school for teaching the magical arts in the New World. As Chsss is fond of saying, the first thing that happens when you forbid anything is that someone is going to find a way around it. Conversely, this may not have been a school—or only a school. It could also have been an entry point for smuggled magical materials."

"Because," Ynamynet said with a wintery smile, "as soon as you forbid something, someone is going to try to find a way around the prohibition. I need to remind the Nexus Islanders of that next time someone suggests raising tariffs for gate transports because we're the only game in town."

Blind Seer leapt to join them, his landing astonishingly silent for such a huge creature. Then he padded over to where the gate was concealed within the tiles. Ynamynet and Kalyndra joined him. The Nexus Island spellcasters had agreed to handle the transitions so that Firekeeper's little pack would arrive in their new location as fresh as possible. After the others had gone, Ynamynet and Kalyndra would ascend via the ladder and replace the camouflage, leaving the ladder behind. Firekeeper suspected that they would not leave immediately, though, but poke around to see what they could learn. That was fine with her. A secret like this could not be kept forever, so the more they knew, the better.

"Blind Seer and I go first," Firekeeper said to her pack. "You come quickly after. No standing about talking. Farborn will make sure."

Then, as one, the wolves stepped forward, melting into silver light and vanishing away.

"Good plan," Kabot said to Uaid. "What will you need?"

"Mana," Uaid replied succinctly. When Kabot's gaze drifted over toward Laria, Uaid added firmly, "That taken from an involuntary donor should be a resort of desperation. You've been holding on to Palvalkay like it's your own private property. Is it?"

It is! Kabot restrained an urge to reach where he had been carrying the fragment close to his heart. He managed an easy laugh instead.

"Not at all. I used it to get us out of Azure Towers, and then in Tey-yo for resonance tracking. Do you want it?" Kabot had to fight to make the offer sound genuine.

Uaid frowned thoughtfully. "Actually, it would be more efficient if you or Daylily used it, then channeled what mana I need. That way I don't need to split my concentration."

"I can do that," Kabot said confidently, "or would you rather, Daylily?"

She shook her head, but her eyes, which she had not changed from the deep green that had so suited Tey-yo, narrowed slightly as if wondering if he had honestly meant the offer. Kabot reminded himself yet again that despite her appearing closer to Uaid in age, she was his senior and more skillful in many forms of magic.

"I think I'd better keep my attention focused outwards," Daylily said. "I'm already maintaining the lights and water purification."

And, Kabot realized suddenly, *Daylily doesn't trust me around Laria. One single panicked reaction—and never mind that my quickness kept us from being captured by Wythcombe—and Daylily's suddenly seeing me as one of the horrors from the grandmother tales of our childhood. She doesn't just mean to maintain the lights. She'll be making sure I don't overreach myself. That's all right. Let me get my hands on Xixavalkay, and I won't need her or Uaid either.*

Alternative futures burst through Kabot's imagination like grasshoppers startled from the grass, confusing and distracting him with their momentary reality. What was happening to him? He really was feeling strange. Well, he had been through a lot. Being aware that Wythcombe was closing in once more wasn't exactly restful.

Should he tell the others about Wythcombe? No. Given their reaction last time, how they'd blamed him, definitely not. Anyhow, knowledge of pursuit wouldn't benefit their situation. Uaid needed to be meticulous as he shored up the loose rubble, not rushed. Once they had Xixavalkay, they'd be set to go after the final one. Kabot could draw on Palvalkay for mana next time he needed to transport them, not the mana of a panicked hostage. He wasn't used to that sort of power, full of a stranger's emotional weight. Doubtless, that explained why he was feeling so frazzled. It might explain why he kept having such odd thoughts. He gave Uaid a confident smile.

"You'll need time to assemble your spells. While I wait for you to get ready, maybe there's something I could eat? Then I'll meditate so I'm ready to offer support. I also wouldn't mind a chance to change my shirt. It's a mess."

Kabot didn't miss that Daylily exchanged glances with Uaid before moving to her pack. "Since neither you nor Uaid thought to squirrel away any food, we have what was in my bag. It's not much. We were going to try steaming some cave crickets later."

"Your foresight is, as ever, appreciated," Kabot said. "Let's hope we're far from here before we need to dine upon your undoubtedly excellent insect-based cuisine."

Kabot ate, then—after he had changed out of the shirt caked in Laria's dry blood—composed himself for meditation. He strengthened his link to Palvalkay, certain he could sense Xixavalkay quivering in response. Kabot wondered if he could use Palvalkay to pull Xixavalkay from under the rubble, but when he tried an experimental tug, Xixavalkay remained firmly buried.

"Ready, Kabot?"

Uaid's words startled Kabot from his trance. Smiling confidently, he shoved himself to his feet, gave Daylily a bow of thanks for the meal, and then walked briskly to the rubble heap. A quick blending of drops of blood let him and Uaid intertwine their mana far more quickly than if they'd had to resort to the tedious dances or songs commonly used in Rhinadei. To guard against Uaid catching the disturbing emotional eddies Kabot still felt swirling through him, Kabot focused hard on assisting Uaid with the intricacies of his spellcrafting. As he immersed himself in meshing sand and dirt so it fused into crystal and rock, Kabot found his appreciation for Uaid rising.

Once Kabot knew precisely how much mana Uaid required, Kabot sent out a spell of his own, a thin tendril that sought to find, then analyze, Xixavalkay. As he probed, he found himself wondering why Xixavalkay was so much weaker than Palvalkay. Initially, he had thought this must be because it had been warded, as Palvalkay had been. Under closer examination, he revised his assessment. The full power was present, but cloven in twain, apparently by something made of iron. Kabot shied away from iron's dangerous taint, then cautiously returned to his probing. The image he built from these quick, careful probes was so fascinating that he almost forgot to maintain the mana flow to Uaid.

Kabot was drawing breath to suggest that they take a break, so he could share his insights, when without warning a shape erupted from the shifting soil and lunged toward him. The human-sized figure moved stiffly, but with a daunting sense of purpose. Instinctively, Kabot stumbled back. Only in grandmother tales did a surprised sorcerer instantaneously launch forth a bolt of lightning or ball of fire. Such attacks took preparation.

What saved Kabot was not his skill, but that Uaid had not finished stabilizing the rubble. The unstable rubble to the left side of the mound shifted, crashing into the moving figure and reburying it—although, judging from the upheaval within the dirt and debris—not for long. Interwoven within his uncompleted spell, Uaid stood as if he himself had become stone. Tumbling to the uneven floor, Kabot grabbed Uaid around the waist and hauled him back.

Caught as he had been within both his own and Uaid's spell workings,

Kabot hadn't really looked at how Uaid's earth magic was transforming their surroundings. Now he assessed them at a glance. Uaid had used his magic to sort the heavier, denser material—stone, bricks, chucks of masonry—from the lighter earth. Then he had fused the heavier materials into a new wall that reinforced and, in some places, completely replaced the walls that had been there before. The lighter dirt had been shifted toward the center, where it was piled beneath a newly created arched doorway. It was from this pile of dirt that something had erupted.

Something, Kabot thought, *that has Xixavalkay within it. Something that, for some reason, views us as trespassers.*

A whimsical thought—Phiona's perhaps—wisped through Kabot's mind, noting that they *were*, in fact trespassers, but Kabot had neither time nor energy to spare for whimsy. The attacking whatever was digging its way out, revealing something human in shape. No human, though, had ever had skin the polished grey of granite, nor eyes without pupil, iris, or white, but that instead cycled with stomach-twisting randomness through all the colors of the gem and mineral-rich earth.

The figure rose and waded forward through the loose dirt: a stocky stone man clad in arcane attire of the more practical sort, such as was used on Rhinadei for field magecraft: trousers tucked into boots, a loose shirt, a vest with many pockets, all ornamented with elaborate runes. The "fabric" of the shirt's breast had been ripped open, revealing a hole rimmed in what seemed to be dry blood. Within the hole throbbed a mana-rich light that Kabot knew was Xixavalkay. The stone man grasped a staff in his hands like a fighter but, from how mana pulsed down its length, Kabot felt certain that the stone man could use the staff as more than a bludgeon.

It was that last that made Kabot leap at the stone man. Kabot wasn't built like a brawler, but anyone who dreamed of earning prestige by healing Rhinadei's corrupted frontier needed to know how to defend himself. Disarming an opponent was a key to defense. Kabot soared forward, pleased that despite decades in stasis his muscle memory retained the proper moves. He continued to feel pleased until he struck his target, discovering that the man-shaped figure didn't only look as if it was made of stone, it felt like it as well.

Pain vibrated up his nerves. Kabot sprang back, muscles throbbing. His confidence had taken a hit, too. Behind him, Uaid was muttering; through the remnants of their blood link, Kabot felt Uaid shaping a working. The mound of dirt flattened and leveled, moving as iron filings spread on a sheet of paper do when a magnet is moved beneath. Kabot immediately understood why Uaid was clearing the loose dirt away. The stone man moved through dirt as easily as a swimmer did through water. Uaid was, quite literally, putting their confrontation on an even footing.

"How about 'Leveling the playing field?'" suggested the voice that might be Phiona's. "*I suggest you hurry. You're running out of time.*"

Kabot thought that Phiona meant Wythcombe and his weirdness of retainers, then he heard Uaid say in a tone that throbbed with true love found, "I want this next thread for me."

"Fine," Kabot said, lying easily, "but first we're going to need to get it away from that thing that's using it as its heart."

The gate carried Firekeeper and Blind Seer into a walk-in storage closet. This was adjacent to a large room which—judging by the slate boards that lined the walls, the long tables, and the speaker's podium—had probably been used as a classroom. Before the wolves had departed, they'd closed the door between the closet and the classroom, as well as the one that led into the outer foyer. When they opened door between closet and classroom, Blind Seer's ears pricked, and Firekeeper nodded in soundless acknowledgement.

As each of the others made the gate transition, Firekeeper held up her hand in the agreed upon sign for "silence." When the last—Farborn—arrived, she turned so that her followers could see her face, then said very softly, "Listen.

Even human ears should hear it. Someones is out there, someones who are fighting."

She saw the humans freeze. Unsurprisingly, it was Arasan, ever sensitive to sound, who nodded immediate comprehension. Ranz and Wythcombe moved carefully to the door, took turns pressing their ears to the keyhole. Farborn landed on Blind Seer's back and waited.

"When we open the door," Firekeeper said, choosing her words with care, "we will be in the middle of whatever is making that noise. No time for chatter. Blind Seer smells human scents but blurred, so he not know how many or who. You remember the map we drew you of what is out there? Trouble sounds to the right. We wolves will go. Follow carefully or wait to see where best you help. No shame in either."

Firekeeper suspected that all three of their human companions would follow, because they had already demonstrated ample courage—sometimes more courage than prudence. She handed the lantern to Arasan, then turned the key she had left in the lock when she and Blind Seer had departed, pleased that the sharp click the key made turning in the lock would be covered by the noise without.

Once the door was open, the wolves bolted out side by side. Farborn soared overhead as high guard. Unlike humans, who would have pulled up short upon seeing the area so transformed from the last time they had been there, Firekeeper and Blind Seer had the gift for both remembering the past and accepting change.

To their right, where before had been a massive pile of dirt and rubble, was now a wide-arched opening floored in dirt. Through the arch was another open area, but their view of what lay beyond the door was partially obstructed by three figures: Kabot and Uaid in close combat with the statue the wolves believed they had laid to rest some moonspans before.

Both men showed fresh injuries. Uaid's nose was bleeding. The side of Kabot's face was raw and abraded. By contrast, the statue looked much as it had the last time they had seen it, with one disturbing exception. Although the front of its "shirt" showed a tear, the large iron spike with which Firekeeper had stabbed it had completely vanished. Instead, around the edges of the wound was a dark orange-red stain, very like rust.

Blind Seer said, *"Kabot and Uaid are sorcerers both. They will not have iron on them. Iron is what you used to stop that thing last time."*

"And I have iron with me now," Firekeeper reminded him. Dreading a fresh encounter with this arcane monstrosity, she had visited the blacksmith before they left the Nexus Islands. Now she drew a cold-forged iron knife from a sheath she had threaded onto her belt alongside the one that held her Fang. This new blade was honed far sharper than the iron spike she'd been forced to use the last time.

"I will distract the sorcerers," Blind Seer said. *"You deal with the statue."*

As much as Firekeeper appreciated her partner's confidence in her, she was not certain it was merited. Last time both of them had been necessary to subdue the thing. Briefly, she considered suggesting that they let Kabot and Uaid wear the statue down, or at least fight it until the sorcerers had exhausted themselves. Then, in a flash, she understood why Blind Seer was not willing to delay. Kabot's pack possessed one highly potent artifact. They had every reason to believe he knew how to tap its latent mana. If he managed to get his hands on another…

Worse, Blind Seer wore around his neck a third artifact. Worse yet, Laria was the prisoner of these would-be experts in blood magic, an art their own people held to be anathema. Humans liked taking hostages as a way to cripple their adversaries. Although Blind Seer and Firekeeper had sworn they would not be hostage one for the other, Laria had taken no such oath and merited their protection. This meant that Firekeeper and Blind Seer must deal with this situation before hostage taking became an option.

"The statue must wait," Firekeeper howled, leaping forward. *"Laria is a greater danger to us and to herself."*

Blind Seer's agreement was given in a deep-throated howl that reverberated off the walls of the subterranean complex so that it sounded as if the full pack cried the trail. Firekeeper's blood thrilled as she ran forward, muscles bunching so she might leap out and around the trio of combatants. She felt, rather than saw, that Farborn soared alongside her.

Despite their desperate situation, Kabot and Uaid had momentarily frozen in visceral fear upon hearing the howling of wolves reverberating through the enclosed area, then again at the sight of Blind Seer charging forward, fangs bared in an impressive snarl.

Firekeeper didn't have time to luxuriate in the honest pleasure of seeing her partner instill terror. She had not forgotten that Kabot's pack consisted of three, and that one of these was unaccounted for. Orienting by sound and smell as well as by sight, the wolf-woman took in her surroundings. A large room, without even a scrap of furniture. Indeed, were it not for the brick walls glimpsed here and there, the space could have been taken for a natural cavern. Even as Firekeeper unconsciously ascertained that there were no windows, no other doors, she located Laria.

Wisely, the girl had distanced herself from the combat, shrinking back against a far rubble heap, one of the ribbons that tied off her braid wrapped around her fingers. Her golden-brown eyes were wide and watchful, but didn't hold the least trace of terror. Indeed, upon hearing the howls, a smile began to spread over Laria's face. She'd been disarmed, but otherwise seemed to have all her belongings. Leaping into the space between Daylily and Laria, Firekeeper motioned with the blade of her cold-forged iron knife.

"Away from Laria," she commanded. As always when she was more wolf than human, her voice came out low and hoarse. "This is iron. Your kind does not love iron."

Daylily's eyes—a brilliant leaf green—narrowed, but blood-lore hungry though she might be, she was no fool. Spreading her arms wide in surrender, she stepped back, taking care not to do anything that Firekeeper might misinterpret as attack.

"Laria, get your sword," Firekeeper growled. "Has this one harmed you?"

"No!" Laria replied with a rapidity that spoke volumes to the wolf-woman. Not only had Daylily not harmed her, Laria felt some gratitude toward the woman. Firekeeper smiled at Daylily, remembering perfectly well that humans often saw her smile as threatening. Laria came running back, strapping her sword belt around her waist, then drawing Volsyl as she skidded to a halt.

Firekeeper nodded approval. "You and Farborn, guard this one. I go help Blind Seer. I would not like to bind this Daylily. If we cannot deal with the statue, she should be able to run."

"Sure," Laria motioned with Volsyl as she spoke to Daylily. "Stand in front of me. Remember, I was raised among those who practiced the anathema art. I'll know if you start a spell."

Farborn shrieked approval and dropped to take up a post on Laria's left shoulder.

Firekeeper paused long enough to ask Daylily one crucial question. "You give your parole?" She had learned the concept of making one's own honor a prison, and tried to anticipate any loopholes. "If you not involve yourself in this fight or do us harm, after we will take time to listen to your side."

Daylily nodded stiffly, outwardly composed although her sweat reeked of fear. "I give my parole. Now go. Your wolf is in more danger than you know."

Firekeeper tilted her head, wishing she had time for more questions but, whatever it was that Daylily was trying to warn her about, there were problems enough. Blind Seer was not affected by iron as so many spellcasters were, but he carried none on him. Neither would Wythcombe, Ranz, or, probably, Arasan—although Firekeeper was not prepared to bet on that last, given the presence of Chsss. Only Firekeeper carried a weapon which could harm the living statue, and she knew that its heart was as vulnerable as that of a living creature.

As she raced across the gritty floor toward the combatants, Firekeeper wondered why she felt something was misaligned. At a quick glance, the situation was as one would expect: Kabot and Uaid had their attention split between the statue and Blind Seer. Through the doorway, she could see Wythcombe, Ranz, and Arasan anxiously trying to figure out the best way to help without interfering with or harming the great grey wolf. The statue was moving with more agility than the last time. Did this mean it had been "awake" longer? It held its staff in a defensive pose, and was backing toward the side of the doorway, where a heap of loose dirt and rubble was still settling.

Why did she feel as if something else was going on? Firekeeper glanced at Blind Seer hoping he would offer clarification, then noticed that he was digging his paws into the floor, as if trying to keep from being dragged forward. As she watched, she saw him plant his haunches firmly on the floor, while at the same time rearing his head back. The stance unsettlingly reminded her of a leashed dog straining against a collar, and brought a flash of understanding. Someone, something, was trying to remove Hohdoymin's necklace. Lacking hands, unwilling to disarm himself by grabbing the necklace in his mouth, Blind Seer was doing what he could to keep his prize.

For a fraction of a breath, Firekeeper considered asking one of their allies to grab hold of the necklace, but she remembered how Blind Seer had refused to give the thing to Wythcombe. Ranz would not be a good choice: not only was he also a spellcaster, he might give Wythcombe the necklace to win favor. And Arasan? Maybe Arasan, but never Chsss.

Howling in the hope of disorienting their enemies, as well as to let Blind Seer know she was coming, Firekeeper sprinted over, straddled Blind Seer. Then refusing to admit that she feared what might happen if she did so, she laid her hands firmly on the multistranded cords of Hohdoymin's necklace.

IX

"Blind Seer!"

Firekeeper's howl lifted the wolf's heart, for not only did that mean she was coming to his aid, it meant that Laria was safe. Blind Seer no longer doubted who came first in Firekeeper's love, but he also knew Firekeeper would not abandon a helpless pup. His partner's howl had not ceased to vibrate on the air when he felt her behind him, long legs over his barrel, clever hands reaching down to grab hold of Hohdoymin's necklace.

That the necklace—or rather one particular charm upon that necklace—was less than pleased, Blind Seer could not doubt. The scent of that displeasure made fresh skunk emission sweet by comparison, but Blind Seer did not have time to wonder what an unhappy artifact might do.

Firekeeper unlooped the necklace from around Blind Seer's throat, backing quickly so he could rise onto all four feet. Even the time for those few motions had been enough for the situation to change. Kabot was no fool. When Firekeeper had entered the fray, Kabot had realized that while two humans—assisted by the artifact that strained beneath his shirt—just might have been able to remove Hohdoymin's necklace from Blind Seer's custody, with the addition of Firekeeper and her iron blade, the equation had shifted against the Rhinadei rebels. Kabot spoke in hushed tones to Uaid, but he had not reckoned with a wolf's sense of hearing, so both Blind Seer and Firekeeper heard every word.

"We can't deal with shapeshifters, but that statue, it looks as if it's made from stone. Can your magic bind it or slow it?"

Uaid replied, the doubt in his tone shifting to excitement. "Maybe… There's something weirdly organic about the matrix but…"

Kabot cut him off. "Then do it! Palvalkay may help me extract Xixavalkay. Then we'll have both."

Blind Seer didn't give them time to confer further. It would be wonderful if Ranz could seal the statue behind a wall of ice or even make the floor too slick for the humans to run upon, but Ranz could not make ice without water.

As for Wythcombe… How he would act, or if he would act at all, was something Blind Seer did not try to predict. Where Kabot was concerned, Wythcombe was clearly deeply conflicted. Chsss? Best never to ask favors of that one.

Blind Seer was gathering himself to spring upon Kabot when a flourish of metallic musical notes, each as distinct and pure as drops of water, echoed through the cavern. After one repetition of the initial phrase, they were joined by a clear voice weaving through the notes, song shaping a wordless counterpoint.

Humans and wolves do not hear in the same range. Wolves hear more, both in higher and lower ranges, and this was doubtless what kept Blind Seer from being captured by Arasan's music. Kabot and Uaid, even Firekeeper, slowed, as if the air around them had become dense and tacky. Then Kabot and Uaid stilled, dreaming on their feet. Firekeeper struggled as Blind Seer had seen her do when wrestling with a nightmare.

Arasan always claimed that his gift was a minor one but, in this music, Blind Seer scented Chsss's odor. At least this time, it seemed that the just-might-be-a-god had proven himself a faithful ally.

Blind Seer did not pause to consider. He nipped Firekeeper on one buttock, the pain breaking her violently from the trance. Knowing they might have little time before Kabot and Uaid also broke loose, Blind Seer ran at the statue. Although unaffected by Arasan's music, it was having problems of its own. The artifact that was its heart was straining to rejoin its siblings. The statue was using all its considerable strength to throw aside bits of rubble, like a rabbit frantically trying to dig a burrow.

Even in the urgency of the moment, Blind Seer felt laughter bubble up. The statue was trying to rebury itself, hoping to make it impossible for any to reach its heart or for its heart to reach for another. The odor of a magical working billowed about it like fog. He envisioned the statue reburying itself, fusing the stone around it, rather as a box turtle pulled itself into its shell. He recalled how the iron nail Firekeeper had buried in the statue's chest had been reduced to rust, and considered that if this thing could use magic to degrade iron, creating a stone shell might be simple.

For a moment, Blind Seer was tempted to let the statue seal itself away, but he'd already seen that burial would not end the threat it offered. He must claim the prize hidden within its breast, even as he had Hohdoymin's necklace. Then, with both of these in his keeping, and the statue hopefully inert, they could deal with Kabot.

As he ran, Blind Seer stretched his ears, hoping to hear Wythcombe and Ranz taking advantage of Arasan's song to subdue the Rhinadei rebels. Hearing nothing but the hypnotic rhythm of the wordless song, the wolf dreaded that Arasan had captured friend as well as foe. That would be very much like Chsss.

Blind Seer wished he could share his conjectures with Firekeeper, but there was not time. He knew that Firekeeper trusted that if her chosen partner was running away from one enemy, toward another, he would have good reason. Such trust was a terrible burden. Worse, he could smell that she still carried Hohdoymin's necklace on her, so she was bringing together two of these arcane powers. But maybe he could use that to their advantage…

Blind Seer launched into a tremendous leap that carried him to where the moving statue swam into the loose rubble, pausing only to toss larger lumps of brick or stone out behind it. The material was not firmly packed, so the statue was having trouble shaping a proper burrow, but Blind Seer didn't doubt that if it was given just a little more time, it would manage.

But I'm not going to give it that time, he thought, flinging himself into the statue from the left. From their prior encounter, he knew the statue would not be quite as hard as stone, more like bags packed tightly with sand. Nonetheless, that was hard enough so that when he hit, he heard his breath explode from his lungs, felt the shock reverberate through his body. The moving statue teetered. Despite the throbbing pain caused by the first impact, Blind Seer rose on his hind legs and pushed. He and Firekeeper had often practiced how he might subdue a human without needing to bite that too delicate skin. His awareness of points of balance made the difference now.

The statue crashed onto its back. Unlike what a human would have done, the statue did not try to cushion its fall, but fell as a tree would fall. Blind Seer flung himself across its legs, Firekeeper onto its chest, her legs spread so that she could use a knee to pin each arm. When she bent forward, the doubled disk charm on Hohdoymin's necklace yearned toward the rust-edged gap on the statue's chest. From that gap was emerging a disk made from sharp-edged crystals of translucent gold, silver, and copper. Minute sparks flickered across the disk's middle where it had been broken, showing how crystal knit into crystal in a partial mend.

Firekeeper angled the blade of the cold iron knife intending to slide it beneath the artifact, flip it loose, then grab it with her left hand. The extraction was proceeding quite neatly when Kabot let loose a scream of rawest fury and wheeled to face them, his hands outstretched, his gaze blank and insane.

Had Kabot not been distracted by the need to assist Uaid, surely he never would have been entranced by the deceptively simple music that rose from one of those who stood among the flickering shadows on the far side of the newly opened doorway. At least that's what he told the Voice when it chided him.

"And so that's it?" Phiona said mockingly. "It's Uaid's fault? You're going to just stand here and wait for that crazy woman and her giant dog to grab Xixavalkay, then take you all captive? Don't look for Daylily to rescue you. She's already been subdued."

Kabot actually had been waiting to see what Daylily would do. If she hadn't been able to help, he'd been willing to be taken captive, because that would mean that the stone man had been dealt with by someone else. He'd figured that being a captive would put him in a position to lay his hands on all three threads at once. With Phiona's laughter ringing in his ears, he couldn't make this plan sound reasonable.

Did Phiona put the next idea into his mind? Maybe, but his thoughts were so clouded by that music that he wasn't certain who came up with the idea. He felt what he must to do, knew it was brutal, but knew he must win the day.

Uaid stood next to Kabot, linked by the blood they'd shared. How easy to reach out, reverse the flow so that Uaid's mana flowed into him. To use that mana to subdue Palvalkay where it rested in his pocket, to redirect Palvalkay's yearning to go to where the other two threads were so that it tried to draw them toward him.

Teyvalkay did not react to its sibling's call, maybe because it was still bound into that necklace, but Xixavalkay, emerging from the statue's chest, the matrix that had held it weakened by the cold iron of the crazy woman's blade, rose of its own accord, then darted toward Kabot.

Moving with more speed than Kabot would have thought possible for a human, Firekeeper's hand darted after the fleeing artifact, but she failed to get a firm hold. Kabot grimaced in satisfaction. Just a moment more and..

Seemingly from nowhere came a flash of motion as a small falcon pounced upon Xixavalkay as it might have a sparrow in flight. The falcon lacked the strength to counter the artifact's forward motion, but it provided enough drag that on her next attempt Firekeeper grasped Xixavalkay between thumb and forefinger.

Furious, Kabot drew out more of Uaid's mana to facilitate channeling his will through Palvalkay. Fortified, he wrestled for control of Xixavalkay, but the crazy woman was not letting go. Worse, now that the artifact was no longer within its chest, the statue had fallen quiescent. This freed the wolf who, rather than racing forward to attack as Kabot would have expected, leaned into the woman, pressing its head against the necklace she wore bandolier-fashion across her torso.

Kabot felt another spellcaster's energy enter the conflict. Not Wythcombe's, perhaps his young apprentice's? It couldn't be the singer; he was still keeping up his music. Unbelievingly, Kabot identified the source: the wolf!

Kabot remembered the warning the Voice had given them, their speculations, forgotten until now, that Wythcombe had linked his fortunes with some shapeshifter. The wolf's control of his abilities was not polished, but the force of his raw talent nearly brought Kabot to his knees.

He screamed in frustration. This wasn't happening! He wasn't going to be beaten! But he was running out of time. What to do? Palvalkay's mana was bound up in the struggle for control of Xixavalkay. He had not yet recovered the mana spent in transporting them here from the jungle. That left no choice but to draw on Uaid's mana, and hope for forgiveness.

Kabot widened the channel between himself and Uaid, then used Uaid's power to enable him to refine how Palvalkay was pulling Xixavalkay to it. To this point, the conflict had been a straight-line tug of war, but now he twisted, hoping to weaken Firekeeper's grasp. All he achieved was to rip the disk along the weak seam in its middle, tearing it in two.

The part of the disk not held between Firekeeper's fingers came shooting toward Kabot—or rather to join Palvalkay. As it fit itself alongside, Kabot felt his knees buckling. The room spun. Instinctively, he reached to draw on more of Uaid's mana to stabilize himself. He was certain he would succeed when he was struck by an inarticulately screeching fury.

Kabot stumbled, falling on his backside in the dirt. Looking up he discovered that the fury was Daylily and what she was screaming was "Uaid!

Uaid!" She'd let her cosmetic magics fall away, revealing a wild tangle of silvery-grey hair, eyes of faded stormy blue, and fragile golden-brown skin coursed with myriad lines.

Running up behind Daylily was the girl, Laria, her sword raised over her head in both hands. Laria brought Volsyl down to swoosh through empty space. Gleefully, Kabot thought she'd missed. Then he realized that Laria's blow had gone exactly where she intended. The flow of mana between himself and Uaid ceased, leaving only Kabot's own depleted stores and the wildly sparkling flow from the entwined threads.

Daylily reached for Kabot's face, her long fingernails curled like claws, her expression wild with aversion. Aversion for him. For what he had done to Uaid. Kabot felt a moment of revulsion himself as he looked to where the youngest member of their triad lay collapsed on his side, his mouth hanging open, his breathing stertorous, his eyes open but unseeing.

But there was no time for regret. Daylily's fingernails were inches from Kabot's eyes. Laria, shining blade in hand, was circling for a clear shot at his back. In panic, Kabot grasped the pulsing power of the rejoined threads. He felt himself pulled away—although he knew not where.

Maybe because Chsss and Arasan had been her teachers, maybe because she was the farthest away, Laria had been able to resist much of the paralysis that their music sent forth. The worst thing was that she really didn't want to resist. The song was so soothing, so restful. It didn't so much bring on sleep as that wonderful state right on the edge of sleep, where you're just awake enough to be able to think, but asleep enough that you don't really need to do so.

What kept Laria from falling into that pleasant numbness was a single very simple thing: Firekeeper had trusted her, had left her and Farborn to guard a powerful spellcaster. Simply put, Firekeeper had accepted that Laria was a member of her pack, and wouldn't fail her. Given that, how could Laria not live up to the wolf-woman's expectation? She kept her gaze locked on Daylily in case the Rhinadeian hoped to use this distraction to her advantage. On Laria's shoulder, Farborn sidled uneasily back and forth, so she put a hand up to stroke his feathers and let him know she was alert.

When Daylily began to visibly transform, Laria was so shocked that the lingering numbness in her limbs vanished. As the beautiful sorceress's dark-green tresses faded to grey, as the roundness of her limbs became more sinewy, as she—to put none too fine a point on it—visibly aged, Laria realized that Daylily was drawing on whatever power remained to her. Laria braced herself, awaiting attack, but Daylily's only action was to speak in a voice hardly above a whisper.

"Please… Kabot's going to kill Uaid. He doesn't mean to—I don't think he does. But Kabot doesn't always think. Please! Let me go to Uaid's rescue. Help me if you can."

Laria had been so focused on fighting Arasan's spell, on Daylily's transformation, that she hadn't had any attention to spare for what was unfolding in the center of the room. Now she saw how Uaid was crumpling, how Kabot was half-bent over something he held in clasped hands over his breast. Although she didn't exactly trust Daylily, she believed her.

"Help you?" she asked. "By letting you go?"

"That sword," Daylily gasped, "may be able to sever the invisible lines that bind spellcasters to each other. If you cut between Kabot and Uaid, you could save Uaid. I will deal with Kabot."

There was something so ruthless in Daylily's voice that Laria did not doubt her sincerity. This was not a time to dither. If she was making a mistake, but, no… Laria didn't think she was. She remembered what she'd heard when Daylily still believed her unconscious. How, from the first, Daylily had spoken against using blood from the unwilling.

"I can do that," Laria said. She thought about adding a threat about what would happen to Daylily if she betrayed her, then decided that was stupid. A threat wouldn't change anything. "Let's go!"

At Laria's words, Farborn launched himself into the fight, shrieking something that made Laria certain he thought she'd made the right choice.

Daylily ran with astonishing speed for someone now revealed to be in her sixties, at the very least. She keened Uaid's name over and over, like a curse, like a promise. Laria realized that it was most probably both—a threat to Kabot, a promise to Uaid. Letting Volsyl correct her balance, Laria ran in the older woman's wake. When Daylily sprang at Kabot, Laria was only a step behind. She saw the astonishment on Kabot's face, the momentary flicker of relief when he thought that she had failed to strike him, his panic when he felt his connection to Uaid severed. Daylily was screaming imprecations, reaching to claw Kabot's eyes from his head when in a burst of golden-blue-green light, Kabot vanished.

Firekeeper pulled up short, tossed something small into the air. Farborn dove down and caught it, then vanished into the shadows above. Arasan's music stumbled to a halt, and he tumbled to the floor. Blind Seer darted to interpose himself between Daylily and Laria. Wythcombe and Ranz stirred. Uaid did not.

Laria slid Volsyl into its sheath. "Blind Seer, please, let Daylily try to help Uaid. Kabot did something to him."

Blind Seer positioned himself beside Uaid and sat, jaws agape. One didn't need words to know he was saying, "Fine. But if she tries anything, she's going to be missing a limb."

Wythcombe was jogging over, moving as if still partly in a dream. Ranz had gone to help Arasan. Firekeeper stood, casting about, clearly uncertain whether Kabot might return as swiftly as he had vanished. Then she visibly relaxed and moved to where she could rest a hand on Blind Seer's shoulder.

By the time Uaid no longer looked as if he was on the verge of death, Arasan had struggled to his feet. Arm over Ranz's shoulder, he came wobbling over to join them. He eased himself onto a makeshift seat on a heap of rubble, speaking almost before he was down.

"Before you yell at me for what I did," he said, "I apologize. I had no idea that my song would have such a widespread effect. I'm still learning how things work."

To Laria's surprise, Firekeeper didn't say something caustic. Instead she smiled at him.

"Is not so good that so many sleep, but you slow Kabot and Uaid when they were a great danger. So, this time, you will not be thumped." She stared at Daylily, as if those dark, dark eyes could look into the older woman's soul. "I tell you, you keep parole, we listen to you."

Laria started to explain that Daylily had not broken her parole, and Firekeeper held up a reassuring hand. "Yes. I not think you suddenly run in a pack with someone who broke parole. You smell to Blind Seer as if your choices is all your own, so now we listen to this Daylily. Then we decide what to do."

Daylily stared thoughtfully at Firekeeper. "What do you want to hear from me?"

Firekeeper gave one of her eloquent shrugs. "So very much. From Wythcombe we know a little about Kabot, but we know nothing about you. How did you end up here? How did it come that Kabot begins to eat this Uaid?"

Wythcombe gave Firekeeper a look Laria couldn't decipher. It seemed equal parts resignation and something like hatred. Hadn't he seen what Kabot was doing? No, he hadn't. Not firsthand, not as Laria had. To give Daylily a moment to organize her thoughts, Laria cut in.

"Wythcombe, Firekeeper's not exaggerating. Kabot did that to Uaid. Even before you all showed up here, I could tell that Kabot had made some different choices than Uaid and Daylily had, and I'm not just saying that because he cut my throat." She held up her head high, so that Wythcombe couldn't ignore the bandaging around her neck. "I know he's your childhood friend. I know you want to save him, hear his point of view, but maybe you're trying too hard to be fair to him?"

The old spellcaster leaned heavily on his staff. "Yes. Maybe so. Before we get into a philosophical debate, do you think it's wise for us to stay here? What if that statue comes back to life? Or if Kabot returns? He's clearly drawing on mana other than his own, and one thing we of Rhinadei know well—even if we do not use blood magic—is that the source of mana can influence how a person thinks. It's not unlike certain drugs: they may make you feel more clearheaded, but maybe paranoia comes with that clarity."

Firekeeper gestured with a thumb back to where the statue lay. "That no start moving again. Go look. Is not statue anymore."

Wythcombe, trailed by Ranz and Arasan, went to look. When they returned, Wythcombe's expression was blank with the blankness of one who has experienced a shock. Ranz looked nauseated. Arasan looked bemused as only Chsss could.

"If I had to guess," Chsss said, something in his tone making it clear he didn't think he was wrong, "I'd say that when things started to go downhill, one of the sorcerers who ran this school or smuggling depot or whatever it was, decided that it was worth dying to make certain that this place remained safe. I have no idea how that artifact"—he gestured in the general direction where Farborn had vanished—"came to be here, but that man decided to both protect it, and use it to protect this place. I'd love to know… No, now that I think about it, I don't think I want to know. Anyhow, somehow he inserted it in his chest and it fused with his life energy. After that, he wasn't really alive anymore, but his sense of purpose was. Maybe he knew someone he thought could reverse the process, maybe he was just suicidal: querinalo can do that to people. Either way, Firekeeper's right. King Tedric doesn't need to worry about the monster beneath his grandmother's tomb any longer."

Daylily's voice showed none of the exhaustion she must feel. "Even so, perhaps we should not remain here. Kabot is demonstrating an astonishing ability to work transportation magics. However, he will have a harder time finding us if he isn't going where he has been before."

"Why make it easier for him?" Firekeeper agreed in her Blind Seer voice. "Arasan, you get the others through the gate. We two will go and tell King Tedric that he needs to set a watch here in case Kabot comes back. Then we will join you."

Firekeeper hoped that King Tedric might be nearby. The old king, although officially still the ruler of Hawk Haven, had taken to spending long stretches of time at an estate he had inherited from his grandmother, Queen Zorana the Great, so that his heirs could grow accustomed to managing without him. The last time she had visited, they had arranged how she could use the alarm that had been in place since the days of that first queen to say she was there. If King Tedric or his wife, Queen Elexa, were not present or were not available, then the estate's steward, who was among the very few who knew of the subterranean complex's existence, would come.

Firekeeper and Blind Seer were prepared to wait. They had just finished a light snack and tidied themselves up when sounds above indicated that the hidden door beneath Queen Zorana's sarcophagus was being opened.

"Firekeeper?" The voice that echoed down the stone stairs was not that of the old king, nor of his trusted bodyguard, but one that made Firekeeper grin so widely she thought her cheeks might crack. "I hardly know whether to shake you or hug you, so get up here so I can decide."

"No shake, please, Fox Hair," Firekeeper said, flying up the stairs and giving Derian a tight hug. "No shake. We have been shaken enough."

Derian hugged her back, then punched Blind Seer affectionately on one shoulder.

Firekeeper bounced in place with happiness. "We was not sure you would be in Hawk Haven already. Is a long journey."

Derian looked self-conscious, as only he could. "Eshinarvash really sped up our journey. Then, when we reached Liglim, we didn't need to wait for anyone to meet with us. Apparently, they had omens of our coming—and that we would need a fast ship, so they had one waiting. I guess we're important now."

Firekeeper was wolf-pleased at this evidence of her friend's importance. "Is you here with king and queen?"

"'Am I' with the king and queen," Derian corrected automatically. "Yes. They invited Isende and me to come visit, where we could have some privacy from prying eyes and—so we learned not long ago—to entrust a few state secrets to us."

As they moved out into the light, Firekeeper could see that her oldest human friend looked very tired. She asked quickly, so he could answer without worrying about embarrassing anyone.

"And this visit, to family, to homeland? Was it too terrible?"

Derian let out a gusty sigh. "It wasn't easy. My parents completely approve of Isende. They're shocked to find that I'm part-ruler of a sorcerous Old World realm. And, as for my new physical attributes, let's leave it at 'They're trying.'"

"Brother? Sister?"

"Glad I'm not dead. Finding it both harder and easier to face all the other changes than my parents are." He forced a smile. "Weirdly enough, I owe to you that it didn't go harder. Turns out that knowing you and Blind Seer had already opened my whole family to the idea that the world isn't quite like we all thought it was. Even so, accepting what I look like, that I'm not coming back to Hawk Haven to stay, that's been tough. I think we were all grateful when King Tedric 'offered' his invitation—phrasing it as a command—so that we could get away from each other and adjust."

"But your family like Isende," Firekeeper said with great satisfaction. "I knew they would."

"We decided *not* to tell them that my new wife may have a small spellcaster's gift," Derian added. "Learning I was married to a girl from the far south was one thing. Learning I'd married a scion of the sorcerers of old… We'll leave that for a later time."

Their conversation had carried them to where King Tedric, Queen Elexa, and Isende—guarded by the ever-present Sir Dirkin Eastbranch—were gathered in a gazebo set within a copse of flowering trees. Firekeeper looked wistfully at where little meat pies were set on a painted plate, but decided that she needed her mouth free for talking.

After greetings—and many hugs—were exchanged, Firekeeper said, "I have news to give and to give quickly, because I have left possible trouble behind us, but I think we can trust Arasan and Laria to manage for a little, and maybe Ynamynet and Kalyndra will not have gone too far in this little time."

Derian looked as if he had dozens of questions, but he clamped his lips tightly, and reached for Isende's hand, letting Firekeeper launch into her account. When she finished, King Tedric—wigless and casually dressed as he had been the last time Firekeeper had seen him—chuckled.

"So, although we no longer have a magical menace in the basement, there is the possibility of a crazed sorcerer appearing to seek you and the remnants of that menace." He turned to his advisor. "Dirkin? Thoughts?"

"I think we can manage a reasonable defense, especially now that we no longer need to fear being attacked when we descend. I will work out the details." The knight looked at Firekeeper. "Do you think that Kabot will return in the near future?"

Firekeeper shrugged, partnering the motion with an unhappy expression, so that Sir Dirkin would understand she wasn't being flippant. "We do not know, because we do not know Kabot. I think that even those who would have once said they knew Kabot do not know Kabot as he is now, but Blind Seer thinks that Kabot will be very weary and very worried, so maybe Kabot not do anything for a time. If you can do some watching, we will go after Kabot. Someone will let you know when Kabot is not a threat. After that, all you have to think about is the gate—and with Derian and Isende here, I think you is doing that already."

Isende nodded. "We have been. Although King Tedric said that he asked you to keep the gate a secret, you did the right thing telling Ynamynet and Kalyndra—we would have been telling the Nexans before long. However, since this gate doesn't go anywhere we have under anything but the most casual supervision on 'our' side, we want to make arrangements, probably with some of the yarimaimalom."

"And I," King Tedric said, "need to discuss with my heirs how much trade we wish to open with the Old World. They are the ones who will need to deal with the undoubted complications that will arise, so they should have a say."

Firekeeper nodded, as did Blind Seer. Then she pushed herself to her feet. "You plan your hunt. We will not howl too soon and scare the prey. Now, we wish so much to stay, but too much is still to be decided. By now, everyone will have rested some and talked and maybe Uaid is no longer unconscious and we can learn more. Time to find out where the trail will take us next."

"Be careful," Queen Elexa said in her sweet, gentle voice, "dear children. You've wandered into something too much like those stories I told you when you were newly come to human lands. Remember, not all of those stories had happy endings."

The humans were deep in discussion when Firekeeper and Blind Seer emerged from the gate into the tiled room, but they turned as one to greet the wolves.

"Did you find King Tedric?" Laria asked anxiously.

"Did," Firekeeper said, sinking down to take a place near Laria in the rough circle. As she did, she assessed what the positions the humans had taken told her. Laria sat next to Arasan, who sat next to Wythcombe. Ranz was beside Wythcombe. Then there was a gap. Next came Kalyndra, then Ynamynet.

Firekeeper grinned to herself that she'd been correct in assuming that the two would not immediately return to the Nexus Islands, no matter what they had implied.

There was another gap, then Uaid, then Daylily. Then yet another gap, which brought the circle around to Laria again. Firekeeper and Blind Seer had slid into the opening between Laria and Daylily, who had moved over politely—or perhaps at the idea of seating herself next to an enormous wolf. Glancing up, Firekeeper saw Farborn was perched on the sill of one of the unbroken windows, busy devouring something the size of a mouse.

"I have the disk piece," Farborn said by way of greeting, "set here on the ledge beside me. Wythcombe has looked at it hungrily a time or two, but I think more because the scent of its mana keeps catching his attention than because he means to seize it. Kalyndra and Ynamynet are being very polite about pretending not to be too interested."

"And you are well," Blind Seer asked. "You have felt no influence from it?"

"These new feet of mine,"—the merlin examined his crystal-enshrouded talons—*let me feel not only that this is not just a bit of pretty stone, but shield me from it as well."*

The conversation between the wolves and the falcon took hardly as long as Firekeeper and Blind Seer needed to make themselves comfortable. Now Firekeeper continued her report.

"We find King Tedric, and Queen Elexa, and Sir Dirkin Eastbranch—and two others, dear to most of this company. We find Derian and Isende, too."

The spontaneous cries of delight would have warmed Derian's heart, reminding him that even if his birth family was struggling to accept all the changes he had been through, he had a community that valued him for what he now was.

Firekeeper gave a quick summary of the meeting, at the end of which Ynamynet nodded in satisfaction. "We will conceal this chamber and its gate until Hawk Haven is ready to open communications. For further protection, we thought to ask one or more of the local yarimaimalom if they would nest or den near here. There are several good possibilities among the creatures who do not roam widely. You will doubtless be off again soon, but we will ask Plik to speak to them for us."

"Good," Firekeeper said. "I think King Tedric would let Derian and Isende come home through this gate, but on this end the way is too small for Eshinarvash. Derian would not let him travel alone."

"We'd actually been discussing that—not Eshinarvash, specifically, but how difficult this room is to get into." Kalyndra said. "There is a door. Eventually, we could excavate the passageway that connects to it. We might even find that some of the original walls remain standing, so all we'd need to do is clear away whatever was used to fill it in."

"I could help," said an unfamiliar male voice. "If you'd let me. I am very good with earth magics."

From how everyone started, this was the first time Uaid had spoken. The Rhinadei rebel still looked pale and exhausted, but no longer as if he was on the verge of death. Daylily quickly offered Uaid a camping mug of something that smelled strongly of stimulant herbs. Uaid began to wave it away, realized he was being overly proud, and accepted it with a nod.

"Up to this point, you have talked around a matter than means a great deal to me and Daylily," Uaid said, "and that's what you plan to do with us."

Daylily nodded. "I've done my best to answer all your questions about what we have been through since we left what Wythcombe calls Mount Ambition. I've even told you about the Voice. I have the impression that Ynamynet is a person of importance on the Nexus Islands—the ruler along with this Derian. Can you at least give us an idea what you will say about us to your council?"

Uaid added, "We left Rhinadei. We don't want to go back. We wouldn't even if we didn't think we'd face execution. We made our choices decades ago, and nothing that has happened has really changed our minds."

Wythcombe couldn't quite hide the sneer in his voice. "So you still are interested in the anathema art? Even after you've seen how easily it can be abused?"

"Anything can be abused," Daylily shot back, "even rectitude. I'd rather learn how to use blood magic properly, which is what I always wanted, than run scared. In any case, in Rhinadei the *best* we can hope for is being made an object lesson. More likely, we'd be executed so we could provide a really *big* object lesson."

Ynamynet was looking with interest at Uaid. "Earth magic? Talent or spellcasting?"

"Both," Uaid said with honest pride.

Ynamynet turned to Daylily. "And you? Your name is 'Daylily.' Do you specialize in plants?"

"I specialize in not specializing," Daylily replied. "I'm interested in how the different magical channels interrelate—which is why I was interested in learning blood magic, because it's one of the very few forms of magic that exists to enhance, rather than having a purpose of its own."

"Interesting…"

Ynamynet exchanged a glance with Kalyndra. Firekeeper didn't need to have Blind Seer's sense of smell to know that, beneath her cool as usual exterior, Ynamynet was excited. Firekeeper knew why. The Nexus Islands was caught in a snare. Its livelihood depended on spellcasting, but recruiting spellcasters from outside the community was extremely dangerous, because the Nexans could never be quite sure if they were recruiting a potential traitor. The two Rhinadeians would feel no conflict of interest between their new home and their birthland, for they could never hope to be accepted in Rhinadei.

"We'll definitely consider your appeal," Ynamynet said, with what for her was a warm smile. "But I'll say right now, Kabot would not be welcome. He attacked Laria. He may have been in a panic. He may have been overwhelmed by that artifact he carries, but we have no room for any who cannot control themselves."

Wythcombe nodded sadly. "No matter what led Kabot to those actions, he has stepped over the line into anathema."

"And now Kabot has two potent magical artifacts," Ranz added, not quite hiding a certain envy, "or one and a half? Or parts of a greater whole. I still don't understand what we're dealing with."

All eyes turned to Arasan, and Chsss raised his arms in an elaborate shrug. "I don't know either, but if you'll let me take a closer look at what we have, I'm willing to make a guess."

Blind Seer growled when Firekeeper rose to let Arasan inspect Hohdoymin's necklace. Chsss waved a hand dismissively in the air.

"Don't bother to translate. He'll find a way to get me if I try anything, even if it means hurting Arasan. I get it. I wish you would trust me more."

"After you put almost everyone into a trance with Arasan's music?" Firekeeper asked. "If Blind Seer and Farborn not hear differently than humans' ears do, then maybe we not able to defeat Kabot."

"I told you I was sorry," Chsss said, but his tone was distracted. "Do me a favor. Take the necklace and rotate it slowly through your hands so I can examine it a little at a time. Thank you." His vision unfocused and his expression went slack, but Blind Seer could smell a new intensity to his aura. After a long while, Chsss sighed, shook his head, and waved to Firekeeper that she could stop turning the necklace. "Most of what is strung on this necklace are mere trinkets, especially the ones that look most like they should be powerful artifacts. A few hold slight charms, depleted from age. I feel certain that Hohdoymin had no idea how powerful an item he had in this doubled disk that our new friends tell us is Teyvalkay. Kalyndra, I believe you said Hohdoymin wasn't a spellcaster?"

"No, or Nalrmyna would have kept him longer."

Chsss nodded crisply. "Firekeeper, take the necklace and go sit next to Blind Seer. Let him reassure himself I haven't taken liberties. Can Farborn bring his prize down here? I'd like to compare it with Teyvalkay."

Blind Seer said to Farborn. *"Bring it down. Give it to Laria to hold. Stay with her. If Chsss tries anything, go for his eyes."*

The merlin shrieked laughter, then soared down and landed lightly on Laria's forearm, carefully setting the torn artifact in her open palm. Laria looked astonished, but obediently extended her hand so that Chsss could examine the broken disk.

"Prettier than Teyvalkay," Chsss said, "even damaged as it is. Do we have a name for it?"

Daylily shook her head no, but Uaid said, his deep voice surprised, "You know, I think I do. I must have picked it up when Kabot was taking liberties with my mana. It's called Xixavalkay."

Once again, Chsss's eyes unfocused as he studied the artifact. "Very like Teyvalkay. Being broken seems to have tightened the conduit through which a user can tap the mana Xixavalkay is tied into—presumably that of the New World." He shivered and, for once, Blind Seer didn't think the reaction was entirely theatrical. "I am not exaggerating when I say that whoever possesses all four of these threads would possess the sort of power usually reserved for deities. And that in handing these over to merely human sorcerers, Jyanee the Unweaver was either very unwise or deliberately courting the destruction of a great part of the world. I'd love to get a close look at Palvalkay, which was apparently associated with Pelland, since Tishiolo is part of Pelland. Did she make any provisions for her own safety?"

"A good question," Ynamynet said, "and not as frivolous as it might seem. I am also from Pelland, but Tishiolo has always been separate—both culturally and physically. The mountains that cut them off from the rest of the continent are only the smallest element in the divide. Recall how, in the story Daylily told us, Jyanee wanted to study at what was probably a small magical academy, although the University of Azure Towers was just over the mountains. It is completely possible that this Unweaver was able to protect her tiny homeland. Perhaps she wasn't a crazed egoist. Perhaps she expected the people to whom she gave the threads to make similar choices."

Brow furrowed, Wythcombe said, "Daylily, you told us that the legend the Voice related to you indicated that there were four threads: Sykavalkay. We apparently have Teyvalkay and part of Xixavalkay. Kabot has Palvalkay and the other part of Xixavalkay. Did your Voice give you any idea where the fourth thread might be?"

"No," Daylily said, frowning. "Kabot may have known more than he told us, but I wonder… He really didn't seem to know where we were, either when we were in what I now know was Tey-yo, or Hawk Haven. He just followed the threads."

"Then that's what we're going to need to do as well," Chsss said, waving for Laria and Farborn to step back. "This time we have a head start. If we believe the legend of the Unweaver, she said that the four threads were tied to the four largest landmasses. Having just spent a great deal of time with Urgana's excellent globe, I can tell you which the fourth landmass is: Rhinadei."

"But where in Rhinadei?" Ranz asked, his voice tight with the anxiety of someone who suddenly feels how very vulnerable his family might be.

Chsss gave one of his eloquent shrugs. "Kabot has a start on us, no matter what we do, so we might as well go back to the Nexus Islands and see if we can narrow down where we need to go, either using the threads or as we did before or by tracking this Voice."

He grinned, and met Blind Seer's gaze with a challenge so direct that the wolf felt his hackles rise. "A Voice who is *not* me, no matter what you're thinking. I'm on your side. Believe it."

His sweat smelled of excitement and something that reassured Blind Seer—of fear. Not fear of Blind Seer. The wolf knew that particular odor well enough. Fear of the one they were pursuing. Not of Kabot, but of the one who had decided to Meddle with Kabot's life.

"Will Rhinadei let us continue our hunt?" Firekeeper asked Blind Seer. The two of them were alone on the mainland not far from the Setting Sun Stronghold, where Blind Seer had gone to hunt so he would be fortified for the next stage of their journey. The humans were also preparing for what they hoped would be their final chase.

"Wythcombe must speak for us," Blind Seer said. "If he is not eloquent enough, I think we will continue our hunt, whether or not they 'let' us. There is too much at risk for us not to do so. And while others might claim to be experts on artifacts, only we are experts on Meddlers. This other Meddler worries me even more than does Kabot."

"Then you do believe there is another? That this is not just our Meddler playing games?"

"I think it is another, but whether 'our' Meddler is also playing games, that I cannot say."

Firekeeper sighed. "I wonder if this other Meddler had been watching Rhinadei for a long while. After querinalo, Rhinadei was the only land with spellcasters of any great ability. But this Meddler needed rebels. One such as Wythcombe would have meekly handed Sykavalkay over to his land's elders—especially since it was created by one who used blood magic."

Blind Seer's ears flickered back in what for a human would have been a slight frown. "You are wrong if you think Wythcombe is meek. Even when starving, a father wolf will regurgitate meat for his nursing mate or small pups. Wythcombe acknowledges that he is part of a pack."

Firekeeper shifted her shoulders to better carry the deer carcass that represented Blind Seer's leftovers. "Yes. But who are Wythcombe's pack now? The Rhinadei counsel? We eight who have hunted Kabot? Perhaps Kabot? Kabot has a hold over him still, even though Wythcombe denies it."

"There I cannot disagree, but even my nose cannot sniff out the nature of that hold, for it is so complex that not even Wythcombe himself understands it."

X

Once again, Kabot awoke to discover that he had escaped the post-overextension hangover. Guilt washed over him as he considered this miracle, because he suspected that his rapid recovery was due to the mana he'd taken from Uaid. But wallowing in guilt would get him nothing, and the best way to pay Uaid back was to turn events in his favor. Then Kabot could apologize, maybe even offer Uaid and Daylily a share of his find.

Pushing himself to his feet, Kabot examined his surroundings. They were completely unfamiliar, but somehow they *felt* familiar. When he reached out to analyze the local mana, the reason for that familiarity struck him like a blow. He was back in Rhinadei. Where in Rhinadei, he didn't know, but definitely Rhinadei. Kabot wondered why he felt so certain when he hadn't had the least idea where they had arrived after the last two transits. Could it be that people actually had a mystic connection to their birthlands?

Then Kabot realized that the reason for his instant recognition was nothing so mystic or poetic. Simply put, his surroundings shared something that he had last felt on Rhinadei—a powerful mana surge.

"Therefore," he said aloud, attempting to push away the creeping aloneness he felt without Daylily and Uaid, "am I actually in Rhinadei, or am I merely somewhere that, like Rhinadei, has mana surges?"

"You got it in one," the Voice replied. Kabot could have sworn he heard the words with his ears, not inside his head. "You're in Rhinadei."

"To answer your question, you are and you aren't hearing me," the Voice continued, sounding less like Phiona than ever. "Let's leave it at that. There really are more important things for us to discuss. You don't think that Wythcombe will not be after you once again, do you? He might catch up even faster this time, now that Uaid and Daylily have been captured and can report on your goals."

"I think you're right." Kabot faced how his friends would react with brutal honesty. "Just a few moments ago, Daylily was screaming Uaid's name as she tried to claw my eyes out. I don't think Uaid will feel any more kindly toward me."

"Precisely."

"Well, at least I don't seem to have arrived in a crumbling ruin this time," Kabot said, turning slowly to examine his surroundings.

"Room" was too pedestrian a term for the massive area in which he now stood. The chamber's floor was black marble, inlaid with an elaborate design in gold. The walls were covered with absolutely impossible quantities of rose quartz. The inner portion of the ceiling was domed, the black marble ornamented with constellations worked in silver and precious stones. The stars glittered in improbable colors, as if they had dressed up for a formal ball.

Kabot almost overlooked the crystalline pillars that defined an elegant circular border beneath the dome, although they were each as big around as a broad-shouldered man. The pillars were faceted on six sides, looking—other than their enormous size—like natural quartz crystals. The room's light was emitted by the crystal pillars, providing ample to see by without washing out the sparkling starscape above. Although this chamber was definitely not a ruin, it shared something with the ruins in which he had been residing of late. After a moment, Kabot had it. There was a similar sense of desertion.

"What is this place?" Kabot asked.

"You could call it the palace of your ancestors," the Voice suggested.

"*My* ancestors?" Kabot echoed incredulously. "My ancestors were mostly greengrocers who took advantage of a tendency toward minor plant magics. Everyone agreed my talent was extraordinary for one of our line, and originated possibly because my mother had spent too much time in the ruined lands. Some whispered that Mama had done more than magic while she was away, but my father was crazy enough about her not to care if I was a bastard."

Kabot suddenly felt very excited. When he was younger, he had spent considerable time daydreaming that his father actually was someone much more interesting than the quiet, steady man Fate had assigned him. He heard something of that younger self in his inflection as he asked the Voice:

"Are you saying that I actually *am* a bastard, and that this palace belongs to my father?"

The Voice sounded apologetic. "Sorry. Didn't mean to open old wounds. No. I was actually speaking symbolically. The last resident of this castle was a woman who did what you dreamed of doing. Onorina was Rhinadei-born, but found her way back to the Old World because she was interested in learning blood magic. While she was there, she became friends with a woman I've mentioned to you before: Jyanee the Unweaver."

"Jyanee? So this was, what, a hundred and fifty, two hundred years ago?"

"Somewhere in there. I will admit, I'm terrible with dates. Going back to my story… When Jyanee gave Sykavalkay to her uncle, she made certain that Onorina knew. When the four threads were separated, Onorina claimed Guulvalkay, the thread tied to Rhinadei, and chose this place to study it. Her reasons were sound: What better place to hide something of great power than amid powerful and erratic mana flows?"

"So Guulvalkay is here?" Kabot asked eagerly.

"It is, although it will not be as easy to reach as the other three were," the Voice warned. "Onorina was very concerned about Guulvalkay falling into the wrong hands."

Kabot—thinking about digging through the ruins of Azure Towers, climbing a gutted tower, breaking the lattice; about spending days stuck in a tree trying to figure out how to steal Teyvalkay from a temple in a village (and still failing in the end); about being trapped in a dank, doorless, windowless cellar, battling not one, but two competitors—Kabot decided to keep his thoughts about "easy" to himself. If Daylily or Uaid had been there, he would probably have mitigated his annoyance by rolling his eyes and mouthing "Easy?" but since he couldn't, his irritation came out in other ways.

"I've been meaning to ask for a while," Kabot said sharply, "just who are you anyhow? You're not Phiona, although you sometimes sound like her. You're not Uaid's 'master,' or whatever man Daylily hears. Just now when you were talking about Jyanee and Onorina, you sounded as if you knew them personally. Who are you?"

"Jyanee called me Zazaral," the Voice replied, sounding amused. "That's Tishiolan for 'Busy Bee.' She said that's what I reminded her of, buzzing in her ear, offering suggestions. I'm the one who suggested the line of research that led to her discovering the threads, I'm proud to say."

"You suggested it to her? So you've been around well over two hundred years?" Kabot was surprised how difficult he found accepting the idea.

"Oh, far longer than that," the Voice—or Zazaral, as Kabot was now determined to think of her—said. "I'm immortal. Now, I mean. I didn't start out immortal, but I rapidly realized that one lifetime really wasn't enough to allow a person to have a proper influence on events, so I set out to extend my lifespan. I succeeded and, well, here I am!"

Zazaral sounded positively chipper, and very, very pleased with herself. Himself? Itself? Kabot decided to settle on the pronoun he was accustomed to, since he didn't think gender mattered for a disembodied spirit. That led to another question.

"We've always encountered you just as a voice. Do you have a body somewhere and are using mind speech or something?"

"Oh, I gave up on bodies long ago. Really, they're so very limiting and they do influence how one thinks. Look at you now. You're one of the most intellectually focused humans I've met in a long time, but part of you is distracted by physical sensations. Your stomach is reminding you, oh so subtly, that the last thing you had to eat was an overripe fig. Your aesthetic sense admires this room in which you find yourself, but your feet are aware that marble floors are extremely hard. Your skin is telling you you're just a little chilly. You're tired, too, although excitement is balancing that for now. When you get over being excited, you're going to be more weary than ever."

"Can you read my mind, then? Feel what I'm feeling?" Kabot asked indignantly.

"Oh, no! Not at all," Zazaral reassured him. "That's why the summoning spell was necessary to bring me to you. Even when I came to you of my own accord, say to bring you a warning or bit of advice, then it was easiest to get your attention if you were a little detached: sleeping, dreaming, meditating. No, dear Kabot, I may have abandoned the limitations of the flesh, but I remember them all too well. It's like when you take off a pair of too tight boots that have been rubbing blisters. You don't forget them just because you're grateful to be rid of them."

Kabot shook his head, suddenly all too aware that he *was* chilly, hungry, and beginning to feel tired and anxious. Worse, he had no one to watch his back while he slept. He looked around the black-floored chamber. There were doors in the rose quartz walls, not so much concealed as made to be discreet. He wondered if any of them led to someplace as prosaic as a toilet.

Immortal, he thought, very carefully keeping his thoughts to himself. *That would be nice, and so very convenient. I have in my possession threads that tap directly into the mana of two continents. I wonder if Zazaral is interested in a companion?*

Zazaral might be immortal, but she hadn't lost touch with what mere mortals needed to function at their best. Kabot had sidestepped the mana-depletion hangover, but his last full meal had been baked duck eggs, cattail tubers, and overripe fruit in the jungle. He had slept in that filthy cave, but rest alone couldn't fuel a body that had been short of proper care for…

He considered. Did the decades they'd spent in a suspended state count? Or should he just count the days since they had been dropped into the ruins of Azure Towers? Even there, accommodations had been less than ideal. If it hadn't been for Daylily's skills both magical and not, he and Uaid would likely have either starved or been taken prisoner by Azure Tower's guards.

When Zazaral directed him to a small apartment in a far less grand area of the massive edifice they had been exploring, Kabot was ridiculously grateful for a clean bed and bathroom with hot and cold running water. When he learned that the pantry was stocked with a variety of provisions sealed against spoilage, he nearly wept.

Properly washed, his hair trimmed, dressed in a clean set of loose trousers and long-sleeved shirt that was among a wide assortment of attire he found in a wardrobe off the bathing area, he felt more himself than he had since this entire debacle began.

"Will someone be likely to show up here?" he said as he put water on in which to cook noodles, set a package of dry beef and vegetables to soak, then began grating some sharp cheese. "Or is this someone's seasonal palace?"

"We haven't tripped the wards," Zazaral replied, "so I don't think anyone will show up. Enjoy your meal, and I'll tell you what we're up against. As I said earlier, getting Guulvalkay isn't going to be as easy as getting the other threads, but I'm confident that you can manage."

Kabot nodded absently. Should he have a glass of wine? Probably not. He'd need a clear head. He settled for sloshing a liberal amount of a dark red over the meat and vegetables. After pouring the noodles into boiling water, Kabot cleared his throat to show he was listening.

"Obviously, something like Guulvalkay would not be kept where any visitor might come across it. Physically, it's as unremarkable as the other threads: just a large coin of polished copper. However, unless appropriately contained, it shows a distinct and very strong magical signature. First, then, we need to get into a portion of the palace that isn't discernable from the outside."

"Underground?" Kabot guessed. He poured some olive oil into a pan and began to heat it. "Uaid would have been useful, but I'm not helpless. So much of being a rising sorcerer in Rhinadei when I was growing up involved searching through what remained of the dwellings of the earlier inhabitants. Much of what survived was underground. I hope we won't need to clear away fill like we did in Azure Towers, though. If I need to do that alone, Wythcombe will catch up before I can reach Guulvalkay."

"Oh, no," Zazaral reassured him. "Nothing like that! The clearing away was done long ago. The problem will be dealing with the obstacles put into place to keep adventurous types from taking advantage of this palace being empty so much of the time."

"Magical or mechanical?"

"Both. Sometimes in combination, sometimes separately."

Kabot nodded absently as he stirred the rehydrated meat and vegetables into the hot oil, added spices, and then set it to simmer, trying to ignore how his stomach rumbled.

"Mechanical obstacles alone may be the harder to deal with," he said. "I can usually find the other sort by reading their magical auras, although…"

"Yes." Zazaral anticipated what he hadn't said. "The mana surges can make that more difficult, especially when they're erratic like the ones here. Still, if I didn't believe you and I could handle this, I wouldn't have said what I did."

She waited until Kabot had drained his noodles, poured the contents of the skillet over them, and had savored a few bites before continuing. "I could help you better if you let me synchronize more closely with you, use your senses."

Kabot frowned. "Surely that isn't necessary. You are already using them to some extent, or so you indicated. You can get into my dreams and talk with me without using sound. What more do you need?"

Zazaral trilled a laugh that sounded heart-tuggingly like Phiona's, but if Busy Bee thought that would sway Kabot, she'd tried the wrong tactic. When he and Phiona had argued, it had most often been over sharing authority.

Perhaps Zazaral sensed this, because she didn't push. Instead, she went off in another direction. "I'm not going to be able to sense Wythcombe's approach as I have before. There's too much else going on magically here to let me read such a relatively small magical signal. I wouldn't advise using Palvalkay and Xixavalkay either. I doubt Wythcombe would be aware of your working, but I can't figure out what that wolf can do. Since he seems to have claimed Teyvalkay, we can't dismiss him from consideration."

"True," Kabot replied, although in reality he was still having a hard time believing the wolf could actually do magic. Not a wolf, a shapeshifter, maybe, perhaps one seriously gone over into its animal nature.

He finished his meal and swallowed a sigh. What he really wanted now was to make some tea, put his feet up, select a book from the collection he'd glimpsed in the other room, and read himself to sleep. But that would be plain stupid. He used the time it took to wash the dishes to organize his thoughts.

"Do you know where the entrance to this off-limits area might be?"

"I have a fairly good idea."

"Then let's get started. Eventually, I will need to sleep—fragile mortal that I am—but so will Wythcombe and his allies. We have a head start, and I'm not going to waste it."

After Laria had caught up on her sleep, she and Ikitata had had a long talk about whether Laria should continue on, especially after how she'd been taken prisoner by Kabot.

"You could stay here and help Daylily and Uaid adjust," Ikitata suggested. "No one would think twice about your choice or label you a coward."

"Except me," Laria said, "because I'd know I was staying because I was scared to go, scared to see Kabot again, scared I'd fall apart if he made a move in my direction."

"You're not seeking revenge, are you?" Ikitata asked, only the force with which she shoved her awl through the leather of the boot sole she was making showing the effort it took to discuss this with Laria, adult to adult.

"Not revenge," Laria said. "I want to prove to myself that I can face what I'm scared of."

"You're not…" Ikitata paused, as she had not when discussing matters of mortal peril, "going because of handsome Ranz, are you?"

Laria blushed, but if she could face Kabot, surely she could talk about a crush. "No. I'm not. I wanted Ranz to like me, more than like me, I mean. I mean, he does like me, even respects me as a companion and friend, but he doesn't *like* me. I don't think he likes anyone right now, or even has room to. He has too much else on his mind, in his heart, all bound up with finding out that blood magic is a lot more complicated than he'd thought. I'm not even thinking 'maybe someday,' because I'm not sure I'd want to live with a sorcerer. Whatever else Ranz is going to be, he's going to be a sorcerer."

Later, Laria went picnicking with Kitatos and Nenean near the New World gate, not so much waiting for the wolves' return as to keep Farborn company while the merlin kept vigil, since Farborn was determined to have the pleasure of giving first report.

When the wolves emerged onto the hill that held the New World gates, Farborn glided down and landed on Blind Seer's back. The trio stood, looking rather like the sort of painting Laria had seen in Nergy's hunting lodge when they'd stayed with him in Azure Towers: silent and noble denizens of the wild. Knowing them better, Laria guessed that Farborn was talking up a storm. Firekeeper didn't even lower the carcass from her shoulders, but stood listening with flattering attentiveness.

Laria saw the change in Firekeeper's expression when she realized that everyone had been waiting for the wolves, rather than, as was more typical, the other way around, and giggled aloud.

Firekeeper grinned widely and called to Laria, "So we keep you waiting?

Still, I think I can drop this venison at the kitchens. We will not leave before you hug your mother, I think."

Laria grinned back. "Of course not!"

With her little brother and sister at her heels, Laria ran off to her mother's cobbler's shop. There were tears, of course, and admonishments, and promises to be careful and even, to Kitatos, who was a little mixed up as to exactly what Laria was doing, assurances that Laria would bring back presents, if at all possible. Then, feeling her family's love warm around her, Laria ran—by herself, but not in the least alone—to join the others near the docks where Chaker Torn would sail them to the island that held the Rhinadei gate.

Wythcombe had surprised them all by not only agreeing to go around Rhinadei's emergency council, but by being the one to suggest that they do so. Seeing the look of undisguised loathing that Firekeeper gave *Silver Lady*, he explained why they were even using the gate.

"I wish I had the skill to jump us across the world as Kabot has apparently been doing," he said, leaning on his staff, his tone wryly apologetic, "but I don't think that—even with Teyvalkay and the portion of Xixavalkay to draw on—this is the time for experimentation. Actually, after talking at some length with Uaid and Daylily, I am not completely convinced that Kabot *has* been working the transportation spells on his own. I suspect that his Voice has been assisting, while letting Kabot believe he is capable of such enormous magics. Why his Voice would do this, I don't know but, from what I've learned about Meddlers, it's doubtless very complicated and 'for Kabot's own good.'"

The last phrase was spoken with an inflection that managed to be ironic without insulting "their" Meddler, a skillful bit of social manipulation that made Laria admire Wythcombe far more than she had been.

It's funny. We went looking for Wythcombe to teach Blind Seer magic. If I think about the magic I've seen him do, sure it's amazing, but when I really admire him is when he's scratching Rusty between the ears and chattering about gardening or how you make different sorts of cheese. I wonder if Ranz realizes that being a sorcerer is only part of the person. I wonder if Kabot realizes that.

Chaker Torn had finished running up the sails, and Symeen motioned for them to board. Once they were settled, Wythcombe continued. "Varelle will doubtless meet us soon after we arrive. Who else, I cannot guess. However, I think she will see why we don't have time for long debates. Gatewatchers are permitted to make solo decisions. Although I cannot transport us halfway around the world, if Blind Seer and Ranz will help me, I *can* take us to Mount Ambition. There we'll have ample mana to draw upon. Using that, we can refine just where Kabot might have gone without needing to tap Teyvalkay or Xixavalkay."

He thoughtfully scrubbed a hand over his mouth and chin. "Although Arasan's song kept me from acting when we last faced Kabot, I was able to watch what happened on a magical as well as physical level. It seemed to me that the pieces of Sykavalkay had—perhaps saying 'an agenda of their own' is too strong, since that implies intelligence—but 'an inclination to be reunited' might not be too extreme."

Firekeeper, who had gulped her anti-seasickness potion at the last minute, so it hadn't had time to take effect, spoke despite obvious misery. "Blind Seer say he agree. Also, I feel Xixavalkay tugging when I hold it. What happen when these four are together?"

"I suspect," Wythcombe said, "that the 'dampening' by the Unweaver's uncle and his allies may be cancelled, possibly immediately. If one of these threads is potent by itself, all four together could be overwhelming."

Ranz said thoughtfully, "Maybe that's why the four threads were separated. Ever since Chsss first told us about Sykavalkay, I've been wondering why did they split up the threads? Wouldn't it be easier to meet the Unweaver's challenge working in collaboration?"

"If they even cared about meeting the Unweaver's challenge," Laria retorted, the violence of her feelings surprising her. "Ranz, you still have no idea what having raw power you don't need to work for does to people."

Ranz looked startled, but whatever he might have said in reply was interrupted when Firekeeper began laboriously checking off points on her fingers

"First," Firekeeper said, "we take gate to Rhinadei, from there to Mount Ambition. At Mount Ambition, we get the scent of Kabot." Looking queasy, she lowered her hand to press two fingers over her lips, but managed to finish articulating her thought. "How then we get to him fast without wearing you spellcasters to uselessness?"

"We can use the mana surge," Wythcombe said with tremendous satisfaction, "at Mount Ambition. Hopefully Kabot will not have acquired the fourth thread, and so the balance between us will be the same as before. Actually, we should have the advantage, because we have four spellcasters to control our portions, while Kabot has lost his allies and not yet acquired others."

The need to reach Kabot before he retrieved the final fragment was what convinced Varelle to let them leave without delay for Mount Ambition. "If we summon the emergency council, at least Orten and Bordyn will argue that the time has come for Wythcombe to turn the pursuit of Kabot over to others less biased. While I might be persuaded on that point, I don't think Blind Seer and Ranz will be. Moreover, portions of Sykavalkay are in Blind Seer and Firekeeper's possession. I can't see them handing the artifacts over to Orten or Bordyn"—her many-colored eyes actually twinkled—"or even to me, who they like so much better. Therefore, we would delay going after a real danger in favor of fighting among ourselves. I suspect the wolves have a proverb about the stupidity of such behavior."

"While the pack fights, ravens strip the kill," Firekeeper interjected in her "Blind Seer voice."

"So there we have it," Varelle agreed, nodding in satisfaction. "I will make explanations. Move along, and quickly. You have very carefully withheld where you intend to go next, but there will be obvious places to check. Some are not as difficult to reach as they once were."

I wonder if she guessed, Laria thought, then shrugged. That hardly mattered. Checking Mount Ambition—Kabot's last stronghold on Rhinadei, as well as a mana surge—would be a logical choice.

"I take your warning to heart," Wythcombe said, sounding more like a courtier than a potato farmer. "Then, if you will excuse us…"

"Go," Varelle said, making shooing gestures with her long fingers. "May Rhinadei be with you." She paused, smiled mysteriously, then said, "By the way, based on what you've told me, how the threads are named for the lands to which they are tied, I would guess that what you seek is called 'Guulvalkay.'"

Kabot had not been at Mount Ambition; the wolves were sure of that. Now Firekeeper stood beside Arasan while Blind Seer and Ranz assisted Wythcombe as he searched for any lead to where his boyhood friend might have gone. Laria had been enlisted as well, and was drawing lines and placing a variety of peculiar items where indicated.

Based on her scent, Laria had mostly given up on Ranz as a romantic prospect but, ironically, seeing Laria in danger had made Ranz almost courtly. He wasn't precisely being romantic, but he was a lot more inclined to pay her attention. Laria was not so "over" Ranz as to not be flattered. For her part, Firekeeper enjoyed seeing the younger woman blossom. Nonetheless, when she considered what they still faced, the wolf-woman grew somber.

Tilting her head in a wolfish query and lowering her voice, Firekeeper asked Arasan, "Have you taken scent of this other Meddler?"

"I have tried not to do so," came the prompt reply. "I trod the edges of the spider's web before because we had no other way to find Laria. Now that we're closer, and Wythcombe can hopefully get us where we need to go, I'm taking great care not to alert the spider. That doesn't mean I've forgotten her. I've been thinking hard about why Kabot's meddlesome friend might have chosen to get involved. The more I consider possible reasons, the less I feel good about what seems most likely."

He paused and Firekeeper made an encouraging noise deep in her throat.

"Both Uaid and Daylily say that their Voice was the one who directed them to go after Sykavalkay. Gaining a thread or two of Jyanee's creation was originally presented to the rebels as a way to gain the power and respect necessary to negotiate as equals when they finally made contact with blood mages. That explanation only makes sense until you know the reality of our post-querinalo magical world. All three of the Rhinadei rebels are quite powerful—especially by our current standards. Any of the Old Country nations would have welcomed them, especially since they would have arrived as supplicants, not conquerors. So, although this Voice's explanation would have made sense to Kabot's rebels, it doesn't when you know the reality."

"So you are thinking," Firekeeper said, alert as if she'd just realized that what she'd taken for deer tracks were actually those of some far more menacing creature, "this Kabot Meddler wants Sykavalkay for herself, but needs human sorcerers as hands and feet. Do you think this one is as you was, trapped, looking to be free?"

Arasan's head shook hard. "No. That doesn't feel right. Then I had to struggle just to communicate. Their Voice is flitting all over the globe, rescuing sorcerers, showing far too much flexibility. Did I ever tell you that most Meddlers come to crave immortality? This other Meddler felt very, very old to me. Now consider this: the coming of querinalo, and the subsequent lack of miracles would have considerably dented the organized worship that supplied mana to the Meddlers."

"And the mana is what the immortal ones eat," Firekeeper finished. "I see. This Sykavalkay ties into ridiculous amounts of mana. Finding it would be like a starved yearling stumbling on a gutted moose at midwinter. Would this old Meddler have the sense not to gorge?"

"I wish I knew," Chsss said. "I'd like to believe so, but hunger and dread are a bad combination. If this friend of Kabot's knows we're on her trail, then I'm not sure how wise she'll be."

"If this Kabot friend gorges," Firekeeper said somberly, "then she could suck the life not from mere living creatures, but from the land itself. Will we be able to stop such a one?"

Chsss shrugged, but with somewhat less than his usual insouciance. The worry lines around Arasan's warm-brown eyes deepened. "I don't think we have a choice. It's stop her or see much of what we love be destroyed."

Dinner—as Kabot chose to think of his glorious meal, having no idea what time of day it actually was—gave Kabot enough energy to set out to find where the entrance to the subterranean complex was.

"You can't just lead me there?" he asked after they had searched one wing of the building.

"I'm sorry. I can't. This place has been remodeled since I was last here. I did show you where the entrance from the wine cellar used to be."

"True enough," Kabot admitted grudgingly. "You did."

In an area rife with mana surges, magical means of detection were all but useless. Kabot had to resort to measurement and routine architectural logic. Zazaral's tip about the wine cellar was useful in one way—Kabot had been able to rule out a large portion of the sprawling palace as unlikely. He was about to expand his search parameters when he found the false back to a larger than usual supply closet. Using spells routinely taught in Rhinadei, he inspected the backing section by section until he found the alarms that would go off unless the proper opening sequence was followed. Worse, in addition to physical locks, there were magical ones as well.

"This is going to be a pain," he said, rocking back on his heels. "Whoever set this up probably had a key or keys, maybe even actual physical keys, since they might have wanted to make sure someone without magical ability could get in here."

"Sorry, I don't have keys, physical or otherwise."

"Well," Kabot said, shoving himself to his feet and putting his hands behind his head for a joint-popping stretch, "then we're going to need to do this the slow way, undoing each spell and lock in sequence. Before I can do that, I need something more to eat and then some sleep."

"There's ample mana to tap here," Zazaral reminded him.

"There's ample water in the ocean, too," Kabot snapped, "but if you want to use it to put out a fire, you still need buckets. I, my dear immortal, am your humble bucket. If you don't want me to leak, I need to restore my focus."

Kabot expected Zazaral to offer some caustic reply, but there was nothing but silence.

Although Laria had paid careful attention as Wythcombe muttered and murmured his way through various workings, she was startled when Wythcombe announced that he was ready to create a transportation spell.

"So you know where Kabot went?" Laria asked. "I mean, you've told us over and over that you can't create a transportation spell until you know where you're going."

"True enough," Wythcombe agreed affably. "Based on the workings we've done here, I'm making an educated guess. There's an old castle in the right direction and general distance that would be the sort of place to attract Kabot. I've been there several times, so I can take us there. Like Mount Ambition, it's located near a mana surge. So if I have guessed wrong, then we'll have ample mana to draw on for further analysis."

He rubbed his chin and chuckled. "It will also take us away from here—which is certain to be one of the locations Orten or Bordyn will check once they realize we have returned."

Laria wanted to ask more, but she decided against it. Firekeeper was looking very tense. Chsss had stopped making obnoxious comments hours ago. If Kabot was there, she'd learn more then. If not, getting all the details in advance would have just been a waste of time. She grinned to herself. Firekeeper was definitely having an influence on her.

Setting up the transportation spell took half a day, even with ample mana to draw on. Ambient mana could save spellcasters from having to draw on their own, but it didn't replace physical exhaustion or increase the attention needed for delicate calculations. When they were done, Ranz's and Wythcombe's usually warm-brown skin was washed with grey. Arasan didn't get any argument—not even from Firekeeper—when he insisted that they eat and sleep.

The wolf-woman did wake them at dawn, but insisted that everyone have breakfast, "Because we don't know when we're going to eat again."

When Wythcombe activated his spell, Firekeeper and Blind Seer dove through the temporary portal as one, with Farborn clinging to Firekeeper's shoulder. The rest followed nearly as quickly, Wythcombe, who closed up his casting behind him, taking care to erase any signatures that would make it easy to pursue them.

Laria stumbled slightly when she exited the short corridor created by the spell and her feet encountered rough, pebbly terrain. Ranz caught her arm and steadied her.

"Thanks!" She flashed a smile up at him, but Ranz wasn't looking at her. When Laria followed the direction of his gaze, she immediately forgot the warmth of his hand where it still gripped her arm.

A dark stone fortress crouched atop a craggy ridge like some impossible creature. The fortress had been built of a brown-black basalt quarried from its immediate surroundings, creating the impression that the building had grown there, rather than being built. Maybe it had been.

The castle's lines were rounded and wandering, with at least two domes rising like humped backs. There were no watchtowers. Then again, set high on the land as it was, this brooding fortification needed no towers to survey its surroundings. Laria shivered as she imagined Kabot—and even worse, his Meddler—staring down at them from one of the narrow slit windows.

"Above us stands the Fortress of the Mended Shield," Wythcombe said, staring into the rough crystal that topped his staff. "Kabot is near, probably within. Varelle and I speculated that this was one of Kabot's likely destinations, but I had hoped we were wrong, because getting inside is going to be nearly impossible."

"The Mended Shield?" Ranz sounded puzzled. "You say that as if we should know the name, but if I haven't heard it, then certainly our outlander friends have not."

Wythcombe sank down to seat himself on a rock. "It isn't a story you would know, Ranz. Even your parents might not have heard it."

Despite her tension, Laria actually laughed. "This isn't another story about how Rhinadei isn't quite as perfect as everyone thinks, is it? You know, I think you people have a problem with facing reality."

Wythcombe looked shocked, then started to chuckle. "Indeed we may. Make yourselves comfortable while I tell you about the Mended Shield. If the senior counsel doesn't like my choice, that wouldn't be the first time."

Ranz let go of Laria's arm and moved promptly to obey. Firekeeper leaned against Blind Seer, who managed to look both alert and impassive. Laria guessed that while the wolf's ears would attend to Wythcombe's lecture, his other senses would be gathering information about their surroundings: magical or otherwise. Farborn had been performing an aerial survey. Now he dove down to settle on Laria's shoulder. Laria felt pleased that not even the Rhinadeians felt a need to ask the merlin if he had seen anything significant. Their trust in his judgement had become unquestioning.

"You will not be surprised," Wythcombe began, rubbing one short-fingered hand over his brow as if his head ached, "to learn that Kabot's cabal was not the first group to attempt to depart Rhinadei for lands where the anathema art was still practiced. During one of those departures—whether by accident or on purpose—the shield that separates Rhinadei from the world without was damaged at this very location."

He waved his hand toward the castle. "I will not go into how many anchor points there are for the shield. That is neither necessary nor politic. What you do need to know is that after the shield was damaged and repaired, additional defenses were erected. A variation of the shield was extended to keep anyone from getting inside the fortress. Lowering this from the outside takes collaboration from an assortment of high-ranking sorcerers."

Ranz shook his head in evident dismay. "I agree with Laria. I think those of Rhinadei could be taught a more honest version of our history. Maybe I need to become one of these 'high-ranking sorcerers' and work to change that policy." The grin he flashed was both impish and impudent, but faded instantly. "Do you think Kabot plans to break the shield?"

Wythcombe nodded sadly. "That seems likely. My divinations show that, as we suspected, the last portion of Sykavalkay is here. If Kabot combines it with what he already holds, he'll have ample mana to shatter not just this point, but the entire shield. Or perhaps he'll choose to leave the shield intact and take some twisted vengeance on Rhinadei. I no longer feel I know him well enough to do more than dread."

When Kabot next awoke, he departed the small apartment, then wandered about the complex until he found a window. Based on the light, he guessed it was about dawn. Which dawn of what day was anyone's guess. Despite a growing sense of unease, Kabot returned to the apartment and made himself eat a decent meal. Then he availed himself of a chance to properly clean his teeth and wash. If all went well, he'd be leaving here today. Who knew when he'd have such pleasant accommodations again?

Zazaral had been very quiet since their disagreement but, as Kabot was packing up his belongings, she spoke. "I've been doing what I can to scout for Wythcombe and his group. No sign of them yet."

The "yet" was slightly emphasized, but Kabot ignored that. Instead he replied with a punctiliously courteous "Thank you very much."

He considered whether or not to ask Zazaral if she was planning to accompany him into whatever was hidden behind the false door of the supply closet, then decided not. What would he do if she said "No" or insisted on renewing their disagreement? After all, whether or not she came with him, he knew where he must go.

Two good meals and some real sleep had done a great deal to recover Kabot's confidence. Once in the supply closet, he tapped into a thin stream of mana that he suspected had been channeled into the palace to facilitate domestic arts. If he had more time, he would have tried to learn if the stream was older or more modern. For now, he decided to be grateful that it was there.

Disarming the wards and locks that held the false back onto the supply closet was easily done. Most Rhinadei mages learned such tricks when on reclamation missions. The sorcerers who had ruined the land had never believed that they were facing a final, destructive catastrophe, so they'd locked up behind themselves, much as a housekeeper heading off to market might, fully expecting to return.

The corridor behind the panel was dimly lit by a pair of glowing ribbons, one near the floor, one higher up. Kabot channeled some of the ambient mana to brighten the higher ribbon, and inspected his surroundings with vision attuned to both magical auras and his more mundane sense of sight.

"Looks as if this corridor was cut relatively recently," he said, not knowing if Zazaral would answer. "The signature is that of a more modern spell."

"Probably done during the remodeling," Zarzaral replied, "when the entry I was familiar with was sealed off."

Kabot placed a hand on the floor, seeking a magical pulse similar to that of the two threads he possessed. Finding it was akin to isolating the voice of a single singer in a choir when you were not even certain if that singer was participating. One by one, he silenced the pulses that could not be the one he sought, then, faintly—when he was about to resign himself that this was not the route to where Guulvalkay was being kept—he felt it. Guulvalkay's vibration was muffled but not sealed, as that of Palvalkay had been. This was closer to how Xixavalkay had felt when buried within that macabre statue: dormant, but in use.

"It's down there!" he crowed. He muted the glow of the light ribbon that ran along the floor, so that its ambient mana wouldn't interfere with his efforts to detect traps or wards. He would have liked to do the same with the ribbon near the ceiling, but then he'd need to carry a lantern. Ah, well, soon enough he'd have memorized the ribbon's particular signature, and would be able to eliminate it from consideration.

The corridor from the supply closet descended, curved, and then intersected with another, much older, corridor. This corridor's age was indicated not so much by dust or dirt as by the fineness of the stonework, and the sophistication of the spells that both lit it and caused fresh air to gently circulate. Eventually, after too many corridors and cross corridors to serve any useful purpose, Kabot realized he had entered into an elaborate maze.

Kabot groaned and ran his hands over his hair. He shouldn't have been surprised; he really shouldn't. The sorcerers of old had loved mazes. Rhinadei's original colonists had found the number and complexity of mazes among the ruined cities of their new home baffling, which argued that whatever purpose they served was specific to the lost culture. One theory held that mazes had been used not only as a simple means of security, but for magical training. Others postulated that there was a religious element, others that they represented an elaborate competition.

Whatever the reason for this maze, it was here and Kabot knew it wouldn't be easy to solve. Worse, Guulvalkay was doubtless hidden in some obscure corner. It was only in stories that anyone hid anything in the maze's heart. That was too obvious. He ground his teeth in frustration. He didn't have time to solve this maze, especially when his pursuers would be tracking him, sparing them any number of wrong turns.

Kabot grinned then, the vicious grin that Wythcombe had said reminded him of a fox who'd just realized the henhouse door was open. Tracking him by scent, at least, wouldn't be easy. The kitchen in the little apartment had been well-stocked with spices, and he'd helped himself to a wide selection that he planned to scatter.

Zazaral did her best to coach him through the maze but, as Zazaral herself had made clear from the start, she was not precisely in the same dimension and therefore was limited in what she could perceive—unless Kabot was willing to let her share his senses. After his left leg was nearly scythed off beneath the knee when he failed to detect a horrid boar-like creature that emerged through the floor, Kabot finally accepted Zazaral's help. He still felt uneasy but—as he told himself while wrapping a makeshift bandage around his freely bleeding leg (and trying not to wish too much for Daylily's eclectic skills)—what good would either pride or caution do him if he was dead?

Given how much Kabot was bleeding, there was no need for him to cut his finger or even perform much in the way of a ritual to draw Zazaral closer. A woman neither young nor old, light nor dark, slender nor heavy, hieratically perfect, without being in the least beautiful, manifested, kneeling next to him and pressing her lips to his wounded thigh. The bleeding stopped instantly. The wound knit closed, leaving only a livid scar.

"Zazaral?"

She rose gracefully, smiled at him, extended a hand that melted into his hand. Spinning as if performing an elaborate dance, she merged herself into him. He felt his lips move in a satisfied smile, heard his own voice say, "Let's go!"

XI

As Blind Seer listened to Wythcombe recount how carefully the Mended Shield had been warded, the blue-eyed wolf found himself beginning to laugh. There just might be a way through the protections, one Rhinadei's humans would not have considered.

"Firekeeper, ask Wythcombe for more information as to what the ward keeps out. Surely it cannot keep out everything. Does it keep out air, rain, insects, passing birds?"

Wythcombe replied with admirable promptness. "The shield doesn't keep out air, rain, or insects. It does keep out magic, so if magic was cast on, say, a swarm of hornets, the insects would not be able to go through the shield. The wards are set to bar humans or magically created creatures. However, wards work best when the parameters are very precise. Therefore, excluding all animals would be difficult. Excluding all avians might be possible, or all reptiles, or all mammals, but the larger the class, the more difficult the exclusion. My guess is that a general aversion, rather than an actual ward, would be considered sufficient to keep most animals away. This would have the added benefit of hindering mounted troops from assaulting the castle."

"You said the castle's ward is a variation on the shield created to ward Rhinadei," Blind Seer pressed. "Surely those long-ago sorcerers were most concerned about other humans, their magic, and what that magic might control."

Blind Seer considered mentioning how excluding birds and insects would have had serious ramifications for Rhinadei's environment, but decided against distracting Wythcombe, now that he had given the wolf the scent of his prey. Blind Seer could tell from her scent that Firekeeper had guessed what he was considering, and that she was very uneasy. Better speak now, before she refused to translate without arguing first.

"Would the ward keep out yarimaimalom?" Blind Seer asked. "We are not human, but neither are we monsters. We may have magic, but what makes us ourselves is not magic."

Firekeeper translated, the words dragging on her tongue.

Wythcombe pretended not to notice, but his scent showed that he was aware of her reaction. It also revealed a sudden flash of interest and excitement: hope where there had been none before.

"I don't know," he said, and might have said more, but Farborn shrieked *"I can check!"* and leapt into the air.

"Impulsive idiot!" Arasan said, springing to his feet as if he might grab the merlin by his tail feathers and drag him down. Chsss's knowledge of great magics lay behind the ferocity of his reaction. "Farborn has no idea what could happen to him! Lightning from the skies such as we saw at Mount Ambition would be nothing to what that shield could do."

Wythcombe was chanting rapidly under his breath, the words unintelligible even to a wolf's sharp ears, the rhythm akin to the beat made by the hooves of a galloping horse. The chunk of rough mineral set into the curve of his staff began glowing with an eldritch light in hues between fire and dawn.

Blind Seer growled.

Firekeeper translated with sulky obedience. "Let the bird try. We need to know."

Wythcombe's spell continued to radiate within the crystal, ready to release should Farborn need assistance. Laria and Ranz stood shoulder to shoulder, unconscious that they'd moved together for comfort, attention fixed on the minute spot that was a small falcon against the blue-white sky. High above the fortress, Farborn darted as he might after a particular agile meal, the light glimmering off his crystalline talons.

Blind Seer thought, *We forgot. Farborn bears a little bit of magic. Will that doom him? Or because that magic is Rhinadei's own gift, will the shield permit him through?*

He howled in wild delight when Farborn began skimming between the crenellations on the battlements, performing an aerial ballet over the fat domes, taking his bow atop an empty flagstaff. The merlin's triumphant screech carried through the still air. Firekeeper translated for those whose eyes and ears were less keen.

"Farborn can go through the shield. He is extremely pleased with himself." She turned her dark gaze, stormy as a thunderhead, on Blind Seer and spoke in Pellish so that the humans would understand. "And you, beloved, you will run into that castle, fight Kabot all alone?"

"*If I must*," Blind Seer replied with a tranquility he didn't feel, for he wondered if his decision would forever rob him of the Firekeeper he knew and loved. "*I would prefer to take you with me. Speak for me, again, beloved, as I explain how this can be done.*"

United, Kabot and Zazaral raced through the maze, every choice extraordinarily clear. Kabot knew where to step, what to avoid, where levers were concealed, even the location of hidden keys that opened secret doors. He knew the coded responses to give to captive elementals, and the snippets of song that would soothe monstrous guardians. His clarity was so great that he didn't even wonder how Zazaral could know all of this. Their course was clear, it was perfect, it was precise. Right up until the moment it wasn't.

If a rainbow could have been played like a harp, it might emit a melody like the barrier that stood between Kabot, Zazaral, and Guulvalkay. Kabot's soul shivered, and Zazaral stood beside him.

"This is where things become interesting," Zazaral sniffed, viewing the barrier with distaste. "Up until now, most of what we've been dealing with was intended to keep out a more general class of trespasser. However, this elegant construction was meant to keep me out."

"You?"

"Me." Zazaral smiled beatifically. "I told you I was acquainted with Jyanee, and that Jyanee and Onorina were friends. Well, just because someone is your friend doesn't mean their friends will like you. Personally, I think Onorina was envious of how close Jyanee and I were, of how I'd helped Jyanee receive the instruction that was being denied to her. When Onorina gained possession of Guulvalkay and resolved to take it to Rhinadei, she became insanely convinced that I would try to seize it for myself. Therefore, in addition to protecting Guulvalkay from general threats, she warded it specifically against me."

Kabot analyzed the thrumming rainbow. "Not *just* you. I can't simply stroll through."

"That's true," Zazaral agreed. "But you have some chance of doing so, while I have none at all."

Like a very light breeze, the thought eddied through Kabot's mind that perhaps Onorina had been right to be concerned, but the worry blew away as he remembered how Zazaral surely could have easily gained possession of Palvalkay, Teyvalkay, or Xixavalkay. Clearly, she wanted nothing for herself. Only after he had needed it, had she risked herself by taking him to Guulvalkay. Dismissing doubt, he focused on the problem at hand.

The rainbow ward sang gentle dissuasion. For the first time since he had let Zazaral borrow his senses, Kabot found focusing difficult. He willed himself to mental clarity, driven as much by a desire not to embarrass himself, now that Zazaral was relying on him, as by anything else.

"There're at least two barriers at work here," he said after laboriously shifting through the energies. "This rainbow's song and something Guulvalkay is intertwined with. That last is drawing on Guulvalkay's own power, so removing Guulvalkay will break whatever that is."

"I suspect," came the very dry reply, "you are correct. The real issue is, can you do it?"

Kabot wasn't about to say "No," not even if he doubted.

"Of course I can."

Although Firekeeper's heart beat painfully fast with barely contained elation, she managed to keep her Blind Seer voice level and measured as she explained her partner's plan.

"Since Farborn and those extraordinary claws can get through the shield, then it is likely I can as well. First, though, I will try to change Firekeeper into a wolf shape, so she can come with me and Farborn. Once we are inside, we will take down the ward so the rest of you can join us."

"Why just Firekeeper?" Ranz interjected indignantly. "If a shapeshifted human can get through, why not shift all of us? I understand magical workings far better than Firekeeper does. Laria could use her talent to 'read' the surroundings. It goes without saying that Wythcombe and Arasan would be useful. Firekeeper would be the least useful of any of us."

Blind Seer snorted. Firekeeper grinned. This time, when she spoke it was in her own voice.

"You would be shapeshifted humans. I will be wolf. Blind Seer says this is because although my body is a human one, my soul is a wolf's. When we are clear of the ward, then he will shape me back." She felt sorrow clog her heartbeat, but pressed on. "When I have hands again, I will help Blind Seer take down the ward or for things like opening doors that a human does easily and a wolf not at all."

Ranz looked as if he would protest again, but Arasan—or rather Chsss—waved him down.

"You've only known Firekeeper a few moonspans, Ranz. To you, she's just a stranger than the rest of us outlander, but in this I agree with Blind Seer: her soul is not a human soul. Blind Seer's plan just might get them both through."

Ranz protested weakly. "But if they're wrong, then Firekeeper going through the shield will trip the ward."

Wythcombe shrugged resignedly. "Then we will need to deal with an elite corps of very worried spellcasters arriving to deal with the breach. They won't be happy to see us here but, if we move quickly, we'll be in ahead of them. If you want, you can stay outside and tell them you tried to stop us. You'd only be telling the truth."

"I'm not trying to stop you going after Kabot," Ranz protested. "I'm saying that Blind Seer is crazy to want to try this."

Arasan chuckled and laid a hand on the younger man's arm. "The very fact that you accept that Blind Seer is capable of working a spell puts you leaps and bounds ahead of just about anyone else in Rhinadei. Think about that." He turned to the others. "Ranz votes against. Chsss and I are for—and we'll let our vote count as one. We know the wolves are for it. Farborn, too. Laria?"

"For, I think. They'll be more careful if they have each other to protect."

"Wythcombe?"

"For." The old spellcaster turned to Blind Seer. "Normally I'd suggest we test if you can get through the shield without breaking the wards, but we don't have time. Kabot's already in there, doing who knows what."

"Ranz?"

The young man gave a stiff little bow. "I withdraw my protest. Wythcombe's right. If Kabot is acting impulsive and crazy, maybe what we need to do to stop him is be a little crazy ourselves." He looked at Blind Seer. "I was going to suggest I loan you some mana, but if you can tap what's already here, maybe that will be better. Depending on the casting, alien mana might trigger the ward."

Blind Seer nodded, panting appreciation of Ranz's offer.

Firekeeper spun in place, elated. "We do this then."

What followed would have been surreal except that Laria's capacity for finding anything weird had been exhausted. To stand in the shadow of an ancient fortification grown from living stone while a wolf paced a careful dance around a naked woman, to know that the falcon who flitted above the castle was scouting out the best possible approach for his ground-bound comrades, to hear the wolf begin to sing high, almost keening notes, and to hear the woman echoing them… All of this seemed, if not normal, all of a piece. Laria sat beside a man who had two souls, one of which might be that of a god, while waiting to find out if a woman might become a wolf.

When the singing stopped, two wolves sat side by side. At first glance they looked remarkably alike: lean, grey-furred carnivores with only Blind Seer's blue eyes to set them apart. Then Laria noticed little differences. Firekeeper's eyes—which were a wolf's more usual yellow-gold—were rimmed in white fur; outside of this was a thick, dark border, as if the darkness of human Firekeeper's eyes had flowed there. The edges of wolf Firekeeper's ears reminded Laria of human Firekeeper's dark brown hair.

Seeing Laria studying her, Firekeeper panted a laugh, then stretched luxuriously. The motion was completely natural, completely graceful, as if this was the body she had been born to. Firekeeper bumped her head against Blind Seer in a wolf hug, then padded to where she'd set her weapon's belt atop her clothes. She nosed the belt over her head, so that it would rest around her neck.

As she was doing this, Blind Seer padded over to Laria, brushing the becharmed necklace that held Teyvalkay against her hand. Laria understood, but she spoke anyhow, aware that she wanted reassurance before touching the artifact the great grey wolf had claimed for himself.

"You want me to take this?" she asked.

Blind Seer nodded. Laria carefully lifted off the necklace, then draped it crosswise over her torso, where it wouldn't tangle with Volsyl. Firekeeper picked up the little pouch that, along with the tinderbox she always carried, now contained the half of Xixavalkay. She dropped this into the hand that Laria extended, then gave the younger woman a gentle bump with her head.

"Well, I don't know if I'm insulted or not," Chsss said, but there was honest laughter in his voice. "Good luck to the both of you."

Without further delay, the two wolves trotted down the slope, vanishing into the shadows that they would cling to as Farborn guided them closer to the Mended Shield. Laria watched them go, remembering the one time when she had been Blind Seer's partner, thinking wistfully how she wished she could join the wolves now.

She was broken from her reverie by Ranz's voice. "Wait! Firekeeper took her knife, but left her clothes. Has she forgotten she's going to be naked when she changes back?"

"Nude, only," Arasan replied gently. "When you know Firekeeper better, you'll realize she is never naked."

Ranz grinned. "I've seen that for myself. I just wish we could go with them, be more help."

"We're not done with this yet," Laria reassured him. "Your ice and snow making may save us yet."

Ranz reached to affectionately pat the large water bag he wore over his shoulders instead of a backpack. After lack of water had kept him out of the fight against the statue beneath Queen Zorana's tomb, Ranz had resolved that he wouldn't go unarmed onto this new battlefield. Ikitata had fit the base of the water bag with a flexible hose, so that Ranz could access the water without needing to remove the pack. Then Ikitata had shaped the sides so that Ranz could press with his elbows and lower arms to increase the pressure. The device was far from perfect, but it should serve.

Wythcombe pushed himself to his feet. "We should get in position for when they disarm the ward—or to be there to deal with whatever happens if they fail. Blind Seer has solved one problem but, as Laria so neatly put it, we're not done with this yet."

Being a wolf was so wonderful it was almost a disappointment, because it was precisely as Firekeeper had always imagined it would be. As she ran behind Blind Seer, the landscape around her was alive with information that her wolf brain neatly categorized by degrees of importance. She knew where there was water. She knew what creatures lived in this apparently inhospitable landscape. She scented their fear when they realized that two very large carnivores were close by.

Best of all, Firekeeper felt as if she was finally perceiving Blind Seer as he was perceived by other wolves. No wonder Moonfrost had tried to steal him away! He truly was magnificent. She felt her ears melt flat in humility that he had chosen her, then perk up as she laughed at herself for such a very unlike herself reaction. Happily, the wind was coming from in front, and her momentary lapse should have escaped even Blind Seer's sensitive nose.

The wash of information didn't overwhelm Firekeeper any more than the myriad colors and fragrances of the flowers in the formal gardens of Eagle's Nest Castle had overwhelmed her human senses the first time she had encountered such massed planting. What use would be hearing that noted the bending of grass stems or the rolling of pebbles if the mind that received the information could not filter what was important from what was not?

Blind Seer's scent held a wealth of information, including his pride that his spell had worked. There was also a level of weariness one would never have guessed at from his steady trot as he led the way up a trail that would have been nearly invisible to human eyes, but was easily detectable to lupine noses because of the number of creatures, large and small, that used it on a daily basis. The area held no human scent at all, confirming their conjecture that whatever means Kabot had used to reach the castle had taken him directly within the defenses.

Wythcombe's instructions took them not to the massive barred gate, nor to either of the smaller doors that flanked it, but to a section of unremarkable masonry tucked behind a curve of the outer wall. The first challenge to Blind Seer's plan would be getting through this door. Wythcombe knew the ritual needed to unlock it, but if that had been changed, then they would need to beg assistance from Varelle.

Sniffing after scents that Firekeeper could not detect, even with her wolf's nose, Blind Seer pressed a paw against a stone mostly buried beneath the earth, then reared on his hind legs to scrape lichen from a brick. He made several more actions that would have been incomprehensible except that Firekeeper had heard Wythcombe explaining their purposes. Finally, Blind Seer pressed his nose against a stone where a door latch would be on a more usual portal. With a rumble that would have been inaudible to human ears, the stones slid aside, revealing a corridor.

Now to find out if the ward would let two yarimaimalom wolves pass, or if the spell had been designed to eliminate all human-born intruders. Blind Seer stepped through first. Firekeeper, heart pounding in an unfamiliar location in her torso, padded after with what she hoped was confidence. She felt a slight tug, similar to what one feels when diving into water, and then she was through.

Blind Seer licked the side of her face. "I was right! The ward neither broke nor reacted more than I saw it do when a dove landed upon one of the walls as we were mounting the trail."

Farborn wheeled overhead, whistling congratulations. "Hurry now! Getting inside is only the beginning! I will go fetch the humans!"

Blind Seer gently tugged one of Firekeeper's ears between his teeth. "Next we lower the ward."

Firekeeper bumped her head and shoulder against him in agreement, knowing her scent would reveal her regret that the transformation would be over so soon, comforting herself with the thought that this would be far from the last time. If she had been raised to believe in deities, she might have prayed. She even considered sending a quick request to her ancestors after the fashion of her human birthland. As she ran after Blind Seer, wolf paws reading flagstones, ears alive to every sound, she dismissed this impulse. Now, when she was finally a wolf, was not the time to become human.

Wythcombe had told them the route to the room they needed to reach, and after racing up stairs, along corridors, they at last emerged into a vast chamber with floor and ceiling of night-black marble, walls of shimmering dawn pink, lit by a forest circle of glowing crystals.

Until this point, the universe of scent had been all but sterile, but as soon as they entered this rom, Firekeeper immediately caught a human scent. Blind Seer rumbled a growl that said, "Kabot."

His nose dropped as if to seek a trail, but he stopped himself before he had taken more than one step after their adversary.

"First we let the others in." He raised his head to examine their surroundings.

Wythcombe had told them that within the seemingly natural veins of the rose quartz walls was concealed a panel that, when pressed, would temporarily lower the ward.

Firekeeper sat to better study the ceiling, appreciating how her fur protected her from the cool of the stone floor without cutting her off from sensation as her trousers did. She enjoyed how her tail balanced her torso, so she didn't need to put a hand behind her or to stiffen her back muscles. She struggled not to lose herself in the pleasure of her new form, to analyze the constellations arrayed in gems and gold on the domed ceiling above, seeking a specific pattern.

"Locate 'Ox Pulling The Plow,'" Wythcombe had told them, sketching the fanciful array of stars that was supposed to represent this. "The line of the ox's right horn will point to the correct wall. On that wall, midway, the veins of the marble shape a rough building." He had drawn this as well, an irregular rectangle with a lopsided triangle at the top. "Stretch your fingers so that you can touch the peak of the building's roof, the two corners where the roof meets the walls, and the bottom of the right lower wall. Push evenly on all these points. This should release the ward."

Firekeeper was mentally tracing the line of the ox's horn when she felt herself returning human. After having fur, the room felt a little chilly, but she'd never let herself get soft, so accepted the change of temperature stoically. She slung her belt around her waist and, as soon as it was buckled, gave Blind Seer a sad smile.

"It was nice," she said, deliberately speaking Pellish, and he whined agreement.

That was all the self-pity Firekeeper would permit herself. Now that she had her human vision with its great ability to discern color, she searched for variations in the color of the rose quartz until she found what might be the correct pattern. She placed her fingers as Wythcombe had indicated, pressed, but felt no change. She was about to press again when Blind Seer nudged her.

"You chose correctly the first time, dear heart. I caught the scent as the ward lowered. Listen! There are the footsteps of our comrades."

"I'll intercept the others so they don't muddle Kabot's trail." Firekeeper ran lightfoot to the door through which their pack would enter the large domed chamber. Farborn emerged first. Next came Arasan who smiled Chsss's wicked grin and extended her pack to her.

"Not that I don't think you're delightful in belt and little else, but you'll distract Ranz and Wythcombe."

Laria shrugged eloquently. "I'd like to say he's being obnoxious again, but he's probably right. I put your clothes in at the top."

As Firekeeper dressed, she gave them a quick briefing.

"Can Blind Seer track Kabot?" Wythcombe asked.

"*I can try*," Blind Seer said, and Firekeeper translated. "*Happily for us, Kabot's shoes hold dirt from beneath Queen Zorana's tomb. That has a distinct odor, since the rest of us have been elsewhere between.*" He dropped his head and cast about. When he raised it, his ears were canted back. "*Here's something to think about. Kabot's trail originates here.*"

"That means he arrived by magic," Wythcombe sighed, "which surprises none of us. We need to assume he has a several-days' head start on us. We should move quickly."

Blind Seer rumbled a warning growl. "*'It is too late to take cover after the prey has been flushed.' Tell Wythcombe to be patient, or we will make him be patient. Where Kabot is concerned, he is a puppy who sees a mouse, and dashes off over black ice.*"

Firekeeper was about to obey but, from Wythcombe's expression she thought that Wythcombe had gotten the import of Blind Seer's growl. She smiled, pleased as ever by evidence that the learning had not gone all one way.

Before heading off in pursuit of Kabot, Blind Seer permitted himself a final sweet whiff of the scent of Firekeeper-As-Wolf. He'd never confide this to the humans, but he hadn't been certain he could actually manage to shapechange her. When he had succeeded, the awareness of what he could do had nearly overwhelmed him, but even more overwhelming was scenting Firekeeper as the wolf they both knew her to be. Had they been on the trail of some prey less dangerous than Kabot—and, more importantly, his Meddler—Blind Seer would have run wild for the raw joy of knowing that Firekeeper could keep pace with him.

Another day. Another day. Certainly there will be another day. But something deep inside Blind Seer made him fear that by his hasty action he had both won and lost his only chance to have Firekeeper run as wolf beside him.

Such worrying about the future was hardly worthy of a wolf, so Blind Seer lowered his head to signal to the humans that he had Kabot's scent trail, although the traces were sufficiently pungent that he didn't need to hold his nose anywhere close to the marble floor. As he led the way from the large rounded chamber, Blind Seer mused that although Kabot had arrived in this gaudy hall, there was no indication that he had returned. Instead, the trail took them away from elaborately decorated areas that, even now, preserved faint scents of incense and perfumed oils, into areas no less well-constructed, but far less ornate, clearly intended to serve the more routine needs of the inhabitants. Here, for the first time, Blind Seer caught a variety of fresh scents, including one that fascinated him.

"Kabot has passed back and forth through this area numerous times," he told Firekeeper. "More interesting than that, his scent has changed. He is cleaner, more rested."

Firekeeper touched his shoulder lightly in acknowledgement, but didn't bother to translate for the humans. These were doing their best to move quietly for fear of alerting Kabot. Blind Seer did not think this mattered. He believed that Kabot was long gone, but what if he was wrong?

"Don't tell the humans yet, but there are multiple Kabot trails here. Only one holds the old dirt and exhaustion. That is the one I will follow first. I want to learn what new resources he may have."

Ignoring various fascinating side jaunts, Blind Seer traced Kabot's original scent trail to where it ended at a closed and locked door. Chsss quickly disabled the lock, then checked to make certain there was nothing unpleasant waiting for the first person to open the door.

"From this point on," Chsss warned, his lowered voice so filled with tension that he seemed to shout, "we go slowly, check every door, every place where we might be expected to hurry. Kabot knows he's being followed. We can't expect him to make it easy for us to catch him."

Behind the locked door was a tidy little apartment, completely empty. Nonetheless, even to the nose-dead humans there was ample evidence that someone had been staying in it for long enough to cook several meals, sleep, and bathe. However, other than the mute testimony of damp towels, of freshly washed plates and cutlery, Kabot had left no obvious trace of himself or his intentions.

While the humans searched the apartment, Firekeeper and Blind Seer examined various of the side trails. Where a human tracker would have found nothing, Blind Seer's nose found a history. When they returned to their companions, Firekeeper reported, her dark eyes shining with anticipation.

"Kabot search much of this part of the fortress. Over and over his trail goes down stairs, so what he wants is below. Finally, his trail tightens near the large kitchens. We show you. It will be faster."

How quickly the humans followed, their lack of comment or complaint, told that their more detailed search of the apartment had found nothing to add to what had been learned initially. Blind Seer could scent the eagerness in the humans' sweat as they followed the wolves, an eagerness that was unmuted when the great grey wolf halted in front of a perfectly ordinary-looking pantry closet.

Chsss carefully inspected the door. "Seems fine, so all the more reason for me to check again." But when a second check showed nothing more, he shrugged and pulled the door open showing a closet for holding cleaning supplies, the back of which had been removed to reveal a downsloping passage. Doubtless the mops, brooms, and buckets now moved to one side had stood in front of the panel.

Blind Seer tilted his head at Chsss/Arasan, inviting them to check to see if Kabot had left some sort of snare. When they indicated that there didn't seem to be anything dangerous, Blind Seer padded forward to take point. Wythcombe held up a hand to stop him.

"This may be a place where Chsss and I will recognize dangers you will not."

Firekeeper answered for Blind Seer. "You forget. He can scent magic. Do you think he such a pup that he not stop then?"

Wythcombe forced a rueful smile. "I did not overlook his gift, but scent alone may not be enough. Although I am not personally acquainted with this particular passage, it must be one of those that leads to the shield. The 'scent' of magic already pervades the entire area. It will only get stronger as we close on the shield."

Blind Seer considered. He wanted to believe his senses were keen enough to sort fresh scent from that of the background, but it would be foolish to risk himself and the others on that belief. He swung his head to gesture Wythcombe forward. The tunnel was wide enough to accommodate them both.

"I take the back," Firekeeper said.

They had barely gotten to the tunnel's end before Blind Seer sneezed.

"Is that cinnamon?" Laria asked softly, "and lavender?"

"And more," Firekeeper agreed. "Kabot is no fool. A sharp-nosed one follows, so he confuses the trail for the nose."

"Maybe his trick will work against him," Ranz offered. "When we get beyond whatever spices Kabot has scattered here, surely some will linger on his person. Blind Seer can use that to trace him."

"We have a bigger problem," Wythcombe said. "I recognize this. We're on one edge of the old maze. When the shield was anchored here, the maze was left in place. Checking all the false passages could take hours, and that's without dealing with the other defenses, some of which are very nasty. Meanwhile, Kabot…"

He trailed off, the frustration in his tone making further words unnecessary.

Blind Seer sneezed again, pawed at his nose, and growled. *"Firekeeper, translate for me. A rabbit may be dug from her burrow, not only followed through the tunnels she has dug. Let us think like wolves, not humans, and consider what digging we might do."*

Kabot began to realize that he'd gotten into something far bigger than he'd anticipated when he felt Rhinadei's pulse twisting through Guulvalkay deep into the beating heart of the land. As soon as he did, he realized that he hadn't been intended to feel this, but Zazaral's repeated reminders that Wythcombe was on his heels had made Kabot acutely paranoid.

Zazaral, ancient as she was, bodiless for so long, must have forgotten how the body competes with even the most sophisticated mind. Doubtless Zazaral had meant merely to blow the wind into the sails of the boat that was Kabot, to move him more swiftly across the ocean of action. But Kabot, friendless Kabot, Kabot who had never been brave so much as brash, Kabot had reached the limits of where fear could push him.

Kabot huddled into his deepest center. He had become a revolutionary more from pride than from conviction. Envy had played a part, too. Envy of the boy he had called Goldfinch, that bright little spark who had grown into a raging fire. Yes. Envy had played a part, too.

Driven before fear's wind, heeling over, about to spill, Kabot sought the center of his personal gravity. He grasped the quietly analytic nature that had convinced him that treason was reason. Steadied, he groped for security, and almost accidentally pulled the ward Zazaral could not penetrate around him.

Did he mean to shut Zazaral out? Not Zazaral as such. Not the kind, comforting Voice, not the almost-Phiona. Only the fear that—had Kabot himself not been so afraid—he would have long realized was as much Zazaral's fear as his own. Kabot only feared shame and death. Zazaral feared dissolution.

Once the force of Zazaral's fear was muted, Kabot could begin to think again. He let the pulse of his heart serve as timekeeper as he sorted through the confusion of mana threads that surrounded him, much as a knitter might sort back into order balls of yarn the cat had rolled across the floor: These shape the general ward; call them lamb's wool. Here is the ward meant to keep Zazaral out: sticky silk.

What is this? Great ropey cords, heavy but flexible. Kabot's breath quickened as he realized that this must be the great shield about Rhinadei, patched at this location, new fibers spun into frazzled old. Within the fibers was twisted in a metallic thread, seemingly fragile, but possessing a tensile strength that made the others seem wisps. He recognized the source of that fiber and swallowed a gasp of pure astonishment. This was Guulvalkay, no mere thread but the lifeline of Rhinadei itself. In Palvakay, in the half of Xixavalkay, Kabot felt this merely as mana, but this he knew as an infant knows its mother's heartbeat.

Suspicion dripped into Kabot, suspicion of Zazaral. When only his intellect had considered what the rejoined Sykavalkay was, Kabot had been able to convince himself that Zazaral was steering him toward a useful artifact. Now Kabot doubted. Sykavalkay was not a mere artifact, a taunt created by a sorceress to display her power to her uncle. Sykavalkay was a halter wrapped around the world, a halter that could be shoved down to become a garrote.

Kabot wondered how Jyanee could have created such a thing. Remembered Zazaral's boast that she had guided that long-ago artificer. Suspicion, as cold as the death he had been fleeing, seeped into Kabot, suspicion that Zazaral saw him not as a friend, an ally, but as a shovel or pick, useful only to extract a treasure.

What would Zazaral do with that treasure? Surely, most surely, she did not plan on letting Kabot keep it. Kabot froze, undecided, aware that to continue could be death, to wait would be death. "Could" is not "would." Caught between them, he realized how little he had valued trust, now, when he could trust in nothing, not even in himself.

Although she knew that the need for quiet had passed, Laria jumped when Firekeeper spoke to Wythcombe in a normal tone of voice.

"You were of the secret here," the wolf-woman said, shooing the others back up the passage. "Can your mind twist to think where, if we is above, we would go to be over where Guulvalkay is?"

"I just might," he said, rubbing the tip of his nose with his fingers, "I just might. But there will be more than dirt and plant roots in your way."

Firekeeper chuckled. "We have thoughts on that. Humans are more like rabbits, sometimes, than wolves. It is a rare rabbit who does not dig a hidden way from its burrow."

Laria glanced at Arasan. This was exactly the type of comment to which Chsss would be certain to respond, perhaps with a quip about preferring to be thought of as a fox, rather than a rabbit. However, both men remained silent.

Laria studied them more closely, and thought that the two men in one body were conversing with each other.

She realized that, despite their moonspans of travelling together, she was likely the only person in their group who would recognize the signs. In her case, the recognition owed much to when Chsss had been her teacher as she had struggled to control her newly awakened talent. She wondered if she should say anything, then decided that she would settle for keeping a careful eye on them, in case Chsss was up to something.

When they emerged from the passage, Wythcombe consulted some internal compass—and possibly some spell Laria could not detect—and began to lead toward the more ornate areas of the complex, explaining as he did.

"Some time ago, for reasons I was never privy to, it was decided to change the location of the entrance into the subterranean areas where the Shield was anchored."

"Did you know about the passage in the supply closet?" Ranz interrupted.

"I did," Wythcombe admitted, "and would have taken us there, but I couldn't be certain that was where Kabot had gone. Firekeeper and Blind Seer's way was much better. Without them, we would not have learned that Kabot has had opportunity to rest and renew. Therefore, we would still expect to be chasing a tired, half-starved, and panicked man.

"Before you ask, I also knew there was a maze, and would have done my best to guide us through it—and still will, if Blind Seer's plan does not work out. However, it is many years since I was in the confidence of any of Rhinadei's governing bodies, and I cannot be certain that the perils in the maze have not been altered many times since I was last here."

Wythcombe had slowed in an area that, while grand, was not nearly as ornately decorated as had been the astronomically ornamented chamber where they had first entered. Here the centerpiece was an enormous fountain featuring a fanciful undersea scene depicting creatures that Laria would have once thought were imaginary. Now that she knew the peculiar reality of sea monsters, she gave them the benefit of the doubt.

Laria spoke without thinking. "The other entrance is under the fountain. I'd bet it, but if you want…" She spread her hands, indicating her willingness to use her talent to confirm.

"That would be good," Firekeeper said. "Feel as you did when we first came through the gate into Rhinadei. If you could find Varelle's hidden gate, you can find if this also hides a door."

Laria pressed her fingers to the lip of the fountain, let her talent wander. She found what she was seeking almost instantly: a sense of purpose that probably reflected not only the construction of the hidden passage, but the spells that protected it.

"It's here. A larger opening beneath the water than would be needed for a drain."

Arasan broke a long silence. "Problem. Unless Wythcombe knows how to disable these wards as he did with the one that protected the fortress, we will surely set off an alarm."

"This wasn't confided to me," Wythcombe admitted. "If you and I worked together, Chsss, we could probably undo them, but it will take time. Perhaps the maze would be best."

Ranz interrupted, enthusiasm lighting his grey eyes. "If I froze the water coming into the basin, then we would have a clearer look at Laria's passage. Freezing shouldn't alert anyone, especially if I leave a trickle of water flowing, in case there is some sort of alert if the fountain clogs. I'm guessing that this is a mostly closed system that recirculates a limited amount of water."

"Good thinking," Firekeeper said as he drew breath to explain further. "Do it."

XII

Firekeeper watched, outward patience concealing inner tension as the water entering the basin froze into an icicle that reminded her of a sword blade.

Ranz studied his work critically as the water level in the basin dropped. "Search quickly. Even if this is a closed system, there must be some means for more water to be added. Otherwise, evaporation would eventually cause the fountain to run dry. I can keep freezing the water, but too much ice would create problems of its own."

Firekeeper glanced at Chsss, usually so eager to show off, saw how Arasan's expression was closed, as if deep in thought. She might have said something, but Wythcombe was already moving forward, motioning for Laria to join him. Together, the oldest and youngest members of Firekeeper's little pack studied the emptying basin with far more senses than those Firekeeper could command, consulting in a soft undertone. She tried not to feel inadequate but, when Blind Seer gently nudged her hand, she knew that her partner, at least, knew her frustration.

"We've worked it out," Wythcombe said, pushing himself to his feet with his staff. "Ranz was correct. This is a closed system. We're fortunate. There's a completely mechanical shut-off, probably…"

Firekeeper interrupted. "Can we go this way or do we need to break through floor?"

Wythcombe blinked. "We can get through here, probably without setting off any alarms."

"Good. We do this. Kabot and his Meddler have days ahead of us."

Although obviously still eager to explain rather than do, Wythcombe recruited Ranz and Laria to assist him. While they were pushing this and pressing that, Blind Seer nudged Firekeeper again.

"Is it Arasan who has you so tense, dear heart?"

"Yes. Chsss is too quiet."

"Maybe so. Maybe not. I scent no great magics from him."

"*A mole's tunnel may break an elk's leg*," Firekeeper quoted.

"True."

Ranz's voice recaptured their attention. "Well, we've gotten it open, but do we dare lower that?"

As one, Firekeeper and Blind Seer padded over. The entire bottom of the fountain's basin had pulled away, revealing a wide shaft that extended straight down into inky darkness. Partially blocking the shaft was a boxy platform large enough to hold their entire group. The platform was suspended by thick ropes run over a series of pulleys. Firekeeper crouched and looked over the edge, her night-seeing eyes perceiving within the darkness. Neither sound nor scent indicated that anyone was below.

Wythcombe was studying the ropes and pulleys. "If we use this, we will definitely trigger an alarm. Is it worth the risk?"

Blind Seer had also poked his head over the edge. "*Translate for me, Firekeeper. Wythcombe, if we scout before you, then make a light, can you create a spell to transport the rest of you? You have said you can bridge what you have seen.*"

"I can but…"

"Can this platform be pulled to one side without setting off the alarm?"

Wythcombe narrowed his eyes and made a few finger gestures. "As long as it does not go up or down."

"How long will it take you to make your spell?"

"I have one prepared for our retreat. I can adapt that quickly enough."

"Good. You adapt. We will go down. When it is safe to do so, we will make light. Farborn will come with us, both to scout and to alert you if we have made a poor choice."

Firekeeper had hardly finished her translation when Blind Seer flexed his shoulders, unfolding from them the moth wings he had created for himself when impulse, rather than wisdom, had chosen the form. Firekeeper knew from experience that those wings could bear them both, and grinned as she lightly set herself astride Blind Seer's torso.

"We go. Is deep but not so deep that a lantern's light will not serve." She extended one hand, and Laria handed over the unlit lantern she carried. Farborn had already darted below. He popped up again, spinning and darting in a fashion even the humans could read as meaning he had detected no immediate danger.

To Firekeeper and Blind Seer, Farborn said, "Below there is a closed door, quite large. Beyond it, I thought I heard something, or perhaps my talons"—he flexed the crystal-covered appendages—"tingled."

Blind Seer bowed his head in appreciation. "If you will go ahead of us, it is possible your talons may warn us further. They are Rhinadei's gift. It is possible this land does not like what Kabot and his Voice are about."

The last time Firekeeper had ridden Blind Seer when he flew using these improbable wings, she had been in a great deal of pain, as well as rattled from a nearly fatal fall. This time, she had the luxury to get nervous. She fought not to hold her breath when Blind Seer tilted his nose down, kicked off the platform's edge, then dove into the darkness. For a terrifying moment, they fell rather than flew. Then she felt the beat of his muscles and heard his wings catch the air, slowing their descent.

They glided down, the steady beat of the wolf's wings pushing them up while, or so it seemed to Firekeeper, the ground itself tried to drag them down. When they landed, her feet touched the ground almost as soon as did his paws. She stepped free, extracting her fire-making tools from the pouch about her neck.

Blind Seer stepped toward the door, his hackles rising, even as he folded his wings against his flanks. "Hurry, Firekeeper. Farborn is right. Something is happening out there. We're out of time."

"Don't tell me," Kabot said when Zazaral began to speak. "Wythcombe is here. He has caught up to me again. This time we can't run, can we?"

"We can," Zazaral assured him, her voice silky soothing. "You have found Guulvalkay, yes? I will help you twine it with the others. We'll have power enough to escape. Even better: the piece of Xixavalkay lies next to Teyvalkay. Through the one, we will hook the other. With over half of Sykavalkay assembled, who can stop us?"

"I'm afraid," Kabot said, speaking part of the truth to hide his more personal fear, "that if I remove Guulvalkay, I may damage, even destroy, Rhinadei's shield."

"What of it?" Zazaral scoffed. "With the power of Sykavalkay, the shield can be remade even better, stronger. The one who does so will be hailed as a hero, even as a god."

Distrust let Kabot hear what Zazaral did *not* say. She did not say "*You* can remake the shield. *You* will be hailed as a hero." Kabot suspected that the one who would be hailed as a god would not be him, but would be Zazaral, and that he—Kabot—would be cast as the adversary in an only partially true recounting of events.

Stalling, he said, "I can try."

Moving Kabot's fingers as she had moved his body, used his spells to get them through the maze, Zazaral said, gently as a lover, "Let me help."

Kabot tried to resist, tried, even, to alter the shape of the spell he felt building, but even with the ward wrapped around him, his body remained Zazaral's to use as she wished. He felt her chuckle rumble through his chest.

"Relax. There is too little time for me to be careless. I do not precisely fear Wythcombe, but there are those I would not give opportunity to interfere."

Kabot's hands shaped complex signs he did not know. He felt Palvalkay, then the half of Xixavalkay flare, lightless tongues of fire that blended without heat, holding an intensity that multiplied, rather than merely added. No longer were they two threads, but were transformed into a fragment of Sykavalkay. As such, they reached for Guulvalkay, but something reached to block them. The rainbow ward? No, something else, something that made Zazaral hiss and curse. Kabot wondered if Rhinadei's shield was more potent than Zazaral had anticipated.

Then he saw, shadows cast by Sykavalkay's lightless flame, two figures wrapped about Guulvalkay. Attenuated, but still somehow female, the pair reeked of power and of age. But, despite the force that vibrated from them, Kabot doubted that these protectors could stop Zazaral and the newly rejoined Sykavalkay, especially since Guulvalkay yearned toward Sykavalkay of its own accord.

Kabot heard himself shouting for help. To his heartfelt astonishment, the name that leapt unbidden to his lips was "Goldfinch!"

Snuffling ineffectually at the far side of a closed door, Blind Seer noticed the door handle was a lever, not a knob or latch.

Surely it is locked, he thought as he reared back on his hind legs to bring his weight to bear, but the latch moved. He smelled the scent of sparks on dry tinder, knew precious breaths would pass before Firekeeper could join him.

"The door is open," he said. "I go to scout. Follow when you can. Let Farborn take care of the humans."

"Wait!"

The speaker was not Firekeeper, but Arasan. When Blind Seer growled softly, against all precedent, Arasan laid a light hand on his shoulder. How had he gotten down?

"We do the dominance thing later," Arasan said. "Chsss has concealed himself deep within me. We need you to guide us to where Kabot and his Meddler are. Now that we're so close, he recognizes her: an ancient, sometimes called Zazaral. Chsss will do what he can to neutralize Zazaral. While he does so, the rest of you must get Sykavalkay from Kabot."

Had Blind Seer been human, he might have argued, asked for explanations. Had he been only a wolf, he would definitely need to discover which of them was dominant. Being what he was, he did neither. Nor did he ask Firekeeper if she had heard, for he knew that she surely had. Instead, his actions became his reply.

Not shaking Arasan's hand from where it rested, Blind Seer breathed deeply, searching not only for Kabot, but for traces of arcane workings. He found both, then stepped into purest darkness. Guided by scent, he led Arasan to a corridor that sloped gently down. To his relief, a glimmer of light showed as soon as they rounded the first bend. From here, Farborn would be able to guide the others without showing a light.

The route beneath the fountain had been made for emergencies, so here there were no traps, no doors, no tricks. Doubtless the closed chamber at the base of the shaft had been intended to muffle the sound of the platform descending. Now that the door was opened, action was all that would matter. Resisting the urge to stretch out his muscles and run, Blind Seer led Arasan, wondering whether putting his trust in Chsss was purest folly.

The chamber at the corridor's end was etched top, bottom, and on all sides with magical symbols. Despite this, the vast space lacked the elegance of the ornamented halls above, but for an eldritch firefly brilliance that filled the air. The swarm of multicolored lights originated where Kabot, his shadow looming larger than it should, was struggling with what, to Blind Seer's vision, was nothing more than sparkle, but to his magic-sensing nose smelled like two human females.

"We're too late!" Arasan gasped. "Kabot has surrendered his will to Zazaral."

Wild defiance filled Blind Seer. "If this Zazaral is anything like you, Chsss, then I can make this one regret assuming a mortal's body. Watch!"

He leapt, swallowing his howl until the fragile moment when he would cross from shadow into the coruscating light. Remembering Laria's face twisted in terror, her blood running down her throat, the blue-eyed wolf could barely restrain his desire to snap Kabot's neck. Then he caught something in Kabot's scent that made Blind Seer wonder if Kabot was resisting Zazaral. If so, then for this moment, they were allies.

Blind Seer slammed into Kabot, knocking the man onto his backside, pinning him with his paws. He smelled urine, felt the sting of a building storm, and leapt clear before a surge of lightning could course through his bones.

As he twisted in midair, Blind Seer scented a cloud with a vaguely human shape oozing from Kabot. He snapped at it, but his fangs slid through the insubstantial form. However, Blind Seer was not hunting alone. With a spring nearly twin to Blind Seer's own, Chsss departed the protection of Arasan's body and latched onto what had inhabited Kabot.

Immediately, Blind Seer knew that Chsss was tremendously overmatched. His clouded shape was smaller than his opponent's, and began to fray, as if being blown apart by a tempest no one else could feel. Arasan raced forward to help Chsss, but what could a musician do against a bodiless demi-deity?

Kabot was struggling to his feet, terror evident on his features, hands rising to cup the partial Sykavalkay he wore about his neck. Maybe Kabot only intended to defend himself, but Blind Seer wasn't going to wait to find out. He crashed into Kabot again, stood with his forepaws on the man's shoulders, lowered his head to within inches of Kabot's sharp nose, and growled.

Kabot's reaction was utterly sensible. He fainted. As the man's limp fingers slid from Sykavalkay, the charms rose in the air and hovered, shifting back and forth between two points. One must be Guulvalkay; the other was doubtless Teyvalkay and the bit of Xixavalkay which remained in Laria's custody. Uncertain what the partial Sykavalkay might do to him, Blind Seer pulled back, but kept his weight solidly on Kabot's torso.

Footsteps thumped down the corridor, announcing the remainder of the pack hurrying to join them. The first to reach Blind Seer knelt beside him with barely a sound. Seeing what was needed, Firekeeper removed short lengths of rope from one of her belt pouches. By the time the others arrived—led by Ranz, followed by Laria, with Wythcombe huffing up last—Kabot was bound. Together Firekeeper and Blind Seer moved to see what they could do to rebalance the unequal battle between Chsss and Zazaral.

"Chsss must have knowed he cannot win," Firekeeper said, her voice tight with frustration. "So if he do this, he do this so we can win. But how with a prey we cannot touch?"

During his battle against querinalo, Blind Seer had gone into spaces where the then-bodiless Meddler had been embodied. He suspected that now Meddler battled Meddler in some similar space.

"Ask Wythcombe, can he make us a way to where they are, fast."

Firekeeper translated, and Wythcombe replied. "If Arasan still has a link to Chsss, perhaps, but I would need more mana than..."

Blind Seer interrupted. *"Tell Laria and Farborn to give Wythcombe the artifacts."*

Firekeeper did, but her slumped shoulders said she wondered if they would ever get them back.

Blind Seer huffed. *"It will not matter if we do not defeat this one. Even now, Chsss dims. When he is eaten, then this other will take all the threads and weave them into one whole."*

"I know. But you won the hunt, and have not eaten from the kill."

"I eat, even if not from the head wolf's portion."

Arasan had hastened to Wythcombe. "What should I do?" He gestured to his knife, spread a hand as if offering to cut himself.

Wythcombe shuddered. "We are not sunk so low. Your music is magic. Sing!"

Arasan drew breath, then, with the aplomb of a seasoned performer, launched into a ballad about a gentleman rogue and a ridiculous gamble. Wythcombe began a chant that blended with the ballad as the howls of wolves young and old blend in songs to the moon. A portal did not so much open as the two struggling shapes seemed more solid. Blind Seer saw them as wolves. He did not doubt that the humans saw them as humans.

Fleetingly, he wondered what Firekeeper saw them as, but did not ask. Chsss-wolf was bleeding from numerous slashes. Despite this, he kept a fierce grip on his attacker's scruff, forcing the other to drag him as, with single-minded intensity, it paced toward what Blind Seer's senses showed him both as a delicious buck and a potent magical aura: Guulvalkay.

"We go!" he howled and, with Firekeeper beside him, Farborn clinging to her shoulder, they leapt forward.

***

Laria hadn't tried to read the artifacts while they were in her custody, but their power had been so intense that she would have needed far more skill at shielding herself to keep them from making an impression on her. Even after she surrendered them to Wythcombe, she remained attuned to the magical currents that permeated the chamber.

Wythcombe and the two artifacts were easy to sense. From there she slid along Xixavalkay to its other half. Beside it was a spicy glow, like but unlike that of Teyvalkay. That must be Palvalkay. Here she paused, squinching shut her eyes to better read the impressions.

With her eyes closed, Laria was aware as never before of the auras of her companions. Then there was Kabot. She shrank from letting her awareness go closer to him, associating him with the sting of the knife on her throat, the crippling panic. She pressed closer, confirmed what she had heretofore only vaguely suspected, then looked for help.

Wythcombe was chanting something under his breath. Firekeeper and Blind Seer poised to spring, Farborn on Firekeeper's shoulder. Ranz hovered near Wythcombe, ready to assist if called upon, but too courteous to intervene without request. Laria tapped Ranz on the shoulder. When he looked down at her, she stretched so she could speak directly in his ear.

"Chsss drove Zazaral from Kabot, but he didn't break Kabot's connection to Palvalkay and his bit of Xixavalkay. Zazaral is drawing on them through Kabot. Can you do something?"

She felt proud when Ranz didn't ask why she was so certain. He only nodded.

"I'll try."

Wythcombe was doing something that Laria felt as realities being dragged into harmony. Arasan had adapted his song. The gambler had cards up his sleeve. Laria hoped that she and Ranz could be two of those cards.

She pointed to where the artifacts were secreted beneath Kabot's shirt, close to his heart. She shuddered. Not just close. They were intertwined with his flesh, sinking deeper. She wondered if the living statue they had fought had, perhaps, taken on its own unlife in this way.

Ranz squeezed water into his hand, froze it into a curving knife blade. With this he slit Kabot's shirt from navel to throat, and then pulled it aside. At the choking noise he made when he saw the artifacts sinking through Kabot's skin, Kabot opened his eyes.

"Do it. I wanted to learn blood magic. I'm having second thoughts."

In those few words, the slight smile Kabot forced to his lips, Laria understood the loyalty Kabot had engendered in his cabal, why Wythcombe still loved him after these many years and so many betrayals. Suddenly, she, also, didn't want to see Kabot die. Nonetheless, the threads of Sykavalkay could not be left where they were, feeding mana to Zazaral.

Ranz showed himself the doctor's son as he dropped to his knees beside Kabot. He reshaped his ice blade into a scalpel, then splashed water onto the peculiarly bloodless wound in Kabot's chest, freezing flesh and artifacts alike. Laria saw the mana that flowed from the threads toward Zazaral slow, and guessed that Ranz had woven a barrier into his ice.

She had to look away when Ranz actually began to cut into Kabot, memories of the hospital on the Nexus Islands flooding her, bringing with them an overwhelming wash of grief, fear, and desperation. Thus she saw how Firekeeper, Blind Seer, and Farborn were fighting something that was one moment human, one moment wolf, sometimes a hybrid of the two, sometimes, weirdly, even a swarm of bees. When it was this last, Farborn was in his element, snatching individuals from the swarm, squeezing them in half with his crystalline talons. The parts that fell to the floor did not rejoin the swarm, while the wounds Firekeeper and Blind Seer inflicted healed at an alarming rate.

Laria bit into her lip. Farborn bore a weapon given by Rhinadei. Volsyl was of Rhinadei as well. Perhaps it would also cause lasting injury. She drew the sword, feeling its delight that it would be able to guide her in such a noble cause. Laria circled swiftly to where she could join the battle without crowding her allies. As she closed, the misty figure became less human, less wolf, more the bee swarm, perhaps because the swarm could split and face many opponents without greatly diminishing its effectiveness.

Growling, Blind Seer spread his wings and took flight, circling above so that the swarm could not escape, buffeting it with the downdraft of his wings. Laria gestured as if to give Volsyl to Firekeeper, but the wolf-woman shook her head.

"Yours! I get my own."

Laria wondered what Firekeeper could possibly mean, but slashed gamely at the edges of the swarm. Her blows were hampered because Chsss—seen as a human who looked a little like Arasan, a little like Laria's late father, Ollaris—

was enshrouded within the swarm. He resisted with weapons Laria could feel but not see, growing weaker with every breath.

Then Firekeeper returned, holding a wildly burning torch that, with every step she took, became less a torch and more a long knife with a blade of white-hot fire. Laria sensed that this transformation was an element of the charm Wythcombe had cast to make it possible for them to reach Zazaral. On impulse, she drew upon her tenuous link to Teyvalkay and willed Volsyl into flame.

Smoke and fire are deadly to bees, hardly less deadly to human or wolf. Zazaral erratically flickered between shapes, seeking some advantage. The link to Sykavalkay that had been an advantage now became a chain. Zazaral severed it with a gesture. The remaining bees in the swarm cradled Chsss in a lover's embrace.

"You have thwarted me," Zazaral buzzed, and nuzzled Chsss. "But I will take you with me so you may make amends."

Chsss must know that neither burning blades nor even Farborn's agile talons could pull him loose. Nonetheless, he forced something of his usual insouciant expression.

"We'll see," he said. "We'll see."

But Laria was having nothing of this noble resignation. Her father had died in her arms. She wasn't about to lose the one who had been a father to her newly talented self. Volsyl could slice through spells, then surely…

Not bothering to shape the rest of the thought, Laria willed Volsyl to excise Chsss from Zazaral's hold. The power of Teyvalkay washed through her with an intensity that brought her down onto one knee and nearly blacked her out. She refused to lose her focus, because to do so would be to fail her father all over again. Volsyl moved in a complicated series of slices that nearly took Laria's arms out of her shoulder joints and made her wrists pop, but it cut Chsss free.

As soon as the swarm parted, Blind Seer dropped down from above, grabbed Chsss and hauled him from Zazaral's encircling hold. As the wolf's moth wings beat with a speed worthy of Farborn's knife-edged wings, Zazaral screamed in rage, collapsing upon herself. Then, with an inrush of air that made Laria's ears pop, Zazaral vanished.

Laria tried to struggle to her feet, fell instead, and Firekeeper caught her. The pride on the wolf-woman's face healed something long-broken in the younger woman. She burst into tears, and Firekeeper patted her.

"You've done well," the husky voice said. "Very, very well."

Kabot decided he was fed up with fainting, but he supposed that doing so while someone excised talismans from his flesh was a reasonable reaction. When he came to, someone had tightly bandaged his wound, which didn't hurt nearly as much as he thought it should. That serious-looking young mage must be something of a prodigy.

The large room was no longer filled with the violent storm of sparks that had erupted as soon as Zazaral had begun to probe the wards. A woman was speaking. This wasn't Zazaral, nor Laria, nor Firekeeper. She spoke with an accent he couldn't place, and though her voice was level and controlled, there was strength behind it.

"We cannot leave Sykavalkay intact," the speaker was saying. "Long since, I suspected that Zazaral had prompted me to create it for her own purposes. Still, pride and anger made me complete it. I hinted to my uncle that he could prove his worth by destroying it, but he only went as far as separating the threads."

Kabot struggled to sit up, found firm hands lifting him, and saw Firekeeper at his side. Guard or nurse? He didn't care. He nodded politely, then turned to face the speaker. In the two ethereal women who now addressed the group, he recognized the aura that had defended Guulvalkay—and himself—from Zazaral.

"Are you Jyanee? That isn't how Zazaral told the story, not precisely, but I guess she wouldn't. Why would she want you to make such a thing?"

A smoky masculine shape said, "Meddlers often crave immortality. One lifetime doesn't seem enough to set everything right. Zazaral seems to have been thinking big."

If he sounded impressed, Kabot didn't blame him.

Ranz asked, "But, Chsss, if Zazaral was so powerful, why didn't she just make Sykavalkay herself?"

Chsss replied, "Having a lot of power and matching ambition does not equal having the ability to implement ideas—a great architect may not know how to mix mortar. And Zazaral *is* a Meddler. We justify a great deal by thinking we're showing others how to best reach their potential."

Laria asked, "But, great ladies, why didn't you destroy the threads later? I mean, when you realized that Zazaral was using you?"

"Zazaral," said the second ethereal form, who Kabot realized was Onorina, "gave hints that soon would come a great disaster, and that the shield defending Rhinadei would fall were it not bolstered. I convinced Jyanee to let me link Guulvalkay, which taps Rhinadei's own magic, to the shield here, where I resided as keeper. She agreed. But Zazaral then came for it, as the least defended of the four threads. We bound ourselves to protect it."

Firekeeper huffed. "Virim and querinalo were like an avalanche, I think. So Rhinadei's shield held because of Guulvalkay?"

"It did. Yet now I realize that the threads must all be untwined," Jyanee said. "Even if they were buried at the planet's heart, Zazaral or some other would find them. Onorina and I have weakened over the long decades of our vigil. Even this time, we could do little more than protect Guulvalkay."

Wythcombe spoke, "What will happen to the Shield without Guulvalkay to enhance it? Will it fall?"

Onorina shook her head. "But it will need more tending than has been given, especially at weak points such as this one. It seems that some responsibilities have been forgotten."

Wythcombe nodded. "I have long believed so. The rituals that once were done seasonally and throughout Rhinadei are now done only yearly, and only at the one remaining gate."

"It will take more than seasonal rituals to preserve places like this"—Onorina's loose hand gesture indicated the Mended Shield—"especially from creatures like Zazaral. She is greatly weakened, but she now bears no love for Rhinadei."

Kabot cleared his throat. "I realize that I'm a doomed man, but in these last hours I realized that I love Rhinadei more than I knew. Wythcombe, if you would speak for me, I would swear an oath, as binding as any wish, that in penance for my crimes I will devote the remainder of my life to tending this shield."

He almost saw the boy who had been his childhood friend in the grin that lit Wythcombe's face. "I could make myself your custodian. The counsel might agree, especially if I hinted that otherwise I will go explore this great wide world that is now open to us. I can be a hermit here as well as on a mountaintop."

Jyanee spread her hands. "You living must do what you can. I cannot be swayed from my course. I wove Sykavalkay. Now here assembled are the pieces, and I will unweave them."

Jyanee and Onorina stood tall and proud as, with a sound like breaking harp strings, Sykvalkay untwined. Right hand clasped in left, the ancient sorceresses made a gesture mingling benediction and farewell. Then, as the artifact that had both extended and distorted their existence swirled apart, they faded, ebbed, and were gone.

"Subtly handled," Wythcombe announced, but Firekeeper did not need Blind Seer's nose to tell that the old spellcaster was shaken. "Nonetheless, there are those in Rhinadei who will have sensed the shield weakening. It won't be long before some arrive here. Chsss, you might want to absent yourself."

Firekeeper looked to where Chsss, to her eyes wearing the guise of a particularly striking creature with a wolf's head upon a more or less human body, stood surveying them all. Although he wasn't completely solid, he was impossible to ignore. He panted a grin half-laughter, half-challenge. Blind Seer rumbled a low warning growl.

Chsss ignored this, though Firekeeper had no doubt he had heard. Instead he surveyed their company, his wry grin not hiding his genuine affection.

"I suppose I must go. If you're not going to force Kabot to bear the full blame for what has happened, you're going to need to mention Zazaral, and mentioning Zazaral will doubtless place suspicion on the head of even innocent, helpful me. I did…"

But whatever Chsss was about to say was cut off by Arasan.

"You could go and not, you know. I mean, you could come back to me."

Chsss's astonishment was genuine. "Our deal was done. Your body was loaned to me, as long as I could keep it from dying. I did. But I won't hold you to an agreement made on such terms, especially when I was the one to break it."

"To fight for us," Arasan replied, his voice taking on his storytelling cadence, "that's why you left. Let's not embarrass each other with sentimentality or gratitude. Let's just say I've gotten used to having someone to talk with when I wake up in the middle of the night. You're welcome here, even if you did, perhaps, withhold just a wee bit about how powerful you still may be, eh?"

Chsss hesitated long enough that Firekeeper wondered if perhaps he would prefer to resume the freedom of the disembodied. Then he chuckled.

"The emergency counsel never even suspected that we two were in your body. Wythcombe now, I think he did but was too polite, but…" The chuckle turned into laughter. "I'll take your offer, Arasan, but on these terms. None but us here will know about my role in Zazaral's defeat. Now that I think about it, do they need to know about Zazaral at all?"

Wythcombe considered. "I only mentioned Sykavalkay to Varelle, not that we suspected Kabot might have an ally beyond his original cabal."

Chsss's grin widened. "Then let them believe that some bit of your magic, Wythcombe—perhaps in combination with Kabot realizing that he'd bitten off more than he could chew—brought the artifact to heel so its creator could destroy it. Yes, I like that. I've always preferred to do my good deeds in secret."

Blind Seer snorted laughter. *"Be quick about it then. I smell a change in the winds. We will have company soon."*

Firekeeper translated, adding, "We wolves go to meet them. You humans, shape words to protect this outlier who wishes to join the pack once more."

She saw Kabot's eyes widen when he realized she meant him. "You'll accept my offer? Even after all I did?"

"Wolves," Firekeeper replied, "know to accept an honest surrender. Why weaken the pack?"

She looked over at Laria, to whom Kabot had done the most direct harm, and saw that the younger woman was deep in thought, tapping her fingers as if counting off some tally Firekeeper could only imagine.

Later, after Firekeeper and Blind Seer escorted Orten, Bordyn, Hanya, Varelle, and Erldon to the shield chamber, Arasan wove a tale explaining what had happened, concluding with a rousing description of Jyanee and Onorina destroying Sykavalkay. As Wythcombe had suspected, those who were associated with Rhinadei's shield had felt when Guulvalkay had been withdrawn.

"Your story is beyond belief," Orten, the Five Spirits Alchemist, snapped. "Would anyone give up artifacts of such power?"

"We didn't give them up," Wythcombe repeated with more patience than Firekeeper thought merited. "Sykavalkay's creator…"

But if Wythcombe was prepared to repeat the explanation, Ranz had had enough.

"As 'beyond belief,'" Ranz interjected, his voice icy with fury, "as that an entire community would give up blood magic?" He used the Pellish term, not the Rhinadeian "anathema art." "Even when that renunciation meant accepting the deaths of mothers in childbed and their unborn babes with them? Even that? Having learned the half-truths that underlie what we're taught as Rhinadei's history, I wonder if the renunciation was always so complete. Perhaps my father's greatest crime was publicly admitting what he'd done."

"*I think Ranz has them there,*" Blind Seer said, shifting his posture in case his fellow apprentice needed defending.

"Ranz, leave your wonderings for another time," Wythcombe said kindly. "They are valid, but we must stay focused on the issue at hand. Counselors, we have presented the truth regarding what happened here. If you stop panicking, you'll realize there is no way we could conceal artifacts of such power from your august selves. What needs to be resolved is whether you will accept my offer—and Kabot's—to remain here and do what we can to bolster the shield now that Guulvalkay is no more. Consider…"

Bordyn, the Chief Elementalist, tried to interrupt, but Wythcombe silenced him with a gesture so fierce Firekeeper resolved to remember it.

"Consider this, if you take our offer, Rhinadei will be in a perfect situation to monitor us. If you do not take our offer, then we will take our leave—all of us."

"Not Kabot!" Bordyn insisted. "He has broken the law. He must pay."

With a cool hiss of metal on metal, Laria drew Volsyl and stepped in front of Kabot. "He's not your prisoner. He's *our* prisoner. Where do you get off claiming the right to punish him? You've been forgetting that most of us don't acknowledge your rule. Our chase ended here, sure, but that doesn't give Rhinadei's rulers any rights."

Varelle asked gently, "Laria, from what I was told earlier, Kabot kidnapped you, injured you. Why are you protecting him?"

Laria shrugged, but didn't lower Volsyl. "Kabot was idealistic, stupid, like a lot of idealists are. I think he's learned. Part of the price paid for Kabot's lesson was my blood, my fear. The only way to keep that from being wasted is for me to believe that somehow good can come out of what Kabot put all of us through."

Erldon, the Lore Lover, turned to his associates. "Even if you want to argue with young Laria's philosophy—which I, for one, don't—she has a point. Kabot is not in our custody. We can accept Kabot's surrender and his desire to make reparations, and so keep him where we can monitor him. We can accept Wythcombe's offer to serve as Kabot's custodian. Or we can fight those who claim Kabot as their prisoner. In the process, a great deal of harm would surely be done. The shield is weak here, and should not be subjected to undue magical energies. Remember, among those who stand here, ready to oppose us, are several potent spellcasters. Even those who do not use magic are not so in awe of us as to stand idle."

Firekeeper grinned a wolf's grin. "Erldon is wise."

Hanya, the Dance Warrior, added, "I would be happy to join Wythcombe in his vigil. The counsel would then have a member in residence."

"I want to stay, too," Ranz said. "I've barely started my training. I think Kabot and I need to learn many of the same lessons."

There was more grumbling, a few protests, but Firekeeper could tell these were the posturing of wolflings who did not wish to be seen backing down too easily.

Blind Seer eased back on his haunches. "*The scents are changing. Orten and Bordyn are now worried where they were not before. Greed is fading in place of fear of what will happen if they push Wythcombe—and us. Varelle—she is the hardest to read—but I don't think she ever doubted our story. Erldon is philosophical by nature, and Hanya has a fondness for Wythcombe, although he will probably never return it.*"

Reassured, Firekeeper let her hand drift from her Fang. Doubtless the humans would continue to argue about the fine points. In the end, no one would have precisely their way, but none would be too shamed.

Blind Seer added, "*What we cannot mention, since we have decided to hide Zazaral's role in this, is that Kabot will have great incentive to keep Rhinadei's shield strong. Zazaral will not easily forgive him his mutiny, weak as it was, and he knows she has his scent. Kabot will need protection, lifelong. Staying with Wythcombe will give him that.*"

"What about you?" Firekeeper asked. "Will you stay here to learn from Wythcombe? I have not forgotten that it was your search that led us here, what you learned here that let you give me—even if for a short time—a wolf's shape to fit my wolf's soul. Rhinadei is not the land I would choose to live in, but I would choose less to go without you. The decision must be yours."

"Let me see how this is resolved," Blind Seer replied. "When I know, then I can answer."

Blind Seer suspected that not all the emergency council had fully accepted the tale Arasan had spun, but their reasons for doubt differed so greatly that he also felt certain they would never come to a consensus. After much discussion, the humans decided that since Kabot's mutiny had never been widely publicized, all that would be said was that he had overreached himself and been trapped for decades. Wythcombe had tracked him down, freed him, then had taken him on as an apprentice, along with Ranz. Why the Mended Shield had been chosen as their new residence would not even be of interest to most, since the fortification's role as an anchor point for Rhinadei's shield was not widely known.

Knowing these members of what had been his pack were secure was good, because Blind Seer had made up his mind as to what he wanted to do next.

When the emergency council had departed, Blind Seer explained, *"I do not wish to stay in Rhinadei. This tormented land, even the 'healed' areas, make my paws itch. I want healthy soil, clean hunting, free from the suspicion that we ingest old secrets with every breath."*

Firekeeper paused in her translation and asked. "But we bring you here to find a teacher, and the teacher we find you, he must stay here."

Blind Seer replied. *"Wythcombe has taught me a great deal. Without him, I would not have learned how to store mana. Nor would I have understood about channels. And the lessons about wizards' tools… I have thoughts there, too. But I have also learned that my magic is very different from human magic. I think I need to hunt after more learning on my own."*

To Blind Seer's pleasure, Wythcombe did not seem in the least insulted. "Goodbyes will be sad, but not forever. Rhinadei will be pursuing at least limited contact with other lands, and if you have questions, you know where I will be."

Blind Seer bowed a long, low wolf bow in acknowledgement.

"So we go to the Nexus Islands, then?" Firekeeper said.

"Yes," he said, "and farther still. Perhaps you and I should go back to the wilder parts of the New World, find an area where we two will threaten no pack. There I could hunt after my own way to channel magic. I wonder if there are other yarimaimalom spellcasters, keeping their abilities secret as I have done."

Firekeeper did not translate this last, but replied only for his ears. "I've wondered about that too. That has made me wonder something else. Why haven't we found any trace of yarimaimalom except in the New World? Oh, there have been a few here and there, but they all trace their origin to the New World. Once I believed we would find others everywhere we went, and certainly we have not seen all the world, but still…"

Blind Seer huffed out through his nose. "*That is a hunt to pursue some other day. For now, I want to go home.*"

Firekeeper grinned, dark eyes dancing with merriment. "Me, too! Derian will be so astonished with all we have done. It's going to be fun to watch him when we tell him there are other Meddlers than ours still playing games."

When Arasan, assisted by Firekeeper and Laria, had concluded their report, Derian—who had returned for the occasion via the Hawk Haven gate—rubbed his face with both hands. "Just when we think we have matters settled… Firekeeper, I'm beginning to believe Chsss is right, and you really are a Meddler. What do you plan to do next?"

"We go to the mainland, run for a while, not meddle in anything," Firekeeper answered, and Blind Seer grinned at how she had learned to summon an aura of almost girlish innocence when needed. "I think Arasan and Laria, they have plans of their own."

Arasan nodded. "Maybe I'll make some goodwill journeys through the gates, especially into the Old World. While I'm at it, I'll sing a few songs, pick up any interesting rumors. Rhinadei has shown that isolation is safe only as long as no one threatens you. Our experience with Zazaral is a reminder that not all enemies may be corporeal. I thought Laria might come with me."

Laria tugged at her beribboned braid, considering. "Maybe for a bit, but I've been thinking that what I really need to do is get some formal education. If the Nexus Islands are going to keep doing business with monarchs and all, we're going to need to be sure they treat us as equals, not just as people who stumbled onto a treasure and are stubbornly keeping hold of it."

Derian nodded. "I've seen how some react when they learn I was born a horse-carter's son."

Ynamynet added, "And it will be long before spellcasters are respected, rather than feared. The Mires might be a good place for you to go to school, or Azure Towers. The nice thing is that with the gates, anywhere is close to home for you."

Blind Seer listened, but felt no need to comment. He thought again of the questions Firekeeper had raised. Were there yarimaimalom elsewhere? If not, why had they originated in the New World, not elsewhere? Interesting questions, but they could wait, as they had waited for centuries.

For now he was content to know that he and Firekeeper would continue to run side by side. With the new arts he had learned, sometimes they would run on two legs, sometimes on four. Most importantly, he felt certain that they would always run together.

GLOSSARY OF CHARACTERS

Note: This glossary is intended to facilitate reading *Wolf's Soul*. Therefore, references to most characters from the first six novels in the series have been removed. A comprehensive glossary of characters from the first six novels can be found at the end of *Wolf's Blood*.

Characters are detailed under their first or best-known name. Initials following a character's name indicate nationality: B.B. (Bright Bay), H.H. (Hawk Haven), N.K. (New Kelvin), L. (Liglim), N.I. (Nexus Islands), R. (Rhinadei).

Amparee: (R.) spellcaster; spouse of Payley; mother of Migyan and Ransom.

Anitra: monarch of Azure Towers.

Arasan: (N.I.) Once Dead. Called "Two Lives." A musician. See also "Meddler."

Bitter: (N.I.) a Wise Raven.

Blind Seer: a Wise Wolf; partner to Firekeeper.

Blysse Kestrel: see Firekeeper.

Bordyn: (R.) Chief Elementalist; member of the Rhinadei Emergency Council.

Caidon: (R.) spellcaster; master of Uaid.

Chaker Torn: (N.I.) captain of fishing boats; father of Junco and Symeen.

Chsss: a new name for an old problem.

Daylily: (R.) spellcaster, ally of Kabot.

Derian Counselor: (H.H.; N.I.) also called Derian Carter; unofficial co-ruler of the Nexus Islands; spouse of Isende.

Dirkin Eastbranch: (knight, H.H.) King Tedric's personal bodyguard.

Elation: a Royal peregrine falcon; also "Fierce Joy in Flight."

Elexa Wellward: (Queen, H.H.) spouse of Tedric.

Elise Archer: (Lady, H.H.) daughter of Ivon Archer and Aurella Wellward; heir to Archer Grant; diplomat; spouse of Jared Surcliffe; mother of Elexa.

Enigma: (N.I) a Wise Puma.

Erldon: (R.) the Lore Lover; member of the Rhinadei Emergency Council.

Eshinarvash: (N.I.) a Wise Horse.

Fash: (R.) a trader.

Farborn: (N.I.) a Wise Merlin.

Firekeeper: a wolf; partner to Blind Seer.

Grateful Peace: (N.K.) former spymaster, currently valued counselor to the Healed One.

Hanya: (R.) the Dance Warrior; member of the Rhinadei Emergency Council.

Harjeedian: (L.) aridisdu serving the Temple of the Cold Bloods; brother of Rahniseeta.

Hohdoymin: (Teyo) a regional leader.

Ikitata: (N.I.) cobbler; widow of Ollaris; mother of Laria, Nenean, and Kitatos.

Isende: (N.I.) Once Dead, spouse of Derian Counselor.

Jared Surcliffe: (knight, H.H.) aka "Doc"; knight of the Order of the White Eagle; possessor of the healing talent. Spouse of Elise Archer; father of Elexa.

Junco Torn: (N.I.) a sailor; son of Chaker, brother of Symeen.

Jyanee: the Unweaver, a legend.

Kabot: (R.) a freethinker.

Kalyndra: (N.I.) Once Dead; mother of Skea.

Kitatos: (N.I.) son of Ollaris and Ikitata; brother of Laria and Nenean.

Laria: (N.I.) Once Dead; daughter of Ollaris and Ikitata; sister of Nenean and Kitatos.

Lovable: (N.I.) a Wise Raven; mate of Bitter.

Mata: (R.) servant/assistant to Varelle and the Emergency Council.

Merial: a general of Azure Towers.

Migyan: (R.) daughter of Payley and Amparee sister to Ransom.

Meddler: (N.I.) a former spirit, now sharing a body with Arasan.

Nenean: (N.I.) daughter of Ollaris and Ikitata; sister of Laria and Kitatos.

Nergy: a retired soldier, current historian of Azure Towers.

Ollaris: (N.I.) a cobbler; father of Laria. Deceased.

Onorina: (R.) a spellcaster.

Orten: (R.) Five Spirits Alchemist; member of Rhinadei Emergency Council.

Payley: (R.) spouse of Amparee; father of Ransom and Migyan.

Phiona: (R.) spellcaster, ally of Kabot.

Plik: (N.I.) a maimalodalu.

Rahniseeta: (L.) junjaldisdu; sister of Harjeedian. Former lover of Derian Counseler.

Ransom (called *Ranz*): (R.) a young spellcaster. Son of Amparee and Payley; sibling of Migyan.

Rhul: (N.I.) spouse of Saeta; father of Loxia and others.

Rusty: (R.) a goat.

Skea: (N.I.) a Twice Dead; member of governing counsel, spouse of Ynamynet; father of Sunshine, son of Kalyndra.

Sunshine: (N.I.) daughter of Skea and Ynamynet.

Sun Diver: a yarimaimalom golden eagle.

Symeen Torn: (N.I.) a sailor; daughter of Chaker; sister of Junco.

Tedric: (H.H.) monarch of Hawk Haven, spouse of Elexa.

Trahaene: Once Dead, spellcaster, Azure Towers.

Truth: (N.I.) a Wise Jaguar; possesses erratic prophetic gift.

Uaid: (R.) spellcaster, ally of Kabot.

Urgana: (N.I.) Never Lived; archivist, member of governing counsel.

Varelle: (R.) the Gatewatcher; member of the Rhinadei Emergency Council.

Virim: (N.I.) a very elderly sorcerer, creator of querinalo.

Wjem: (R.) servant/assistant to Varelle and the Emergency Council.

Wort: (N.I.) a Twice Dead, member of the governing counsel; quartermaster.

Wythcombe: (R.) a hermit, a spellcaster.

Ynamynet: (N.I.) Once Dead; unofficial co-ruler of the Nexus Islands; spouse of Skea; mother of Sunshine.

Zebel: (N.I.) Twice Dead; member of governing counsel; a doctor.

Zazaral: a busybody.